Theron
and The Wolf on the wall

Forward

Have you wondered how Bigfoot could appear and disappear without being discovered? Have you imagined strange worlds that touch the boundaries of science fiction? Theron Salter had never thought of such things, he never though he was any different than other ordinary boys, yet, he was. In the days ahead Theron will be faced with the strangest of beasts, wondrous lands and a struggle for life and death. Travel along with Theron and experience his reality. His reality might be right where you live. Are you ordinary? I don't think so; you may be the next to keep the balance.

When the world began it was composed of matter. More worlds were made of matter of various kinds. This allowed seven worlds to exist in the same space in the heavens and operate independently of one another. Each world was populated with humans and creatures indigenous only within that world. If we could peer through a magical window perhaps some question would be answered. Questions like why we can't find the legendary Loch ness monster, mermaids, or the master of legendary creatures, Bigfoot.

Before Theron Salter the balance was kept by trusted souls that each was given seven gifts, these gifts were designated to repair tears and bubbles in between worlds. The balance of worlds is delicate and with seven worlds all in the same space certain collisions occurred, tears turned to bubbles and creatures wondered from one world to another. Socrates, Michael Anglo, Magellan, and Samuel Clements all were among the keepers of the balance. And now in 1957 a new balancer is born. Experience the chronicles of his life as the newest keeper of the balance.

TS and The WOW

Theron Salter and the Wolf on the wall

<u>Dedication</u>

Growing up in the southwest, we had no idea that our lives would blend, twist, and mingle with the winds of the atomic tests. Although my father and other relatives lost their lives to the radiation fallout, I prefer to remember the sweetness of my child hood in the high desert.

This book is dedicated to the memory of my father, my children who inspired me, and my loving muse. My father once told me that because of who I was I could do anything.

My gifts to you are my father's words "**you can do anything**."

Today as you learn who Theron and Twila Salter are perhaps you will see you're self in them and know that you are not ordinary but you have the strength to do anything your mind and heart desire. To my children that brought this dream to reality I love you all and challenge you to take your dreams to reality. From your father "**you can do anything**."

Written: by Don Hadley
Cover Illustration: by Jon McNaughton
Edit: by Margie Lynch

Theron Salter and the Wolf on the wall

Contents

Chapter 1   **MYSTERIOUS WATERS and THE BOX OF STONE**

Chapter 2   **THE TREE IN THE YARD and TWO FOR THE PRICE OF ONE**

Chapter 3   **WALL BACK IN SCHOOL and THE WOLF ON THE**

Chapter 4   **CRYSTAL STONE and WAVES OF SAND**

Chapter 5   **THE STEERSMAN and CROP CIRCLES**

Chapter 6   **TROLLS UNDER THE BRIDGE and BALANCE IN THE WORLD**

Chapter 7   **TURNED INSIDE OUT and MRS. SWEENEY MEETS THE NEIGHBOR**

Chapter 8   **BUSHER'S POND and MEBO**

Chapter 9   **A PARENT'S DREAM and UNDER ATTACK**

Chapter 10   *THE NIGHTLY NEWS*
                  and CREATURES IN THE FOREST

Chapter 11   *THE HIDDEN PLACE*
                  and ARLIS ALGER

Chapter 12   *THE TWO-FACED MAN*
                  and THE WORLD OF TOMORROW

Chapter 13   *THUNDER LIGHTING BOLTS*
                  and TERROR IN THE CANYON

Chapter 14   *THE STONE*
                  and THE NEVER SEEN

Chapter 15   *TO RIDE LIKE THE COWBOYS*
                  and WATER DOGS

Chapter 16   *WHERE THE WIND BLOWS*
                  and HOLES IN TIME

Chapter 17   *VALLEY OF THE MOUNTAINS*
                  and WATER THEIR ROOTS

Chapter 18   *THE TRAVELING COIN*
                  and WHISKED AWAY

Chapter 19   *HIDDEN*
                  and 1918 RED RIDER

Chapter 20   *RETURN TO THE CANYON*
                  and PHOTO IN THE FALLS

Chapter 21   *HOME AGAIN*
                  and LOOSE AMONG US

CHAPTER 1

Mysterious Waters and the Box of Stone

The summer bugs glowed as they twisted and turned in the last moments of the night's darkness. Two identical fireflies flirted with the water on the pond. Frogs croaked a mysterious song as the illuminated pair dipped near the edge of the water and the long reeds. The snap of a single sticky tongue shot into the air at them. Only a single firefly retreated over the pond bank across the dry wash and into the neighboring civilized yard with its fine-cut grass. In full-winged fury it smashed into the clear clean window of the Salter home in the early morning light.

"What was that?" asked the woman, packing her bags, only looking up for a second, and then readjusting her focus.

"Where is that boy?" Adeline Salter said, while thrusting her hands into the air in frustration. Adeline continued to pack the two suitcases, one for her and the other for her husband George. Both suitcases lay open on the bed, already overflowing with intended contents. Soon they would be on their way to a vacation they had planned for the past eleven years.

TS and The WOW

They had been drawn to the canyon and, for some unknown reason; they knew that they must go there this season. Even before Martin, their only child, was born they had both felt the call of the canyon.

"Have you seen Martin?" Adeline asked. George had entered the room and was quickly brought to attention by his usually timid spouse.

"I think he's shooting some hoops outside," George said.

"It's barely light. What's he doing out there already?" she asked.

The front door opened and in walked Martin, talking to someone.

"Who's with you?" asked Adeline from the back room, her hair in curlers and not wanting the world or one of Martin's friends to see her that way. Adeline heard the basketball hit the floor and roll to the wall. "Martin, you put that ball away!"

"No one, Mom. It's just me." Not wishing to be caught reading out loud, Martin rolled up the comic book he was reading and tucked it into his back pocket. Adeline's fairy-like qualities shined brightly as she flitted from bedroom to kitchen and then back again.

"Now Martin, you will water my plants, won't you?" she said, not wanting her favorite pastime of growing things to end

TS and The WOW

while she was away. Adeline loved George and Martin, but something was missing from her life. Perhaps she would find it in the canyon that she had so longed to visit.

George Salter had given up his dream of riding across the country onboard a motorcycle to plant roots and become a father. He settled for the restoration of his prize possession, a red 1910 Flying Miracle motorcycle. Time was fleeting before the trip, so he worked on his toy, installing the new brake pedal he had fashioned.

"There, that's nice and tight," he commented as he twisted the last bolt snug with an extra tug. Mostly the motorcycle sat in the garage covered by a blanket.

"George, would you come and help me?" Adeline called, hanging out the back door and using that voice she was famous for to get his attention.

Martin's basketball rolled down the stairs, bounced on the concrete and rolled into his room. He also bounced down the stairs and closed the door behind him. Martin tucked the ball under a shelf and returned to his mother's side.

"Mom, what are we going to eat?"

Adeline had forgotten breakfast, but Martin hadn't.

"Just make yourself some bread and butter and some bottled peaches or the Cheerios," she answered, continuing her frantic packing.

TS and The WOW

Martin was the only child. He always wished he had a brother or sister, but his parents were silent about the subject whenever he asked why he didn't. Martin made do with an imaginary friend, Abernanthy.

"Martin, are you talking to Abernanthy again?"

"No, Mom," he said, knowing that it upset his mother that he had this strange friend.

"He worries me," she said tucking the last of her items into the over-stuffed suitcase.

"Well, let's not worry about that right now. We are going on vacation and Martin will be with your sister and all her kids for the next week," George said, closing the suitcase she had sat upon to help close the latch. The car was loaded and hugs and kisses exchanged with their Martin.

"Aunt Mary will be by about ten to pick you up, so you be good. Love you!" Adeline said, giving her last instructions.

"You too, Mom," Martin said, waving at his dad with a gesture of love.

Adeline needed to stop several times at the filling station for a "woman's break" she called it, but over the years George had become patient with her needs.

"Fill 'err up, sir?" asked the attendant.

"Sure, and would you check the oil?" George replied. Adeline closed the heavy door behind her as she got into the car.

"Ask him how far to the canyon, honey."

"The sign said 40 miles about five miles back."

"That will be two dollars, sir."

George paid the man and they were on their way once more. It seemed no time at all had passed when they rounded the turn to discover the end of the drive and beginning of their adventure. Adeline saw it first and called out "Lee's Ferry!"

The pontoons of the raft gracefully floated on the water of the Colorado River as the Salter's were about to discover secrets that had been held silent within the majestic walls for thousands of years. Grand cliffs shot from the river's edge a thousand feet into the blue-white sky.

"What is it that drew us here?" Adeline wondered as she gazed up at the rusty-colored cliffs. No answer came to her unspoken question. Secrets were calling them to the canyon. She felt solemn, apprehensive like a young girl on her first adventure to the playground. The first day had been a time of calm and becoming acquainted with the ways of the river.

"So, has everyone had their fill of grub?" the boatman called out his rhetorical question to the passengers. All were fed and the sun fell away, leaving the passengers to gather at the fire with the boatman and his stories of the river.

TS and The WOW

"Play us something on that box," George requested to the young boatman that had guided them this far down river to their first encampment. The boatman's fingers strummed the strings of the guitar coaxing from them a tune. The song "Blue Moon" rang from the weather-beaten box. The moonlight on the waters of the Havasupi bubbled past in rhythm on its way into the Colorado River. The melody rolled a cacophony of pleasure from wall to canyon walls. The muted coral-pink cliffs of the Grand Canyon blocked the sky, except for a pathway of stars and a glaze of the moon were all that made it possible to know they were still on planet earth and not in an alien world as the landscape portrayed. Adeline could not resist singing her favorite song. She began to sing, "Blue moon… and we were dancing alone… without a care in our heart…"

The moment seemed everything she had hoped for this trip to be. "Finally away on the adventure of a lifetime with my man," she thought. In an instant her moment was dismembered when an unnatural cry stunned the tune. It died to silence, leaving only the popping of gasses from the logs on the fire. Again, the unrecognizable scream came from down the river, smashing its echo on every wall of the canyon, as had the music before its interruption. Everyone stopped what they were doing, frozen captives. Their souls for the moment bound in its grip. The fire flickered as if the breath of the screamer had disturbed it's comforting glow, tossing it to and fro.

Adeline and George had saved pennies, nickels and even pop bottles to exchange for enough money for this, their once in a lifetime vacation.

"Why had they been drawn to the river and the canyon?" questioned George. All their lives they had been pulled like a pair of magnets to the bottom of the Grand Canyon. Why? he wondered. With their dreams to come to the canyon finally realized, Adeline now felt as though her home, her warm bed and the safety there, was the only place she wanted to be. Thoughts of home only served to make her more terrified of the strange scream, more so of the screamer. What had been a festive mood had died as the sound of the screams slowly faded.

"George, what do you think it was?" Adeline softly asked, holding her arms around him for protection, from whatever was out there in the night.

"Perhaps we were welcomed or told to get lost. I can't decide which." George felt like an invader here in this ancient place, intruding on graves of the long dead. There was no way to escape, so whatever the creature was going to do they would have to face it.

When morning came without incident, Adeline found that George had leaned against a rocky outcropping all night, staying awake as long as he could, ready to protect his wife. All

that resulted from the events of the night was the stiffness he felt
in his neck and the gooey glaze that covered his eyes when he
awoke.

"The river smells different in the morning," Adeline
thought, breathing in the cool air coming off the river across the
bush and tamarisk. The raft was pushed back into the water
where Adeline felt just a little safer. Being back on the river put
distance from the rocks where the sound had come from and her.
It felt great to be on the river again. The sun was warm and the
water pushed the raft ever closer to the canyon's wonders and
further from the reach of the screaming creature. Or was it closer
to the entity that had cast a spell on the travelers aboard the raft?
When it came time for lunch the rubber raft was landed at the
foot of a beautiful waterfall. Long before landing the raft Adeline
pointed her finger at the waterfall.

"How spectacular!"

"I've never seen anything like it," replied George, who
had regained his enthusiasm for the experience of the canyon.

"Look at the rainbow," said the boatman, who had seen
it many times in the water spray of the falls. As the water would
fall it would twist as if it were dancing, chasing its own rainbow.

"Come on George let's go up to the falls." Adeline and
George climbed across painted stones. They climbed to the place
where the falls splattered on the rocks watering the green ferns
and filling a small pond. The fresh water filled a pool at the base
of the cliff. Droplets landed on the couple's faces as they

TS and The WOW

approached the waterfall. It felt good, cooling them from the heat of the day. Slide-like ruts were cut in to the sandstone where the water poured over the pond's bank and across the rock down the hill and into the river. George wondered how many hundreds of years of water had passed there to cut the channels. The rest of the passengers had made their way to the same spot, marveling at the water falling from some hidden ledge many feet above them.

"How high do you think that is," Keyon Ranch, a fellow passenger said, while looking up to find from where the water fell. Yesterday, at the first turn on the river where the canyon walls shot up on both sides, Keyon had started to yodel. It was interesting, but rather weird. Keyon was a round man with massive arms. Nelda Ranch, his wife was ten years his junior. It took both her arms to surround one of his arms in a hug. She also gazed up at the edge of the cliff from where the water fell. She answered his question.

"I think it's at least 200 feet." All this water appeared to be escaping the desert lands, traveling down into the cradle of the canyon.

"It must be hotter than Hades up there! Even the water wants out," Keyon declared.

"George, isn't this wonderful?" Adeline said while running her hands into the cool of the falling waters. George did the same,

"This water is clean and cool." He wiped it onto his forehead. Then Adeline undid the laces of her shoes. She took

TS and The WOW

them off, placing them carefully by a rock to keep them dry. George was a little less ready to remove his footgear. Cowboys prize their boots and he wouldn't be caught dead without them on. But the water was too inviting. Cowboy or not, he just had to cool his burning feet in this heavenly liquid. His boots were placed next to his Addie's before he strode into the cool of the pond. Two of the young girls from the raft sat down in water that ran down the stone slides. Water built up a pressure behind them, sliding them down the slide into a pool at the edge of the river. Soon everyone was sliding, everyone but Adeline and George. They were wading in the cool water in the waterfall's pond.

"Hold my hand," Adeline said, finding the rocks too slippery to stand on. She held out her hand to George. George reached toward her, but his feet slipped on the slick rocks. One foot went behind him and the other into the air, and his arms flailed aimlessly. The splash he made only Adeline witnessed. She laughed with that laugh that only a wife has when her husband makes a fool of himself. George spit and coughed the water from his mouth and throat, struggling to right himself back on his feet. He looked like a turtle on his back wrestling to turn over. The realization hit him that he was only in water a couple of feet deep. He moved to a sitting position on the pond's bottom, still a head above the water line. He began to laugh at his predicament. Adeline had lost her footing also and narrowly avoided falling headfirst into the pool.

TS and The WOW

"What's this?" George asked, his hand resting on something that was lying on the bottom. It felt manmade, strangely familiar. George rolled to his knees where he could see the object. "It's a sword," he said. He reached to the bottom, grasped the handle, and pulled to try to remove it from the water. It was stiff, smooth, and made of hard steel.

"It can't have been here long. There is no rust on it," he said. He pulled on it and it began to rotate to where the handle rose from the water. At the same time a large round rocky slab behind the falling water rolled from its place. It traveled in a groove, sliding aside and grinding against the other stone as it did. Where the stone had been an opening was exposed in the cliff. There was a cave behind the falls, barely noticeable, even with the stone rolled away. He pushed the handle down and the rocky door rolled back in to place. "Did you see that?"

Adeline's mouth hung open, a look of disbelief on her face. It took a moment for her to reply and then it was just, "Uh, huh."

George first looked to see if the rolling door had been noticed by any of the others from the raft. It hadn't, so he pulled the lever again moving the door open just enough that he might enter into the cavity behind it.

"Was this the reason that they had been drawn to the canyon for so many years, or was this…?" George left the thought unfinished as he climbed into the falls, dripping water from his clothes on the already wet stone floor. It quickly trickled away into many open cracks.

The hole behind the falls was a cave, hidden until now for possibly hundreds, maybe even thousands of years. At least that was the way it seemed.

"Adeline, come up here. You have got to see this!" George said. His own echo startled him as he spoke. He continued to climb further, sliding his body past a fallen rock to where the cave opened.

Adeline had watched, focused on where she had last seen him. "Wouldn't you know he would find something up there?" she said under her breath. She struggled for her first grip on the rock behind the falls, and then popped into the cave, wet but pleased with herself. George was waiting for her and the Kodak box camera that she carried on a strap around her neck.

"Take a shot from here," George said, pointing out at the waterfall. She removed the camera from under her shirt where she had concealed it, hoping to keep it dry. The water spread a curtain over the opening, hiding the activities inside the cave. The camera's flash illuminated the green mossy covering on the walls of the cave, which glistened with a sparkle of droplets of water and showed remnants of carved stone steps. Someone had been there before them. George noticed the steps carved into the stone, took Adeline's hand to guide her, and together they ascended the steps. The steps wound around in a spiral and were part of the wall of the cave. They showed generations of wear.

TS and The WOW

"I wonder who did this?" George thought as he envisioned an ancient people striking the stone with a chisel to cut the steps. The walls of the cavern were rough and, moist and water seeped from the falls and into the staircase. They climbed upward inside the cavity of the mountain, step after step, until the mossy cushion under their feet disappeared.

"What is it?" Adeline whispered to George. Instead of growing ever darker as they had expected, the walls of the chamber intensified in luminance.

"Look. It is getting lighter," Adeline said. They could see the water trickling down the walls and onto the steps, the beginning of a tiny stream.

"Addie, do you believe this!" Adeline and George had reached the top of the staircase, holding tightly to each other's hand, and were now standing in a room hewn inside the mountain. Light filled the room in the hollowed rock. The roof of the room was natural isinglass. It let in a drifting prism light. The rainbow of light came through, reflecting upon a finely polished sheet of metal, partly caked in dust. In the center of the room stood a pillar and basin cut from stone. It was all that remained from the rock that had been hewn away, leaving only the basin and stand apart from the rocky floor. On top of the pillar was the stone basin. The basin was partly filled with crystal blue water, a color that, at first, appeared to be projection from the prism's colors of the ceiling. In the center of the bowl floated a ball that rolled as the water poured from its center. The ball's

TS and The WOW

translucency allowed them to see a second ball within its center and another inside of that ball, each varying in its transparency. In all, George counted seven of the spheres from which the water flowed.

"There are seven. How does the water come out of them?" He was puzzled. The water seemed to come from the balls, not through them. "Where is the water coming from?" asked George again.

"There's got to be a hidden spring," Adeline replied. Adeline cupped the water into her hands, first sniffing. "I think it's fresh." She placed it to her lips, sipped it and then drank a couple of handfuls. It was sweet, cold, the most wonderful water she had ever tasted. As she drank, her body tingled, almost sparking with pleasure. "This water's is wonderful." She encouraged her husband to drink. George scooped his hands full of azure water and drank it.

"That's fantastic!" He drank until he was filled. "Watch this, Doll." He pointed to the inside of the ball as they watched the bowl fill from the spring within it. He wiped the remaining wetness on his hands across his Wranglers.

At a glance, the room appeared mostly empty, except for one small curious stone box that caught his eye. The box was shaped like a multi-pointed star. George could not resist picking it up. As he held it in his hand, he wondered if this was the reason that he and Adeline had been drawn to the canyon.

TS and The WOW

"Look at this little box," George said, showing it to Adeline. She was the first to point out the strange carving on the side of the stone box.

"What does this mean?" She pointed to the carving.

"Don't have a clue," was all George said, before tucking the box into his backpack. Carvings of the same kind covered the cave walls.

"Have you seen these?" Adeline asked, and then knelt near the polished metal sheet. She wiped away a century's worth of dust, leaving only her fingerprints on its surface. The walls were covered in carvings, a symbol-like language foreign to anything that George had ever seen. George examined the walls, running his hand over the symbols cut into it. He turned to his wife.

"We're going to be missed," he said. Excitedly, they hurried back down to the falls and to the others.

"We can come back when we are alone," George whispered to his wife. They felt lifted as they climbed back down from the cliff to the base of the waterfall. Perhaps they had discovered the reason they had been connected with this canyon for so long, or had they discovered something that would change them forever?

"I feel great," Adeline said.

"Me too," George replied. It was hard for them to tell whether it was the intrigue of their adventure or that fabulous spring water they found that made them feel this way.

TS and The WOW

The moon rose over the canyon with its full presence, lighting the cliff opposite the encampment with a lunar glow. Water lapped against the raft, pushing it into the sandy beach time and time again. The campfire danced almost in time with the guitar music and the songs washed away the thoughts of the scream, the cave, and all the events of the day.

"George, let's go to bed," Adeline said, a twinkle in her eye that matched the moonlight. The laughter paused as the bedrolls were placed on the sand. Mountain sheep began to traverse the face of the cliff. The ewe, led by her kid and followed by an older ram, stepped surely as she came down the cliff face to the water.

"How are they doing that? Those footholds wouldn't hold my finger," George said, lying on his back, watching the animals from his sleeping bag. Adeline laughed as the sheep crouched on the cliff's face, almost agreeing with what George had said. It seemed as though the ewe had had enough of this trail, when the old ram placed his horns on her behind and gave her a shove. She gave him the look many human women give their husbands, and then moved on, crossing the sheerest part of the rocky face going down to the edge of the water to drink. After watering, the sheep climbed back up the cliff to disappear into the memories of the trip down the river.

All the sleeping bags were scattered throughout the Tamarisk bushes that lined the sandy beach. George and Adeline had found a spot that was more alone, away from the rest. As the moon

TS and The WOW

passed over the edge of the canyon, every bush was light and every nocturnal creature was exposed. A ring-tailed cat pranced down out of a rocky crevice, its tail floating behind him in the air, appearing weightless. The rafters were asleep, except for Adeline and George, who watched as the cat walked across the sleeping bag of Keyon Ranch. The cat went on to retrieve a piece of meat from the scrap trash bag, and then moved away as silently as he had come, back over Keyon's sleeping bag and off into the night. Hours later, when the moon had passed the canyon by and finished as guardian of the sleeping, something strange happened. In the shadow, George's backpack began to produce a faint glow, a prism light, the same as the one that had shone through the isinglass in the chamber behind the falls. There was no more moonlight, no source for such an event, yet it glowed brighter and brighter in the little hidden corner of the sand bar where the Salter's slept. The flap on the knapsack unfastened itself, leaving the glowing stone box exposed. The box was of fine workmanship, a masterpiece of workmanship. It began to shake, rocking itself back and forth, dancing, and spinning. Its shape changed from the star shape to a ball, then came to rest in the shape of a three-pointed triangle.

George slept, sound and deep influenced to dream by the star box. His body was weightless, flying in the night sky, looking down on the canyon and traveling back in time, as if all time had rewound itself to the gathering, to the gathering of all the materials that composed Earth. Then it started! Sparks flew in the darkness of the cosmos where winds began to whirl. Energy of a power unseen, a rocky core spun, attracting light, matter, and the frozen liquids that formed where nothing had existed. The first core of matter molded, begging a world. Then a second core of matter folded and molded, then a third. On and on it went until there were seven layers of spheres, each formed of different matter and each occupying the same space, yet spinning at different rates, causing them to phase into worlds separate one from another. Worlds upon worlds formed, seven times and with seven different set of rules to govern their base elements. George's dream ended and he rested, unaware of the box in his knapsack.

The glow from the box ceased and the flap closed, covering the box within it. George rolled over in his sleeping bag and sat up to an awakening world. Two large birds swooped, dipping into the water and catching fish. From where he sat, he watched the boatman beginning breakfast. The smell of the wood burning entangled with the aroma of things cooking coaxed him from the warm bag. He was still softly remembering his dream of the seven worlds.

This was the last day on the river and George was already planning the return trip when they would visit the cave one more time.

TS and The WOW

Enterprise was their home; a town name that showed the desire of the folks that lived there to be industrious. Those folks were good, hardy stock from old Mormon pioneers who had settled the place in Utah's high desert, a lonesome valley with as much wildlife as the human presence allows. There was certain peace of mind existing in this small town where life moved at a slow pace.

In the early morning, an eagle flew as servant of the mountain, with a tilt of his wings, he swooped into the valley. Something of importance to him passed the pond and the wash where the water trickled past. He passed over the line of cottonwood trees to circle above a tiny yellow house, watching for something, something yet unseen.

Adeline had to have a yellow house. That was all she wanted. No picket fence, just the house filled with lots of kids. Adeline kissed George goodbye. He patted her swollen belly with one hand while holding his black lunch pail in the other.

"Goodbye, Honey," she said.

"Don't have that baby without me," he said, and then went out the door. George was the superintendent of the new electrical system, a lineman for the utility company. He loved electricity and all the electrical challenges it brought. The 1957 Chevy pickup with utility boxes sat idling in the driveway. It contained only one occupant. Dewy Tanner sat in the driver's seat.

TS and The WOW

"Come you love birds. Cut it out. We have work to do."

"Work to do? You mean I have work to do," George thought. He knew Dewy was a man who seemed to always be looking for a way to avoid doing any work. After all, he was the boss.

"Alright I'm coming!" George let the glass door close and headed for the truck. Adeline waddled back through the snow to the house, after watching the truck reach the stop sign at the corner, which was her custom. The door clicked as it closed. Adeline unloaded the two new loaves of bread from the oven, laying them on her kitchen counter for cooling.

"You look good this time," she said, basting the warm crust with her butter brush. The aroma of bread was rich and the crust was golden brown. "Ouch," she said, putting her fingers into her mouth to cool them after touching the hot pan. The heel, or "butt end," as George called it, was the best piece of the loaf of bread. "My favorite slice," she thought. "The fresher the better, besides, butter melts better on hot bread," she mused as she smothered butter on her hot treasure. As she did, something strange happened. The house began to shake. Not the walls or floor, but the entire contents of the house whirled and darted about. As the commotion started, she screamed, tossing the slice of bread into the air. It also began to spin as if it were possessed. Steam, still rising from the open end of the loaf, left a vapor trail as it shot into the adjoining living room. The other loaf of bread slid on the counter. Adeline grasped a cabinet with both hands.

TS and The WOW

Her knees weakened and her balance was failing, a sick green feeling in her stomach, as the house danced all about her. The drapes on the windows didn't move at all, yet everything in the house spun. Cushions on the couch bounced off walls, the bread floated in the air, and the table and chairs in the kitchen whirled like tops. As suddenly as the building's contents had been brought to their abnormal motion, all commotion ceased. As the whirling derby terminated, Adeline stumbled her way to the living room, where everything had come to rest.

"What the heck is going on here?" Everything was back in its place, like nothing had ever happened. She rushed back to the kitchen, still wanting to toss her cookies. "Freaky!" The kitchen also was in order, the bread resting on the counter in its place. Even the end piece that she had bitten sat on the counter. Not a crumb seemed to out of place. Nothing was out of place except for the triangle box that hovered above the counter, glowing like the isinglass room. The box had changed shape, adding a new fourth corner and becoming a square. The box had not been there when all this started. The business of floating in the air was more than she could take.

"Where the heck did you come from?" Adeline thought, afraid. "He has got to get rid of it." It was the box George had brought back with him from the cave of waters. It had been in George's lockbox in the garage; however, now it sat next to the cut of bread she had buttered. "How could it have gotten in here?" she thought. Then she saw it, the photo she had taken at

TS and The WOW

the falls on their river trip. Adeline looked closer at the photo
that had mysteriously landed on the countertop. A watery form
of a man's face was blended in the black and white image of the
waterfall. Fear gripped her. She rushed from the house into the
backyard. "Anywhere is better than a haunted house," she
thought. She stood like a statue, stone hard with an equally stiff
stare at the house, not wanting to be anywhere near that box.
Adeline didn't feel the winter's cold as she stood in the yard,
covered in snow above her ankles. It was nearly an hour that she
stood there, her mind running rampant, raising blisters on her
thoughts while trying to make sense of what had happened.
"What's that?" She felt a warm sensation. Suddenly she was wet.
Her water had broken. The baby was on its way.

The baby had not been due until January, but five days
before Christmas the babies were born. Not one as they had
supposed, but two bundles of joy, twins.

"What a Christmas present!" George said. We have twins,
a little girl and boy. It was totally unexpected. No one had
thought there were two.

"Our little miracles," Adeline lovingly said, cuddling her
son while Martin held his sister.

They came home on Christmas Day. Adeline had dressed
the twins in warm sleepers and then placed each tiny body into a
candy cane striped stocking. These babies were a gift that the
family had thought would never come. Martin never struggled for

a moment with giving up his Christmas Day to bring the infants home. He treasured them. Being a big brother was the best.

"Mom, look at this." Martin showed her a spot on the boy's head where his hair grew in a red circle.

Adeline examined her little girl. She had an identical red spot, but on the opposite side. "I guess I am Irish." Adeline had supposed that her father was of Irish decent, never really knowing because he had mysteriously disappeared when she was a young girl. Her mother died soon after. She had grown up with her mother's mother, Grandma Judd.

The only thing that had surprised her more than the red hair circle on the twins was the strange tree that had grown overnight and in the dead of winter. The tree had appeared directly in the spot where she had stood as her water broke. She had only been away a few days in the hospital with her new babies and now she also had her new yard baby. They had decided to name them Theron Lee and Twila Marie and simply the Winter Tree. The strange tree had sprouted and grown three feet seemingly overnight. Adeline welcomed the tree. She felt like he was one of the kids and she always had room for more children.

When George heard the story of the box and the house quake, he retrieved the box from the counter where it still lay.

"Time to break you open, you little pest," he thought, worried that it could be a danger to his family. "Let's find out what makes you tick," he said, talking as if the box could answer

TS and The WOW

him. His conversation with the box continued. "So, speak your piece, little box. What do you have to tell me?" The box lay silent on the workbench. The vice squeaked at each turn as George opened its jaws. He placed the box in the waiting jaws, twisting the handle until the jaws gripped snug. George picked up his coal chisel and hammer from his workbench. "Smack-ting" rang the sound of a hammer striking the chisel. He swung the hammer again, hitting the chisel and hoping to break open the box. Nothing happened. The box held its secrets. George lined the chisel up with what looked like the point where the lid fit on top of the box. He swung the hammer again. Nothing happened. He clanked the hammer against the chisel several more times without even scratching the surface of the box.

George had never been able to explain the change the box had made while in his pack or in the kitchen. All of this had him disturbed, maybe even scared. "Maybe you're not a box at all, but something else." He had come to believe that the box was a key fashioned to unlock something or a part of a machine of some kind, but now he had to wonder. "I am sure that you have a secret inside." The box took his licks, smack after smack with a hammer, to no avail. "Come on, little one, give me your secrets," George said. An hour passed while he worked, determined to open the box, yet it would not open. George brushed his hair back with his fingers, turned away, and walked in the house. He left the box snug in the vice, unchanged. He muttered under his breath, "Please give me your secrets."

TS and The WOW

The next morning George returned to the shop to examine the thing once more. To his surprise, the box had opened. How had it opened and why, he wondered as he emptied the jagged golden arrowhead shard from the box into his hand. "This must be something," he said, while turning it over and over in his hand. "I've had enough of this." He put the treasure from the box into his pocket. The box lay open on the bench only for a moment. Then it began to quiver, shake, and roll, closing its own lid. The stone box, with its carved exterior, rested on the bench like nothing had ever happened.

CHAPTER 2

The Tree In The Yard and Two For The Price Of One

"Twins! How does anyone survive them?" Adeline asked herself while shaking her hands over her head, a pose that Martin had become very familiar with. In 1959, the twins, Theron and Twila, were now toddlers. "The terrible twos." Adeline said.

"They got that one right." Martin replied adding, "What do you call two twos that are in their terrible? Torture," Martin said, and then laughed. Adeline put her hands on her knees, tossed the glance that mothers do to smart alecks, and then laughed with him.

"You are a pair." Martin picked up his little sister to get her away from the white bread flour she had covered herself with. Adeline had already put Theron into the kitchen sink to wash away the broken eggs that he had sat in after pulling them off the counter and breaking them on the floor in the flour. Both twins' golden-brown curls were pasty white, caked in flour. Their red spots might be pesky, but the red clutch on the right side of Twila's head and on the left side of Theron's, each about the size of a silver dollar, had shaken themselves free of any dust. They were the color of sandstone and grew faster than the rest of their hair.

"How weird was that?" Martin thought, watching the hair spin about all on its own. "Not to trend-setting for hairstyles, but pretty cool." Their red hair would find a place, or find a reason some time in the future. Right now, being babies, it was hard to tell them apart. Same skin color, same size, same hair. All that was different were the sides of their heads where the red spots resided. "Theron's always right and Twila's never left. That's how I tell them apart."

Their birthmarks were helpful. Theron had a mark on his right shoulder, composed of three perfect circles linked and intersecting each other. Twila had her mark on the left shoulder. It was similar to Theron's, the difference being the number of circles. She had four in a pattern similar to her brother, but with four intersecting circles. It was odd for the position of the marks, let alone the way they were so close to the same, but after all they were twins. Then the real difference was, of course, one that was a boy and the other a girl, a natural slight difference.

"Twins double the fun, double the trouble," were the words Adeline repeated whenever friends came to see her little matched pair.

TS and The WOW

The Salter's had lost all thoughts of returning to the Grand Canyon. The twins' needs had consumed them, both in time and energy.

Another morning crept its way into the world. Adeline could hear whistling coming from the kitchen where Martin, her 10 year old son, attempted to fix breakfast for his mother.

"What a night." She had spent the night in the twins' room again, sleeping in the chair. Martin had already gathered the eggs from the henhouse in the backyard and was making French toast, well, egg toast. Martin had sliced a loaf of Adeline's homemade bread into slabs, not one slab the same. Some were two or so inches on one end, then tapering paper thin on the other. The kitchen bellowed with smoke from the melted butter in the frying pan. Adeline, in her robe and fuzzy pink slippers, stood in the doorway watching her son, never prouder. Martin stood next to the stove, a spatula in one hand and dripping freshly battered toast in the other. His whistling stopped while he showed a grin of satisfaction.

"Martin, I love you," she heard herself say. Adeline slid open a window for the smoke-filled kitchen. Her smile was warm. "This is why I like being a mom," she thought.

Martin became the watcher of the twins. He watched them on long summer days. He would take the twins to the

TS and The WOW

backyard to play. He watched them, entertaining them in the cool of the morning, and through sun-drenched afternoons, they rested on his bed in the cool of the basement, while Martin read them stories from one of his books. This made it possible for Adeline to catch up on all her chores and to produce a meal with substance. Adeline leaned out the door that led to the back yard and called out, "Martin, come and please help me with this!"

Martin rose from playing in the sand with the twins, and then went to help his mother, leaving the twins playing alone in the sandbox.

Theron pushed his jeep through the sand. "Vroom, vroom." He made the noise of a car running while Twila shoveled sand into a painted pail that had big flowers all over it. She dumped the sand all over Theron's toy jeep. Theron put the jeep over Twila's head and dumped the sand on her. Sand streamed through her hair into her jumper and filled her diaper. The red hair circle spun and twisted, throwing sand in every direction, cleaning itself. Twila responded to the sand drenching by crying. She cried a howling cry, tears streaming down her face and streaking through the sand, making mud.

"What's that?" Martin heard her crying and darted for the yard. He leaped out through the screen door, which slammed as he jumped off the porch. He ran toward the sandbox as quickly as he could, fearful that something had happened to

TS and The WOW

his sister in his absence. He looked back when Adeline called his name.

"Martin." He turned only for a moment to look for her while still running. "Smack. Ker plunk." Martin ran full stride right into the Winter Tree.

The tree cried, "Ouch!" and Martin was flipped to the ground on his behind. He was stunned for a moment, more from the cry of the tree than from the double bounce he had taken, once hitting the tree and then bouncing onto the grass.

"Where did you come from?" Martin said, talking directly to the tree, a habit he had gotten from his father, who often talked to inanimate objects. This one apparently could respond when he wanted to. The tree had not been there before. It had moved itself from the spot where it had grown.

"How did you get over here?" The grass had torn a hole where the tree had been. His roots were deep and solid, as if that was where he had always been, right where he now stood.

"Mom, Mom!" Adeline was watching Martin during his accident. She had scampered to Martin as he maneuvered to his knees, still on the spot where he had landed. He laughed. Twila cried, still dirt covered.

"Are you okay?" She asked.

"I'm okay Mom," he replied. Twila sat in the sand sniffling and rubbing the sand from her eyes.

"What's the matter, little miss?" She was rescued by big brother Martin while Theron was disciplined with a scolding and smack to the bottom by Adeline. The Winter Tree was another story.

Through the years the family would become used to the tree and its moving about the yard. Martin grew tired of patching the holes he left and even scolded the tree a time or two. The Winter Tree always had its leaves beautiful green, always keeping watch over the Salter's, especially the twins. One day when the twins were about six years old, they bounced out the back door, leaving the screen door quivering in their wake. The backyard was their playground and they loved it, from the swing set to the sandbox, with running room on the quarter acre of green lawn. It was a kind of paradise. The Winter Tree had grown nearly seventeen feet tall. He spread his branches, giving cover to wherever he came to rest in the yard. Today the sun was hot and the tree's shade was welcome over any spot on the big lawn. Garden water flooded the back lawn for the Salter water turn. Two inches of water from the ditch covered the grass where the twins usually played. That was okay, for the little brunette pair, covered with clumps of grass and with clothes dingy brown from the soil, they enjoyed the cool water and the new game

TS and The WOW

it made for them. Theron slid on the water and grass after running a bit. Twila, however, was content to just sit in the cool water, pretending the clouds in the sky were animals.

"Look, that one is a castle." She pointed at a billowing thunderhead that would surely pass out of the county before it dropped any rain. The Winter Tree began to shake his limbs and to mumble undeterminable things. He twisted his limbs into something like a braid you might see in girl's hair. Then he unleashed his branches, uncoiling like a tornado. At first it moved too fast to see, whatever it was he was tossing from his branches. A long harried white cat sneered its terrified snarl as it flew into the air and out from the branches. Winter Tree's branches rustled, settling back into their normal position. The cat landed in the water next to Twila. They were eye to eye in surprise. The weary cat locked its one green eye on Twila's brilliant blue ones. The mysterious cat was crouched, prepared to leap directly into her face, his faded gray eye focused toward an entirely different intention. Escape. Twila reached her hand out to touch the wild-eyed cat.

"Here kitty," she said, reaching toward the animal. It was as if the rubber band inside the animal burst. His feet went four directions all at once, rolling in the water and mud and grass, and then spurting with all parts churning. The once fluffy white cat shot like a rocket to attack the unprotected little girl.

TS and The WOW

Normally, Martin would have been there to chase the cat away, but today it was Mom's job to keep an eye on the twins. She was in the kitchen making lunch and watching them through the window. The wild one struck, launching to attack the little girl, but in that instant, a branch from the Winter Tree swung, slapping the cat into the air, cat howling and screaming. The cat took flight in sheer terror, knowing it was about to lose one of its nine lives. The animal landed in the neighboring vacant yard near the wash in several clumps of brush. All four feet running when it hit the ground, scurrying as fast as it could into the undergrowth, it disappeared. Twila sat in the water, calling, "Kitty, here kitty."

The next day, the tree had moved to the far corner of the yard where the other trees stood in a line on the ditch bank. He stood proud, erect. His limbs folded as if he had arms.

"If that tree had a face, it would have a smug look on it. Master of his domain," George said, looking out the window. It seemed like the tree might stay in that spot for awhile. Glad the tree had been there to protect his little girl, George muttered quietly, "Thanks, old boy."

Weeks had passed since the cat had been ejected from the yard and the Winter Tree had stood guard along the ditch bank, not moving, not showing any hint of his real nature. He just soaked up the water from the ditch, growing another foot. His leaves shimmered in the evening breeze while

TS and The WOW

Martin cut the lawn beneath him. The Winter Tree stayed in that spot through the winter, only unfolding its limbs to reach toward the sky, shaking for a moment to loosen the snow so it would fall to the ground. For a time, he seemed to be quite content. Most families would have been bothered by the tree moving about the yard, but the Salter's had decided that their tree was a special gift, and what good would it do to tell anyone about their moving tree anyway? They would just say they were crazy and lock them all up.

"Let me see the news." George was worried about the state of affairs in the country, fearful that his son would be sent into the conflict. "Turn it up." The black and white picture was a marvel and Walter Cronkite gave the totals of the dead that day in Vietnam. His sober voice gave the grim words even more reality.

"Those poor mothers!" Adeline exclaimed. Martin, who was now nineteen years old, was in boot camp in Alabama. The twins were eleven years old and watched with a new reverence. The entire family had their fingers crossed, praying Martin would not be sent to the war. It had become a nightly ritual to keep up on the five o'clock news. Tonight there were fourteen boys lying on the ground motionless, blankets draped over their faces and their boots exposed. They said they were dead. "That isn't going to happen to Martin. It couldn't," thought Adeline.

"Did you mail the letters to Martin?" George asked, directing his inquire to Adeline.

TS and The WOW

"Yes dear and we got one from him," she replied, waving it in the air. George read the letter aloud. It was all about how well Martin was doing in training, especially the shooting, which he had done since he was a boy.

"At least he can defend himself." Somehow the war wasn't here, so it wasn't real. The news ended and on came "Rudolf the Red Nosed Reindeer."

"Theron," George said as he shook Theron's shoulders. "Wake up, son. It's time to go to bed." Theron had grown to the point when it was too hard to carry the boy to bed. George stood him on his feet. Theron, still not awake, stood balanced by his father. George stood behind his boy, hands on his shoulders, and began to walk him in his dazed state. He walked him to the front door, opened it and guided him out the open door. He continued walking him to the edge of the yard. George then turned around, leaving Theron standing in the cold. George hurried back to the house, where the rest of the family watched giggling. Twila held her hand over her mouth as she giggled, muffling her sounds. Adeline smiled at Theron as he awoke enough to realize where he stood. It was in that moment that a revelation about who Theron was became exposed. He turned toward the house while rubbing his eyes. As he stumbled back to the door, the blueness of his eyes intensified in its brightness and a glow encompassed his entire face. George, Adeline and Twila were all shocked at his appearance.

TS and The WOW

"Son, are you okay?" Adeline inquired. His face glowed as bright as if the sun was shining from his eyes, not with yellow light but with a light blue as the ice of a frozen glacier. Theron looked for the snowman that he and Twila had made in the yard. It was gone, it had disappeared. His eyes mellowed, returning to their former appearance.

"What is that?" Adeline knew, as did Theron, that something was wrong, very wrong. Now on the lawn, where the snowman had been, grew a bent-over tropical palm tree. Coconut-like fruit hung under its fronds. The grass that had been covered with snow was gone and a small pond with swamp grass surrounding it had taken its place.

"Get into the house!" George pushed on Twila's arm and Adeline's back, recognizing danger. The whole of the front yard had been changed. Even the neighboring yards looked like the everglades. An extraordinary thing always seemed to happen to the Salter's and tonight was no exception. The palm tree rose from the swamp and was not a palm tree at all. It was a reptile that had been resting in the warm steamy waters of the swamp. The neck bent and the palm branches were not branches at all. They were a collar around the reptile's neck. The face of the beast was round with a tubular snout, something like the trunk of an elephant, until the mouth opened, exposing four rows of teeth undulating in waves to draw whatever entered deep into the throat.

TS and The WOW

"How is this happening? Something like this could not have existed in the hills of Utah," George thought. The word ugly only touched on the nature of how hideous the monster was that possessed the body rising before them. The titan's fearsome, wide-open mouth was reaching down to devour Theron, who had not yet reached the safety of the front door.

"Hurry, Theron, hurry!" George waved his hand in the signal to steal second base, waving his son on to a double. Theron dropped to the sidewalk, narrowly being missed by the palm-necked monster. Theron leaped to his feet, no longer in the grip of sleep that had muddled his mind. Diving with all the power in his legs, he leaped through the threshold of the open door. George slammed the door with a force that quaked the glass in the windows.

"You're safe, son." Theron made it into the house when it had seemed he was about to become food for that monster.

"What was that? Theron squealed in his unchanged little boy squeak.

"Is it still out there?" Twila pealed back the curtain from the window to see. She didn't understand how this had happen or how the creature had gotten in the yard. Where had the snowman gone? "He can't get in here, can he?" Twila thought that her family was about to be eaten by a giant slimy coconut monster. She commanded, "You go back to where you came from you

TS and The WOW

skazbit, you!" Her voice was penetrating. It was not loud, yet it pierced the fabric of space and time. The monster withered, its head whipping back and forth, disappearing with the sound of the popping of a bubble. The swamp was gone, along with the grassy marsh that had surrounded it, being replaced by the shining white snowman that stood like a sentinel in all his glory.

George looked out the window, surprised that everything was back to normal. He opened the door that he had braced himself against moments before to protect his family from the monster on the other side. He marveled as he walked over the yard, leaving his tracks in the clean white snow.

It was true. Salter's could do anything. Just like George had always said.

CHAPTER 3

Back In School and The Wolf On The Wall

Theron was the first in the class to raise his hand, but as usual, it was as if he were invisible. He waved it frantically for recognition.

"Kathy," Mrs. Sweeney said, while pointing at a girl in the second row who had long blond hair that was curled to perfection and a pale blue dress that complemented her angelic face.

"It's the dodo bird!"

"That's right. The dodo is extinct. Now, where did the dodo come from originally?"

"Theron's house," Jack Sweeney said. The whole class burst into laughter, everyone except for Theron and Twila.

"Jack that will be enough of that!" Mrs. Sweeney said, scolding her son Jack who was always trying to get Theron's goat.

Usually Theron had a snappy reply that made Jack look like he was a half-wit. However, Theron knew that, in a class taught by Jack's mother, it wasn't prudent or the place to get the 'one-up' on him.

"When did the dodo bird live on the earth?" Mrs. Sweeney questioned. This time she called on Becky Burk, a girl with short brown hair and dimples. She wore one of the two dresses she owned. The once bright yellow material had faded, but was clean and freshly ironed. Theron was kind of sweet on Becky, but he was considered a dork by most of the girls. Becky smoothly gave her answer

"In 1681, they were considered extinct." She smiled and relaxed in her seat.

"Why are they extinct?" Mrs. Sweeny always had another question to ask.

"Because they taste like chicken!" Jack spouted out. The class laughed. It was the scolding his mother gave him with her eyes that sent tension throughout the classroom.

Theron swung the hall pass that Mrs. Sweeney insisted they carry just to go to the restroom. The pass was a stick that looked as though it could be used to paddle someone's bottom. Its real purpose was to allow other teachers to know that the child was doing what they were supposed to. Even though he had to go and felt the urgency, he dragged the stick along the wall acting like a waddling dodo bird. "Doo, doo diddle do," he sang all the way to the bathroom.

It was then that the air shifted or the alignment of molecules migrated into a new pattern and when extraordinary things were launched.

Theron had just come out of the bathroom when he realized that the building was undergoing some kind of change, a transformation. The lunchroom wall was gone. It had disappeared and now opened into a rolling, hilly slope, a grass-covered plain. At the edges, where the worlds came to together, it blended seamlessly. Who was to tell where one world started and the other ended? Theron stood on the threshold, his mouth gaping open and his chin nearly scraping the floor. He was marveling at the color of the sky. His red locks of hair had started twisting and untwisting in spastic movements as if they had intuition. His early warning system was in full operation. The New World was so different. It was brighter in colors and the smells were crisp. Different than anything he had ever seen or smelled. The smell felt like tasty tickles of flavor. They were experienced by more than one of the five senses at the same time.

"What the heck is that?" Theron wondered. A herd of something clattered as hoofs crossed a rocky hillside and then went on to the grassy plain, where they came in to full view. The noise increased in the seconds he stood there as they

TS and The WOW

came closer and then a herd of wild white horses burst through the opening.

Theron dove to the ledge where the coats hung to get out of their way. Hoofs clamored and clanked down the hallway, leaving muddy horse prints in the path where they had traveled. As soon as they had passed, Theron poked his head out from behind the coats to check out what was happening. The stallion reared on his hind legs, grazing the horn on his head on the tiles of the ceiling. He turned his harem about, wanting to escape from the building that had captured them. It was then that Theron recognized what kind of animals trampled through the school. He gasped.

"Unicorns!" he said, both with shock and delight in his voice. He then hugged the wall of the coat rack again while the unicorns bounded past him, and thundered by as he watched through the coats. Then, once more, they were off onto the grassy plain with clumps of grass and mud flying from their hooves.

"Woo, that was cool!"

Theron had just stepped out from the security of the coat rack to watch the unicorns as they ran off into the distance, when the floor began to quiver under his feet, inviting the rest of the school to do the same. The school shook with the fury of an earthquake and the entrance to the grassy plain

TS and The WOW

popped like a bubble and faded away. The wall was a wall again and the hall was littered with purple clay and grass from the unicorns' hooves, leaving neither hide nor hair of the animals. They had left just the tracks, remnants that shadowed their existence.

Doors on every classroom opened and teachers' heads poked into the hall where only one person stood: Theron. All Theron could say when Mrs. Sweeney, followed by the twenty three members of his class, arrived was, "Man, the janitor is going to be mad!"

For reasons unknown to Theron, Mr. Roper, the principal, and Mrs. Sweeney wanted to attribute the whole mess to Theron.

"But I didn't do it!" he pleaded. However, it seemed, someone had to pay. Who else stood in the hall alone with the biggest single mess that the principal had ever seen?

Twila knew Theron's story was true. She had fought with her locks of red hair during the stampede, trying not to let them bring attention to her. She knew her brother had gone through the twisty turnies with his red hair. Besides, not even Theron could make a mess that big in so short a time, she thought. Not a person except Twila would listen to Theron when he told them how the mess was made.

TS and The WOW

"I'm not kidding. It was a herd of unicorns that ran through here!" At first they marveled at his imagination and then they laughed at him.

"You're just crazy," Jack said.

After school Theron's punishment was to write one hundred times on the chalkboard, "Boys make messes, not unicorns. I will keep the hall clean. Theron." Jack was delighted with Theron's punishment.

"Theron Salter, you're such a loser," Jack said. As he passed him, he bounced his shoulder off Theron's shoulder, making him scribble on the chalkboard. Theron just shrugged it off. This kind of thing was always happening with Jack, so he went on writing.

"What's the matter? You chicken!...Bock, bock." Jack was taunting him, hoping he would come after him and then he could tell his mother how Theron started it and he would be in more trouble.

Becky Burk walked past, holding a book against her chest with both arms. She smiled at Theron.

"I believe you, Theron." she said, then walked out the door to go home. He liked that she thought he was telling the truth, but all he could think of was how someday Jack Sweeny would "get his." However, Theron had been in this position before with Jack. It seemed to be just a repeat of a week ago

TS and The WOW

when Theron was accused of throwing food at Jack in the cafeteria. Mrs. Sweeney always took Jack's side on everything, so Theron had decided not to let it happen. He was in control of his own mind and his own body. He had learned that from the experience with the snowman and the swamp creature. His Dad had taught him that God had sent all of us to earth to learn how to make choices.

"We all have the right to choose," he said. "Choosing either right or wrong is up to each of us. God called it free agency." Theron had thought this was kind of like when a baseball player's contract was done and he could choose to stay with the team or join another team. Theron was exercising his free agency not to let Jack get his goat. Mrs. Sweeney came back into the room,

"Jackie, it's time to go home." Theron liked it when she called him Jackie.

"Girl's name." was all Theron said. Jack glared at him.

"Let's go home, Theron," she said. "Time to go." That meant freedom for Theron. Freedom from the bondage of the chalkboard and, since the janitor hadn't wanted Theron's help cleaning up the hall he was free for the rest of the day. Theron plucked his coat from the rack, slipped it on and met his sister, who had waited at the door. Twila had always been there whenever Theron faced any challenge. It was big sister to the rescue. She was his left hand, as he was her right. She was three minutes older and a head taller, but they were partners. Whatever had happened to one was happening to both of them. As they walked toward home Twila pushed her brother for the skinny or the details on the incident in the hallway.

"What were they like?" she said, meaning what were unicorns like, having never seen one herself.

"They were kind of like Dad's horses, a bit bigger than his mustang mare 'Peanuts'."

"Were they white? That's the way I imagined them."

"They are white, but kind of blue, too. Oh yeah, they have kind of a spiny, twisty-looking horn on their heads. That's how I knew they were unicorns."

If you had seen Twila and Theron from a distance, you would have noticed that their red hair stood at attention, each twins pointing toward the other twin as they walked home, still discussing their newest mystery.

A mystery of a different sort was why Twila was taller than all the boys her age. Most of the time she enjoyed the advantage that gave her, but it wasn't what she wanted. She had found that she would rather admire the boys than fight them, especially Rex Twinkle.

"Twila, Rex likes you," Allie Jackson said.

TS and The WOW

"He told you he liked me?"

"No, but I saw him staring at you while we were eating lunch." The girls giggled. Twila was excited to hear that Rex might be sweet on her. Sweet on someone was the way her daddy, George, described a crush or being twitter-pated. All through the day in class, Twila watched Rex. She would smile and duck her head whenever he happened to look her way. Her shyness showed like a beacon on top of the highest tower, although she tried to be unnoticed.

"He's watching you." Allie said, and then giggled as Rex looked right at her. Rex was kind of like Theron, a head shorter than most of the girls, but he was so handsome, the most popular boy in school, unlike Theron who was considered a dork. George would say, "A dork was someone who farted in the bathtub and would bite at the bubbles on the way up."

Twila was the envy of all the girls who thought that Rex might like her. The romance between Twila and Rex was one where they never talked, never looked at each other, and never held hands, but everyone knew that they were in love. When Rex came near, she would duck her head and blush. Theron was always teasing his sister. First it was, "Rex and Twila sitting in a tree, k-i-s-s-i-n-g." You know how the rest of that rhyme goes. Then it was the thought of the name Twila Twinkle. Theron really liked that thought. He would

TS and The WOW

say,"its Twila Twinkle, the newest star in the sky," or "Here comes the wood fairy, Twila Twinkle and her baby Tinkle Twinkle." Then something so bizarre happened. Theron and Rex become best of friends.

"This is too strange," Twila thought when she first heard that they were best friends. She felt a little jealous. She had always been Theron's best friend. "But it would be okay that Rex was, too," she thought.

Rex had been coming to the Salter house to hang out in the tree house and to help build the fort on the hill, but Theron had not wanted Twila to be a part of those things anymore.

"Rex is coming over. We're going to work on the train set," Theron told his mother. Twila had listened in on the conversation.

"Rex is coming over," she said to herself, holding both hands over her mouth, muffling her own words. A flurry of outfits landed on the bed. "Is my hair okay, Mom?"

"Just as cute as a bug."

"Bugs are not cute Mom."

"You're just fine, honey."

Cold and calculated, she entered the room where the boys were setting up an HO train set. Theron saw through the whole thing. "Theron, Mom wants you," Twila said while

TS and The WOW

walking down the staircase like she was Scarlet O'hara in "Gone With The Wind."

"Oh, hi Rex. I didn't see you." She stumbled and fell three steps before catching herself with the handrail.

"What a train wreck," Theron said under his breath. Theron ran upstairs to see what it was that Adeline wanted him for, leaving them alone in the same room for the first time. "We don't like dumb girls," Theron said as he passed her on the steps. His face bore a scowl, his freckles connected by the red in his face.

"Twila, is Theron down there?" Adeline yelled.

"No, Mom, he came upstairs."

"Would you to go out to find him?" Twila blushed as she came up the stairs.

"Sure Mom." She bounced as she walked a step ahead of Rex. They pushed the door open, exiting to the backyard. The Winter Tree was standing in the center of the yard with its lower limbs drawn close so as not to expose his inner trunk, hiding something as Rex and Twila passed under him. Passing by without noticing anything unusual, Twila said, "Let's check the tree house. We can see all over from there."

The day was warmer than most of the winter days, but this year had been very different. Theron had climbed into the Winter Tree and peered out from behind a blind that the tree

TS and The WOW

had made for him with his branches. He watched as Rex and Twila climbed into the tree house in the neighboring yard atop the wash bank. The old cottonwood tree was the foundation of the tree house that Martin had started and now Theron was finishing. The Winter Tree's branches unfolded as Theron slipped down from the tree and followed the unwary combo in his stealthy manner.

"It's time to morph into a bush or something like Morph Man would," Theron thought, frustrated that he couldn't turn into a bush. Morph Man was his comic book hero. In fact he carried issue six, "Morph Man Meets Megawatt," with him at all times. It was a crinkled worn-down copy that his big brother Martin had given him before he left to serve in the armed forces. First, Theron hid in the ditch behind some brush thinking, "I'm morphed to brush," and then behind a big cottonwood tree, becoming a tree in his mind.

Rex and Twila surveyed the countryside, not seeing Theron anywhere.

"Where would he go?"

"My brother is strange that way sometimes."

From the tree house they went on to the wash. Theron could hear them talking and laughing about something. He wished he could hear what they were saying.

"If I were able to morph, I would become a listening device," he thought. He simply was not close enough to hear more than a laugh. They passed the edge of Busher's Pond with Theron sneaking ever closer to hear the conversation. He had deduced that they were on their way to the black fort. This had become a cool game to Theron, spying on his two best friends. Twila was doing her thing, that girl thing. You know, when they talk their hands dancing through the air like they added expression to the words spewing from their mouths. She was looking over her shoulder, making those stupid smiles.

"What a geek." Theron would have been disgusted, but he had decided this was fun. At the right moment, he would hide and then jump out when they reached his hiding spot. Theron wasn't even breathing hard after running up the hill and dodging Rex and Twila, hiding and then running, then hiding again so as not to be found out. He was sitting in the spot waiting where he knew they would pass under him. Their voices were still distant. He could no longer see them, yet he knew that he would have to just wait quietly. Then he would jump out and scare the life out of them. He could no longer hear them talking, but there were footsteps making rocks clatter, with some rolling down the hill. Theron crouched behind the bush, holding his breath and readying himself to leap into action and cause Twila to pee her pants.

TS and The WOW

The footsteps were nearing. The moment had arrived. Theron leaped off a rock over the bush into the air, screaming like a banshee. But the surprise was his and not his friends'.

The travelers walking the path were large and hairy. Shock rested on their faces and terror was etched on the face of the leaping boy. Theron darted left. The Big-Foots leaped over a stand of rocks and went left. As Theron ran down the hill, he stumbled over rocks, plopping through a bubble that he had not noticed. Somehow, he had entered the boundary of some other world and now he was back where he had come from. Theron rolled to a stop at the feet of Twila and Rex.

"Theron, where did you come from?" Theron had no reply. His red hair had matted itself flat to his head. Twila held her hand over her red hair, twisting it like she was playing with it. She had felt the same activity as her brother had, covering their secret the best she could.

"Theron, sometimes you are a weirdo," Rex said, laughing at Theron's appearance behind them. Twila and Rex helped him up, dusted him off and they began the walk back to the house.

"So you really can morph, but when do you turn back to a normal boy?" Twila had to tease him because she could.

Twila was just a friend to Rex after that and it was all back to normal with Twila and Theron.

Smoke rose from the yard barbecue where Adeline was preparing dinner, one of her fabulous barbecues. George had built the barbecue from native rocks. It had taken him all last summer. The table was set on the patio and spring had swept in, along with the first onslaught of mosquitoes. It was the bugs that sent Theron into the house early. He hated them, but they loved the taste of him. Twila rested on the back step where the sun had warmed the concrete all day. George and Adeline sat back in the lawn chairs holding hands. Theron would say that was gross, but he was glad his folks loved each other and were not afraid to show their affection. At home it was okay, just not in front of his friends or in public. Theron had gotten himself ready for bed. Tonight he was extra tired, the new warmer spring air he had supposed.

Going into Theron's room was like a trip to the baseball hall of fame. His room was lined with baseball posters and his Arrow of Light from the cub scouts hung over a drawing he had done of a horse. His favorite things rested on his dresser, things he found, like that old French coin with the lady half rubbed away from being in someone's pocket perhaps. Coins from strange places sat alongside his real treasure: his prized possession, a Don Drysdale rookie card. Theron would say that he was the best left-hander the Los Angeles Dodgers ever had.

TS and The WOW

The only other item on the dresser top was a photo of his older brother Martin in his Army dress uniform.

The twins were similar, but definitely not the same. Gender, of course, gave them some distinct differences. Twila's room was lined with fuzzy and furry stuffed animals. She loved them all, but mostly the ones that had been given to her by Martin, her big brother. Her favorite she had named Martintee. The rest of her bedroom had dolls, a shelf full of books and the same photo of Martin that Theron had on top of his dresser. So some things were the same.

Theron folded back the bedding and turned off the lights, leaving the door slightly ajar. Theron knelt by his bed and offered his private prayers. He rested in his bed listening to the others coming into the house. Drowsy, heavy eyelids closed and he faded into the world beyond the waking time. The room became darkened. It was not so much as blackness. It was more the feeling of something bad contained in an inky gray cloud. Theron's red hair spastically thumped against his pillow, waking him. Startled by the action of his hair, his eyes opened to see what was going on. Now his hair was fluttering like a squid being chased by a hungry whale. As his eyes cleared, the light in his room was growing dimmer.

"What's going on?" It was only a few seconds after his red hair had awakened him. He settled back to rest. His hair lay still in silence. "What's that on the wall?" It looked like a crayon

TS and The WOW

scribble at first, until he saw that it was moving across the wall. He supposed that it was a group of spiders. Nervously, he watched as it grew large. The lines defined themselves and become a sketch, then a shape. Fear grew inside his chest. The shape became an image of a dog of some sort. Scared, but intrigued, he watched it moving on the wall.

The lines on the wall had become more of a shape. Bulging on the wall was a face, now recognizable as a wolf.

"It's a wolf," he uttered under his breath, feeling his impending doom. The wolf was moving ever closer to the open door. With terror in his heart Theron realized that the figure, now half of a wolf on the wall, soon would be alive and loose in his room. The wolf on the wall was trying to reach the door to close it. Inside Theron was sure that if the wolf closed the door before he himself could reach it, the wolf would surely devour him in a gruesome way.

"Theron!" Twila screamed bounding from her bed, her red hair twisting away in a warning to go to Theron's aid. In a race for his life, Theron rose from his bed and, with all his agility and strength, he dove for the open door, sliding half of his body in the opening. At the same moment, the wolf on the wall reached the door, budding into a gruesome face of teeth and terror. Theron wiggled and scrambled to get out of the room, his legs still in the opening of the doorway. Twila reached her brother, "Are you okay?" Both George and Adeline followed her.

TS and The WOW

George swung the door aside, revealing an empty room. With the wolf's attempt on the boy thwarted, he leaped from the wall, as a fully formed wolf. The wolf turned toward the spot where it had first appeared, changed its shape in a darkened shadow into a half wolf-half man, and turned his head only for a moment to glare at Theron where he lay in the doorway. Then the wolf was sucked into the wall and disappeared.

Theron had not had time to scream, only to act. He stood in the hall, shaking, while Twila held him, cradled in her arms.

"What was it?" she asked.

"It's a wolf, a wolf on the wall." The wolf on the wall meant nothing to Theron, but the vision still hung in his mind.

"The red hair warned me," Theron said.

"Mine warned me, too." She had experienced her brother's terror, just as she had experienced other moments in his life, sometimes thinking it was her own encounter and not noticing he was involved. The opposite had occurred once with Theron, feeling Twila's cut on her hand when she herself had not felt it. Together they have sensed something more was about to happen, but at the moment, it was distant and in the future.

Theron pulled the blankets from his bed and slept on the floor of Twila's room, as they had done for years when they were scared. Tonight they were scared and it would be a long night.

TS and The WOW

CHAPTER 4

Crystal Stone and Waves Of Sand

Theron and Twila had passed their eleventh birthday and ever since the palm-necked monster had appeared and disappeared in the front yard, things had been pretty weird. For example, the behavior of the Winter Tree on their birthday, what a day that was. The house was filled with kids, both boys and girls, nearly everyone from Mrs. Sweeney's fifth grade class. That included Jack Sweeney. Adeline had insisted he come to the party.

"It's time to blow out the candles on the cake," said Adeline. She led the group to the patio in the back yard.

"It is an unusually warm winter day and it would be less mess in the yard," thought Adeline. All the candles on Twila's cake were lit at the same time as those on Theron's cake. The boys circled around Theron and the girls, in their bright party dresses, encircled Twila.

"One, two, three, blow them out!" Adeline said, clasping her hands together and smiling at her children.

Twila blew, puffing only once to get her candles out. Theron had sucked in a big breath that he was sure would blow out eleven candles. He was wrong. Three of the candles stayed lit. In his second breath he was sure that he would blow them all out, but the others that he had blown out re-lit themselves. He blew and blew with everyone laughing at him as the candles re-ignited each time he tried to blow them out.

"You will never get them out," called out Jack to frustrate Theron.

The sound of leaves on the breeze arose and, since it was winter, there was only one tree that had its leaves. Suddenly, a breeze came right from the Winter Tree. The wind increased until the candles on the cake were dimmed. The boys alone were in the wind. But the girls all stood aside, watching the boys being tossed forward. No wind blew the girls, their hair or their dresses. Some of the boys were hanging onto the table, hoping not to be blown down. Jack stood opposite the table, facing the wind, Theron his back was into the wind. The cake was blown off the table and landed smack in Jack's face. The candle stuck to his shirt and re-lit.

"Help me!" screamed Jack, as he plucked candles from his clothes.

"Good job, buddy," Theron said, knowing that this was a Winter Tree prank. The tree was now a towering presence in the yard. It had become hard for it to stand in line with the trees on the ditch bank. He overshadowed them, blocking their sun. So he moved on occasion to the middle of the lawn, right about where he first grew, spreading out his limbs like he was stretching in relief from his confinement. Theron had noticed that his leaves were as green as the moss in Busher's Pond in the middle of summer.

Night fell and, when morning came, the world was different. It had stormed in the night. Few of the Winter Tree's leaves were showing through the snow he was carrying on his branches. The Winter Tree sagged in the heavy snows, his branches creaking under the weight of the water-filled covering of white. It was then that the antics of the tree began again.

Theron watched the tree from the window. The tree twisted itself like a dishrag being wrung out. All his limbs went into the air, leaving his trunk bare where the twisted limbs started. Then it unleashed, unwinding with a snap and flinging snow, which splattered on the window where Theron watched. He jumped back, startled by the impact. As it reached the end of the twist, the remaining snow flew and, when it landed on the window, it formed the words "Happy Birthday to Us!"

Theron had seen some strange things, but he had no idea that the Winter Tree could write or that he knew that today was their birthday, even though they had the party yesterday.

TS and The WOW

"Twila, come and see what the tree has done," said Theron.

Twila rushed to the window to see what was so exciting. As she did, three names appeared in the snow that ran down the window, "'Theron, Twila and Tarel," along with the words, "Happy Birthday to Us". Theron and Twila stood back from the window to read the bizarre greeting card. Reaching out to touch their side of the window, the snowy names changed, melting and running down the window.

"Tarel. That has to be his name," Theron said, pointing at the tree.

"Happy birthday to you too, Tarel." Twila said.

"The three T's," Theron said, the tone in his voice rising then dropping, changing as young voices do.

Twila was growing in different ways than her brother. His voice was changing. Her vocabulary was increasing. Sometimes Theron couldn't understand a word she said. She was giddy and giggly like the other girls her age. Theron thought she was getting too strange for words. She liked boys. What was up with that? Theron still thought girls were weird, except for Twila, who was his best friend, at least at times.

Theron and Twila dressed for the snow and went to the yard to see what the tree was up to. Eventhough he revealed his true name, he would be forever 'The Winter Tree" to the family.

TS and The WOW

He was being active again and they didn't want to miss the fun. The Winter Tree had been up to something; he had moved to the ditch bank and turned so that the moss on his north side was now south. The tree whispered so lightly that his words at first were mistaken as the wind rustling through his leaves. Theron and Twila turned around to find the tree had moved again and was right at their backs. The low voice of the Winter Tree said only one word:

"Follow."

They would have been shocked that a tree could talk, but this was the Winter Tree and they knew that anything could happen when he was involved. The word was so brief and meaningless. They waited to hear more from the tree, but an answer never came, only the silence of the snowstorm. The word hung in their minds, haunting them with wonderment. What did he mean and why did he say "follow" to them?

"What does that mean?" Theron yelled at the tree, stabbing into the silence, hoping for an answer. No answer ever came. The word "follow" became an unsolved mystery.

Snows melted and spring came, once more freeing the twins to roam the countryside. Martin's wonderful tree house on the edge of the wash was where the twins set up their home base. Martin and George had hung a rope swing that dangled from one of the highest branches. The swing was a challenge of courage. Neither Theron nor Twila had ever swung on it across the wash. The twins leaped out the back door to run across the lawn past the Winter Tree.

"Watch out for that hole," Theron said. Twila did a little arabesque spin around the hole and jumped the brush.

"Theron, are you going to do it?" she questioned.

"You'll see," he replied.

Hand-over-hand they climbed up the board ladder to the platform where the tree house stood. The rope swing had dangled lonely ever since Martin had turned sixteen and lost interest in the tree house. Theron stood next to the edge of the platform where the rope hung, looking down into the wash.

"That's a long way down," she said. "Don't do it,"

He had wanted to do this from the first time he saw Martin swing out over the wash on the rope, but he was scared. Martin had been the master of this swing. Now it was Theron's turn to prove he was as brave as his big brother. Twila didn't need to prove how cool she was, but Theron had

TS and The WOW

to prove he was as big as his mind told him he was. He grasped the dangling rope in one hand, twisting it until he had the grip which made him comfortable.

"You're going to kill yourself," she said, almost singing it.

Theron leaped into the air above the seat, reaching to grab the rope with the other hand. He slid his bottom onto the board where the rope's end passed through it and where a knot on the opposite side held it. Theron's second hand missed, and as quickly as he mounted the board, he found himself losing his grip. He swung across the wash and was hanging by his knees on the board seat.

"Theron, you're gonna die!" Twila screamed.

Theron swung like the catcher on a trapeze, first across the wash and then back toward the tree house, watching the sand pass under him. The Winter Tree heard Twila's scream and moved to the yard's outermost limits along the ditch bank. Theron was on the return swing when Twila plopped her behind to the floor of the tree house, her legs hanging over the edge. She had all intents of catching him as he swung close to the tree house. She reached out as far out as she could. She caught him only by a strand of red hair that seemed to be reaching for her as it untwisted.

"Let go," Theron whimpered. She let go, not wanting to rip the hair from his head or cause him to lose the grip with his

TS and The WOW

knees. Theron swung to the middle of the wash before his knees lost their grip and he tumbled head over heels to the bottom of the wash.

Twila screamed, knowing he would never survive. He saw the rocks, then the brush, then the sand, and then heard a thud as his feet and hands hit the ground. His face kissed the sand, his breath gone. Twila's long gangly legs swung back to the platform and she started down the ladder, jumping off to the ground midway down. She then made her way through the fallen barbed-wire fence, down the wash bank through the rabbit brush. Then she lifted Theron's head from the sand. He seemed to be breathing. He spit sand from his mouth.

"Are you okay?" Her voice showed fear. A tear ran from the corner of her right eye. She tried to pick Theron up to roll him over, but his feet were stuck in the sand up to the knees. She stood him up. He sat onto his posterior.

"Are you okay?"

"Yes, I'm fine, but I'm stuck." He pulled on his legs while Twila tried to move the sand with her hands to no avail. He was stuck and stuck solid.

"Woo!" he screamed. "That was awesome! I'm invincible!" he roared, holding his hands over his head.

"You're a shortie, " Twila teased, still scared and shaking, hoping nothing was broken. His legs were buried so deep that his head reached only to her waist.

"Twila, it was so strange. When I hit the sand I heard a thud, but it didn't hurt. It was like landing on that old bed Grandma has, the one made of feathers."

Twila stopped her digging and got behind Theron, wrapped her arms about him and pulled, with all her might. As she pulled she noticed a disturbance up stream in the sand. It looked like a wave in the sand and it was headed their way. At first sight she thought that she was seeing things, but it was a wall of sand well above Theron's head, coming right toward them. She struggled harder to pull him free. It wasn't happening. He was stuck and stuck in a way that it would take superhuman strength to set him free.

"Twila, get to the wash bank. The sand wave will cover us both!" But she would have none of that.

The wave was about to hit and Theron still had not moved. He felt like he was being pulled from the other side of the sucking sand. Twila pulled with all her might, groaning from the strain, when the sand around Theron's legs took the shape of a pair of lips and spit Theron and Twila to the bank. The sand wave passed, leaving the sand as if nothing had happened in the spot where, moments before, Theron was nearly buried. They

TS and The WOW

had narrowly missed being swallowed in a sandy grave. Theron was covered from head to toe with particles of sand. They both sat still in the brush on the bank, resting and hardly believing what had just happened. A second wave passed in the same motion. Then the wash fell silent. Not even a sign of the hole where Theron was stuck remained.

The massive branches of the Winter Tree hung as far over the property as they could without leaving the yard. Twila and Theron cautiously stepped on the sand they needed to cross in order to get home. First Twila placed just a toe on the sand.

"It seems firm." She settled her whole foot on the sandy bottom of the wash. Then she maneuvered her other foot to that spot, recognizing the sand was the same as it had always been. "It's ok," she said, being fully committed with both feet in the sand of the wash.

No sooner than they had both feet exposed to whatever danger lay beneath the sand, Theron, at first a bit wobbly in the knees, they ran as fast as they could across the sandy trap. The twins had had enough of the waves in the wash for one day.

They passed under the sentinel in the yard that had stood firm, awaiting their return. As they passed beneath the Winter Tree, his rigid posture slumped in relief, knowing they were safe.

Until they could find out what was happening under the sand, they were staying out of the reach of whatever it was that propelled the sand down the wash as a giant wave. From that time on, the twins crossed the sand in the wash with the utmost caution. They only crossed the wash, never meandering along its bottom as had been their practice in the past.

Strange things seemed to happen to them at regular intervals. Was something out to get them? Why them? Clearly, the Salter family was being stalked. At least Theron was.

The Winter Tree had sensed the coming of the wolf, lingering as close to the house as possible the night the wolf came. He was unnoticed, with his limbs waving in the air as if they were being blown in the torrent of a great wind. Yet, that night was not windy. Not even a breeze blew. That was just like the Winter Tree, who at first was so scary to Adeline and George, but now was more just a member of the family. He was always watching out for the children, even showing his frustration for not being able to leave the yard when he wanting to follow after them. If he had had his way, he would never have let the kids to leave the yard or be out of his protection. He knew something that they didn't. Whenever the twins returned from one of their treks off the property, the Winter Tree preformed a sort of victory dance, always bringing laughter to the twins. One day, when Theron was gathering the eggs from the henhouse, Twila was all alone in the yard. She hung laundry on the clothesline. As she did, she kept one eye on the Winter Tree, waiting to see it move to the center of the yard. No one had ever seen it move

TS and The WOW

from place to place. She thought she could pull a sneaky one and catch him. He was at the edge of the yard where nothing was going on.

"Hey Sis, look at this egg." Theron held an egg twice the size of all the other eggs in his hand. She wanted to look, but restrained herself, still focused on her target.

"That tree's too snoopy to stay there while I'm out here." Twila thought. "This is my chance."

The tree was bound to move and Twila was going to catch him in the act. It was as if he never really moved. He seemed to just be there, wherever there might be. Hanging each towel, she slyly kept an eye on the tree. The tree didn't move, but she just had to catch him. She hung one end of the last sheet, wondering if she could fool the tree into thinking that she wasn't looking. Her face was partly covered by the white cotton bed covering, but one eye remained solidly open, not blinking, ever watching. The second clothespin slipped over the middle of the sheet and on the line, securing the cloth to the temporary host. The third pin she placed in her teeth and dragged the sheet carefully, not letting it touch the ground, to the spot where it would have its last pin placed. Then her work would be done.

"Come on move!" she thought in frustration. She worked slowly, expecting the tree to move before she was done, nothing happened. "Silly bob!" Twila said a word she had made up to express her frustration.

"Twila is the most stubborn of all the Salter's," Adeline said. That was natural. After all, Adeline's father was the first man to ever squeeze blood from a turnip. That may or may not have been true, but it accounted for the tenacity of her only daughter, Twila, to stick with whatever she did to the end.

Twila thought she knew the habits of the Winter Tree. He always made it back to the center of the lawn. All she had to do was catch him one time and that would explain how the tree moved about the yard. Twila plucked her laundry basket from the ground, pulled it tight to her waist and turned her back to the tree.

She muttered, "I will catch you." She walked to the house, never looking back. As she rounded the corner of the house, she increased the speed of her movements, tossed the basket aside and hugged up against the edge of the house, peering back at the tree like a spy. She waited for the tree to move. He stood tall and erect, like he had been in that spot for fifty years.

"Twi, what are you doing?" asked George, who had just stepped out of the truck, returning from work.

"Dad, I'm sure the Winter Tree is going to move," she whispered.

George stood over his girl and leaned around the corner so as not to be noticed. He wanted to catch that tree moving as bad as she did, also hoping to learn his secrets. They had waited nearly an hour when they heard a grinding growing sound. They deduced it was coming from somewhere in the back yard. Now was the moment they had waited for. The tree was about to move and they were ready to catch him. Twila held her hand over her mouth, about to giggle. The tree had decided that no one was watching and it was time to move. The grind turned to a creek, but nothing had moved, not yet. It was all Twila could do not to giggle with excitement, for she had caught the Winter Tree and was about to learn his secrets.

Theron came out of the house, slamming the screen door as he had time after time. Twila and George spun around, just for a second, responding to the noise. Their heads sprung back like they were tied to rubber bands. When their eyes focused, on the spot where the tree had been was now vacant. The Winter Tree was swaying back and forth, solid and rooted in the center of the lawn.

"Theron, what's wrong with you? Didn't you see?"

"See what? "

"The tree. It was about to move and we had him," Twila said. "You messed it all up."

"There will be another time," George said. "You two go and play."

That was enough for Theron. He waved his hand at Twila to follow him. She did, kicking at the ground, but when they reached the wash, he paused. Nervously, he stood on the bank, not wanting to be trapped in the sand again.

"Oh, come on, we're okay," she said, tugging on his arm.

He placed one foot on the sand, holding back the other. It was the same as it had always been. Theron placed the other foot cautiously in the sand to follow his sister, then ran to the other side. Nothing happened. They were safely on the other side.

The trail led through the stand of new small cottonwood trees on the bank of Busher's Pond. They made their way past the pond and onto the hill that was called "The Black Ridge." It was a lava-covered hillside that was laden with caves, places to hide and ledges to climb.

Theron bounced from rock to rock testing his shoes, "tennirunners," as he called them. His tennis shoes had a red dot representing a ball on the heel. It was as the commercial said: Red Ball Jets make you run faster, jump higher and Theron knew that was true. Theron was out to prove them right as he leaped over each rock, finally coming down in front of Twila as they walked toward their fort.

TS and The WOW

At the top of the ridge where the lava had bellowed from the hillside a thousand years or so ago, there was a natural shelter in the hollow of the rocks. Theron and Twila had started to stack more flat lava rocks on the edge of the hollow to build a wall on the downward hillside of the cavity.

"Twi, get some more rocks." Theron commanded.

She had already climbed out of the hole to get more rocks. She wanted to tell him to get his own rocks, but she tossed him a couple of loose ones from the lava flow. Then she climbed down to where the cliff dropped off fifty feet or so. She sat down on top of the rocky pinnacle. She loved to swing her legs when they dangled over the edge of anything. She swung them back and forth until one shoe fell off.

"I should have tightened my lace," she said aloud. Her shoe tumbled down the rocks, wedging in between two boulders. Twila watched as it fell. "Stop, you stupid shoe!" Next time she swore she would tie the laces tighter. The lava rocks were tearing at her foot, now only covered with her sock. She moved slowly down to where the shoe was. She retrieved the shoe, but before she put it on, she brushed away all the lichen that had gathered on her sock, and then placed the shoe back on her foot. She tightened both the laces.

While bending to tie the laces, Twila had noticed a cave that they had never seen before. The cave opening was a perfect oval, which was unusual in a lava rock, but there it was.

"Theron come down here! Hurry!" she yelled. Twila ducked her head and entered the cave. She was only going to explore a little way, then go to get Theron and show him her discovery. At first the cave's small opening made it hard to see much. The opening led into a hollow that had been hewn from the stone and had a pedestal in its center that rose three feet tall and had a bowl on its top. Twila had supposed that it had been a relic left by some Indian tribe long gone. There was something exciting about being somewhere that no one had been in many, many years, a discovery of something from another time. Twila moved into the center of the room after noticing that there was something in the basin.

"What's this?" It was a small round ball nestled in the bottom of the bowl. It seemed to be made of crystal and was perfectly round. As she approached, it began to glow from within. Then it started to spin around and around itself, driven perhaps by her presence. The Orb rolled around the inside of the dry bowl. A sparkling light shot bursts of tiny lighting-like bolts around the room, at times narrowly missing Twila. She made her way back out of the cave, scared.

"Theron! Theron!" she screamed in a tone of voice that meant she thought she was in trouble. Her head poked out from

TS and The WOW

the rock where her brother could see her. He leaped from rock to rock, making his way to her.

"What's going on?" He could see she was okay.

"Come quickly. You have to see this."

Light was leaving the cracks that were on top of the cave. Crystal white light came from the mouth near where Twila stood. Something was generating the light. Theron wanted to know what it was.

"What's making the light?"

"It's coming from a ball I found in there."

"A ball? What kind of ball?"

"It's a crystal ball."

"No, what is it really?"

"A ball you can see through."

Theron lead the way back into the cave. His sister hung onto his arm, putting finger dents in his biceps. The red hair had spun while Theron was on top of the hill, but now it was working overtime, knotting and unknotting as they made their way into the chamber. Their hair was not weaving in a warning way but more in an announcement of excitement and intrigue.

The ball rolled, increasing in speed until it began to hover, still spinning and spitting light showers in the air. Twila stood back from the orb near the opening to get out of the cave if need be. Something was happening to the orb.

"It's opening," Twila said in surprise. It opened like the petals of a flower blossoming, opening to greet the world. Smaller flecks of light bounced about the room, filling it with calm bliss.

"Look at that." Theron's eyes were as wide as two slices from the center of a watermelon.

Twila wanted to see what was inside the ball. She crouched, bending her knees she dodged the tiny lights that darted at her. They would dart at her and then pause at her face until she realized they were miniature humans with wings.

"Fairies," she said with an expression of astonishment. Her mouth hung open and her eyes bulged as the fluttering lights began to gather at her face.

"Theron help me!" At first it was all she could do to keep from swatting at them like mosquitoes. To her amazement, the tiny ones began to speak, not in words because their voices were too small to be heard; rather it was in thoughts they spoke.

"You're the one," said their leader, hovering in front of Twila.

The one speaking was female. She wore lavender jeans and a soft white shirt that flattered her. Again she asked, "You are the one, aren't you?"

TS and The WOW

"What's the one?" When Twila spoke, she used her mouth, not her thoughts. As she did, her breath blew the miniature crowd about six inches further away from her. They batted their wings until they recovered and moved back into place.

"The one in zee world, as you might call zee balancer." Even in this method of communication, the little ones were hard to understand. Some words sounded like they had a Z, at the beginning, much like the French when speaking English. But that wasn't what made the statements hard to understand. They were asking for something about which Twila had no knowledge.

"No, not me. Anyway, I don't think so." She was unsure about any of this.

"Yet you open zee door to our world. "

"What did you do?" Theron asked.

"I guess I opened something, but I don't know how."

"We must return to our world. You can call when you need us." As that was said, they began chasing the orb. As it spun, they retreated into the opening of their world. The fairies accelerated to speed, then were sucked into the orb.

"Wait, what's a balancer?" Twila called after them. Twila knew she had found new friends as the orb's petals closed behind them.

TS and The WOW

"What was that all about?" Theron asked, only hearing what Twila had said. The spinning of the orb slowed and it rolled around in the basin, finally coming to rest in the bottom of the bowl. The light died and the cave fell dark.

"Let's get out of here." Twila plucked the sphere from where it rested and put it into her pocket. When they got outside, Theron wanted some questions answered.

"Twi, what is this balancer thing?" She had no idea, but apparently she was one or the orb would not have opened the bubble to the world of the fairies.

"Did you see that? This is so awesome!" Twila said, holding out the orb trying to look inside. Twila suddenly became worried. The sun was going down and coyotes had begun to howl a canyon or so away.

"Theron, down here," Twila said, wanting him to hurry toward home with her. Theron climbed down to where Twila stood and together they hurried on down the hill. As they walked, Twila showed him the orb.

"How did you talk to them?"

"It was more like sending thoughts back and forth."

"How did you find their cave?"

She pointed toward the cliff. As she did, she said, "I dropped my shoe right there." As she pointed, she noticed the

TS and The WOW

rocky hillside had a face. The face was long with a cave that appeared to be an open mouth.

"The cave is there," she said, pointing toward the cave. A nose hung near the mouth like a roof shedding the rainwater and was probably the reason they had never seen the opening before. Stone eyes seemed to follow them as they hiked away down the hillside. The focus of the eyes faded in perspective as Theron and Twila searched for answers to their new questions. How could fairies be real and what was a balancer?

CHAPTER 5

The Steersman and Crop Circles

Main Street ran the length of town coming off the old highway and progressing past the bridge that crossed the wash. Main Street continued on to the one attraction that brought people into the area, which was a set of beautiful lakes in the hills above the town. The lakes were exactly twelve miles out of town. Theron knew it was twelve miles because he had ridden his ten-speed bicycle up to the lakes, along with his cousin Randolph. The reason he remembered it so well wasn't their ride up to the Lakes. More than likely, it was the cold night they had spent there with only fishing poles and a six-pack of the Farmers Friend soda pop and, oh yes, the flint stick and his pocket knife that built their fire. They had planned to catch some fish and roast them for dinner and, after all, they had the soda to drink. What more would they need?

Theron shivered, moving closer to the fire. It was a lot colder than either he or Randolph had expected. Randolph decided to put a soda on the fire next to the flat rock where one fish they had caught was cooking.

TS and The WOW

"How are you going hold that, to drink it?" Theron asked. The boys used teamwork, squeezing a pair of sticks together get the hot can out of the fire.

"Don't drop it," Theron said when Randolph nearly tipped the can over as they set it down. They placed a second soda on the coals. Both boys soon held a can of the brew in hand, each wrapped in one of their socks after they realized that the can was hot and could warm their hands.

"No coats, no sleeping bags. What were we thinking?" Theron asked in a rhetorical fashion while walking around the fire shaking his head.

"Your turn to get wood." Randolph crowded closer to the fire that was growing smaller.

"All right," Theron said, not wanting to go off into the darkness by himself for more fuel to keep the fire and their only source of warmth burning. "There is some brush." He loaded his arms until he could barely see over his armload. Sparks rose quickly into the air as Theron put three of the brush stocks on the fire.

"Woo, they look like flies lit on fire.

"Yeah, fireflies." Both boys laughed.

In the cold of the night they tried to rest under the starlit sky. The water of the lake shimmered and sparkled in the starlight.

TS and The WOW

"What was that?" Theron asked, startled from his moment of sleep. He was sure he had been awakened by something in the water. His red hair had twisted, forming a chain. When his eyes cleared up, the water of the lake was boiling. The water had boiled with what he thought was a school of fish, until he saw a massive tail slapping the water.

"Did you see that?"

"See what?" Randolph asked. He was still wiping sleep goobers from his eyes. The tail was from something much bigger than the trout that inhabited the lake, something that surely did not belong there.

"What could it be?" Theron wondered. His eyes locked on the water, watching the wake as it disappeared while he was waiting for the swimmer to rise and surface again. The water settled to a solid sheet of dark green as it always was on a calm cool morning.

"There it is." Randolph pointed to the opposite shore. In the dim morning light, an entire school of trout was airborne, escaping the creature that had been next to Theron and Randolph through the night. The water bubbled and shimmered and then the lake returned to its normal placid beauty. Theron's red hair settled down, returning to its plain strands, no longer excited.

"Let's go home. I want to get some sleep." Both boys mounted their banana seat bicyles. Shivering as the sun rose; they headed for the highway back to town.

"Let's not tell anybody about this," Theron suggested. Randolph agreed. Theron peddled toward town, racing at times with Randolph. Theron sprinted, taking the lead from Randolph on the downhill chunk of the road. Soon he was far ahead of Randolph. Too far he thought, looking back to find him. Theron stopped and waited.

"Come on!" he yelled. Then he started back to find out what had happened. Perhaps he fell, or worse. When Theron reached the top of the hill he saw Randolph, his bike in one hand, pushing it, and the bike's chain in the other hand. He waved the chain so that Theron could see it.

"I broke my chain," he called out. The chain that propelled his bike had snapped. The keeper link was gone, along with about an inch of the chain.

"Oh heck, what do we do now?" Theron said, looking at the remaining eight or ten miles home.

"I'll just push it and ride down the hills," Randolph said. Off they went toward town and, after the first downhill portion, Theron became the tow truck. As they rode, Theron's red hair would mat itself flat to Theron's head. Randolph sat behind

Theron on his bike as he was towed home with an old rope that they found. "A long twelve miles," Theron thought.

The downtown portion of their high desert oasis was centered around three buildings. The oldest building was small, now used for a gathering place for the Daughters of the Pioneers. They sewed quilt after quilt there, chatting up the world's problems as they did. The other old building had been a church, but was retired to be the place where dances and town activities occurred. The third was the new church. The grassy area and baseball field were all part of the town's high desert charm.

It was just across the street where the Mercantile stood, a two-story block building. The many coats of paint had taken away the once rough texture of the exterior of the structure, leaving it as smooth as a baby's bottom. A large framed sign hung on the front of the building, little change from its frontier old western days. The sign read "TAYLOR'S MERCANTILE." Other businesses lined the main street, a bank of course, and a rickety barn used as the fire station housing an antique fire truck. The opposite side of the street was just as sparsely covered: a single building used as a pool hall that doubled as the only restaurant called the Blue Bird Café. Taylor's Merc. contained everything under the sun: shoes, canned goods and potatoes, or spuds as the farmers called them. If you looked into the right corner or a hidden nook, you could find anything. Once when Theron and Randolph were browsing through one of those

TS and The WOW

hidden corners, they discovered just what "anything" meant. Beside the horseshoe nails and behind the stack of pop bottles in their wooden crates was a row of boxes covered in dust. The boxes had been there for longer than anyone had memory.

"What's in here?" Randolph asked the store owner Kent Taylor.

"I don't know. They have been there since I got the store from my pappy."

"You never looked?"

"Nope, never needed them. Guess I never will. In fact, I'll pay you boys to get rid of them for me." It was like a treasure hunt for the boys as they took the ten boxes out of the store and loaded them into the red wagon.

"No one has looked into these boxes for more than fifty years," Theron said excitedly.

Each box was filled with the oddest things. One just had horseshoes. Another contained wax candles and Watkins Carbolic Salve in brightly painted cans. It was the last box that made the treasure hunt a success. Eclectic was the only way to explain the contents of the box.

"What's this for?" Randolph held up a steel ring that was strung with skeleton keys. Eight of them to be exact.

"Those are skeleton keys."

TS and The WOW

"Why do you need a key for skeletons?" Randolph was puzzled, tossing the keys back into the box. Theron laughed, trying to picture the key poking into the nose hole of a skeleton, twisting the key, and making it dance. The things in the last box were not like anything that should have been in a mercantile store. A dingy ivory elephant carving, a tarnished bronze dagger and some curious coins, were some of the treasures from far away places, right down to the wooden treasure box., laden with more odd, old things hidden in the bottom of the box.

The main street was a-buzz. Mrs. Sweeney had just walked out of the bank to greet her friend who stood on the sidewalk.

"Thelma, how are you today?"

"Well, I'm peachy. How about yourself?"

Thelma Jennings, together with Mrs. Sweeney, composed the pipeline to all the local gossip. If there was a partial truth to be told, one of them was doing the telling.

"Did you hear…" was interrupted with,

"What, hear what?"

Then the story of the how the fellow called Steamboat Wilson had cheated a bunch of folks up in the Beaver Valley.

"He's missing. No one has seen him in a couple of weeks," Mrs. Sweeney said.

TS and The WOW

"You mean he might be dead?"

"Dead or something worse. Now you didn't hear me say anything that would be gossip and you know I would never gossip," Thelma Jennings said. The two women parted, waddling off in separate directions. Mrs. Sweeney was on her way to the Taylor Merc. across the street. Thelma had noticed a man walking up the street and, of course, she had to find out who the stranger was, always wanting to protect her little town from the evils of the world. At least that was what she told herself. What she really wanted was to be first to know all the gossip. She hadn't notice where he had come from, just that he was headed her way. She had searched the street for his car, but no auto was found.

"It was impossible to get to Enterprise without a car. This is the middle of nowhere," she thought. That surprised her a little.

This man was different than the farmers that lived around her town. He wore a white cotton shirt with the sleeves half rolled up. His shoes were strange, possibly from a foreign place, and his trousers were also white and baggy, similar to what a sailor would have worn. He carried a white linen sports coat that matched his wrinkled trousers, certainly strange for Enterprise, a desert farm town. But it was the hat that shaded his face and head from the hot sun that first caught her attention. It was a Panama style. As he approached, he slowed down as if he wanted to talk to her.

TS and The WOW

"Hello, Madam," he said with an island accent. Jamaican, she thought, or was it French Cajun? It was neither. Thelma began to blush; never having heard what she thought was such elegance.

"Can you direct me, ma'am, to the Salter family abode?" His eyes were that same brilliant glacier blue as Theron's and Twila's. Thelma had decided that she was talking to Grandpa Salter. She gave him the directions he had requested. He thanked her, bowed in a sweeping old-fashioned way swinging his hat from his head in one hand, rolling it once and placing it back on his head. The man walked across the road toward the church center. Quickly, he passed the smallest pioneer building and the line of twenty-five feet tall pine trees that guarded the old buildings. Thelma looked to see where he had gone, but it was though he had disappeared into thin air.

It was Theron's job to gather the eggs every morning. He would lift the clucking hen from the nest with one hand while plucking the egg from the nest with the other.

"That makes six red ones and three white." On cold days, the warm underneath of the hen warmed his fingers, but today it was a job just getting done. He repositioned the hen back on the nest.

"Bock, bock," the hens clucked.

TS and The WOW

"Bock, bock," Theron clucked back at a hen, his way of thanking them for their eggs. When the eggs were delivered to Adeline, it was Theron's next task to mow the lawn. The mower started on the third pull, chugging out several puffs of black smoke. Theron revved up the engine and began to mow the lawn.

"That looks like so much fun," Twila thought. She sat on the back step and watched Theron cut the edges of the lawn in a large square, as was his habit. Twila had noticed that Theron was playing a game while mowing. He kind of looked like he was dodging something or maybe dancing with the mower. The Winter Tree must have moved to the edge of the lawn when he heard the mower in the front yard. It was obvious that he didn't like the mower. Not one bit.

"Theron," and again louder, "Theron!" Twila yelled to be heard over the mower's noisy motor. Theron went on mowing, not hearing a word. Twila was not content to watch. She wanted to do some of the mowing. She rose from the porch and walked up behind Theron. Before she could tap him on the shoulder, he turned to face her, their red hair sending signals as they had become accustom to doing. Before she asked if she could mow, he did the twin thing.

"Read your mind again," he laughed. He had heard her yelling his name or he had felt her thoughts. She believed him because they often would let each other know things that way. Lately it happened a lot.

"Not for real," he said. He had been watching her and recognized his sister wanted something. Sometimes it was just regular normal and other times it was twin normal. It was just more fun to let her think that he could read her mind anytime he wanted to.

Twila looked at him in the way he had hoped, bewildered about how he was able to read her mind. Sometimes she was able to read his mind, but not so often as he read hers.

"Twi, you have to go all the way around the square," Theron said. He had no more said his piece when she took off, pushing the mower as fast as it would cut. Half way around the square, Twila had begun to wonder why she thought this would be fun. Sweat dripped from her forehead and her arms felt weak.

Theron sat on the porch smiling at his sister. She smiled at him and stuck her tongue out, shaking her head from side to side. Twila pushed the mower harder, hitting a bump. She stumbled and the mower took off on its own. She rose to her feet to chase the runaway mower.

"Stop, you stupid galzlop." It dodged her and cut an incredible pattern, as though unseen hands guided it. Theron rolled off the porch, yelling at her

TS and The WOW

"Catch it, catch it!" He held his sides laughing.

"Stop! Stop, you!" was all Twila could mutter, too slow to catch the racing mower. As she called for the machine to stop, it did. The mower seemed compelled to obey her command. The mower shut off and Twila once more grasped its handles in her hands. She pushed the mower to where her brother sat still laughing at her.

"Here, take this crazy thing."

"My, who's crazy, you or the mower?" Theron said. "Would you look at that?" he said pointing at the pattern in the grass. Twila turned around and, for the first time, noticed the pattern in the grass.

"What's going on Theron?" It wasn't a jumbled mess cut by a runaway machine. It was a series of circles.

"Twi, let's get on the roof of the house." Theron knew that the higher they got the better they could see the whole picture. Together they took the ladder down from the rack in the garage and carried it to the house. The rickety weathered wooden ladder shook as they climbed. Once they were on the roof, the circle pattern seemed to be more than a random act of a mower gone mad.

"What do you think it means?" Twila was sure that it had something to do with how she had been feeling inside lately. She was not alone. Theron had felt the change also. It was a

TS and The WOW

crop circle like those the news reporters found in England.
Twila rested her head in one hand, her index finger stroking
her face. Her other hand was on her hip, which was cocked
to one side.

"Maybe we need to squint our eyes like this." She narrowed
her eyes to only slivers. Theron placed his hands on his hips.
Together they looked like a crime-fighting duo studying their
latest mystery. The pattern in the grass consisted of circle
upon circle and some connecting lines. Suddenly, the red hair
on both of the twins became electrified, standing on end.

"Not now." Twila swatted at her hair to put it back in place.
Twila's hair had been braided and it was unraveling itself.
Theron's hair was shorter, but stood at attention like the
Queen's guard in front of Buckingham Palace, guarding their
post.

"What do you think it means, Theron?"

"Well," was all Theron said in response. He had no answer.

"A circle here, a line there. This makes no sense. I was sure
that from the roof we would make sense of this." Startled,
hearing a foot sliding on the shingles, Twila and Theron
turned to see what had made the noise.

A man wearing a white cotton shirt with the sleeves rolled
half up his arms, with his Panama hat covering his face, stood
on their roof. Twila stepped closer to Theron.

TS and The WOW

"What do you want?" Theron blasted the words at the stranger.

"Don't be afraid, my children. I am here to help you." The twins had seen a lot in the past year. Most of those things didn't seem to be happening for their good.

"I am your steersman. My name is Arlis, Arlis Alger."

"Mister, what are you doing on our roof?"

"Dad!" Twila yelled.

Arlis held his hands in front of himself so as not to appear no threatening. He looked into Twila's eyes. Then he sat down on the roof.

"I will just sit right here."

"I'm here to help you."

"What do you want?" Theron repeated his words.

"Have you become troubled lately?"

Both Theron and Twila knew they had been confronting some pretty weird things, but the question was how did he know that? Was this man trying to beguile them? Was he the wolf in sheep's clothing? Or the wolf himself? They stood their ground, away from the man.

"Theron Lee Salter, what does the circle message say?"

"How do you know my name?"

TS and The WOW

"I have known you from the day you two were born. I have been watching you two for a long time, waiting for you to reach the age of balance."

"What is balance?" Twila asked the man with eyes as brilliant and blue as were hers and her brother's. The match of his ultra blue eyes to theirs was the disarming factor. Their worries lessened, not disappearing totally, but causing them to listen to him. Arlis began to explain his role to them.

"I am your steersman. You would call me a guide."

"A guide for what?" Theron thought, as Twila said the same words.

Understanding their confusion, Arlis told them he knew the tree in the yard.

"His name is Tarel."

"You know the tree?" Twila said, confused.

As Arlis spoke of the tree, the Winter Tree reached his limbs toward them, his effort to let the twins know Arlis was trustworthy. Arlis now stood next to the twins, their hair still doing strange things, although somewhat more relaxed. This had happened before, but never quite like this. The hair pointed to the other twin and swayed in rhythm

Arlis turned the twins about to face the circles in the grass. Then he instructed them to hold hands. Twila slid her hand into Theron's hand. Sparks flowed like tiny stabs of lightening through them. Not a shocking sort of spark, but rather connecting sparks. Their minds glowed with understanding. It was like they had always understood what was written in the grass.

Arlis waited confidently, knowing that the twins were in a moment of discovery. Theron's mind tangled with Twila's, opening the meaning of the crop circles.

"So that's what it means," they said, their words in perfect time.

Arlis was delighted to find the twins to be so bright. Certainly, this had never happened before, not a brother and sister as the balance in any world. Through history, no woman had been the balancer, and now here was both a male and a female, the perfect balance.

Something had been upset in the cosmos to bring this about, Arlis had thought many times since the birth of the twins. He only knew his time was nearly at its end as the Balancer. Soon it would be the twins' time to play the role in the balance, just as he and those throughout the ages had.

Twila and Theron rested on the roof, absorbing all that had been thrust upon them and contemplating the responsibilities now theirs. It was like a flash across their thoughts and now they understood all that had happened to them in the past.

TS and The WOW

Arlis stayed with the family for nearly a month, teaching Twila and Theron all he could about the balance. He showed them wonders beyond their tiny part of the world. Each day they would greet the Winter Tree in the yard, exercising and meditating underneath his limbs.

The cool morning air was sweet, a reminder to Theron of God's hand in all things. He knew that he was a tool in the balance of worlds. Just one of Gods tools.

The time passed quickly with Arlis. He had become the grandfather they had never known. Sadly, the time came when he was to return to his home.

"Twila, may I speak with you?" Arlis asked. They went into the yard, not near Theron or the Winter Tree. "Twila, you are special. You must remember that a time will come when you will be the thread that holds the balance together. You must remain ready both in body and spirit." She listened to all he told her and told him she would remember him in her prayers each day.

The time came when Arlis hugged his new family, kissing them on both cheeks. Then he simply walked away, just as he had come.

CHAPTER 6

Trolls Under The Bridge and Balance In The World

The Fairy Orb seemed mystical to Twila. Often she would place it in her hand and attempt to coax the tiny winged fairies to come out.

"Come on out. I know you're in there," she would say, trying the same exercise a dozen times or so with no result. Each time the crystal would just lie in her hand, nothing changing. Today she was ready to try to get the thing to flower again, to open up, letting out its captives so she could talk to them. She had some questions she thought they might answer. Arlis Alger had tutored both Twila and Theron in the job of a balancer. For everything he taught them, more questions came about.

"Perhaps the fairies could make sense of the quandary I have inside," she thought. She was more confused about who she was, more confused than ever about so many things. Being eleven and a half was a lot to deal with. Girl stuff and boys. Boys had become beautiful to her and she was wondering what had changed. Just a year or so ago Theron was the only boy she even

TS and The WOW

liked, but now it was different. She had these weird feelings for lots of boys, feelings she sort of liked. Being a balancer was a part of her life that she was unsure of. In fact, she wasn't sure she could even do what Arlis said she was born to do.

"Maybe if the orb was back in the cave, it would flower," she thought. "Theron, are you ready to go?"

Theron stood in the doorway leaning against the doorjamb, with one leg crossed over the other at the calves.

"Just waiting for you," he said.

"Come on, let's go then."

It was only a moment before they were in the back yard. Twila held the orb in a cloth bag she had made to keep the fairy world safe. Passing under the Winter Tree, they were startled when the tree shuddered and dropped leaves all over them as if fall had suddenly come. Theron looked up into the tree and said, "What's the matter old boy?" never expecting a response. Then they walked on toward the Black Ridge and the cave of the orb. Neither Twila nor Theron had noticed the pattern in the leaves that had fallen from the Winter Tree. The leaves were a message of warning to them, "Wolf."

"Twi, what do you think we can do with this ball anyway?"

"It's not the ball, it's a world with people inside. I think they can help us."

TS and The WOW

They passed by the edge of Busher's Pond. Theron tossed a couple of rocks, skipping them across the water.

"Did you see that one?" The rocks would glide on top of the water, almost floating, and then sink into the green things that covered the bottom of the pond. From the pond bank, it was a short distance to the foot of the Black Ridge where the cave was.

"There's the face on the rock," Twila said, pointing to her landmark. She thought the Indians must have used the same landmark hundreds of years ago, or maybe they had even carved the face in the rocks. The cave was dark when Theron first looked in.

"This time I'm prepared." He pressed the on switch of the flashlight he had brought from his father's workshop. It didn't work. He shook it. The light flickered, and then came on.

"Don't jiggle it or it will go out again." Twila was always telling Theron the obvious.

He entered the cave, followed by his sister. They stood inside for a while before their eyes focused.

"Put the ball back where you found it," Theron said.

Twila rolled the orb back into the bowl of the basin. The ball rocked back and forth rolling around the smooth surface at the small of the bowl and coming to rest in its center. It rocked back and forth until it stopped. Twila hadn't noticed that the ball fit perfectly in the bowl's bottom.

TS and The WOW

"Look at this." She rolled the ball, spinning it around the edge of the bowl. The ball circled the surface again and again, finally coming to a full stop right in the same cupped spot at the bottom of the bowl.

"Twila, roll it again." Theron focused the flashlight on the inside of the bowl. Twila scooped the ball from the dry surface of the basin.

"Here it goes." She rolled the ball even harder than she had the time before. A whistling noise came from the spinning ball.

"Maybe now it will open up."

It made moves up and down the wall of the basin, no longer just spinning, then being overcome by gravity. It was like the ball had taken control of its own destiny. Water began to flow from the ball like a thread tying worlds together with waters flowing from one world to another.

"Look, it has water coming out of it!" Theron said, surprised to see water coming out of the ball and not out of the ground or some natural place.

The ball began to float upon the water. At first the water was dark, but as it flowed over the edge of the bowl, it cleared. The water became a beautiful electric blue, filling the bowl and a channel in the floor apparently cut for the purpose of guiding the water into the floor.

TS and The WOW

"This is incredible." Twila dipped her hand into the water and poured it onto the floor. The ball floating on the water began to spin, glowing from a light within. Light reflected off the water and the ceiling and danced like sparkling jewels. The spinning ball lifted from the now aquatic bowl, droplets falling from the ball and sending ripples through the waters of the bowl. The ball light grew and grew in intensity, along with Theron and Twila's ever-widening eyes, until the flowering happened.

"It's happening! They are coming!" exclaimed Twila, excited over her success. The blossom brought about a shockwave of light, blinding the twins.

"Twila, can you see it?"

"No!"

Both twins rubbed the sting from their eyes. As they regained their sight, they saw the flowered ball, floating in the air with water flowing from its base, but nothing else was the same. The room had dissolved away and they stood in the middle of a field of something like grain stocks colored with bright red tints. Each stock was twisted the same way that a woman would curl her hair. The open sky above them was a pasty green like from a child's drawing, a green that you could find on a stock of broccoli. Twila's red hair was twisting and untwisting at the same rate, as was Theron's, like a nervous twitch.

"Twi, I don't think we're on the Black Ridge anymore."

TS and The WOW

"What's happening, Theron?" His best guess was that they were in another world.

"That's kind of obvious," Twila said.

"What happened to us? Are we dead?" she said.

"We're not dead."

Theron noticed something in the distance. It was a city, he thought.

"Maybe someone over there could help us," Theron said. As they started to walk in that direction, the flowered ball followed behind them, still watering the ground as they traveled, new plants springing from the soil, from seed to full growth in seconds. The ball was spinning, the way a helicopter would fly behind them. To Twila's surprise, not a single fairy had come from the flower to answer her questions. Instead, they were in the middle of bigger questions.

"Not too close. We had better see if they are friendly before we knock on a door." Theron felt uneasy. His red hair had taken on the shape of the curly grass. As they neared the city, they could see the houses.

"Are those homes or bridges?" Twila said, while crouching down in the grass as she saw Theron doing.

"Looks like they are bridges. Hundreds of bridges."

TS and The WOW

"Do you think anything lives under those bridges?" Twila asked.

"Maybe some animals."

Each bridge connected to the other, but none of them led anywhere. The closer they got, the more it looked like spaghetti strung every which way. The ball spun its petals like a propeller after them, sometimes hovering in the air, still pouring water on the grass. Grass was still popping to life from nowhere.

"If we get on top of that one, we can see where to go," Twila said, already walking toward the closest bridge.

Their steps were as light as leaves dropping to the ground in the fall. They started across the first bridge, thinking that if they got high enough they could find someone to help them get back home.

"This is one of those places Arlis told us about," Theron said. A light going on in the memory portion of his brain told him he should pay closer attention when offered wisdom from older folks.

"I would never have believed that a place like this existed," Twila declared, now standing on the top most part of the bridge.

"How are we getting home from here?"

That was the one thing Arlis had neglected to tell them, how to get out once they got in. A gruff voice came from under the bridge.

"Who dares to cross my bridge?"

Theron was startled. He wondered if they should run, but decided he should announce their presence instead.

"Theron and Twila, sir," Theron said.

The voice from under the bridge abruptly called out, "No more of you goats can cross my bridge!"

"We are not goats. We are humans."

A door on the face of the bridge swung open and a head slowly peeked out. Only the face was exposed.

"What kind of goat is a human?" the voice said with a new curiosity, only having dealt with regular goats crossing his bridge in the past.

"Humans are boys and girls," Twila softly said, not wanting to offend the person under the bridge. A dwarf-like man came from under the bridge. Others from under the neighboring bridges began to gather next to his bridge. They were all like him, short and stocky.

"You are human? What be a human?" The question came from a small pasty-faced woman in the crowd.

Theron stuttered, "Well, well… a… a… a…."

TS and The WOW

He was interrupted.

"What you doing on my bridge?"

"Just trying to get home, sir," Theron said, nervously sweating and fearful of the growing crowd of onlookers.

"What bridge you live?" questioned the odd little man whose bridge they stood atop.

"Far from here in our world," Twila said in a submissive tone.

"Oh yeah," Theron remembered, "I'm suppose to say..."

Before he could say the word Arlis had taught them, the orb shot water out over the crowd, spraying them all. They ducked back into their bridge homes, where everyone hid.

"It's just water!" Twila yelled.

The orb hovered for a few seconds, drenching the low ground where new growth sprouted in response to the taste of water. The orb left a trail of growing life as it flew back into the red grass. No one had expected the flying waterfall that poured from the orb onto the heads of the trolls. Windows in the bridge homes framed peering faces in their swishing curtains, all wanting to see the humans.

When the orb retreated, the community came out one by one from their shelters into the open. Only Theron and Twila had not run for cover from the water. The emerging short folks

TS and The WOW

had reason to run when the waterworks had begun. Each of those that had been doused in water now had a hairdo that curled and swirled in every direction.

"What happened to them?" Twila laughed as each one emerged from the security of their bridges.

"We are balance!"

There. He finally got it out. Theron was saying what Arlis had told him to say if ever he was swept into a different world by accident. He was sure this would either put them in more trouble or get them home.

"These guys seem almost human, short and very hairy humans," Twila said in observation.

Their heads were too big for their very muscular bodies. Their feet seemed to begin almost at the knees and they looked like they were smiling all the time because of their enormous teeth.

"Not a one of them can fully close their mouth," Theron thought.

To Twila the people under the bridges might be human-ish, but were more like the stuffed animals sitting on her bed at home. They barely had knees, so walking was more like waddling. They looked like they were skipping when they moved. The guy upon whose bridge the twins stood skipped his way onto the bridge and over to where they stood.

TS and The WOW

"Well, well balancers we be," he said, pointing to himself with both of his stubby hands. He then said, "Oh, me Klin."

Twila recognized that Klin knew what a balancer was and that he was trying to welcome them. The other Klinomens as Twila dubbed them, had watched, but seemed to be guarding their own bridges.

"Balance!" Klin said drawing a circle in the air with both of his hands, ending with all ten of his chubby digits pointing at his chest. "I be balancer," he said, trying to remove the confusion.

"You're the balancer in this world, right?" Theron half questioned.

"Twila, he is a balancer."

Twila was relieved, sure he could get them home. Klin took the twins by the hands and led them back under his bridge. It was much different than it had appeared from their approach through the curly grass. Klin opened a heavy set of double doors, the ones he had come out of from under the bridge. Inside, a staircase led underground into a shortened version of grandma's house, except for the paintings on the walls of billie goats in various states being chased to the hills.

"What got here?" said a klinomen seated in an overstuffed chair, his big feet propped up on a stool that must have once been a tree stump, now carved to look something like a turtle with an enormous butt.

"My brother Tuck."

"What these in my place?" He was polite but to the point, Twila was glad he was kind because she didn't want to admit how scared she was.

"This humans."

Both Theron and Twila nodded.

"Nice to meet you," Twila said.

Klin was notably proud of his home.

"Sit." Klin directed them to a pair of wooden stools. The door opened and in walked a female Klinomen. She tossed a woven bag filled with the red curly grass onto the chopping table in the open kitchen.

"Who these big ones?" She wanted to know what they were doing in her house.

"Balancers from other world." Klin said patting his wife on the shoulder and letting her know it would be okay. "We go."

Klin lead the twins out the door. The orb had passed over and over the red grass, watering it.

"Look how tall the grass is over there." Theron pointed at the tall grass near where they had come to this world. The grass appeared to have grown, but it had only uncoiled, becoming much taller in patches. The orb zoomed to resume its position behind Theron and Twila.

"No let in hair." Klin was worried about the orb pouring water on his head and held his hands over it just in case.

"Where are we going, Klin?" Theron asked the question, but Twila was just as interested in the answer. Klin totally ignored the inquiry as though he had not heard it.

The curly red grass grew smaller in the direction they walked. The tree line was just ahead, if you could call the mushroom toppers and asparagus stocks trees. At least they looked like mushrooms and asparagus to Twila. The forest blocked the light from the sky, and as they traveled deeper into the forest, the taller and taller the foliage was. Less and less light penetrated the mushroom tops.

"Is this the way to our world?"

Twila was scared by her surroundings. From the undergrowth emerged the weirdest animal Twila had ever seen. She screamed. Klin jumped to her protection, quickly placing his body between her and the animal. Klin put his arm back to push Twila away from the Smoo. He had encountered many a Smoo in his time and knew that the hairy beast with its long sticky tongue could snatch a tasty thing like Twila and runaway with her before you could say 'what's for dinner'. Klin locked eyes with the bulging eyes of the Smoo, knowing there was only one way to beat a Smoo beast.

"Run, my Twila!" Klin yelled.

Twila turned. Already in full stride she ran away, followed by her brother, leaving Klin to fight the Smoo.

The Smoo wanted her. She looked tender. His tongue snapped from his mouth, unrolling long enough to catch her leg in the sticky ooze that covered it. Twila screamed as she fell to the ground. Theron tumbled over her into the bushes. The Smoo's tongue latched around Twila's leg and began to pull her toward his gaping mouth.

"Twila, grab my hands."

Theron had hooked his feet in the small stocks of asparagus, leaving his hands free to hang on to his sister. And the tug-of-war was on.

"Theron, you're pulling me apart!"

The Smoo's tongue grew taut as he pulled. He also locked his legs into the mushroom stems, working his suction cup toes all around them. Like a winch, he worked his tongue to pull in the tasty treat.

"Hang on!"

Twila's fingers were slipping from Theron's grip. Klin climbed up near a mushroom stock as far as he could, pulled off

TS and The WOW

a handful of the fleshy gills under the canopy, and then slid back down the stock. He flipped open the carrying pouch he had on his shoulder, stuffed in one of his stubby hands, and brought out a fistful of plant life. It wiggled like a bug in his hand. He crushed the two plants, rubbed them together, spit on them, and then poured it on the Smoo's tongue.

"Not so tasty now," he said as the tongue's sticky goo sizzled, erupting in multiple tiny explosions.

When the mixture reached Twila's leg, the Smoo lost his grip on her. His tongue recoiled to his mouth and he yelped like a wounded dog as he retreated into the forest. The orb doused Twila with water, easing the sting of the sticky ooze.

"Come, come," Klin said, waving his hand and motioning them to go with him as if nothing had happened.

The forest opened into a meadow of colors that were never seen in nature, at least on earth. Some plants shimmered in the light. Others glowed from within, not needing any other sources of light. It was the most beautiful place Twila or Theron had ever seen.

"Wow!" they collective sighed as their mouths fell open with amazement.

Water trickled down from a pink and green hillside, feeding a pond on the end of the meadow. Just beyond the meadow, where the mushroom trees parted, stood a wooden structure, housing a single door not large enough for a building. Just a door.

"There it be."

Klin pointed to the door. The door was round, as round as the tiny man was tall, the door an extremely large ball. It sat on a pivot and spun on its axis to open. Soon they all stood in front of the doorframe.

"Must be enough water here," Twila said.

The orb had followed them, pouring water from its bottom and watering everything in sight. Yet when they entered the meadow, it had stopped sprinkling. Now the orb floated in the air behind Twila, its flower-like petals spinning and its body pulsing with light as it had done the first time the fairies came from it.

"Not now. We don't need them now," Theron declared.

"They will rescue us!" Twila said excitedly.

Klin calmly plugged what looked like a three-sided skeleton key into the door, twisted it three times around, and then removed it. As he turned the key, the ball door rolled to a pocket inside the ball. The orb landed in Twila's hand and ceased to spin or glow. She slid it into the pocket of her jeans. Klin directed them to enter the scooped-out part of the door. It rolled closed and disappeared into a hole in the wall.

TS and The WOW

"Hey, that can't be right. There's nothing back here," said Theron. He noticed the mushroom timbers were holding a freestanding frame. The doorway stood by itself, nothing at its back on that side of the timbers. But on the open side was a series of tunnels, tunnels that went in every direction.

Klin took the tunnel to the right, which quickly turned in to another group of tunnels. He then went to the left, and then left again.

Theron whispered, "Twi, are we going around in a circle?" He was sure they were, but Twila said, "No."

The tunnel abruptly ended. The door at the end of the tunnel opened with another key from the ring of keys that Klin carried. Flying balls of every size flitted about in what appeared to be their home and the balls seemed to be communicating one with another.

"Where are we, Klin?" Theron just wanted a bearing with which to find himself.

"Is this the fairies' world?" Twila had questions of her own.

"You in Tween now," Klin responded.

They were in the Tween, the control center for balancing this world.

Arlis Alger sat on a large chair made from a mushroom tree top in the corner of the room. Klin led the twins to his chair. Klin said, "Just like you told us, they're here."

Arlis reached out to grasp a ball out of the air.

"I see they found you." The ball closed and fell at rest in the palms of his hands.

"They do find us here." Klin said, as he turned and walked to a stool and sat down.

"What are we doing here?" Twila asked. Both she and Theron had an onslaught of questions.

Arlis stood from the chair and placed the ball on a table, then put out his hands-shaking them to stop the questions. Arlis had expected the ball to bring them here.

"This was training for you both. I brought you to the Tween."

Bursoa was a kind world, a friendly world to the balncers. Other worlds were less congenial. Arlis sat back in his chair and motioned for the twins to sit on a stool made from the same materials. Questions were answered for a long time.

Klin sat on a mushroom stool and gazed at something he had carried in his bag. It looked alive as it struggled not to be eaten.

"Come with me," Arlis said, ending that portion of the teaching time. They walked to a room behind the chair. It was shaped like the cave on the Black Ridge. Even the basin was similar and the Aqua blue waters flowed from a large crystal ball in it.

"Is it time to go home?" Theron asked. Twila nodded in approval.

"Let me have your orb." He held out his hand and Twila placed the orb in it. Arlis plugged their orb ball into a spot above the center of the watering ball and the ball began to float in the air and then spin, opening again as a flower. The light smashed against the walls. The orb floated back into Twila's hand. They saw the walls fall away. As abruptly as they had been taken away, Theron and Twila were back home in their cave on the Black Ridge.

CHAPTER 7

Turned Inside Out and Mrs. Sweeney Meets The Neighbor

Theron awoke to the crowing rooster again.

"Shut up!" he yelled out.

He rolled over in the bag, and then slid free from it, leaving the sleeping bag where he slept under the Winter Tree. Theron liked camping out. It was one of his favorite things to do, even if it was in his own backyard.

The tree rustled his leaves and something from his branches fell to the ground. Theron was puzzled. When he stepped on the grass, it was wet with snow that had fallen in the night.

"Snow in July?" he questioned. It was the middle of the July and cold wet snow covered the ground around the Winter Tree.

"How could it have snowed?" he thought. The snow was piled around the perimeter of the Winter Tree, forming a circle about twelve feet wide.

"Wouldn't you know I would be the target of a freak storm?" Theron said, listening to how strange his words sounded, even to him.

The view from high in the air above looked like the bulls-eye on a target, composed of a green, leafy center and a white circle of snow. Not a hint of a cloud languished in the sky. It was only covered by the brilliant blue of a summer morning. As the world took on its light, Theron noticed footprints in the outer edge of the snow ring. The snow was melting rapidly and there was no way to tell if man or beast left the prints in the snow, yet they were footprints.

"Is the world out of sorts, or is it just me?" questioned Theron. He could see that the tree had been watching over him in the night while he slept. "Natural things are never natural in this yard." Theron thought, wanting to know why the snow had fallen and what it meant. Inside, he knew he probably never would know the answer to that one.

The rooster crowed again as the sun passed the mountain edge, burning its rays and melting winter's glory rapidly away. The sun brought the changing of the guard from nocturnal to diurnal activity, showing day had begun. The only footprint within the circle was Theron's at the bottom of the sleeping bag. The tracks that encircled the outer edge of the snowy circle disappeared into the green grass.

Theron had slept through the night with only the stars and the Winter Tree for company. At least that was what he had supposed. The Winter Tree shook his leaves vigorously.

"Hey, you infernal tree!" Theron was immediately half covered in the remains of snow as if all the snow from the Winter Tree's leaves were channeled on top of his head. The tree rolled from side to side, his way of laughing at his joke.

Twila let the screen door slam as she walked to the chicken coop to gather the eggs.

"Don't slam that door!" Adeline said from inside the house.

Twila swung a tattered old basket about as she walked.

"Twila come over here. Look at this."

"That's snow. How did you do this?"

"I didn't. It was the Winter Tree."

"It's not winter," she said, a bit perplexed.

Theron pointed to the tree. "It was him!" He said firmly.

The charismatic tree immediately began to rotate his limbs in friendly recognition, just to gloat. The snow melted quickly in full view of the sun's quantum rays, leaving no evidence of what had happened. It was one of those days at the Salter house.

"Everything has a place and today we are putting everything in its place," Adeline had announced, ardent that the house would be cleaned.

TS and The WOW

Twila washed all the cabinets and reorganized all the dishes. Theron had been assigned the fruit room. There were bottles stacked in boxes and bottles lined the floor, some full of fruit, some filled with corn, and others waiting for the season to render its produce for winter storage.

"Why do I get banished to the fruit room every time?" he grumbled, going down the stairs to the basement room where all the bottled food was stored.

Theron took all the empties up the stairs to Adeline, who was waiting to clean them. She was getting ready for the next week's corn and bean harvest. He then went back to the basement and swept up the dust from the bare cement floor.

"What's this?" There, in the dust of the floor, something shiny caught Theron's eye. He bent to one knee to examine it.

"Where did this come from?" he asked. With his finger, he brushed away the particles that hid the brilliance of the object. He plucked it from the floor and stood to inspect it in the light from the single bulb over his head.

"This is cool." there was the lighting shard that George had hidden in an empty Kerr jar a few years ago. The jar must have fallen and broken and the lightning bolt must have slid to the corner under the shelving. The parts of the jar were long since gathered and disposed of, leaving only the lightning bolt, hiding in the dust on the floor.

"I wonder what it's for?" Theron ran question after question through his head. The lighting shard went discretely into Theron's pocket.

Twila worked all morning on the cupboards and dishes, first pulling all the dishes from one cupboard.

"Mom, how about this one. Keeper or throw away?"

"Got to keep that one. It was your dad's grandmothers."

"The family heirloom pile then."

Twila started scrubbing with a dishrag that had been soaking in a big bowl of soapy water. The doorbell rang.

"Can you get that, honey?"

Twila slid out of the cabinet. She had half her body inside while washing it down. "Got, it mom."

The vacuum-like seal on the door broke and the outside light rushed in. There stood Mrs. Sweeney. She was already talking in a full stream of barely audible words, something about how Mrs. Phelps had said the best sweet corn in the world was grown in the Salter's garden. That was true. It "was" possibly the best in the world.

"Hello, Mrs. Sweeney."

"How are you, sweetie. Is your mother home?"

Adeline appeared at the door.

"Hello, Dorothy. Won't you come in?"

Adeline was always cordial to everyone. Twila thought she was the kindest person in the world.

"I just wanted to see if I could get a few ears of corn for tonight's dinner."

To Twila, it seemed that Mrs. Sweeney was begging for some of her mother's corn. Twila watched as her mom walked out the door, with Mrs. Sweeney tagging behind her. She followed after them as they walked into the cornfield. Snap, crack, squish. The sound was like the rubber of a bike tire recoiling after it had been stretched beyond its limits. Adeline broke the first ear of corn from the stock.

"One, two, three… twelve, thirteen, a baker's dozen. That ought to do."

Adeline had loaded the woman's arms to the point that she was barely able to see. Twila looked up, seeing something of interest. The Winter Tree had moved. He was standing alongside the raspberry patch, shading it again in an effort to tease Adeline. She hated it when he blocked the sun from her prize berry patch. He would move there whenever Adeline went to the backyard.

"That's the biggest ear of corn I have ever seen!" Mrs. Sweeney said.

"Bigger is not always better," Adeline replied.

Twila covered her mouth, not wanting the women to hear her giggle, thinking she had gone mostly unnoticed as she followed them. The corn stocks leaned toward her. Their ears rolled around to listen when she snickered. Neither of the women noticed a thing, carrying the corn they had picked to Mrs. Sweeney's '52 Chevy. The door on the Chevy closed with a clunk.

TS and The WOW

"Would you like a few berries for desert?" Adeline asked. She was so proud of the things she raised in the yard. No matter who arrived at her door she would share it.

"Well, if you have enough to share."

The two women meandered around the yard. Adeline pointed out the plums on the plum tree and the not quite ripe peaches on the peach tree, all while they walked around the house to the backyard. When they reached the backyard where strawberries grew along the wall of the house, her green thumb had been crowned with superior marks by the judge.

"You must have two green thumbs, Adeline."

"I just love working in the garden and this is my reward," Adeline said, plucking the plump strawberries. "Twila, would you run and get a bag to put these in?"

Twila hurried in the back door, coming out nearly as fast as she had gone in.

"Here's a bag, Mom."

She handed the midsized brown paper bag to her. When the bag was half full, Adeline stood, groaning from the strain on her knees.

"You must have some raspberries," Adeline said to her guest.

The raspberry patch grew next to the workshop. The raspberries were Adeline's favorite plant, so hard to grow.

"What are you doing there, you stupid tree?" Adeline suddenly burst with her frustration over the tree's new position in

TS and The WOW

the yard. Without thought, she began a flurry of scorns, directed at her wooden child of the yard. "Not another one of your holes in the yard…and…!" she scolded.

Mrs. Sweeney watched in wonderment. She thought that Adeline had, without warning, slipped a cog and gone off the deep end. Adeline paused and looked at her neighbor. She blushed and then ducked her head, realizing how she must have looked.

"Oh it's, it's…"

She tried to back out of the embarrassment she felt. Mrs. Sweeney put her hand on Adeline's shoulder,

"It's okay, dear. I understand menopause."

The Winter Tree had waited for her reaction, thinking he was pretty clever. Twila had found a good spot to watch the event unfold. She laughed at her mom from the roof of the house, a safe distance, she thought. The ears of corn leaned, creaking toward the backyard, still listening in as well.

"Try some of these raspberries."

Adeline handed four red, ripe berries to Mrs. Sweeney. The uncomfortable moment passed after Adeline picked the raspberries and handed them to Mrs. Sweeny. Who, without looking, rolled them on her tongue while gushing words of complement to Adeline.

"Your patch is so lush, not like mine. I have a brown thumb."

TS and The WOW

With the tree incident all but forgotten, Mrs. Sweeney described the patch of raspberries she must have had a million or so years ago as a child.

"That's unbelievable. No way!"

It was hard for Twila to imagine the enormous woman ever having been a child. Twila plopped her bottom end down on the warming asphalt shingles while the women turned their backs on the spot where the Winter Tree stood. As they did, the tree shook its limbs, moving air over its leaves as though a gust of wind had blown through the yard. "Here comes the show," Twila thought. Both women reached for their hair, bracing themselves against the wind that was sure to muss their hairdos. Nothing happened.

"This is awesome," Twila said under her breath.

It was like a game of "Simon Says" played by the pair of old ladies, thought Twila. "Simon says hold your hair." Then she laughed.

The tree was winning without trying. Adeline turned to look at the tree, realizing his mischief making.

"You stop that," she whispered, her eyes in a mother's roll of disgust.

Twila had moved to the edge of the house to watch the women as they walked away from the backyard, Adeline scooting Mrs. Sweeney away from the Winter Tree. Twila screamed as her

TS and The WOW

foot slipped on one of the shingles and she tumbled from the roof.

"Time has stopped," Twila thought, falling toward the sidewalk, her arms behind her to catch herself. The stop was sudden, yet not the jolt she was braced for. Adeline ran to her child's scream. Mrs. Sweeney, a much larger woman, lumbered a few yards behind. Twila rested, cradled in the limbs of the Winter Tree. He had caught her in mid air, then gently rolled her in his limbs. Adeline knew that she had fallen from the roof, but Mrs. Sweeney was none the wiser, thinking Twila had just been playing in the tree the whole time.

"Young lady, you nearly gave me a heart attack." Adeline scolded. When Mrs. Sweeney turned to leave, the Winter Tree set Twila safely on the ground.

"Mom, not so hard."

Adeline pulled the snarls from Twila's hair in the evening ritual. The only spot that wasn't tangled was the red spot that had untwisted itself, standing like a wire out of the way while Adeline combed the rest of the hair.

"Mom, what is the Winter Tree?"

"What do you mean? He's a tree."

"He is more than a tree, isn't he?"

TS and The WOW

Twila probed to see if her mother knew more than she did. "Ouch that hurt!"

"I never really thought about it." Winter Tree had been there for so long and watched over whatever happened in the backyard. "Well, I guess he is more than a tree. At first he scared me some."

"Why would a tree scare you?"

"It was just that he was something new, I suppose, and new things take time adjusting to."

Adeline had begun to remember the day when the Winter Tree grew in the yard. "He was something special, not another one like him on this planet," she thought.

In the living room, George and Theron were watching TV. The black and white picture was so cool, George thought.

"This is real entertainment, huh son?" George said.

Then on came the nightly news that always disturbed the whole family: riots on the college campus, the war in Vietnam. The entire world seemed in upheaval. That was everywhere but in the corner of the world where rabbits ran free, where Theron and Twila Salter explored the lava hills and floated their raft on Busher's Pond. "It is nice to be hidden kind of from the rest of the world," George thought as the news rolled on.

TS and The WOW

The day was bright. Fear of the wash's, sand waves and other worlds splintering into Earth had come and gone from their hearts. So it was back to exploring the lava cave and just being kids on summer break. Walking through the sage brush, Theron asked, "Twi, do you think I will ever do anything important, you know like Yuri Gagarin, or John Glen?"

He and Twila walked through the brush on the wash bank. Both Gagarin and Glen were space men, one a cosmonaut and the other an astronaut. That was one thing that seemed okay in the world, the space race. Both of Theron's heroes had accomplished amazing things in space, yet somehow he related more to his comic book hero, Morph Man. Morph Man was a lot like Theron, a mild mannered, nerdy guy, thrust into a metamorphic change and then expected to save the world.

"You ARE someone great. You're my twin, little brother." Twila jabbed at him.

"I guess I just see my funny paper side, not my comic book hero side."

"I guess you're right, Beetle Bailey."

"Well, I'm serious. I'm so short and I know that I get called geek and nerd."

"You're not a geek or a nerd, trust me." She said, still looking for the right thing to say. He might be different, but that was a good thing.

TS and The WOW

"Then, what am I?"

"You're a dope!" she laughed. "No, Theron Lee Salter, you are just a boy, a boy that has a family who thinks he is great."

"Do you think that?"

"Sure, little brother." Twila loved to play the older sister card. Theron stumbled over a clump of brush while looking back and talking to Twila.

Woo, thump, grunt. Theron landed belly down in the brush. His right foot, snugly tied inside his Red Ball Jets, was wedged in a hole and trapped by a metal object. Twila laughed again at her brother.

"I guess you are a nerd." Twila said.

Theron looked up at her, propping himself up over the bush to get it out of his face. He then twisted to sit up.

"My foot is caught," he said while tugging, trying to free it.

Twila started digging around the edge of the hole. She took a stick and began to pry against the metal and the shoe that had trapped Theron. With the earth removed from around the metal ball, it rolled aside in the diggings and Theron's foot was finally free.

"Cool, "Twila said, cradling the ball into her hands. She was becoming famous for her use of 60's slang, even building

TS and The WOW

words of her own. Theron's favorite was 'insmackulatious', which meant something was extremely good.

"Don't you mean, insmackulatious?" Theron said, teasing.

By its appearance, the ball had been buried for some time. It was caked with dirt, yet still still looked like a lost treasure, possibly from Spanish conquistadors that had come into the area centuries ago with Cortez in search of the seven Incan cities of gold.

"What is it, Twi?"

Twila was still assessing the object. It was heavy, maybe a cannonball, she thought. But as she removed more of the crust of hardened dirt, it shone, not dull like the iron shot they made cannonballs from. Theron and Twila sat in the dirt and together they cleaned away the remaining earth from the object.

"It's a perdunkalung," Twila said, her word for something that was beyond her understanding.

When the metal piece was cleaned, they saw that it was more an oblong piece with a gear imbedded in its end. The body of it looked like it was made of gold.

"Is this gold?" Twila asked.

"No, it's too hard. Gold is soft," Theron said as he tried to scratch it.

"Is there anything else in the hole?"

TS and The WOW

Theron took Twila's stick and began to dig in the sandy dirt. The hole was quickly opening to show that it did have something else within its grip, this thing was much larger than the geared egg-like object. Twila put the geared thing on the ground and together they enlarged the hole, moving away the dirt until only a crusty layer hung on the metal hull.

"What do you think it is?" Theron asked in his nerdy way.

"Judging from the metal skin, it's a machine."

"Duh, I can see that."

"What do you think it's used for?"

Theron kept peeling away the crusty layer.

"Hey look, the egg shape must have come from here!"

Theron placed the egg gear down into the open space that he had just cleaned. It fit like a piece from a puzzle. The machine was not like anything that either Twila or Theron had ever seen. The bronze exterior was glazed with the green coating of time. It was apparent that it had been left in the earth and lay below the growth of brush for centuries.

"Do you think it's Spanish treasure?" Twila was sure it had some kind of importance.

"It's some kind of treasure."

"Dad will know what it is," Twila said.

TS and The WOW

However, George didn't know what it was, but he was determined to figure it out. It was late that night when George, Twila, and Theron put the machine to rest in the corner of the shop next to the Red Rider motorcycle, which hid under its blanket.

CHAPTER 8

Busher's Pond and Mebo

"What a weird summer," Theron thought. It was nice just to relax and be a kid. Theron and Twila had watched the movie "Sinbad the Sailor" on the television just last night. After that, all Theron could talk about was being a sailor and searching for the golden fleece.

"Argh, matey! That's sailor talk," Theron said. Twila smiled at him.

"Come on sailor boy, let's go."

With their towels in hand, they were off, on their way to cool down from the summer heat at the best spot to be on a sunny day, Busher's pond.

"This is an incredible day." Theron thought. Not more than a breath of air blew against their cheeks as the sun caused their foreheads to sweat during the trek to Busher's Pond.

"Do you feel that, Theron?"

"I don't feel anything." His red hair had stayed in rhythm with the rest of his hair. The thought rose and fell that there might be something watching them in the woods. They were on to the pond.

"Last one in the water a big green frog," Theron shouted at his sister who was steps behind him. They raced to the bank of the pond, tossing their towels on the small bushes and leaping into the clear, cold water.

"Man, this feels so good," Twila said, pulling her wet hair back into a ponytail. The water only reached the middle of Twila's chest and Theron's shoulders.

"You're a frog." Theron dove under the water, coming up ten feet away near the green things that clung to the bottom of the pond.

"I'm not a frog!" Twila splashed water at him.

"Hey, let's build a raft." The warm sun felt good on their wet skin as they dragged the last log, big enough to support their weight, to the spot where they were building the raft.

"Get a push pole, Theron." Twila was lashing the poles together with the twine they had taken from George's workshop. She had never before tied a knot other than those that belong on a dress, but today she was lashing the poles like an old sailor. Theron dropped the push pole and then began to help Twila tie off the rope.

TS and The WOW

"You're going to push our raft, aren't you?"

"Of course, I'm the captain." Twila couldn't help but squish her toes into the mud lining the bank. It was cool, and before Theron could push the raft away from the bank, she was knee deep in the pond's water. Theron pushed the pole into the dry part of the bank. The raft glided into the water.

"Hurry, get on. We're sailing." Theron hollered. Twila plopped her bottom on the raft. With the sun on their faces, Theron boarded the raft, pushing off into the water of Busher's Pond. The water was clear and cold on this summer's day. If they were to fall off the raft anywhere on the pond, the water was only deep enough to reach Twila's chest and Theron's chin. This was not something that was a threat to life or limb, just a fun adventure.

"Theron, look at the things on the bottom of the pond," Twila said, pointing at some long green spires. They had grown there since the last time they had been to the pond.

"Where did they come from?"

A week ago, there had been nothing lining the pond bottom, just a muddy coating. Today there were lush green things shimmering in the clear water.

"Theron look, I'm a pirate," Twila said, holding her right hand on her hip and thrusting the other hand in the air, swishing it about like she had a pirate's cutlass. Theron sat down on the

TS and The WOW

raft, dangling his legs over the edge of the raft and into the cool water.

He sang, "It's a pirate's life for me. Yo ho, yo ho. It's a pirate's life for me," something he had gotten from another television show.

The green things swirled about his legs, running their tips across his toes and tickling his legs with their broad leaf-like bodies.

"Stop that!" Theron said while swishing his legs around in the water, attempting to avoid the green things. Some of the things loosened from the bottom of the pond, shooting straight up and flying onto the raft. Soon there were enough of the green things to nearly cover Theron.

"No, no!" screamed Twila as she swatted at the things with the push pole. They were gripping one another, wrapping themselves around each other to make a chain right to the bottom of the pond. They bound Theron's hands and his legs, pulling at him and working to slide him from the raft and into the water. Twila fought violently against their attack, the whole time screaming, "Let go of my brother!" Her fierce defense ripped some of the green spires in half, but that only created more of the leafy organisms. Terror gripped the souls of both brother and sister as the green things snatched Theron's mummy-wrapped body from the deck of the raft into the water.

"Help me!" was the last scream that Twila heard before Theron was swallowed up by the bubbling water.

Twila dropped to her knees and then to her stomach, reaching into the water after Theron's one loose hand, still visible. Their fingers touched, and Twila slid her hand into his, grasping him by the wrist. Beginning a tug-of-war, the swarms of plants pulled, moving the raft with the girl and the boy toward the more numerous members in the center of the pond. Theron struggled to get his head out of the water for a breath, finding himself quickly smothered again. The look on his face told Twila that she was his only hope.

"Fight them!" she screamed. Her arm was being pulled under the water and her grip, was loosening.

Theron had lost his hold on Twila's hand. Abruptly, the battle ended with Theron being pulled by the green mass of life into the clear water and to the bottom of the pond.

"No, this is not going to happen!" Twila yelled, diving into the water and swimming after her brother. The pond had never seemed so deep or so hard to swim in. She swam deeper and deeper in pursuit of Theron, swimming right into the green things.

The green things had no interest in her. They seemed only conscious of Theron. They pulled him tighter into their clutch and formed a circle around the boy, then disappeared into

TS and The WOW

a bubble of water that erupted from the murky muddle of silt. The bubble tossed the girl back to the surface of the water. Gasping for air, Twila sucked a Goliath breath into her lungs and stood on the pond bottom. Now the water was only chest deep as it had always been. She searched to find Theron, but the green things, the raft, and Theron were all gone, swallowed up by the bubble.

Theron had passed out while holding his breath. When he awoke, he lay on a stone floor, his clothes still wet and the reaming puddle of water rapidly evaporating around him. In less than a minute, he was totally dry. There was no sign of either the pond or of where the green things had gone. Apparently, Theron was someone's prisoner.

"I've been kidnapped. Twila, are you here, too?" he shouted. His words echoed on the stone wall. He was sure he had been kidnapped. The door was stone, lifeless and gray, as was the room. Even the water had escaped his dungeon prison. "Where is Twila? She must have gotten away, I'm glad" He thought. Theron had to figure this out.

"How would Morph Man get out of here?" he wondered. In his mind's eye, he could see his sister fighting for his life. What must she think? She had last seen him drowning. He wanted to be home. There was no way he was going to be able to escape, he thought. The walls looked to be six to ten inches of thick stone. Who was he kidding? He wasn't the real Morph Man after all. The massive door would be too much for him to move.

His red spot of hair began to swirl, ringing the last drop of water from it. The water quickly evaporated as it hit the floor. The stone door began to roll. It rolled aside leaving a fine powder on the floor.

In the doorway stood an extraordinary looking man. His bulk absorbed the light that had come through the opening. His long hair hung in strands or clumps, covering part of his face as he ducked to enter the room.

"This must be my captor," Theron thought. He carried a stone bowl in his hands. It contained something round. "A fruit or melon," Theron thought. Theron backed his body to the wall, feeling tiny and afraid, never having seen a man so large or this particular shade of green. "Who's green anyway?" Theron's thought was interrupted.

"Eat your food," the man commanded with a grate to his voice that was like the groan of a starting train. He placed the bowl on the table in the corner of the room. Theron's thoughts flashed as a vivid picture fired across them: "If I run fast past him I might escape."

The giant was watching him as he worked his way toward the door. "Not going to get away," he said, shaking his head from

TS and The WOW

side to side. He cut him off, letting the boy know he would never make it. All it would take was for this monster of a man to put out a hand to knock him down. Or worse, he might step on him. Theron's vision of escape dwindled as reality set in.

Theron examined the fruit. As the door rolled to a close, he had no choice but to resign himself to being a prisoner, at least for the time being.

"What's this?" Theron eyes fell upon a coin wedged in a crack in the floor. "Just like a coin to be stuck somewhere," he said to himself. He worked it loose, rubbed it against his pant leg and stuck it in his pocket.

The day had been a hard one. The fruit was full of water. It was sweet and tasted something like a dry-land casaba melon, Theron thought. One fruit was plenty. It filled him up and quenched his mounting thirst. "I will save this one for later." He patted the melon like you would a good dog.

"What's this?" In the bottom of the bowl, underneath the second melon, was a melon that had been flattened. It wasn't rotten. It just seemed to be an empty rubbery skin. Theron removed the skin from the bowl, placed it on the table, and poked it with his fingers. It was unique, not like any fruit he had ever seen. When he laid it on the tabletop, it folded over. Theron folded it again and again, fascinated that it was like an empty basketball, but more flexible. When it was folded, it was small

TS and The WOW

enough that it fit into his pocket. Theron picked up the remains of the melon he had eaten and tossed the leftover half of the melon rind over the top of the folded skin in the bowl. Water spilled on the skin, as the melon traveled over it. The skin absorbed the moisture and began to swell, unfolding itself.

"That's cool." Theron poured more fluid on the skin making it swell even more. Finally, the skin made a popping sound, something like the sound of a tire reaching full when filled with air on the metal rim. The expansion caused it to bounce on the table, reaching full size. It looked similar to a basketball, complete with the same indentions as the lines found on a basketball.

"Woo! Would you look at that? That thing is alive." The ball rolled itself around, attracted to Theron's voice. It exposed a face to Theron.

"Wet be good. I like water," it said.

Theron jumped back, surprised by what he was witnessing. The ball bounced up and down a few times on the table as if it were stretching after a long sleep. Theron felt that the ball thing was okay. Somehow he was glad for its company, regardless of how bizarre it was.

"There, you got's a name?"

"Yes, I'm Theron Salter," he said hesitantly.

"Mebo!" the ball exclaimed.

TS and The WOW

"So that's your name, Mebo?" Theron ask still feeling strange that he was conversing with a ball.

Perhaps this was the answer to his dilemma, a vision. Inside his head, he could see the Mebo ball in his deflated state sliding underneath the rolling door, then water being poured on his skin to inflate him and rolling the door aside.

"Can you?" Theron paused before he asked.

"What I can?" questioned Mebo in return.

Theron formulated his thoughts before he spoke, not knowing the do's and don'ts of Mebo's kind.

"Do you do that thing often? You know, empty all your water out."

"Mebo just be resting."

"You mean that's how you rest? Would you rest for me?"

Theron convinced Mebo to rest, reassuring him that he would wake him with water as soon as he slid him under the door and explaining that the door would roll aside as he swelled. Mebo closed his eyes and water leaked from his body until he was as flat as a pancake. His water evaporated as it hit the stone floor.

The guard was confident in his prison and had no qualms about taking his morning nap in the shade. His snoring rang out, the only sound in a hollow world. Theron folded Mebo twice and slid him into a triangle-shaped spot where the door was not quite

TS and The WOW

closed. It was a little tight and he hoped he had not hurt Mebo. Theron rushed to the table and brought the remaining melon nearer the door. He split it open. The melon's insides were moist, just as tender as the first had been. He scooped a handful into his hand, careful to guard the watery contents. Then he squeezed it over Mebo. Mebo began to swell almost immediately.

"Are you okay?" Theron said as Mebo began to awaken.

"Tight," he said in a squashed voice, his skin making a rubber pressure sound as it expanded against itself. His ball-like shape was distorted, some bulging outside the door and some inside pressing against the door.

"Mebo is okay," he said in a higher pitched, squeezed voice. The stone door held fast in position as Theron poured more fluid on Mebo. As he swelled, the door first groaned and then made the sound of stone grinding against stone as it rolled slightly open. Mebo assumed his normal ball shape and rolled free, leaving an opening at the door base.

Theron was quick to make his escape from the walls of his prison. Both arms went through the opening and then he pulled and pushed his body out into the world. For the first time, he was glad that he was not as tall as Twila. He thought that sometimes smaller is better.

Mebo watched as Theron made his escape. Theron monitored the activity or inactivity of the gatekeeper as he struggled. Finally, he was free. He brushed some of the fine grindings of dust from his clothes.

"Come on, Mebo, let's get out of here," he whispered. Mebo rolled into the space. It was too small for him to escape at his present size. Again, water poured from the ball's body, evaporating almost as it appeared. Mebo rolled easily through the hole that now seemed quite large. The guard snored louder, then sputtered and spit.

"Quick, hide."

The pair of escapees hid behind the corner of their prison. The stones were different on the outside. They were more gray, more lifeless, much the same as the world in which Theron now stood. The inside had been hidden from the forces that rule in this world and seemed much more alive, if the walls of any prison could be alive. The guard's massive body nearly covered the wooden porch where he slept, spewing spittle as he snored. Mebo's eyes shuffled from side to side to see around Theron's arm under which he was tucked. Theron moved slowly down the slope to ensure that his guard would not see the escape and alert the crowd of giants in the distance that would surely chase after them. The slope suddenly changed, becoming a cliff and canyon to rival the grand one on earth.

"We can't get down there. We will have to go back," Theron said, turning to go back to where his captor slept. The porch boards creaked under the weight of Theron's feet. Not even his Red Ball Jets could stop the sound.

"Just my luck," Theron said under his breath. The biggest pair of feet he had ever seen blocked his path and there was no way around them.

"We're going to have to step over him," Theron thought as he lifted his leg above the giant green gatekeeper.

"Mebo watch you go," said Mebo, cranking one eye in a contorted way to see the mug of the guard.

Theron raised his leg carefully above the legs of the guard. He was halfway over when the sleeper rolled to his side, catching Theron's legs with a force that threw him from the porch and into the pasty white dirt. He lost his grip on Mebo, who was flung down the trail and was still rolling when Theron raised his head and spit the dust from his mouth. He climbed to his feet.

"He's awake. He's awake!" Theron's mind was saying to run. His body, however, wasn't working. He was stone-cold in his tracks. The giant was awake and stumbling to his feet.

"Got to get going!" Theron told himself while watching the giant gaining his balance.

Suddenly, it was like a starter pistol had fired and they were off. Theron raced to the last spot where Mebo had rolled. The giant's lumbering body was in pursuit. He only stopped long

TS and The WOW

enough to puff his cheeks like a New Year's balloon, and then blew into an animal's bony skull that he used for a horn. The horn blared, its alarming alert. Now everyone knew there had been an escape. Soon, lumbering, green giants were coming from all parts of the worn-down village, some carrying clubs and others riding on the backs of Vendalus, two-legged beasts big enough to carry the giants.

Each Vendalu wore the same pasty white face as the depleted soil that Theron still wore on his. The Vendalus were fast and that meant Theron and Mebo had to be faster. Theron opened his arms as Mebo bounced, snagging Mebo like the perfect pass in a game. Theron ran toward the trees of a dead forest. The forest was foreboding, but Theron had already decided it was their only chance for escape. Theron was afraid to look back, feeling a Vendalu's breath on his neck. Mebo chanted, "More faster, more faster," as he watched the growing hoard that appeared. Ten or more were chasing them. The trees were bent over the path ahead, and Theron hoped they could reach that spot before the giants and their beasts did. Just before Theron and Mebo reached the edge of the forest, a Vendalu bounced to a halt in front of them, white powdered dust rising at his feet and the biggest ugliest giant straddling his back.

"Stop, you human!" commanded the rider.

Theron looked, just for a second, behind himself to see where the others were and then ran straight for the rider and his mount.

"I'm not stopping for anyone!" was his battle cry. He ran right between the legs of the Vendalu, who had parted them to balance the giant's heavy body weight. The Vendalu tried to turn, twisting his legs together like Twila's hair when it was braided. The crash was great. Old trees cracked and snapped and dust rose over the fallen bodies of the giant and the Vendalu. Amidst the crash, Theron could hear the approach of the hoard.

"We've got to get out of here!" Theron exclaimed. Mebo's contorted eyes looked up at Theron.

"Vendalu. There be a Vendalu," he said, warning his ride.

They had to escape into the woods right now, or it was back to being a prisoner. With Mebo tucked under his arm, Theron dodged the fallen tree behind the new Vendalu, who was trying to turn about. It tossed his rider to the ground. Apparently, these giants bounced. "Not much of a Cowboy," Theron thought. The green giant man groaned when he landed on his back, half across the log. The woods were still a short distance away.

Mebo cried out, "Bounce faster!" meaning Theron should run faster. Theron didn't need coaching. Instinct had already taken him by the seat of the pants and inspired an all out effort

TS and The WOW

for escape. The trail wound down a hill through the dead trees. At the bottom of the hill, he could see that the forest was growing thick, so thick that, if they reached it, the giants could never follow them.

Suddenly, it was like Theron was back on the rocks, leaping his Red Ball Jets into the white powder of the trail. A green, oversized hand, reached out to catch the boy as he leaped into the air and he run faster than he ever had, avoiding the hand. For a moment, all had seemed lost. The giant was chasing them, an arm's length away, and then Theron ducked under a low branch that smacked the giant green man directly in the chest, knocking him and the other two behind him into the dust. One rolled down the hill into the forest.

"Got-zem. Wa hoo!" Mebo squealed.

The rest of the giants tramped over the hillside. Some were riding on Vendalus, others on foot, all filling the narrow corridor behind them. There were so many that they stumbled against each other. Theron and Mebo darted through an opening in the straggly patch of fallen trees. The stone-like trees became so dense and so thick that none of the monster creatures could continue to chase after them.

Theron gulped in needed breaths of air.

"Whoosh, I think we are safe in here," he said, looking about and wondering if they had escaped or if they were in worse trouble than they had been.

"Voice grumble back there." Mebo had noted the voices behind them, still concerned. They could hear the voices of the giants as they tried to decide how to pursue.

"I think we're safe for now."

Theron crept deeper into the woods, choosing to stay off the trail.

"Mebo, how do we get out of here?" Theron had become nervous about the depth of the forest. It was beginning to seem more like a trap than the freedom he hoped for.

"Mebo remember this way." He tried to point with his lips. Theron followed the direction and soon was on a trail. Mebo bounced his way into the lead. "You come, follow Mebo."

The forest was growing thin, as was the light of day. Theron wondered why the giants had captured him anyway. What did they have against him? Mebo left a single print in the dirt as he bounced and Theron left the bipedal prints of his Red Ball Jets on top. How different he and Mebo were, but today they were best friends. The sun dropped quickly into what he thought was the southern mountains and Theron's red hair began to twist and untwist. He was sure that something was about to happen.

"Where are we going?"

TS and The WOW

Mebo glowed in the dark, lighting the path.

"We be there soon."

Theron noticed torches lighting the night across the ridge behind them. Were they still being followed, he wondered?

"Where is Twila when a fella needs her?" thought Theron. Theron's next step sent him rolling down a hillside. He tumbled into the dark, landing in a parched dried bush. Mebo rolled to a stop while looking for his partner in the darkness.

"I'm down here," Theron called, as he saw the glow of Mebo's skin.

"What you do down there? Let's be go, Theron!" Mebo said, sounding kind of Irish.

Theron was tired, banged up and wondering if this odyssey would ever end. He lay in the bush a few more seconds before he rolled onto his knees and climbed back to Mebo. When he was about to crest the hillside, Mebo screamed as a large green foot stepped on him. Water gushed out all over Theron, and then evaporated. Mebo's light went out as he was flattened. Theron immediately dropped to the ground, hoping he would not be seen. His eyes adjusted to the dark and he watched the giants as they fumbled about, searching for him.

"Where is the boy?" one of the gruesome figures said.

"Not here," another said. Then they walked away, supposing that Mebo was squashed and dead. Theron waited, listening for them to be far enough away that he may be free to help Mebo. This time, Theron just folded Mebo as tight as he could and tucked him into his pocket. Since he had no water to raise him from his hibernation, folding him up was his only choice. Theron's red clump of hair still had not stopped twisting and turning about. There must be something still out there, something about to happen.

"Why did you get squashed, Mebo?" Theron was feeling so alone. A sense of foreboding engulfed him, alone there in the darkness of the world of his captors.

Twila, Adeline, and George searched for the third day in the cave, all the time calling for Arlis to help them find Theron. But Theron had the orb in his pocket when he was taken to the bottom of Busher's Pond. Theron was in trouble, and at the moment, it seemed that the family had no power to assist him.

"What can we do?" Twila said, frustrated with the situation. George was a man with conviction. He knew that man was not alone and that there was a way to help Theron.

"Have you asked a prayer, Twila?"

Twila's red hair twisted and untwisted until the prayer ended. Then it rested as if peace had come to it.

Theron awoke after an abbreviated night. Nights and days were shorter here in this world. In fact, lots of things were different here. Theron had slept in the woods near where he had fallen in the night. He was dusty and his throat was dry. He wanted water, just a drink, and now he was so hungry that his stomach grumbled with desire to be fed.

"One of those melons would be great right now," he said out loud, startling himself with the sound of his own voice.

First, Theron found his hands and knees and rose to his feet. He surveyed the horizon for any sign of the giant green ones. Not a one in sight.

Theron wondered how he was going to get out of this world and home. Surely his family was trying to find him after two days, or was it more since he had been taken? The sun was dropping in the west, ending the day. It was one of the hottest days that Theron could remember.

Another day had passed since Theron had been taken by the green things in the pond. Twila's red hair spot twisted like the spinning blades on a helicopter.

"Yes!" she screamed with excitement. Twila remembered something that Arlis had told her. "Think, concentrate," she told herself over and over. All at once, her red hair stood at attention, straight and tall, as rigid as the Queen's guard at Buckingham

TS and The WOW

Palace. Twila scrunched her eyes closed, tighter and tighter, seeing something that did not lie in front of her in this world.

"Theron," she called. Again she called "Theron, where are you?"

Right there in the living room of the Salter house, a storm arose. The wind blew with the fury of a tornado, whipping Adeline's curios, furniture and potted plants around in its funnel of wind. The windows bulged out, barely holding in their frames, yet Twila knelt directly in the center of the storm, not a hair out of place, lost in total concentration.

"Open!" she commanded with authority. At her command, the storm halted stone still, the entire complement of objects suspended in the air right where they had been drawn by the wind. The windows relaxed again, flat in their frames. Twila's face was effulgent with sparkles of light. Her eyes closed, for she was seeing something outside of the earth world.

Theron rested in the darkness, glad the sun had gone down, leaving the world cooler.

"Mebo, I wish you were not sleeping. It's getting pretty lonely here."

Theron unfolded his friend. A tear fell from his eye onto the deflated ball. The water was not enough to change Mebo. He remained in hibernation. Torches lit the hillside above the hiding place where Theron rested.

"I'm so hungry. Maybe I would be better off to give myself up," he thought.

"Theron, Theron." It was Twila's voice out there in the darkness.

"Twila, where are you?" he said, trying to keep his voice low enough not to give away his hiding place. She was not out there. He was so tired and hungry that he was hallucinating, he thought. First a speck of light appeared in the bushes below Theron, right where he had heard Twila's voice.

"Man, I'm going crazy," he said to himself, just wanting to hear his own voice to reassure him that he was sane. The light burst to open a window where Twila sat in their living room at home.

"Twila!" Theron yelled, not caring who or what heard him. The bubble fell open, framed by the darkness of the dry world. Theron stepped through. He was dirty, tired and hungry, but home.

"Mom, Dad!" Twila cried out. "He's home!"

CHAPTER 9

A Parent's Dream and Under Attack

George awoke in night's deep hours for the third night in a row. The waters of a cold sweat had drenched his nightclothes.

"I need to sleep," he said in frustration. Haunting dreams were devouring his attempts to rest. His dreams were something he didn't want to talk about. He was keeping them from his wife, Adeline, but it was the kind of fear or dread that often consumes fathers. The dream had placed George in the forest under the darkness of night. His whole family rested inside their canvas tent beneath the massive Ponderosa pine trees. George had propped himself in a lawn chair in the warmth and glow of the campfire. The limestone rocks had taken on heat from the fire, and even in the dream, their heat radiated from them. The trees glowed in the flicker of the flame, and George thought he was right where he wanted to be, until the cry from the wild. It was the same cry that he had heard in the Grand Canyon before the twins were born. No creature had shown its face, but George knew, yes, he knew, that it threatened his family. "Was it dream or was it reality that

TS and The WOW

so clearly exposed their impending doom." George wondered to himself as he sat in the darkness of his bedroom. Yet, George could do nothing. There was no way to fight a dream. Morning came. The rooster crowed just like it did every morning.

Theron, who was already walking to the hen house, whistled,"Oh, I wish I were an Oscar Meyer wiener."

Gathering the eggs was never his favorite chore to do, but sometimes, you just do the doing because it needs to be done.

Adeline and Twila were in the kitchen when George finally agreed that it was time to toss back the warmth of the blankets and be resurrected from his bed and his nightmares. The dreams had been so real that George still wore the fear in his eyes.

"Not like you to stay in bed so long honey," Adeline said, as her husband hung his arms over her shoulders, resting his head next to hers.

"Better grab your breakfast, sweetie."

George sat at the table and ate a small stack of pancakes that Twila placed in front of him.

"Morning, Daddy." She kissed him on the cheek. He smiled. She bounced back to the stove and her pancake duty.

"Honk." Just one brief toot, and up drove the power truck.

TS and The WOW

"Dewey's here," Adeline called out.

Adeline kissed George on the lips, Twila kissed him on the cheek, and Theron, still at the table downing his second stack of cakes, mumbled through the mouth full. "Bye, Dad."

Adeline chased George to the truck caring his black lunch pail. "Don't forget your lunch, honey!"

He turned, took the pail and finished his climb into the passenger seat, then closed the door. George drove off to his normal day's work, never hinting of his terror or saying a word. "There is work to be done," Twila said, tossing the orb into the air over Theron's head. "You have to come now." she said insistently.

Theron was sitting cross-legged on the floor in his bedroom reading the adventure of Morph Man. The comic book lay on the floor in front of him.

"Can't you wait one minute?" Theron said, frustrated because he was about to learn who was behind the mask of Morph Man's nemesis, Megawatt. He set a baseball card down to mark his spot in the comic book and went into the living room to see what was up. Klin was waiting, showing frustration upon his face which matched the frustration on Theron's, who would just have to learn Megawatt's secret another time.

"What a mess, what a mess my world be!" Klin said, shaking his head and acting as if he were defeated. The world was in havoc, not just Klin's world, but earth world as well. It was as though all portals, or bubbles as Theron and Twila named them, had opened, spilling over into the earth all at once. After Klin explained they were needed in the Tween, a bubble opened, taking away half of the house and leaving the grassy plains of Inovda, the world of the Unicorns, in its place.

"Come now, we must be gone." Urgency colored Klin's voice, his desire punctuated by the missing half of the Salter house that was lost somewhere in the Tween. Before the trio could move out the door, the house was back, and the bubble had closed or shifted to the backyard. The bubble now was hovering next to the Winter Tree, where three unicorns were grazing on his low leaves. The Winter Tree swung a limb with a snap to the rear, causing them to bolt and run away. Suddenly there were bubbles opening all around them as they ran toward the cave of faces on the Black Ridge.

"We have got to hurry. This is a disaster!" Twila called out, as she ran ahead of Theron and Klin. Twila turned to look back at the others, and in that moment, they were gone.

"Oh no!" she screamed, knowing that they had been caught up in a stray bubble and could be lost in any of the other worlds. Twila knew she had to get to the cave to use the orb to find Arlis.

"Twila," someone yelled as she entered the cave. She turned, just for a second, to see who followed her.

"Who's there?"

Klin entered the cave.

"Where is Theron?"

"He ran into the world of large hairy ones with immense feet." Klin looked down at his feet, thinking they were small in comparison.

Twila had already cast the orb into the basin's water. A jolt of both light and energy erupted as Klin's head rose from admiring his feet. At the same time, Klin felt sucking from the cave to find they were standing in the field. The field was not far from Arlis's workshop. Arlis was waiting for their arrival.

"Come with me, you two. We have work."

So far this summer after the raft was swallowed, nearly every day had held some adventure.

"Where is Theron? We need him, too."

Arlis had taught them that they were more than just a couple of kids. They were a team.

"No got him," Klin announced. For a moment Arlis was irritated.

"I sent you for both of them."

Klin had no defense, but he had tried.

TS and The WOW

"The bubble swallowed him," he cowered in the doorway.

"Come on, we will have to do our best with you and Twila."

It wasn't an apology, but they had pressing duties.

The balls of crystal buzzed about, one following them to a portal, and they were shot off into the opening of a bubble. It closed with the pop of energy and reconnected as they entered, leaving its sticky residue on their skin. There would be a flash of light, and then a bubble would open. As they watched, a series of bubbles surrounded them. World after world, bending and bleeding into one another, all connected right where they stood. The entire army of flying balls stood fixed, several in front of each bubble, each spinning and throwing off tiny lightning bolts directed into the bubble in front of them.

"What are we doing?" Twila was scared. The inbalance made her stomach queasy. When she looked at Arlis, his body flickered like the television when it is off the air, and he disappeared. Then the bubbles would come back with some strange creature, and then they would bubble off again to wherever that animal belonged.

"Stand still," Arlis called out, before he faded away.

Twila and Klin stood their ground, not moving out of the pentagon of worlds.

TS and The WOW

"Where could we go, anyway?" Twila thought. Arlis faded in and out several more times, and the bubbles closed one by one. At his return, he seemed exhausted.

"You have done well," he said, opening a bubble of his own. "Follow me."

He waved his hand for them to walk in behind him. For a moment, it was calm as Arlis lead them to the room where assignments were handed out by a yeti that spoke English with an accent that Twila had never heard before. An extraordinary map broke into seven parts across the wall. It looked like globes cut in to halves. It was not of any territory or world that Twila had any knowledge of, except for one. It was the earth.

"We are in trouble. We are losing the battle," Arlis said.

Any thought that this was going to be a fun day had long ago slid away from the young girl. The sober moment was clear on her face. The red hair on her head lay limp, giving no warning as it usually did. Arlis stood near the map.

"This is the map of all seven worlds," he said for Twila's information. "We...." he hesitated. It was almost despair on his face. Arlis raised his hands over his head, and then slapped them on his sides. "You're just a kid!" This was the first time that he had called Twila or Theron kids. Arlis turned toward Twila and Klin. "I guess I must go."

"Go where," they said in unison.

TS and The WOW

"To stop him," he said. Twila had just gotten used to the idea that there were worlds all coexisting on top of one another, now there was a great battle of the bubbles!

"What next." she sharply thought.

"You must find Theron and return with him here to keep the balance." Arlis turned to the tunnel in the rocky wall of the room and waved his arms, opening a bubble. Twila was afraid that this might be the last time she would ever see Arlis.

Theron had not been able to avoid the bubble that swallowed him up. Now he was in the world of Palltare or "Yetiville" as he called it when he and Twila talked of the worlds that they knew. This time things were different. Bubbles were opening here, some into all the worlds.

"If I'm quick enough, I could jump into the earth world," he thought, watching the bubble open into Inovada, the world of unicorns. A unicorn ran through the bubble and was trapped there with Theron.

"I can't leave you here alone." Theron reached to the unicorn with his open hand to reassure the animal. The steed was the whitest horse he had ever seen, other than the animals that had nearly run him down in the school. This animal had to be from that herd.

TS and The WOW

"Come here, boy." Theron had pulled some watermelon grass that he thought would appeal to the unicorn. He waved it at the beast. "You will like this."

The unicorn sniffed at the grass, blew a burst of air from his nostrils, and then ate the grass. Theron moved closer as the animal ate, rubbing the muscles along its neck.

"You are going to be just fine," he said calmly. When the grass was nearly gone, a bubble appeared behind the unicorn. It was the earth world. "There's our chance!" Theron said aloud, while grasping the hair along the back of the unicorn's neck in his fingers and swinging his leg over the animal's back. "Come on boy! Let's go."

The Unicorn leaped to attention, feeling something on his back. First he bucked and then kicked, bouncing up and down like his spring had sprung. He bounced and bounced right into the bubble. As suddenly as Theron had been trapped in the bubble, he was back on earth. The unicorn was confused and ceased bucking. They were back on earth, but it seemed strange to Theron. The trees were thick oaks, he thought. Theron slid his body down from his ride and walked toward what looked like a trail or road. The unicorn followed after him, as if he knew being with Theron would be better than being here alone. It was a road. It had to be his best bet for getting home.

"Come on." He waved for the unicorn to follow him. As they rounded the bend on the lonely state road, it became clear where they were. The sign read "Gladwin 10 miles." It was the sign next to that one that tied things together for Theron. It read "Michigan State road 18."

"We're in Michigan. How the heck are we going to get home?" Theron took a look at his companion, a horse with a horn on his forehead. "That's great. Anyone sees you, we're sunk. Hope no one lives in Gladwin," he thought.

A 1950's truck was coming down the road. It was too far away for the driver to see the horn on the horse's face, but soon he would be close enough for him to count the freckles on Theron's face. Theron took off his shirt and wrapped it around the horn. The stripes on his shirt made it look like a barber pole was growing from the animal's face. The truck stopped, its clutch clanking as the man let it out. The farmer wore bib overalls, just like the farmers at home. The man smiled through his missing front tooth.

"You okay boy?" he called out.

"I'm fine," Theron called back.

"Strange horse you got there." The barber pole had not gone unnoticed. Theron had to think fast before the man decided to get out and examine the unicorn closer.

"A bit cross eyed. Got to train him with this contraption. Well, you be good now," the man said. He put the truck back in

TS and The WOW

gear and started on his way. Then, for some reason, the man stopped fifty feet down the road. Theron gasped, but didn't look back, hoping the man would go. It was to his delight that the engine wound up again, and the truck went on down the road.

Klin had finally zeroed in on the whereabouts of Theron. Not an easy thing to do just using a flowering orb. He and Twila had first traced him to the Yeti world on Palltare. That part was easy. They had seen him enter there, then return back to the earth world. Twila opened a bubble in the field where the trees would hide most of it, hoping Theron would be the only one to see it. The bubble burst open and Twila ran through.

"Theron, we're over here," she called out. Theron had never been so glad to see anyone.

"Twila, how did you find me?" His question went unanswered as they rushed to the opening bubble. The unicorn trotted behind them, still flinging the flag-like red, white, and blue tee shirt from his horn.

"What is he wearing your shirt for?" Twila asked. The window in the field outside Gladwin closed, and they were on the hill below the cave of faces. "That shirt is more your size, don't you think." Twila laughed a bit. Theron removed the shirt, from the swirl horn and led the animal back to his father's horse corral.

"The unicorn will be okay here until we get back," Theron said, putting back the slip rails on the gate to the corral. The unicorn ran to greet the mustang named Peanuts. They sniffed each other and bounced their heads up and down as if one recognized the other.

"Hurry, we have to get back. Arlis needs us."

Twila had seen Arlis go into another world, which changed nothing. Bubbles were still opening all over the Black Ridge. Arlis had wanted them to find Theron and return as soon as possible.

"Why was Theron so important?"

"Watch out!" Twila warned Theron of an opening bubble. "Can't afford to lose you a second time, little brother."

"I was never lost. I knew right where I was all the time."

Klin watched, perplexed, as they bantered back and forth. The orb quickly lit the cave, and in a second, they stood in the field next to the glen just a hop, skip and a jump from Arlis's cottage and workshop.

"What are we suppose to do here?" Theron asked, wondering what Arlis wanted them to do. Neither Klin nor Twila could answer that question. They were as bewildered as Theron. They were just following the request that Arlis had made of them to find Theron and bring him here. Orbs flitted frantically about the room when they entered. Theron ducked to avoid being smacked in the head by one of the glowing white balls as it passed. Another dodged Twila, spinning itself into the wall.

"It's mayhem in here." Twila always had the big words and Theron always wondered what they meant.

"What does that mean?" Theron wondered.

"It means everything is out of order. No order."

Klin placed a ball into a slot on the wall. It could be heard rolling away. He placed a second one in a basin where it began to spin. This time there was no light from the ball. Klin just dissolved into particles and was gone. It was only moments until both balls reappeared with a loud snap. Klin was not with them. "Where had the balls sent him?" both children silently wondered. The room flickered with light, and Arlis's Panama hat floated to the ground. Twila caught it as it fell.

"Look, a note."

The note bore only one word. "Wolf." It was scribbled in blood.

"Theron, what does this mean?" Twila showed him the note. He took the hat and placed it on his head as if it would help in some way. When he read the word "wolf," he shuddered, thinking that the blood must be Arlis's.

"We have got to do something, Twi."

Theron always jumped before he thought. It was Twila who knew they couldn't go unprepared or they would be in the

TS and The WOW

same trouble as Arlis. Maybe the note was just the wolf's way of getting them on his territory, Twila suggested.

"Dad would know what to do," she said to her brother.

Both of the twins were shaken by the word "wolf" on the note, feeling an urgency to help.

"Theron, what would Dad do?"

"First, he would pray to Father in Heaven for understanding and guidance, like we do every morning."

"Let's do it." The twins knelt on the hard floor of the room and reached out with all their faith for help. The words that occupied their minds came straight from the Bible: "The Lord helps those who help themselves."

"What did that mean?" Theron thought.

Twila had received the same message. She understood it and proceeded with an idea that she had decided upon years before. Her father had told her to examine her life, try to see what might happen in the future, and decide how you might face that challenge. She had never predicted the events of this day, yet it was the same kind of situation as the one she had prepared for. George had told her that she should kick and fight and scream if anyone tried to kidnap her. In that situation she had decided she would fight with all her might. It was Arlis who had been taken this time, not her, but the same plan still applied.

TS and The WOW

"Over here, Theron. This is the room where the bubble was."

"The one where Arlis went?"

"Yes."

They went through a tunnel in the rock wall of the workshop. On the other side of the tunnel was a room where a single bubble opened on the wall. It rotated worlds all in the same space.

"Which one did Arlis go into?" Theron asked his sister, who was counting the windows as they opened and closed.

"Seven. There are seven," she declared.

"Which one is Arlis in?"

"I don't know!" she said in frustration.

At the same time she felt her red hair spot tugging at her head and pulling in the direction of the bubble. The hair pulling stopped as the bubbles rotated, one opening and then another right in front of her. Both her hair spot and Theron's red hair spot yanked on their heads, pulling them closer to the fifth bubble.

"It's this one." Twila felt the tug as the bubble passed. "Get ready. When it opens again, we jump through."

Twila reached to hold Theron's hand. When the pulling bubble came around, they leaped into the opening and into a different world.

"I recognize this place. It's where the giants are. You know, Mebo's world."

The heat was like the deserts of Arabia. The withering forest struggled to grow, but most of it was gray and lifeless.

"This is an odd world."

Twila had already felt the water from her skin coming to the surface as sweat. The sweat was evaporating as soon as it beaded on her skin. They had made their way to the trees where even the dead gray ones gave shade from the parching rays of the sun.

"We have to wait for the sun to go down before we can go very far." Theron was sure of himself, remembering his capture and escape from this world.

"Okay, do you have any water?"

She was so thirsty. Theron shook his head no. The sun was dropping in the sky, the forest cooling down, and Twila was nearly exhausted from the heat.

"Come on, Twila. The prison is this way."

Theron walked into the woods and up the hill. Twila dragged both feet, following after him. Within ten minutes, they could see a decaying stone building on the hilltop. The building was a castle of sorts and the prison lay below it. The castle was not the kind where you would have found King Arthur, but a castle nonetheless. It covered the entire top of the lonely peak. The castle was made of sand, each grain linked to other grains to build the walls. From a distance, it had appeared to be the contents of a giant bag of crinkled potato chips, some lying flat and others propped into the air, held there by strange forces of nature unknown to earthlings. Periodically, it would reshape into a new figure, camouflaging the entrance. By the time Theron and Twila reached the spot where the door had been, it had reshaped, looking like the feathers on an Indian's war bonnet. Theron's eyes flickered in the fading light of evening, throwing off a spark. Then, suddenly, he could see each of the sand grains. Their round bodies had several tiny hands attached to them, and the particles were holding hands to keep the shape of the castle.

"That's amazing. I've never seen anything so strange."

"What are you seeing?" Twila couldn't see anything more than the sandcastle walls.

"Just these little sandy people." He poured some of the sand into Twila's hand.

"That's just sand."

A million little voices cried out, "We are Doids, not sand."

TS and The WOW

The particles that had run through her fingers were calling out to her as they reformed their selves into a ball. The ball rolled over to the castle edge and bound again with the parent building.

"Doids, I can hear them!" Twila said, shocked once again.

"And I can see them," Theron said, just being matter of fact about their discovery.

"Things just get weirder and weirder," Twila thought. Theron was past the weirdness of things. "Maybe this was a good thing," he thought.

"Twila, tell them to give me a door."

"Mr. Doids, can you make my brother a door?"

They responded like one voice. "We will comply." The entire pile of sand shifted, reforming into the shape. It reminded Theron of the front of a steam engine repeated in a circle several time to make the castle round. Theron watched as the Doids let go of one another's hands and rolled about like tiny cogs into their new position, grasping hands in a locking formation. The engine-cowcatcher-looking front gate opened, leaving a doorway into the castle. No life seemed to grow around the castle, not even lonely tumbleweed.

"Arlis has to be inside." Theron was sure that he was here. It was a whispering inside that told him that was so.

TS and The WOW

"I'm so tired, Theron, I need to sit awhile." Twila sat with her back against the sands of the castle.

"I have to find Arlis. You understand, don't you?"

"I understand." She was weary.

"Stay here. Warn me if the giants are coming."

Theron was off to find Arlis. Twila sat in the sandy soil, watching. She watched the gates where Theron had entered the castle. He had just slipped in when four brutes wearing hoods came from the same direction as Theron had gone. "They must have missed Theron," Twila thought as she hid from them, hoping that the darkness would conceal her. It was her friend as the hooded ones lumbered their huge bodies away from her.

"I have to be calm," she held her breath. "What can I do to help them," she said not realizing she was talking out loud. The cool of the night air soothed her. Her sense of wellbeing returned. She would watch all the happenings around her, searching for the opening she needed to creep into the castle before it changed again. She knew if she waited too long, the hooded ones would come back.

It was now or never. She felt a surge of adrenaline, instant energy. The walls of the castle were wiggling under the touch of her hands as she worked her way to the gate where she had seen Theron enter into the castle.

TS and The WOW

Theron had been near silent. His Red Ball Jets had worked their magic, deserving of the name of sneakers. The castle was busy, alive with activity from the figures wearing hoods that canceled their faces, some leading Vendalus' carts loaded with cargo.

"I'm glad Twila stayed outside," Theron thought. "Where would they keep Arlis?" Theron analyzed the building. All castles have dungeons. "I wish I could turn on my Morphing powers like Morph Man. I would just become a crate on that cart. Wait, I can do that," he thought, and as the cart passed, Theron climbed aboard, hiding in the middle of the crates. Theron got as low as he could on the floor of the cart. A noise was coming from the box next to his face.

"Is some in there?" Theron asked.

"We are here," a single voice spoke for the group. All of the chatter ceased. They waited calmly as though they were just on board for a bus ride.

"Are you okay in there?" Theron imagined children locked inside the tight dark confines of the boxes. The cart bounced over a stone in the floor, jolting Theron.

"Oof!" he cried in an uncontrolled response.

The cloaked figure paused a second to look around and then led the Vendalu and its cart into a chamber where crate after crate was stacked, nearly to the height of the ceiling. Voices came from the boxes, voices that sounded like children stacked like a commodity on a store shelf.

"I can't leave these children here alone." Theron was figuring out how he could rescue them. "What about Arlis, he needs me," Theron thoughts were conflicted.

He climbed out of the cart just before it stopped for unloading, hiding behind a stack of boxes. In the middle of the room was a tower with a great dish in its center. Something rested in the dish, hidden from view below.

Twila had made her way into the castle where she had encountered three of the hooded ones. At first her heart leapt in her chest, knowing she was caught, but her thoughts changed.

"I'm just one of you," she suggested. That was exactly what they saw as they passed her, just another hooded figure. She would not have believed it if she had not seen it herself.

"That was the freakiest thing I've ever seen." Her mind was able to cloak the minds of the hooded ones. All she had to do was to think what she wanted them to see, and it was so. "This will be cinchiosious."

Crumbled stones were strewn on the floor as though no caretaker monitored the building. Flattened Mobo like creatures were all over the floor, all in hibernation, their water emptied from their skins. Theron's heart pumped with a kind of excitement that had only been present in his life since meeting

TS and The WOW

the spinney-necked monster in the front yard. He thought that he had become a comic book super hero. He secretly called himself balancer boy.

Theron had to save the children in the crates, and that would take all the courage he could muster. A dark cloak brushed his leg where he hid, as the hooded one led his Vendalu back up the path

"Boy, boy, help us." The children in the boxes called out to Theron.

"Quiet, they will hear us." Theron shushed the kids trapped inside the crates, already taking action. He pried the top board off a crate that sat alone on the floor. The board snapped, breaking as it came loose. The second board revealed different content inside the box than Theron had imagined.

Twila had ice water running in her veins. Her dad would say she was as cool as a cucumber. She wondered why she was calm as she watched, peering first down the staircase and then into the hall from where she had just come. Down the stairs it was dark, and there was an old muddy smell like dewdrops under a toadstool. It was little surprise that was the direction that Twila chose.

"Smells like Theron's socks," she said to herself while her hand that was touching the wall felt the Doids changing the outside shape of the castle, but nothing changed on the inside. At

TS and The WOW

the bottom of the dark corridor, a wooden door with iron bars hung on the wall. It was ajar, open just enough that Twila could see inside. In the dark corner of the chamber, two of the hooded ones were building a fire. They placed several long bars of iron on the flames, and down into the coals to heat. The light from the fire grew, and a third person's presence was revealed. The shadow on the wall reflected the image of the prisoner. It was Arlis, chained between two hefty poles anchored to the floor.

Theron had broken loose crate after crate, releasing the captives, each one grateful. With all the crates empty, it was time to get everyone out of there.

"They are coming!" a tiny voice called to the group that huddled around Theron.

"Everyone, behind the boxes!" Theron whispered, re-stacking as many of the empty crates as he could, trying to make it look as normal as possible to the hooded ones. They came, with their Vendalus into the room, stirring up a dusty cloud as they did. There was a hush, almost a holding of breath, as the last of the crates found its place in the stack. Dust settled on those hiding behind the boxes, glazing their skin with a coating that looked like sugar. Theron covered his nose, trying to stop the sneeze he felt was coming. An eruption of sneezing bounced from one to the next, coming from all the corners of the hiding places. In an instant, they were discovered. At first only the two hooded ones responded, still holding back their Vendalus from bolting for the door.

"Go, go, everyone! Head to the door!" Theron commanded the ball creatures, knowing confusion would aid the escape. Ball creatures bounced in all directions, some climbing the stacks of crates and toppling them to the ground. Others bounced and rolled right past the hooded figures that were reaching and grabbing in all directions to capture them again. Mayhem filled the air, ball after ball bouncing past the guards and out into the dreary desert world to safety. The room drained like water from a broken dam, leaving only Theron.

"The mind thing, Twila thought, casting out the idea that Arlis had escaped. The door opened in a hurry, and the two cloaked figures ran clumsily from the dark chamber.

Twila had stood behind the door hiding in the cavity it left. "This is too easy," she laughed. Most of Arlis' clothes were torn away from his body. Only straps of cloth still held them together. He had been beaten, and much worse was about to happen had Twila not arrived. Twila tugged on the remainder of his shirtsleeve. He winced.

"Twila, get out of here, the wolf."

He was afraid she would alert the vermin that walked these halls, worse yet, the wolf.

TS and The WOW

The turmoil gave Theron enough warning to hide before the man entered the room.

"What's going on in here?" the howling voice demanded.

Theron's own breath sounded like winds of a tornado to him as the man passed. He didn't dare look for fear he would attract attention. This man's gate was awkward, dragging one of his feet. He stopped on the opposite side of the crates from where Theron was curled into a ball, hiding and attempting to hold his breath.

"It was easy getting in here," he thought, "but will I get out alive?"

As soon as the man had passed, Theron looked to see his tail swishing back and forth in the air. It was strange to be inside the fortress of the wolf man, the mad man that wanted him under his power or even dead. It had to be him, the wolf from the wall, which had just passed.

Twila was being led by a feeling toward the newest door of the castle. Theron also could feel the drawing powers. They were being called from different spots in the castle. Their red hair swung as if it were dancing at first and then sprung, bouncing like the hands of a compass pointing the way out.

"I have to find Arlis," Theron thought, still intent on rescuing his surrogate grandfather. He ignored what the red hair was trying to tell him. He had a job to do, and as George had

TS and The WOW

always told him, "If a job was worth doing it was worth doing well." This might not have been what George had meant, but Theron had found himself following the man with the tail, trying to stay where he could see his shadow on the wall.

The man ranted and raved over the escape of all the Mebos. He was tearing the robe and hood from one of the hooded ones when Theron peaked around the corner. Other hooded ones cowered on the ground at the feet of the man. It was the fury of viciousness within a wild creature committing the act against the now willowy, green creature that had been behind the hood. Claws extended like switchblades on the man's fingertips. With only a couple of swings, the creature was no more than a pile of wood stacked atop his empty robe. Light cast a grizzly shadow of a man-wolf upon the wall. Fear rose in the young boy's soul. What had been a game suddenly seemed much too real.

"Take this one to the dungeon. He will suffer."

The other hooded ones gathered the wood remains of the stick figure into their arms and carried it, following after the man thing. The pile of wood was still alive, trying to escape whatever was about to happen to it.

"If I..." Theron's words were low, almost silent, but when the man looked his way, his words fell dead, mid sentence, frozen in place. Theron ducked to hide from the view of the man, who

TS and The WOW

turned and continued ranting about how the others would suffer if they didn't do something. Theron couldn't hear what that something was.

"I have got to be more careful," Theron thought, ducking into a dark shadow in a cavity in the wall.

Twila had released Arlis from the tethers that had held him. The two of them were making their way out of the bowels of the castle when Twila noticed someone coming.

"We have to hide," Arlis said. Then he coughed.

"In here," Twila said. She propped Arlis up, keeping him from falling to the ground. He was weak from his wounds. There was an awful commotion in the passageway. The hood of one of the hooded ones was violently torn away by an old man. The victim was slashed, screaming for his life. For a moment everything was hushed. Twila had hidden her eyes, not wanting to see. Then the man walked on with the others following after him, the robe bundled in one arm. The sticks in the other arm were quivering and trying to escape his grip. Something invaded the dark cavity where they were hidden. It came in, stepping backward, faceless. Twila didn't dare speak. She prepared to hit it with the only thing she had, her fist.

"Theron," Arlis whispered.

TS and The WOW

The figure that stood in front of Twila jumped and turned slowly about to face the voice. Twila recognized Theron's face and threw her arms around his neck.

"Theron, it's you!"

" Shush, sis. They'll hear us."

"You must open a bubble here, right now," Arlis said, focused on Twila.

Twila focused, also, thinking "Bubble home, bubble home." The bubble opened on the Black Ridge above Busher's Pond. As they stepped through out of the desert world, the bubble closed. Theron turned to see the castle crumbling and the Doids rolling away, escaping. The cry of a lone, injured wolf echoed through the bubble, abruptly ending, as the bubble popped closed.

CHAPTER 10

The Nightly News and Creatures In The Forest

The nightly news had given the totals of those killed in Vietnam that day. They showed the covered bodies, lying on the ground with only their boots exposed to identify them as human. They read the names posted, while all the family watching the TV held their breath. Martin's name was not among them. Theron and Twila always said Martin was the best big brother any twins ever had. Once a week, the family would hold a family evening. That was the night that was set aside to write letters to Martin who was stationed, "in the country" as he called it. The family called it Vietnam. That was the night when only family members counted. No one else was allowed to intrude, just family.

"Family night is the best," Theron said, rolling the dice on the monopoly board. George and Adeline would play games with the children sometimes. It was like they were kids, too.

"Everyone, come into the kitchen and let's have our treat," Adeline said.

TS and The WOW

Adeline was the one who loved family moments the most.

"Mom, is it ready?"

"Yes, honey." Adeline's famous egg custard was divided into four bowls on the counter.

"I wish Martin were here." Adeline brushed away a tear, having been thinking of her son so far away. The moment had become sober. It was during nightly prayers that Martin was always remembered. They all would ask that God protect him in the jungles of Southeast Asia.

Martin sat in a midst of other boys who were in the same lonely place. He was reading a letter.

"Dear Martin. The whole family misses you. Dad told Theron he would be much taller if so much of him hadn't folded under. I think he means his feet are too big."

Martin smiled at his sister's words. He reached for his backpack and rifle that were at his side while tucking the letter inside his jacket, savoring it and knowing it was there inside his jacket anytime he wanted to touch home. The corporal called out. "Mount up men."

They all scrambled to stow away the things they had taken from their packs. Martin said a silent prayer, asking the Lord to protect him and those around him. "It's hard to be so far away from home and in a place where people were trying to kill

TS and The WOW

you," he thought. "I wish that...." His thoughts paused. He was about to wish that his dad were there, but really he would never want to have anyone he loved in this horrid place. At that moment, he saw Corporal Hunsaker waving his hand to take cover. Each of the boys slid into the undergrowth at the edge of the trail and blended the best they could with the jungle. They lay in the underbrush as a platoon of Vietcong wandered by with searching eyes for their prey. It was hard for Martin to breathe. He tried to think of what they taught him in basic. No way could he think of these fellow human beings as animals. Not that he wouldn't defend his family, but there would be something wrong with shooting them from hiding. Then, for a moment, one of the young men in black pajamas and sandals stared right at Martin. He was sure that, if his eyes flinched, he would have to shoot. The pajama man turned his head and walked on as if he had been told to walk on by some unseen force. Martin was relieved when they passed without incident. He felt that he could take a breath again. The platoon had just taken to their feet when the Corporal waved them back into the bushes. There was a rumble under the ground and a rush of air passed the point where they lay. Several large hairy creatures, walking upright like they were men, followed the trail. They were covered from head to toe with long white fur.

"What in the heck? Yetis!"

TS and The WOW

They were much taller than men and walked heavily, kicking up dust with their enormous feet. The Yetis marched on down the trail, seemingly stretching the air and disappearing into a bubble that wrapped around them.

"Salter, did you see that?" Jenkins croaked.

Before he could answer Jenkins, a herd of horses bounded onto the trail in the midst of the jungle.

"What the heck is going on?" Martin half said, more a mumble than actual words.

"This is like a circus parade," Jenkins said, then went silent, paralyzed because one of the animals' approach. One of the horses stopped in front of Martin and turned its head, sniffing just like the horses at home. But it wasn't a horse at all. It was as bizarre as the Yetis. Martin was amazed at what he saw, yet anything had to be better than those men in the PJs, he thought. The unicorns popped through a bubble.

"What was that?" the soldier next to Martin questioned.

The whole platoon couldn't believe their eyes.

"Did Cong spray us with something?" Private Conners asked.

"It must have been a hallucinogen."

The commander agreed that the enemy had sprayed them with something to cause sightings like this.

TS and The WOW

"Yeah, that had to be the answer," the commander said.

Martin knew better. He remembered the episode Theron had had in the school, and he personally knew the Winter Tree. Things like this were commonplace for him. However, this was the strangest thing he had been a part of, in a while.

"This jungle is no picnic, so let them think what they want."

They took position in formation back on the trail. Night began to fall and several clicks had been covered on the jungle path.

"Camp here for the night. No flames!" the commander said.

Martin settled back in his spot to get what rest he could. He hated the night, with everyone assigned to his own spot. It was lonely and nerve racking.

"Oh, great. Could it get any worse?" Rain began to fall on Martin, covering the jungle with a curtain of mist. Martin thought that it was better to try to sleep in the rain because there was hardly ever an attack in such conditions. He ducked his head so that his helmet would shield the rain from his face and dozed off to sleep. It was late in the night when the bombs started landing all around them. In an instant, Martin was wide-awake, bombs bursting on all sides of his platoon. There was nowhere to go. He felt that he would just have to sit where he was and pray

TS and The WOW

for a miracle. Praying was something that he did a lot here in the jungle. Prayer was something he had carried with him throughout his life. God had listened whenever he prayed.

"Father, deliver us from this battle. Take me home, if it be your will." Somehow he knew that a miracle would happen if one could happen.

The commander was yelling, "Retreat!"

Soldiers were scrambling in the only open direction to retreat. Martin stood, muddy and wet, ready to withdraw in the same direction as the others had. They ran like rodents being hunted by a hawk, scrambling through the undergrowth. Martin thought he should be terrified, but for some reason, he was not. As he ran, he thought of the way he used to run in the wash and along the bank of Busher's Pond.

"Kaboom!" The crash of a mortar hit on his heels and he was tossed into the air. His pack and rifle twisted in front and were slung away from him. Martin landed in the fresh cold waters of a pond where his entire troop was already standing up to their waist in the cool of the clean water. All Martin could hear when he rose from the water was the sound of birds and he felt the warmth of the bright sun on his face.

"What happened to the rain?" he questioned. As he looked about, the calm of familiarity rose in his heart. Could it be? Were they now standing in the middle of Busher's Pond?

TS and The WOW

They must have passed through one of those bubbles like the Yetis and the unicorns had yesterday.

"Yahoo, yahoo!" Martin yelled, throwing handfuls of water into the air.

Hunsaker called his troop to attention on the bank.

"Salter, come here!" he commanded, waving his arm in the same signal as when they had taken cover in the jungle. Martin responded with the smile of an angel.

"Yes Sir.'"

The commander didn't share his joy because he had no idea where they all were.

"Salter, where are we? Obviously, you know something I don't."

"We are home, Sir."

"What do you mean, soldier?"

"This is the pond behind my house, Sir."

Not understanding a thing of how they got there, he questioned. "Home? How could that be?"

"I don't know, Sir, but we are definitely in Utah." Hunsaker trusted Private Salter, which was not hard. After all they had been through, Salter had earned his trust. Wisdom said that Salter knew more than he did, the commander thought.

TS and The WOW

"Lead us to your house," commanded Hunsaker.

Martin took them on the trails he had traveled his whole life. Then there it was: the Salter's backyard. It was the Winter Tree and home. Yes, home. It was a miracle.

"Are you sure, Salter?"

"Sir, its home," he said excitedly. Tears collected in his eyes.

"Are you sure, Salter?" the commander repeated.

"Absolutely!" said Martin.

"Camp here!" Hunsaker ordered his men.

The platoon set up camp on the back lawn in the mountain town. Martin dumped off his pack on the grass and ran to the back door, entering and letting the screen door slam behind him as he had done all his life.

"Who's there?" Adeline called from the back room.

"It's me, Mom!"

At first she was sure it was Theron that had answered her. After all, Martin was in southeast Asia. Then, recognizing the voice, she ran into the living room, still not believing her senses. Her eyes filled with tears and joy filled her heart, displacing the disbelief.

"Martin!" She leaped toward her boy, who was covered from head to foot with the tatters of the jungle. She didn't bother to ask how he got there. She just savored the moment.

"We have wounded," Martin said. He went directly to the phone and dialed. "Doctor Jones, can you come to the Salter house? And hurry, please."

"Martin, is that you?" Dr. Jones questioned.

"Yes, can you hurry? I will explain later."

The doctor arrived within minutes to find an entire platoon of soldiers resting in tents under the Winter Tree. Only two were taken to the clinic. All other injuries were minor. Late that night, under the branches of the Winter Tree, Martin rested with his fellow soldiers.

"Father in Heaven, thank you for my miracle," he prayed in thanks. It was several days before the armed truck rolled into town to take the soldiers away. When they did, Martin was reassigned. The army was hushed about the whole thing. This time, Martin went to Fort Ord in Washington State.

The bubbles were opening more and more all over the world. Up until now, Arlis had been able to keep the earth world from being aware that life was becoming multi-dimensional, but there were strange flies on the wall, bugs that just did not belong. They were coming from minute bubbles in the wall opening and then closing, leaving the bugs behind. Some had two heads and others could leap from one wall to another having legs like tiny springs. They were in the room one minute and gone the next, gone to who knows where.

"Look at this one, Twila." Theron had a spring-leg bug in one of Adeline's Kerr jars.

Arlis had protected as much as he could, but the seams of reality were bursting and the overflow was right in the middle of the Salter home. It must have been the balance of the twins that skewed the edges of all worlds so much to this particular spot. Theron liked the creepy-crawly bugs, especially the strange ones. The bright red ones made him nervous, since that meant they were dangerous in earth terms, but what did pink and chartreuse-colored ones mean?

"Twi, want one of these?' Theron squeezed one of the bright purple bugs between two fingers and pushed its slimy body in Twila's face. Twila's shrill scream somehow burst the open bubble into the other world. The bug in Theron's hand popped and disappeared back through the bubble to its world.

"That was weird."

"Just a normal day with you, Theron."

It was a normal day, however odd it was. Night fell without any further incident. In fact, it was rather mundane. The television told its stories and Adeline had cooked her most extraordinary fried chicken ever. The stars glittered through the

TS and The WOW

night sky as Theron slept in his bedroom. Twila resettled, searching for peaceful sleep in hers. It was late into the night, in the wee hours betwixt midnight and dawn, when the fog rolled in across the hills, slowly engulfing Busher's Pond in its bodiless fingers. It then crept to the wash, enveloping even the massive cottonwood trees that lined the wash. The Winter Tree franticly rustled his leaves when the fog swallowed him in its hedge of silence. Twila had been uneasy. Her nose pressed to the window as she peered out into the darkness, watching the lights in the distance. The fog moved in, covering every living thing. In the fog, faces formed and placed a nose against the window to look back at the girl. She bounced back, startled at the innocuous face that watched her. It pulled away and fog filled the frame of the window. Twila's heart pounded. Frightened, she rested back on her bed and crossed her legs.

"What was that?" she called out to herself. She slid under her bed covers, tucking in every edge snug so as not to allow anything to enter in the night. Finally, she pulled the covers over her head, then struggled off to sleep for the last three or four hours of the night.

Trees grew tall and straight in this forest with twisting narrow paths between them. It was near impossible to see any given distance, any direction. Moss hung from most of the tree limbs, many wrapped in the green coat of wormy sprawling

TS and The WOW

tentacles, reaching for the next host to carry them to the moisture. Theron looked down at his feet.

"Where are my shoes? "he thought, wondering why he would be in the forest without his Red Ball Jets. He wiggled his toes. The moss felt good on the bottom of his feet. "How did I get here?" he wondered, noticing he was in the forest.

Something caught the corner of his eye. It darted past a tree and over a fallen log. A tiny plastic-looking face peered around the tree, hugging up against it for protection from the thing that had invaded his forest. With surprise, Theron realized he was the invader. Several other faces appeared. They looked similar to the plastic-faced creature, but not exactly. They joined the one with the plastic face in an instant. Obviously, they were of the same species. Theron felt a tug on his foot.

"Wake up, the chickens need watering."

Theron was surprised when he left the world of the plastic-faced ones, finding himself back in his own bed.

"Okay," he said in his grumble voice.

The sun had risen and burst into his window, ensuring Theron's rise to face the day and tend to the chickens. Gone were the thoughts of the forest and the strange dream. It was understood by the Salter family that all the strange, wonderful, and terrifying happenings were incidences kept to themselves.

TS and The WOW

Life was hard enough without their neighbors and friends thinking they were all off their rockers.

"Bock, bock," Theron mocked the chickens who strutted around the chicken coop, their heads bobbing with each stride they took. He poured the two buckets of water into the metal pans. Steam rose from the water. The chickens strutted around the pans, then dunked their beaks into the water and tossed their heads back, letting the water roll down their throats.

"Bock, bock, bock," the henhouse rang out with each of the thirty-five chickens greeting morning and the fresh water. Theron closed the wooden door with a latch made from a chunk of wood that spun on a nail. Theron walked under the Winter Tree on his way to the house. Leaves rustled and Theron said, "Good morning, buddy."

In the house the last dish made a ringing sound as it came to rest in the stack of bowls in the cupboard.

"Twi, are you ready?" Theron prodded. Adeline looked at her.

"You can go."

Theron and Twila brushed past the kitchen table, walked through the doorway and then bounded off the back steps. They went down the street toward the center of town. It was only five blocks to the ball field. The game was already underway. The pitcher swung his arm around, the softball reaching an arch and then flying hard from his underhand sling.

"Strike two!" The ball popped into the leather of the catcher's glove. Dust, looking like smoke, was coming from the catcher's mitt. Theron and Twila climbed to an open spot in the wooden bleachers.

"What's the score?" Theron asked Mrs. Sweeney, who had poured herself across the space of several seats. Jack Sweeney stood next to the water fountain, spraying younger children with the water nozzle and then filling balloons full of water.

"Stop that, Jack!" Mrs. Sweeney yelled, and then turned her attention back to Theron's question. "its three runs to two in favor of Rankle Farm."

Rankle Farm was the home team, so being up one run was good. The wooden bat cracked as it connected with the softball. It was a hard hit. The ball soared up over the second-baseman and kept climbing as it crossed into the outfield. The center fielder took an angle on the ball's line of flight. His head nearly rested on his shoulder as he twisted to watch the ball. He raced toward the fence and leapt with all of his reserve energy into an empty sky. His glove reached far above his head, snatched the speeding ball, narrowly averting the home run with a man on second. The fielder came down with his legs on top of the outfield fence and he toppled over headfirst into the softly-

TS and The WOW

plowed dirt. He rose to his feet, still clutching the ball in his glove and realizing the man on second had tagged the bag and was headed to third.

"Get him, get him!" yelled the crowd.

Theron watched in anticipation of the throw that was about to happen. It would be a miracle if the runner didn't score. After all, the player that had made the catch was in the deepest part of center field with a fence in the line of throw. The runner was headed to third. He rounded it.

"He's going for home!" the second baseman screamed. It looked like the runner would tie the game easily. Then Buwhen, the fielder, unleashed a throw that consumed his whole body. He had twisted his strong, young figure into a contortion, and as he unwound himself, the ball shot like a rocket, missing the fence by three feet directly in line with home plate. The second baseman watched as the ball shot directly at him, only at the last second deciding not to reach out and stop its travel. The runner dove headfirst into the catcher who was trying to watch the ball and not thinking of the impact the runner was about to have on his body. Dust swelled around the play.

The umpire yelled, "You're out!" while making the motion with his hand and kicking his knee into the air to emphasize the call. The crowd had risen to its feet to see the play and even Mrs. Sweeney leapt into the air, cheering for the extraordinary throw and the tag. As the players traded the field for the bench and their turn at bat, the dust settled. The umpire swept home plate with his little brush and no one noticed the change beyond the fence. That is, no one but Twila, who had been trying to keep the clump of red hair in place since. It had started to twist and tug at her again.

"Stop it. I said quit it. Now."

Perhaps her commanding it would help. She had feared that Jack Sweeney would notice what her hair was doing and then what torture that would bring on her. Twila had noticed something going on in the outfield. Suddenly, trees were there that had never been before, and it seemed that more were just popping into place. Fully-grown trees were appearing. In seconds, a veritable forest just materialized right before their eyes. A bubble!

"No one sees the change," she said.

"What change?" Theron answered his focus on the players in the infield. Twila tapped Theron on the shoulder and he turned to see what she wanted.

"Look beyond the fence." She pointed to the deep outfield. Theron's hair had spun, but was short enough not to be as obvious as Twila's long locks.

"Just a minute." He pushed her hand off his shoulder. The player that had made the amazing throw stepped up to the

TS and The WOW

plate and swung the bat twice in the air, showing he was ready for anything. His team whooped and hollered for him. The fielders crouched ready for the batter's attempt to hit the ball. The pitcher started his windup and then flung the ball in the underhand sling at the batter.

"Strike one!" the umpire called out. The batter turned and gave him a look of disbelief, then reloaded his bat with a swing in the empty air. The pitcher slung the pitch. The batter swung and hit the ball hard enough for a homerun. The ball was headed into left field. He slowly dropped his bat on his way to first base, watching the ball as he trotted. The left fielder was determined to snatch the homerun away from him as he had done to his teammate.

"Drop it, drop it!" the heavy man leaning on the fence near the dugout bellowed. The fielder approached the ball the same way as the batter had done before. He was running to the fence when, to everyone's surprise, a tree become visible in centerfield. Then, more trees appeared throughout the infield. The ball smacked against one of the trees and dropped to the ground at the base of its trunk. The fielder stopped just short of an appearing tree.

"Where did that come from!" he spouted out as he fell backwards on the ground. He was immediately swallowed up in the encroaching forest. Players ran in from the field and the batter stood firm on first base, watching the emergence of trees

TS and The WOW

all about him. The left field was lost somewhere in the new forest. The folks, who had once been unruffled in the stands had retreated behind the row of automobiles parked on the street. Theron and Twila stood alone on the bleachers as firm as the player still standing on first.

"Not here, not now!" A fire of resolve shot from Twila's eyes. She was determined to close this bubble and save her hometown. The populating forest stopped near second base where a bubble hung in the air undulating its skin up and down and distorting the view into the forest world with a fish-eyed look.

"What's coming from behind that tree?"

Peeking out from behind the tree where the ball had landed was one of the plastic-faced creatures that Theron had seen in his dream.

"They're real!" exclaimed Theron while pointing out the plastic-faced man to his sister.

"I see it. What is it?"

"It's a plastic face like I saw in my dream."

Sometimes Theron showed no fear of what caused others to quiver in their tracks. He leaped from the stands and strode with determination through the gate and onto the field. The bubble melted around him as he popped into the forest.

TS and The WOW

"Help me!" cried the ball player when he saw Theron. He had been stranded in the forest.

"It will be okay," Theron said.

"How do I get home?" It was clear that he was disoriented and shaken.

"Go back that way around the tree and you will see the ballpark."

Theron pointed out the pathway back into the earth world. Theron was still heading directly to where he had seen the plastic-faced creature.

"This is your sphere, I am sure." The plastic-faced creature held out the ball he had salvaged from the new undergrowth at the base of the tree where the ball had impacted. A second plastic-faced creature emerged from the cover of the forest. He was leading the lost right fielder by the hand out into the sunlight. Soon, the two plastic ones and Theron stood on the infield face to face, partly hidden in the new trees. The lost player retreated to first base, joining Twila and the player who had become fixed on first.

"Where is my brother?"

"He is with the things."

"What things?"

"The plastic men. I don't think they will harm him."

TS and The WOW

Twila stayed near first base with the player that seemed to be made of stone. He now stood at Twila's side, resting the bat he had retrieved for protection on his shoulder. The two men were opponents now, ready to protect the youngsters and all others. From where Theron stood he could now see the players. He raised his hand looking at the player with the bat and shouted. "It's okay they won't hurt anyone!"

"We visited you in the night talks."

"Who are you?"

"I am Jalick of the house of Lick and this is Jamoon of the house of the Moon." Each bowed as they introduced themselves.

"We saw you in the night talks."

"You mean my dreams."

"Yes, in your dreams," said Jalick.

"We need your tilt," said Jamoon.

"My tilt? What is my tilt?" Theron was confused. Then it hit him. "You mean my balance. Like to close a bubble or something, right?"

Back on the curb, where the crowd stood, the armchair quarterback, Mrs. Sweeney, was tossing out thoughts. "Are they invaders from outer space?" Mrs. Sweeney asked the ballplayer standing next to her.

TS and The WOW

"That has to be it," he replied.

"What is that boy doing with them?" another man asked. The crowd watched, ooing as Theron conversed with the aliens. An alien was the only way they could explain the appearance of the trees. The creatures seemed to be wearing masks made of plastic which had trapped their faces without emotion. The two aliens were about the same height as Theron. Theron was not sure what to do. Surely Dad would be upset if he were to be exposed as a balancer. It was not much of a secret that something way beyond the ordinary was happening.

"Theron, what's going on?" Twila yelled.

"Just give me a minute." He waved his hand in the hold-on gesture.

Theron withdrew something from his pocket and held it in his hand. The object was too far away to identify.

"Here it is. I hope it helps." He handed it over to the plastic-faced man. "Are you sure that will close the bubble?" Theron questioned.

"I am sure it's the key."

"The key? How does the key work?"

Theron was trying to wrap his mind around the object as the key that opened or closed a bubble. A gentle breeze was blowing or sucking, depending on which side of the bubble you stood. It sucked on the earth side, pulling paper and small objects to the gateway of the bubble, and pulling all sorts of things from the forest. The wind grew quickly, reaching hurricane forces. Trees folded like blades of a pocketknife, crashing to the ground with limbs smashing into millions of splinters. Theron, Jamoon and Jalick clung to a massive rock cluster that seemed well grounded, imbedded in the earth or whatever this world was. On the other side of the bubble the players still stood on first base along with Twila, where now not even a breeze blew. Once in awhile, a gust would escape the bubble, causing it to swell, bulging, quivering, and then belching through the barrier as if a giant mouth had burped on the other side of the bubble.

"Theron, come back through. Get out of there!" Twila yelled at her brother, frustrated that she could only watch what was happening to him. The plastic facers clung to the rocks, their bodies swaying in the wind like a flag high on a pole. Then it happened. Jalick lost his grip and spun out of control into the air. He was swept away into the twisting grip of the wind. Twila's face showed the thoughts that ran through her head. Her tight lips puckered in determination and her eyes narrowed in search of the one thing it was that would free her brother from the winds.

"We've got to help that boy." The baseball player tugged on the sleeve of the man still standing on first base.

TS and The WOW

"Yeah," he said, returning from the trance-like state he had fallen into. Together they cautiously approached the bulging bubble entrance into the other world. Twila continued her vigil, watching Jamoon and Theron being whipped by the storm. At that moment, she noticed that there was not a drop of water in the air. "All that wind and not a cloud, either coming or going, she thought.

"Help, I can't hold on!" Jamoon was about to lose his grip and be blown from his spot on the rocks.

"Grab my hand." Theron leaned as far toward Jamoon as he could while he held on with one hand and the Red Ball Jet he had forced under a rock.

"I can't reach you."

"You have to. Come on. Stretch!" commanded Theron. The ball players had come as close to the bubble as they deemed safe. They were brave men, but neither had seen such a sight. Twila ran to the edge of the bubble.

"Theron get him. He's l..."

At that very moment, Jamoon lost his grip on the rocks. Theron let go of his grip, grabbing with both hands for Jamoon. There they were just beyond the bubble. Theron stretched into the air, hanging on to Jamoon like the string on a balloon. Trees were crashing to the ground, shaking the earth and breaking loose the rocks holding Theron to the ground.

TS and The WOW

"This is too much for me. I'm only eleven years old," Twila thought. But even as she heard her own thoughts a whisper came to her heart. It said, "You have the gift." The whisper came again, "Trust your gifts."

"Okay," she thought. "What am I suppose to do?" It was not an official prayer, but nevertheless, it was just that. A prayer. Twila stood at the bulging bubble with a ballplayer on either side of her. She seemed so small between them. Lightning flickered, and the crash that followed shook loose the last thing that bound Theron and Jamoon to the rock. Theron's shoelace snapped in two, freeing them into the air. They shot like they were aboard a rocket, being swept away. The crowd behind the row of cars screamed.

"Stop right there!" Twila commanded. Her command was simple, but effective. They stopped in the air. Somehow, Twila had become the string that tied them to the ground.

"Don't let him go, Theron."

Theron had kept his grip on Jamoon. Gradually, Twila reeled them in, using her mental tether.

"Just like fishing on the lake," the ballplayer at her right said. The other player, still not believing what he was seeing, stood frozen. Plop, plop. The pair was on the ground at Twila's feet. The bubble bulged with a fury toward the ballplayers, stretching toward them like the finger on a glove, and then

TS and The WOW

disappeared. Everything disappeared, fallen trees and hurricane winds and Jalick somewhere amidst the torrent, still raging in its own world.

Theron sat on the infield grass with Jamoon at his side. Twila threw her arms around her brother's neck.

"I thought I lost you again."

"Can't lose a bad penny. They just keep turning up."

She pushed her hand against his head.

"You're a knot head." She smiled, glad he was not where Jalick was. Jamoon's plastic face swelled with water from the earth world, making a small un-crinkling sound as it became rounded and earthlike. He no longer looked like the alien that Mrs. Sweeney had declared him.

"We have to help Jalick," said Jamoon with a pleading in his eyes. "That is, if he is still alive," thought Theron. A siren howled from the end of town, headed toward the ball field. It had to be Teek Truman, the county sheriff. He was tall and slender, had a mustache and wore the traditional cowboy hat and boots. His complexion was dark and rugged, making him intimidating.

"We had better get out of here," Twila said, recognizing they already had too much to explain. The Chevy pickup came to a stop as Jamoon, Twila, and Theron turned the corner toward home.

TS and The WOW

"What happen here?" Teek asked Mrs. Sweeney who usually was full of gossip and answers.

"It was aliens," she started.

"Aliens, is that right," he said skeptically.

Mrs. Sweeney heard her own words.

"I think I just got too much sun. I need to go home." And with that she left. The ball players resumed the game as if nothing had happened. Teek sat down in the bleachers and sipped on his Pepsi Cola to watch the game.

"I guess I'm better off not knowing what went on here. Aliens," he thought and chuckled.

Jamoon's hands, feet and whole appearance had changed. He no longer looked like an alien.

"What's going on with you?" Twila asked, wondering why his body was changing.

"You mean, why am I changing?"

"Yes. You're swelling."

"That's why we came for your tilt, your balancer."

"You don't have a balancer in your world?" Theron questioned, having been told by Arlis that there was a balancer in all worlds.

TS and The WOW

"Jalick is the balancer in our world, but all our water is being stolen. We're drying up and Jalick can't stop it."

So that was the reason that had brought the plastic-faced people to the baseball field. Normally, the world of Lucabald was beautiful, green and lush. It was full of water. Today, it was being torn apart by increasing winds in the ever-drying dieing, lifeless countryside.

"So what can the balancer from our world do to help you?" Twila wanted to know what they thought a couple of eleven-year-old kids could do to change a thing like a drought.

"Our problem is coming to you here in this world, unless we stop it in my world." Jamoon gestured with both of his hands, indicating that soon the earth world would be dry, dieing, and barren the same as Lucabald.

Jalick soared on the wind, changing his appearance into that of a flying creature from his world that had a wing span of four feet, making him an impressive sight in the skies of Lucabald. He was glad his mother had been a changeling. Without that gift, he would have smashed into the ground and been torn to bits to wither away in the dry, increasing heat, However, with the winds at his command, he could soar to the water's edge and find the reason the water was being siphoned away.

TS and The WOW

"Where is the water going?" he said to a passing bird. He spoke in the language of the phoenix whose shape he had taken. He flapped his wings and turned into the wind, driving his new body high into the sky above the winds. He flew, strong and proud, toward the source of the winds. Not knowing how much time had passed, he continued his search.

"I'm probably too late to stop it," he thought. "Besides, I will need the earth world balancer to help me."

Theron, Twila and Jamoon were in the backyard of the Salter home under the covering limbs of the Winter Tree still working on the combination to open the bubble into the world of Lucabald.

"Theron let me try." Twila wanted a turn, seeing that her brother had little success in his attempts to open the bubble.

"Besides, sometimes it takes a woman's touch," she declared to her brother.

"You mean a girl's touch, don't you?"

She shrugged her shoulders.

"Woman or girl, they are both powerful in their own way," she thought, without acknowledging his comment. She focused her thoughts on the bubble that she wanted to open. This was all still pretty new. It was difficult to think of a bubble and then which world you wanted to open. Arlis had told her it was just like opening a door, only inside your head. Someone had

TS and The WOW

slammed this one shut and locked it tight. All she could see inside her head was Jalick being taken away into the twisting winds of his world. She squeezed her eyelids shut in concentration, and the focus inside her head changed. She could see something new. It wasn't a thought like the others had been. This was a vision, a vision of something with wings, flying in the air above a spot where water was being vacuumed out of the entire world of Lucabald.

"This has to be it." Twila's words brought curiosity from her companions.

"'It's what?" Theron's question was answered with a disturbance in the yard. Where the trees lined the ditch bank on the west edge of the yard, a bubble opened. Trees disappeared and the bubble flexed toward the group. The bubble then rested, leaving a clear tight window into the world where it opened.

"Is this Lucabald?" Theron looked at Jamoon.

"Let's go. It's my home."

Twila had done the girl's job like a woman would. She had opened a bubble into the very spot where the water was being drained from Lucabald. The wind was calm here. The ground was covered in vegetation. Creatures of all kinds and shapes had gathered along the river of water that flowed to the bubble in the world that joined Lucabald to another of the seven worlds. The creature that Twila had seen in her mind circled

TS and The WOW

above them, gliding its giant body to land at their feet. The phoenix chattered in the phoenix language. Theron pushed his sister behind, holding his ground and ready to defend her if he had to.

"Wait, wait!" Jamoon stood between Theron and the enormous bird.

"That's Jalick!"

"Jalick is a bird? How can that be?"

Theron still stood in a defensive position. The massive wings of the bird folded and twisted. Shrinking, it turned back into the Jalick they had met in the ball park hours ago.

"Theron, it is Jalick and he's okay!" Twila had worried that he had been killed in the windstorm. Jamoon hugged Jalick.

"Good job. You brought him." Jalick had to have Theron's help to close this bubble and stop the flow of the entire world's water into the parched deserts of the world on the other side of the bubble. Through the bubble, it appeared that the waters were already changing the intersecting world into a rich, living world.

"Use your thoughts. Let's close this bubble!"

Jalick, Theron, and Twila stood shoulder to shoulder, facing the sucking bubble. Jalick began to change his form. The small plastic-faced man swelled, becoming plump and round the same way that Jamoon had when he was in a world with all its water. His concentration was intense, as was Twila's and Theron's. The bubble quivered. It quivered again, and then popped. The waters disappeared that were in the river by flowing away into the other world. The water now filled the low plains and everything was set to return to normal.

"Where was the water going?" Theron was anxious to know.

"There is a legend in our world of a land where all their water is hidden beneath the ground."

"Why is it underground?" Twila wanted to understand the reason the water would be so hard to get.

"It was because of their king. He disappeared and the one good and one bad, sons battled for his kingdom."

"Who won the battle?"

"It was the son they call the Wolf. From that time on, most creatures hid from his rule. Even the water hid its life-giving fluid from him. Now he wants our water."

Theron and Twila understood how evil the wolf was. They knew him firsthand. The lasting question for Theron was: Why does he want me?

TS and The WOW

CHAPTER 11

The Hidden Place and Arlis Alger

George built a vault of cement. It was at least eight inches thick on the sides and the bottom. The top was ten or more inches. It was a very solid, secure place for something of value. That was where, for some time, the stone box had been hidden away. The vault was beneath the rock barbecue at the edge of the patio where one large stone lay loose. Under that stone was where the vault rested and the stone box lay hidden.

"Some things just are not meant for the whole world," George thought as he placed the lid back on the vault. He then slid the stone over his hidden treasure box. "Still in there. Addie will be happy to hear that."

Ever since Adeline's encounter with the shaking house, George had been cautious with the box and its contents. At first he would keep the lightning bolt in his pocket, but after the second time his pocket caught fire, he had to put in a place where it would be safe. He had tried the Kerr jar in the fruit room, but after the jar had broken and Theron discovered it, he had placed it back in the box. Adeline and Twila had gone into the city to

TS and The WOW

shop. George was in Veyo, a tiny hamlet nearby that rested at the foot of the volcano. He was running maintenance on the hydroelectric power plant that was fed by the mountain stream.

Theron was home by himself. He was planning to spend his day finishing the fort on the Black Ridge. Theron trudged up the wash. Today, the sand worked against the energetic youth. In fact, Theron was feeling worn out. It had been a long time since he dared to walk on the sand for any length of time.

"Man, I am so tired," he said to himself, (one of his quirks, was talking to himself.) He had only been up for a few hours, but was running out of energy. "I should just sit here awhile."

Theron found a spot clear from underbrush and shaded by the towering cottonwood trees. It was only eight-thirty in the morning and he not only wanted, but needed a nap. Theron settled into the wash bank where sleep was almost immediate.

Twila placed two grocery sacks on the kitchen counter. "Theron! Come and help us with these bags!" she yelled. The sound fell through the house like leaves in a forest, unheard. The red hair on her head lay limp. That usually happened when she was sick.

"It's just like Theron to be hiding so he won't have to help unload the car," she said, also talking to herself.

A full hour had passed since Twila had first called for Theron. "Where is Theron?" Adeline asked Twila, like she should

TS and The WOW

know. Twila didn't like it when everyone assumed being a twin meant that you read each other's mind. Of course, that was something they did all the time, but sometimes she liked just to be Twila and not Theron and Twila. Theron liked to show off when others were around, reading one another's minds, so Twila would play along. Right now she wished that reading each other's mind wasn't part of being twins. She tried to find out where Theron was in her thoughts. She could not read his thoughts, but she could sense that her red spot of hair was telling her something. What was it?

"I can't find him, Mom."

Theron still lay on the wash bank. It was nearing five in the afternoon.

"Mom, I'm going to look for Theron." Adeline nodded her head in a yes motion, also feeling the need to find him.

"Try the wash honey."

The screen door banged its hollow ring after Twila passed out the door and into the backyard.

"That darn door," Adeline said.

Twila went over to the spot where the Winter Tree had moved. The tree seemed to be exploring the entire yard. Twila had noticed there was one place that it wouldn't go and that was next to the chicken house. Right now it rested near to the back of the garage, shading part of the garage and her mother's raspberry patch. Just like a kid, this was his way of telling Adeline that he wanted her attention. Twila thought the Winter Tree was teasing

TS and The WOW

Adeline. Every time it stood in that spot, Adeline would go to the backyard and stand there shooing the tree away wanting it to move to the other end of the yard. You should have heard the gossip that went around town when Mrs. Sweeney came by to tell mom about a Daughters of the Pioneers meeting and found her in the backyard cursing at the tree and demanding it to move. Twila wanted to ask the tree where Theron was.

"Tarel, do you know where Theron is?"

The tree smoothly rocked its limbs toward either the tree house or the wash. Twila turned to run that way. Then she turned around and yelled, "Thank you, Winter Tree."

She climbed the ladder, expecting to see Theron sitting in there on the platform of the tree house. When she reached the top rung on the ladder, high enough to peer onto the platform, she found it was empty. There was no one in the tree house. The inactivity of her hair told a story of its own. Twila was beginning to worry.

"The tree said he was over here, so he has to be somewhere around here."

Twila walked up the wash, the same way they had for the past few weeks, going to the fort on the Black Ridge. There was something on the wash bank. It was Theron's gym shoe, one of his Red Ball Jets. Twila ran to where it lay in the dirt. She picked it up to examine it, knowing that Theron loved those shoes. The laces were broken and the shoe torn.

"Theron where are you! Come out! It's not funny."

TS and The WOW

Twila knew that something had happened, but she didn't want to admit what she already knew. The spot where the shoe had been, showed the signs of a struggle, knee prints and butt prints. Now she was sure that something had happened to Theron. Maybe he got away.

She rushed to the face of the cave in hopes that Theron had gotten away and was hiding there. Twila's eyes scanned the area, snapping back and forth as she watched everything about her. She was nervous that whoever had attacked Theron was lying in wait for her. She was carrying the orb of the fairies with her, suspecting she might need the key to the Tween world and Arlis Alger for help. The fairy ball she carried rested in the pouch she slung over her shoulder. It bounced against her side as she ran around the obstacles in the woods in a hurry to reach the cave.

"There it is," she thought. The face nature had carved on the hillside blended with its surroundings. She knew that the face was there, or she might have walked right past the opening. She rushed to the cave that looked like the mouth on the face and ducked the whole time calling Theron's name. Her words only echoed off the lonely walls of the chamber. He wasn't there. Twila entered swiftly and drew the ball from her bag. She placed it in the basin. It flashed light into the cave and opened the bubble into the Tween. She arrived in the meadow near the stream that led into the glen where Arlis's cottage was concealed.

"There it is. Now I will get help."

TS and The WOW

In a moment she stood at the front door of the cottage that reminded her of the witch's gingerbread house. After she knocked, the door opened. To her surprise it was not Arlis that came to the door.

"Tuck, is Arlis here? I need him quick."

"Not, not here at all."

Arlis Alger was not there. Tuck rested in his big chair with both feet sticking out over the edge of the seat and his short legs snug on the seat bottom.

"Miss Twila, I'm seeing you. What you be doing here?"

She placed her arms around the troll's neck and began to cry. Amidst the tears, she said, "Something has happened to Theron."

"Wait, Miss Missy. Where be little brother?"

Twila told Tuck that something or someone had taken Theron away. Tuck jumped down from the chair and reached out his hand to her. He waddled to a booth. It was more like a capsule that you would see on a spaceship, not inside a cottage in the woods. He led Twila by her hand to the metal-polished chamber.

"Come, Little Missy," he said.

They entered the chamber and were followed by two fairy orbs. They were smaller than the one she had left in the basin in the cave. Tuck placed them into the metal basin of the chamber. The orbs spun in opposing directions. They spun faster and faster until Twila couldn't see them anymore.

TS and The WOW

"I hate tight spaces," Twila thought, closing her eyes. A noise cracked like the sound of two boards being smacked together as the orbs impacted one another. The explosions burst the orbs changing them into nothing but light. Twila opened her eyes in surprise. The light enveloped both Tuck and Twila like fingers inside a glove.

"This is not like a bubble opening."

Twila had felt like they were riding on the light itself, or maybe they were part of the light, she thought. They were swept into a cosmic storm, and in two shakes of a dog's tail, they stood onboard a sailing ship.

"What's, I mean, where are we Tuck?"

As they landed onboard the ship, which was in full sail, it lurched upon a wave, slapping them to the deck. Immediately, Arlis Alger reached a hand down to help Twila back to her feet. Tuck was already standing, having a much broader understanding as George would have called his large feet. The size of his feet gave him an advantage while standing on a rocking deck or on just about anything.

"Arlis, Theron has been taken," Twila announced. The spray of a wave came over the bow of the vessel. The spray wet the deck and their shoes. Twila told Arlis all she knew about Theron's kidnapping. She told him the whole story about the dead red hair and the gym shoe and how she couldn't read a single one of his thoughts. Arlis stood well-footed on the deck, steering the boat toward some creature swimming to the right of them.

"Where are we?" she asked.

"Scotland, on the Loch Ness Lake," Arlis spun the loop of his rope three revolutions, like any good old frontier cowboy. His loop shot from his hand out over the water. The loop rested over the head of the creature next to the sailing vessel.

"Time to go home, Nessy." With the rope around the amphibious dragon, Arlis led her through a bubble that had opened on the edge of the water. He sailed right into the bubble, right along with the monster he led. On the other side of the bubble the ocean water was calm and the sun cast a deep orange glow on everything. The ship moved silently to where the creature was released.

"Okay, that's where you belong, old girl." Arlis talked to the monster like he had done his rope trick many times.

"Was that the Loch Ness Monster?"

"Sure enough was, young lady."

"Incredulocious!" That was Twila's way of saying how cool was that.

It was hard to get used to the time of day change whenever they passed through a bubble. Now it was early morning, but that was not the only thing that was strange. Twila had never seen the ocean before, not in land-locked Utah. Her face was green and her stomach fluttered with butterflies. The trees on the shoreline were so tall their trunks were green and

TS and The WOW

bore bright purple leaves, resembling leaves found in an impressionist painting.

"Are we going to find Theron now?" Twila said, trying not to toss her cookies on the boat's deck.

"Well, I guess we had better see if we can't find him. What do you think?"

Twila just nodded her head in agreement while holding back her lunch. Theron was in need of rescue and this was his best hope. Arlis and Tuck dropped the sail. The boat came around and then steered into the dock. With the ship docked, Twila leaped onto the planks and the world stopped bobbing to and fro.

"This is better." Twila's stomach settled back into its silent place in her body. Arlis stood quietly for a few seconds and a bubble opened into the Tween. Obviously, there were things that he had not had time to teach Theron and Twila. Or maybe they weren't yet ready for that knowledge.

"Come, Tuck," Twila had been attentive to Arlis but Tuck was still tying off the rope to dock. Tuck looked up at her to see Arlis already passing into the Tween. Twila scurried quickly behind him and Tuck waddled as fast as he could, the bubble closing only seconds after he passed into the Tween.

Theron awoke, remembering scattered fragments of a dream about fighting with an animal or a person on the wash bank. What had happen to him while he slept? Nothing had awakened him from his nap. Now he was inside a domed mud

TS and The WOW

hut, buried to his waist in an ever hardening mud pile. The structure in which he was captive was made of grass, sticks, and mud, showing age by the holes of light streaming into the room. His body was stuck inside the mud pedestal. Perhaps he would be able to get free if he could reach a big stick that hung from the ceiling above him, he thought. Theron reached as hard as he could for the stick. "That hurt," he groaned, now realizing he hurt all over.

"Where am I?" he said, not expecting any answer. The voice that answered him was low and recoiled against the walls or was a part of the walls.

"You're mine, Balancer." Theron could see no face, but felt the chill of terror run up his spine.

"Who are you?" the boy demanded.

The dirt on the floor of the room darkened as water sprang from the ground, forming a puddle in front of Theron. The water soaked into the dirt like it was stirring in a bowl of chocolate pudding, but this pudding had a difference. It was alive. The mud sucked in air, inflating and taking the form of a man. The mud man oozed, absorbing all the mud as he approached Theron. He was liquid, with mud flowing down his body and then pumping back to his head to flow down again.

"Why do you want me?"

The mud man drew closer to the boy.

"You're a thief!" Mud splattered as he spoke.

"I haven't taken anything from you."

TS and The WOW

The mud man's imposing figure stood over the half-buried boy, who had no way of retreating with his legs still embedded in the dried mud pile. The mud man became infuriated with the boy's claim. He swung a fingerless hand over Theron's head, dripping mud that splattered the walls of the hut. Oozing, gooey mud poured onto Theron's head and slicked his hair tight to his head.

"What is it you want from me!"

"The life fluid you have stolen from my world."

"Life fluid? What the heck is that?"

Water sprayed from the ground and puddles formed in several spots about Theron. Puddles of mud grew and mud men arose from each of the mud holes.

"Life fluid."

"You mean water," Theron interpreted the meaning of life fluid. "You think I took your water?"

The mud men stretched out of their pools toward the boy.

"It's not me. I didn't do this."

The new mud men were smaller and the mud from which they had sprung was quickly drying, leaving hardened dry shells of the creatures that had been mud men moments earlier.

"You have doomed us, doomed us all," called out one of the mud men with his last words as his fluid texture hardened to a crusty layer of dried clay.

TS and The WOW

Arlis Alger put his hand into the air and swished it in front of himself, leaving dust floating in the wake of his hand. At first the dust was brown like the dust in any storm. The particles began to gather and form a transparent square. He held his hand next to the dust screen and vivid colors appeared on it, just like the in the pixel of a television set. In that moment, they could see the Winter Tree and the back of the house, even Adeline who stood with both hands on her hips and her face wearing the look of a tortured parent. Then the picture changed as Arlis moved his finger in front of the view area.

The ship docked in the world of the ocean monster, Nessy. He continued moving his finger and the screen moved from world to world. Then within the viewer, a village of domed buildings appeared, atop a cliff from where a waterfall had once spewed to the canyon far below. Now there was nothing more than a trickle of a leaky faucet.

"That's it. Theron is in there," Arlis said.

"How do you know that?" Twila asked.

Arlis didn't bother answering her question. He placed his hands on the ends of the square and pulled the corners, enlarging it into the shape of a door. Tuck handed Arlis the two balls that had earlier burst into light, now back in their original shape. Arlis tossed them into the air over his head. The ball that floated near his shoulder opened and sucked in the dust box in the shape of a door. A stream of dust and distorted shapes simply disappeared into it. Twila watched the mysterious preparations with a growing

TS and The WOW

feeling of urgency. She was uneasy when her red hair just lay flat on her head, telling her nothing.

"Come on, tell me something about Theron." She patted her red hair trying to awaken it. The red spot lifted away from her head only for a moment and then fell flat again as lifeless as it had been before.

"Twila, we are ready to go for Theron."

Arlis wore his calm demeanor as easy as his baggy white trousers. Both seemed to fit his persona. He seemed comfortable in any situation and this was no exception.

Arlis and Twila entered the rectangle which reminded Twila of a phone booth. Twila was more than a little bit claustrophobic. When the door shut, she felt like she could not breathe. It was just like she had felt when she and Tuck had gone to find Arlis. A dark cave was one thing, but an upright coffin was something else.

"Are we there yet?" Twila, breathing rapidly, had closed her eyes and just wanted to be in the open air once more.

Before she knew it, the balls crashed into each other, exploding into a brilliant light. She moved her hands from her eyes, just for a second, to watch the light show as they had before. The bursting balls smashed, changing to pure light, and enveloping them as part of its particles. The light dissipated, and they stood in the woods above the dirt blister dwellings. The waterfall had ceased, leaving nothing but a steep cliff that guarded the dome huts on the other side.

TS and The WOW

"Do you think he is here?"

"He is here. Can't you feel him?"

The red spot of hair was tugging at her.

"He is here."

She smiled for the first time since she had begun her search of her brother. The dirt mound guards were silent, lifeless statues along the path to the huts.

"What are these statues doing here?" Twila had never seen anything like them. They seemed to have been piles of mud, dribbled down from the head and flowing to the ground. The canyon contained the barren falls before the water went under the stone and dirt bridge. Arlis put his hand on Twila's shoulder and pulled her back into the cover of the rocks and trees.

"Wait here."

Inside the hut, Theron's red twist of hair stood on end. Twila's did the same where she hid behind the rocks. The creature that held Theron captive acted as if he sensed something. Theron ducked his head away from the creature and slid his free hand over the red spot to keep the mud man from seeing the sudden activity.

"Stay down," Theron muttered to his hair, hoping it would remain unnoticed.

"Well boy, the game has begun," the mud man taunted, still fluid enough to move about the room.

TS and The WOW

"What game? I just want to go home. I didn't do anything," Theron pleaded.

"You are the bait in the trap," was all the creature would say. The mud man was watching for something that he expected to happen.

"What's going on?" Theron questioned.

Arlis had left Twila on the rocky trail as he made his way up stream on the dry riverbed. He entered the riverbed as a man, but as he began to cross, his feet began to morph. Bones twisted, creaked and popped, until they had become paws. Almost at once, he had totally shifted his shape to that of a native Paragorina, a hairless tiger that could blend with the surroundings, like a chameleon. He seldom used his ability to shift his shape because he hated the process. Arlis moved up the river to where the riverbed split, dodging and darting around the rocks, nearly invisible. He climbed from the riverbed up the steep, rocky canyon wall to the mud hut, using the grasping toes of the animal he had chosen to become. Arlis made his final morph at the top of the wall where he became Arlis Alger again. As he morphed, it was obvious that changing might have its advantages, but it also took a toll on him. It was prudent not to give away all your cards in any game where you might need a little surprise on your side, and this was no exception.

Twila watched the events somewhat in shock, learning that Arlis could become whatever creature he desired.

TS and The WOW

"He is the real Morph man." For awhile she had lost sight of him as he blended into his surroundings. Suddenly, there he was, Arlis the man once more. She had almost cheered as he morphed back into his human form. She watched as he reached the passage to enter the mud village, and was left in despair when two mud men captured him as if they had been awaiting his arrival. Inside the mud hut, Arlis found just what he had wanted to find.

"Are you okay, Theron?"

"Silence, Balancer!" the mud man forcefully commanded.

Theron nodded that he was okay, without speaking the words.

The mud men had cast dried bonds around Arlis's hands, holding him prisoner.

"Arlis Alger, I should have known you were behind this thief."

"I am here to help you, Shma."

Shma had always been suspect of anyone from outside his world, especially those who were not a part of the soil.

"You and this bit of flesh have taken our life fluid."

As he spoke, one of the guard's legs became fixed to the ground and dried, becoming a statue like the others.

"We want to help you."

"Why help us? We are soon dust."

"This is McFarland's work. He is draining your life fluid."

TS and The WOW

The guard finished his drying, becoming frozen in his tracks leaving only Shma and a single guard.

"Let us help you, Shma."

Shma pondered the thought of help from this flesh man.

"What is left to do," he thought as he felt his feet becoming part of the soil, affixing him in his tracks until he was dust.

"Let them loose." He commanded.

The guard touched the bonds surrounding Arlis's wrists. Arlis broke away the dried mud that had trapped Theron for so long.

"That feels good," Theron said while rubbing his legs to help the blood to circulate.

"Shma, we will help you," Arlis, the flesh man promised. "Hurry, Flesh Man. Time is gone."

Theron and Arlis emerged from the mud hut. Twila had waited and watched for their emergence. They were fine and headed toward her while the red hair leaped and twisted, reflecting what the girl felt inside.

Twila thought of herself as a small, frail girl in a foreign place, facing the great threats. It had seemed like she was always in some mess ever since this balancing thing had come about. Right now she was just happy to see the other half of her twindom alive and well.

"Theron, over here!" She leaped up and down, clapping her hands in excitement. Hurriedly, Arlis led Theron toward Twila.

TS and The WOW

"We have to stop the water from being taken from this world." Arlis knew more than he offered the children. They were young, and although they had experienced many new things since becoming balancers, they were not ready to face all that they would come to face.

"We have to get up stream as fast as we can." Arlis returned to the shape of a Paragona, knowing he would be able to travel much faster in that form.

"What the heck?" Theron watched as the transformation took place and Arlis the Paragona raced up stream, vanishing with his natural camouflage into the background.

Theron and Twila rested on the rocks above the dry falls. Paragona tracks were all that were noticeable from the travel to the headwaters of the river. It seemed like magic when Arlis morphed into his natural form.

"This is it," he said aloud, watching all the water that should have run down the river pour into a bubble resting in the middle of the stream. With his mind, he burst the bubble to the other world. Water rushed down stream, soaking into the riverbanks and again allowing mud to be freed along the way.

"Do you hear that?" Twila asked. It was the sound of water filling the riverbed. Soon water spilled over the rocks of the fall and drenched the soil. In the village of the mud men, the solid statues were dark and muddy, full of life fluid once more. Arlis bounded off the rocks as a Paragona, coming to rest at Theron and Twila's feet before changing shape.

TS and The WOW

"Shma and his people are safe for now," Arlis said, startling Theron from his transformation.

"You're just like Morph Man," Theron said with a spark of enthusiasm.

"Who is Morph Man?" Arlis inquired.

"Long story short, he is a character in a book and Theron's hero," Twila said.

Arlis nodded his head, seeming to understand.

"Can we go home now?"

Arlis Alger was aloof and mysterious, only allowing the Twins enough information to keep them from any real danger. He was the teacher and that was the way he had been taught. It was their faith in the Lord above and the fact that they never relied on their own human powers that kept them safe. Arlis had watched them as they said their prayers. He saw that, when others were taking substances into their bodies, Theron and Twila remained clean. Their abilities were gifts from God, accessible by those willing to live a life of value.

CHAPTER 12

The Two-Faced Man and The World Of Tomorrow

The world shook at 4 a.m. that morning. The walls of the house moved a foot and a half from one side to the other.

"Don't you get out of bed," George said as he held Adeline across the chest, keeping her from getting up. All she wanted to do was rush to her babies, Twila and Theron. George knew that if she were to get out of bed in a quake like this one she would find herself nose down on the floor, or worse.

"Just wait. It will be over soon."

The ground shook under them as if a train had hit the walls of a tunnel, sliding and bumping its way toward a crash... As suddenly and alarmingly as it had started the quake ended.

"Now you can go," George said, releasing his grip on his dear one.

"Twila! Theron! Are you okay?" she called, running into the hall. Nothing seemed to be out of place, except for some dishes that had fallen to the floor. Twila came from her room wiping the sleep from her eyes.

TS and The WOW

"What happened?" she inquired.

"An earthquake," George said.

"Where is Theron?" Adeline asked excitedly in a quivering voice. The door of his bedroom had been twisted by the quake, locking it closed.

"The house must have shifted," George said while pulling on the door to slide it over the carpeting.

Adeline wanted to rush into Theron's room, but to her surprise, Theron was not there and neither was his room. It had tumbled away and all that was left were fragments and a gaping hole that looked like that train they had imagined had passed right through Theron's room, taking him and his room on with it wherever it had gone.

Adeline fell to her knees in the doorway, tears streaming down her face, her heart aching, and with a cry of true loss in her voice. "Not again. When will this all end?" She cried. Twila whimpered, too, cowering in the corner, and George stood over them both in total disbelief, for Theron was indeed gone. Twila's red hair rubbed against her head with a soothing caress as though it knew something she didn't.

Looking into the gaping hole, she said "He's got to be down there. He just has to be."

George launched search and rescue efforts. Quickly, he retrieved all the rope he could from the garage. Adeline had recovered enough that she wanted to be part of the search.

"Hurry, honey. He could be in trouble," Adeline said, not wanting to find herself again in that place her heart had been. The rope unraveled toward the bottom of the hole.

"Go. Go get our boy!"

George wrapped the rope around his waist, and then rappelled into the hole.

"Theron, Theron! Where are you?"

No answer came back. Soon George was in the darkness of the hole. It was filled with all the remains of Theron's room. His baseball glove rested on a portion of the wall that leaned against the rocks. Some of his clothes were tossed to the rocks. The closet was demolished. Only splinters remained. The clothes rod was wedged between two rocks with his clothing still hanging on it. George noticed a folded basketball tucked inside one of Theron's clothes pockets.

"George, have you found him?"

George scanned every part of the cavity with his flashlight in the settling dust. Twila watched the light, unable to see her father. Somehow she knew her twin was still alive.

"He's not down here!"

TS and The WOW

A frustration came over Adeline. Where was her son?

"Are you sure he's not there?"

"He's not down here, honey."

Twila had seen what she thought were strange events transpiring. First, there had been a growing effort for something to take Theron away, and now his disappearance a second time, right in the same room where the wolf had appeared on the wall.

"Dad, the wolf has him."

"What are you talking about? The wolf can't cause an earthquake."

"He has him, Dad. I just know he has."

Twila had felt her red hair spot twisting, almost yanking at her head.

"What do you want?" She grabbed her hair with her hand to hold it still. Twila wanted to find her brother in the worst way. He might have been a dork to others, but he was her twin and partner in ways that no one could ever understand.

"Mom, why don't we ask God to helps us? That's what you have taught us all our lives." Twila remembered the time when Martin had been in the hospital and no doctor could find the reason he was so sick. Then the family knelt had beside George and Adeline's bed to pray. They had folded their arms and George had begun to offer a humble prayer. He began,

TS and The WOW

"Dear Father in Heaven. We come to you in need of your help. Our son and brother is ill and we do not think his time on earth is complete. Please help the doctors understand his need and bring him back to health." He had closed by using in the name of Jesus Christ, then amen. The family felt as though Martin now would be okay. Dr. Stults had been persistently working to figure out Martin's problem, even asking some prayers of his own. It was that very day that he had found an illness called "Sarcoidosis" in one of his books. "That's it," he had said. When he read those words he knew that he now could save Martin and did.

So Twila knew that a prayer would help this brother just like it had Martin because she knew that God loves us all. George, Adeline, and Twila knelt in the hall outside Theron's door and what was left of his room.

"Twila, you ask the prayer," George said.

She started her prayer, "Father in Heaven…" a long pause, she waited to listen for what God might want her to say. Then she said, "We need my brother." She felt so alone without him that a tear choked her words. Then she continued. "Help us find him and give him the aid he needs to return home." That same felling of comfort she had felt for Martin warmed across her soul as she ended in Jesus' name and said amen. Twila now knew that her twin brother was going to be just fine with God watching over him.

TS and The WOW

Four hours after the quake, the dust sifted into the air as if a giant blanket had been shaken and it was slowly settling in the silence back to Mother Earth.

"We can't do anything until daybreak."

George had the girls sleep in the living room away from the windows and close to the front door, expecting aftershocks. None came and the sun rose, unexpectedly. It was suddenly just there.

"It's time we figure things out," announced George, who had not slept the rest of the night. He had sat in the darkness, watching over his family and pondering what to do concerning Theron. Twila had spent the night tucked under her mother's loving arms in contemplation of her lost brother. Today it was her father that commanded the moment, planning to go after his son. Twila's red hair began to spin in warning of something or someone approaching. She had come to recognize the different signals it would give her. She rushed to the front window to peer out. A knock fell on the door before she could reach the window. The pounding on the door rang with resolve. Someone wanted in without delay. George rotated the door open on its hinges and there stood Arlis Alger.

"Is he here?" Arlis said.

"No," said Twila, approaching from the living room.

"Do you know where he is?"

TS and The WOW

Adeline, now standing with her hands on George's shoulders, interjected, "I fear the wolf is at work here again."

Theron had escaped his grasp before and Arlis thought his luck might have just run out. "Twila, you must concentrate on Theron." Twila sat in the big, gray rocking chair, which always comforted her. She rocked back and forth and the old chair creaked.

"Close your eyes and think of Theron," the old man said.

Twila seemed to see her brother in his Red Ball Jet tennis shoes leaping, almost bouncing, from rock to rock on the Black Ridge. Her red hair wilted, appearing to rest with her in the rocking chair. Mother, father, and mentor stood, three faces with one expression, waiting for a revelation from the little girl. In the eye of her mind, Twila saw Theron pulling something from his pocket. "What is that?" she thought. "He's okay, but I can't tell where he is."

In her thoughts, Theron held the object in his open palm. Twila searched within her twin connection to visualize the object. She was unable to observe the object, yet somehow she knew what the object. It started to spin, increasing in speed until it opened, flowering as she had witnessed before. A crackling, smashing, banging like a jet going supersonic, then the room filled with light. The Orb had come from her thoughts into the room. It floated in the air, spinning tiny fairies who were dancing all around it.

"No!" Twila screamed. The Orb closed, still spinning, then came to rest on the floor with a final turn. The old man reached down and brought the Orb into his palm the same way Theron had in Twila's vision. He groaned as he brought his body erect.

"I saw him!" Exclaimed Twila. Arlis smiled, just slightly stretching his lips at her, showing his approval.

"You have done well," he said. "What did you see?"

"I saw him. He's somewhere dark. He was holding something in his hand. I didn't see what it was, but I felt it."

"Anything else?"

"Just one thing. I kept seeing the word "eclipse" in my head. What does that mean?" Arlis paused. "Eclipse is enchantment of worlds." It bothered Twila when Arlis spoke in what she called circles.

"What the heck does enchantment of worlds mean?" she probed. Arlis drew his hand to his whiskered chin and sighed out a breath.

"The worlds have always been, at least the matter that they were created from has always been. In the beginning of the balance, all the worlds co-mingled freely, passing from one world into another, separate, but like brothers and sisters born of the same parentage, living in the same house. But the time came when the worlds were separated and the balance began."

"So is that eclipse?"

"No." He paused again, searching for the correct words. "Eclipse is for all the worlds. Earth, Bursoa, Lucabald, Inovada, Palltare, Shopera and Eltergo. They eclipse one another, invading each other's space and blocking the reality of the other. To keep them apart, seven treasures were hidden in seven cities."

"What treasures are you talking about? Where are these treasures?"

"Let's focus on finding Theron right now." It seemed that Arlis was reluctant to answer her question. "Why was that?" Twila wondered. For now she would just have to wonder about this eclipse. Arlis then brought about a change, focusing back to Theron who was still missing.

"Arlo McFarland has Eltergo. I think he caused the quake," Arlis said.

"Eltergo? Which world is that? Arlo McFarland? Who?" Twila asked, knowing that their Earth was not the only one that needed balance. She had really wanted to know about all the worlds.

"Eltergo is the center of all worlds. Balance begins and ends there. I began there. Arlo, is The Wolf."

TS and The WOW

Arlis stopped himself, afraid of disclosing too much.

"So are you saying that Theron is on Eltergo with that thing?"

"I'm almost certain of it," Arlis replied. Mother and Father were anxiously awaiting some plan.

"What can we do?" George asked, somewhat understanding the controls over the forces of nature that Arlis possessed.

"This will be something that I do alone." Arlis held his hat in his hand until then. He placed it on top of his head, preparing to exit the front door.

"What are you going to do?" asked Adeline. George had readied himself, not understanding that this was a bigger moment than he was prepared to face. Arlis knew that he was alone in the moment. No sense risking Twila's life along with Theron's.

"Bring our boy back to us," Adeline said, watching Arlis exiting the door. He left through the backyard, walking right under the Winter Tree, who seemed fully aware of his presence. The tree bent to the ground as Arlis passed. Soon Arlis had distanced himself to the wash bank and out of sight. Now all that remained was in the hearts of the Salter trio.

Footsteps echoed in the cave where Arlis trod. He worked deeper into the earthen cavity, farther than Theron or Twila had ever ventured. Water seeped from the ceiling, pooling

TS and The WOW

on the floor in milky ponds. This hole in the hillside cloaked something that Arlis had hoped would remain hidden forever, but he had no choice. No choice. Theron's life would depend on it. Eltergo had been Arlis's birthplace. He was connected to that world, a connection that he sometimes treasured and sometimes regretted.

"Eclipse!" he commanded. His word initiated an action, long silent under the cover of the milky pond. It began to bubble and boil. Rising from the pool came the very thing that Arlis had hoped would remain hidden there forever. The milky waters rolled away, dripping back into the pool from where it had come. A thousand years it had been hidden in the depths, revealed again, born from the fluid ready for its first breath as it rose.

Eltergo was much different than it had been when Arlis was young. He remembered the forests that had been where he now stood amidst a dead fallen forest of trees, lying in dry, parched, lifeless soil where lush meadows of crimson once rested. Mounting dunes of sand emerged, overtaking the landscape. The riverbeds had once thrived where rock had bathed in the fresh waters. The rocks here were once living creatures and had suffered a dry, choking death, left lifeless and covering the dry bottom of the riverbed. Arlis thought that the rocks must have suffered a coughing, gasping, death without the river's life fluids. With no way to escape, they simply expired.

TS and The WOW

The sun's short cycle, almost setting in the west and rising within a few hours in the east, baked the land of Eltergo. The mountains in the distance were Arlis's destination and he knew there would be perils in his travel. Yet he had to face this trial. He carried the one tool in his hand that could free Theron from Arlo McFarland. He carried it carefully, not wanting to disturb the substance inside. The sun lit the morning sky, never releasing Eltergo from its rays. Only for a moment would it release the world as it set before the rising of the moon. Arlis mopped the sweat from his forehead, then replaced his hat a top his head. He looked off into the distance, knowing that this was the only way to reach the castle of Arlo McFarland without being noticed. It was imperative that he was not detected. He knew that the boy was only bait, luring him to his nemesis.

The second sun set in the west and the moon rose. Creatures began to awaken on the desert landscape. Eyes shined in the moonbeams where nothing had traveled all the day. A square-toed truthlimite rolled down a dune, tucking his three feet under him and becoming the shape of a football. He bounced at the bottom of the dune, and then spread his tripod legs out, catching himself and landing on his square-toed feet. Arlis was surprised to see a truthlimite. He had supposed that, since Eltergo had dried up, the truthlimite would also be extinct. He was glad to see that the truthlimite had survived. He had had one as a pet when he was a boy. Life was everywhere in the sandy world and everything seemed in a hurry. Something was chasing a Smatia cactus. It appeared to be hoping to get a drink of the water that the plant spewed into the air. Smatia cacti absorbed water from the air and could only live if they expelled it like other animals expelled carbon dioxide. If they took on too much water, they would explode. The pale white skin of the cactus glistened with water on his needles as he raced away and over the dune.

Arlis, too, was in a hurry, racing against the sunrise. He had spent too long in the parching breath of the sun and needed relief if he were to survive in the new Eltergo. A second Smatia cactus ran past him, soaking his clothes. It felt cool and soothing. He rang the water that soaked his shirtsleeve into his mouth.

"I needed that," he said.

The mountains were soon within reach. The cool night had not been wasted. When the first sun rose, all the creatures of the night had burrowed or hidden themselves up in a dark crevice to await life in the night once more. All hid except the man who held a Panama hat and the Smatia cactus that now stood firm in the sand, leaching water that quickly evaporated in the heat of the sun. Here in the hills life was somewhat better. Still hot. Still dry. Yet, every few steps, there were growing signs of life. Red plants grew in clumps, a plant that Arlis identified as musk weed. It was one of those hardy plants that needed water only to root itself and then it could live forever with next to nothing. If musk weed became uprooted, it would simply walk to the next spot where it

TS and The WOW

would be protected and send a tap root down to hold it from blowing away in a breeze.

Arlis worked his way to the top of the mountain, finding more and more living things. He knew that Arlo McFarland would least expect him approaching this way. There were trees and piles of dead rocks for cover. He crouched behind a large outcropping of rocks that seemed to still be alive. They were breathing, still sucking water from the ground. Arlis surveyed the castle as it changed shape. Doids were chattering in high-pitched babble as they released their handgrips to form the new shape of the building. Guards walked the perimeter of the castle grounds in anticipation of his arrival. "Or, were they awaiting some other event?" Arlis wondered. A man leaped from the bushes and heaved something large and round at the back of one of the guards, then ran right to where Arlis crouched. The guard fell to the ground onto his face, but quickly got to his feet, his robe covered in the fine white dirt. The attacker funneled his body into the underbrush. Finally, he crouched, inches away from Arlis. His eyes were closed as though he thought that if he could not see, then he could not be seen.

"Vard!" Arlis said softly. Vard opened his eyes, and then turned his body around, facing Arlis where he exposed his second face. The second face had a personality all its own, so it was much like two people inhabiting the same body. The second face had never cared much for Arlis or perhaps he was just a little

TS and The WOW

jealous of the first face. It and Arlis seemed to be able to talk about anything. Still Face Two was kind of glad to see him again.

"Arlis, you have come to save us." They hugged each other. Vard had been Arlis's boyhood friend. There was a time when they caught slimy rocks in the river together. They both remembered Daka, Arlis's pet Truthlimite.

"I wish your father were alive. Things were so much better when he was King." Arlis nodded to show he was fully agreeing with the Vard's. The way life had been when they were children was clearly much better, and it showed throughout the land and in the expression on both of Vard's faces.

"Things have changed," Vard's second face said.

"I have missed you, old friend," Arlis replied to the second face, surprising him. "I have missed both of you, my brothers."

The guards had not seen where the dead rock had come from that struck one of their numbers, but they were searching. A guard in his hooded cloak worked his way toward the top of the rock where Arlis and the Vard's hid.

"Quiet." Arlis held his finger to his lips shushing the Vard's. The guard stood on the rocks just above them. A whimpering cry came from the rock who wanted the body off his back. The guard responded to the whimper and moved on, still in search of the rebel that had clouted his confederate. When he was a safe distance away, Arlis began to present his problem.

"Have you been here long?"

"For a few hours. That's the second rock I hit them with," Vard's number one face said.

"You mean we hit them with, right?" said the second face, making sure his contribution was noticed.

"Yes, we did it."

"Well, what I need to know is, have you seen a boy being taken into the castle?"

"I don't know if it was a boy or what, but they brought in something tied up in a bag two suns ago," the first face said.

"It was a wiggly one," the second face said.

"That has to be him."

The castle Doids' shrill chatter alerted Arlis and the Vard's that the castle was about to change shape. The castle shape molded, twisted, and contorted until it looked like a giant Dagwarp, a beast that resembled a combination of a Rhinoceros and a Shar-Pei dog sitting on his back legs. The horn above its wrinkled nose hung above the castle door, an intimidating spire. It seemed nothing like the home Arlis had once known. Now it was nefarious, vicious like the animal it represented. Arlis remembered the fantasy shape his father ordered on the castle to

TS and The WOW

become and how much it delighted his mother, brother, and himself. That memory was a child's memory and had long ago passed away, as had his parents.

"I have to rescue the boy," Arlis announced to his friends.

"You're going in there?" the second face blurted out. It was an ominous thought to meet Arlo McFarland on his own ground after all he had done, yet Theron was being held captive in there because of a battle between two Eltargoens. Arlis simply nodded his head yes, as he fumbled with the object that rested in the bottom of his pocket. It squealed and tried to climb out.

It was easy getting past the guard and into the mouth of the Dagwarp castle. Once inside, Arlis stayed close to the walls, searching out the next place to hide before he proceeded on. Should he morph as Theron and Twila called it? Should he become a Paragorina?

Theron had been in the clutches of the faceless man for nearly two days. It was dark and moist in the cell, deep in the bowels of what Theron thought was the castle where he had rescued the Meboen. The large wooden door opened and three hooded figures half dragged, half pushed a man into the cell. Soon the man was chained to the wall, apparently more of a risk than Theron was. They were alone in the darkness, the man barely moving. It was more the sound of him breathing that let Theron know he was still there.

"Are you okay?" Theron inquired. The man, in a whispered voice, said he wasn't hurt.

"Can you help me get out of these chains?" The chains bound both of his arms to the rock in the center of the room. The rock was the closest thing to furniture that there was in the room. The man moved each time the rock breathed. It was worn smooth from use.

Theron pounded a dead rock onto the chain. Snap! Pop! Sparks flew in the darkened room. "Hit it again!" the prisoner commanded. Theron smacked the rock to the chain. It broke, releasing one arm. The second arm was not as easy. It took many strikes to snap the chain free.

"Woo, that's better," the prisoner said, rubbing his wrists where the shackles had been. "Are You Theron?"

"How did you know that I was Theron?"

"Arlis sent me."

"There you go again. Don't you mean he sent *us*?" said a second face that had been silent until now.

"We're Vard," the first face said, appeasing his other face.

"Now, that's more like it."

TS and The WOW

"Wait a minute. Are there two of you?" Theron was confused, hearing two voices but sensing only one man in the darkness of the room.

"We are two-faced," Vard's first face said, moving into the part of the room where a sliver of sunlight shined on him. He turned his head around, exposing his other side. That changed the way Theron thought of being two-faced. He had always thought that was someone who talked behind your back. Perhaps this was where the expression "talking out of both sides of your face" came from, he thought. It was strange to see a man with two faces, but at the ripe old age of eleven years, Theron was a veteran to the weird.

"Vard. Is that your name?"

"Yes, that's us. There's not much time. Arlis is about to..."

Before Vard's face one could finish his statement, an explosion rattled the castle. All the doids lost their grip, and for a moment, the outer walls of the castle crumbled into a giant pile of sand. The wooden door of the room where Theron and Vard were imprisoned collapsed under the weight of all the sand doids. The doids chattered one to another in the sand pile. Theron, led by the Vard's, climbed over the sand doids to escape. Guards were buried to their necks in the sand, and could only watch as Theron and Vard quietly walked away. Arlis stood, watching the

TS and The WOW

wake of sand still moving away from the point of shock, the point where he had assaulted the doid castle. His weapon was already tucked back into its place in his pocket.

"Now I have you!" The voice from behind him growled. Chills bit on his skin, and the hair on the back of his neck curled as he turned to face the embodiment of the voice. The two men locked eyes as if they knew each other, neither one allowing the other to see any weaknesses.

"It's been a long time," Arlo McFarland said in his sinister voice, almost taunting Arlis.

"I haven't missed you," Arlis replied.

"Not just a little?" he coaxed, then laughed, his chest bouncing and swelling to an unnatural size and then deflating, showing his bones beneath his skin.

"Well, I guess it's time to finish our unfinished business, don't you think?" McFarland spewed out his rattling words. They circled around each other, each taking a pose for combat.

"What is it you want?"

"I want it all, first you, then the boy, and then everything else." McFarland struck with the fury of a wounded Caterziph, a cross between a dragon and a baboon. Airborne, fists flying, he dove toward Arlis. Arlis stood in his tracks, his posture resembling a Greek Olympian, preparing for his medal to be

TS and The WOW

presented. He only moved his upper body to avoid contact. McFarland fell past, rolling on the ground.

"Nothing's changed Arlo. You're still too slow."

Arlo was now on his feet, one hand in the dry dust, balancing his body like a Truthlimite on his three legs. He was prepared to exact revenge upon Arlis, his arch enemy.

"You can try to kill me, but you never will," Arlis said while calmly facing him down, not flinching a muscle.

"We're not children any longer," Arlo said, sniffing in a deep breath and recalling memories of long past encounters with the man he had lured to his doom. Arlis, himself, had memories of the past, a time when his father ruled the kingdom where they now stood, locked in battle. He could see his own image, his spot of red hair twisting just like something that was happening to his brother. But those memories were of so long ago. His brother no longer existed and the red spot of hair was now bright silver. It still reacted when there was need for warning the same as it always had. Arlo, too, had a spot of hair that was once red and once lively, but now it was just a spot of coarse rugged molting, straw-like, purple hair. It was thinning, leaving the spot nearly bald.

"Wouldn't Daddy be proud of his precious boy?" Arlo said, taunting Arlis, hoping to work on a weakness.

"Father was always proud of his sons," Arlis rebutted, nothing wavering. The posturing settled into a dance as they worked to find any advantage one had over the other. Arlo struck a pose for his attack, and it happened. He leaped into the air, his hands swinging and his feet kicking in anticipation of striking his target. At the same time, Arlis took defensive motions to ward off the attack. As the first blow impacted, Arlis reeled and landed on his back in a pile of sand Doids. The sand Doids were still chattering, trying to rebuild the castle. They had paused, lying in a pile, disoriented from the blast from the ancient one.

"You're no better than I, and I will crush you beneath my heal like a slithering Crawlax."

Arlis was no serpent and neither would he let a creature like Arlo have the upper hand, yet he knew Arlo may well crush his head if he didn't strike first. He had no more time to think. He had to react or perish. He rolled out of the way of a crushing stomp just before it would have smashed against his face.

"Arlis!" Theron yelled just in time to warn him of the next blow that he had not seen coming.

"Get out of here, both of you!" Arlis had come to his feet, pulling his weapon from his pocket when the Doid castle knitted itself back together, engulfing Arlo McFarland and the weapon inside.

"We must act quickly if we want to escape. He has one of the treasures."

The guards that had been incarcerated by the sand were now free and soon would be after them. Retreat was wise now that one of the seven gifts had fallen somewhere in the Doid castle. It now looked like a patch of coral from the bottom of the sea.

"I've lost one of the seven." Arlis said. The Vard's mumbled something about wishing that Arlo had been buried alive, but neither Theron nor Arlis could understand their words. "We will get it back," added the Vards

.

It had seemed like nothing had happened. Theron was home. Twila's red hair was in its correct place. The only thing that gave any evidence that anything had happened was the gaping hole where Theron's room had been. Boards now covered the space, keeping out the weather.

"I guess I can sleep in Martin's room for awhile," Theron said.

"Not on your life! You're sleeping in here until your room is back," Adeline said, pointing him to the bed she had made on the floor in her room where she could watch over him. "In fact, tonight both of you are sleeping right here." They felt a mother's love.

CHAPTER 13

Thunder, Lightning Bolts, and Terror In The Canyon

The trio's pickup rolled off the pavement onto a graveled country road. They were already choking on the dust from the truck ahead of them. Theron was doing his best to sleep, although the confinement of being seated between his father and his uncle made him almost as uncomfortable as being seated on top of the broken spring in the seat. Sleep was a losing quest. The spring poked him each time they hit a rock or a divot in the road, arousing him to consciousness. The gray, tattered 1956 GMC pickup had brought them down the back country roads many times, yet it still seemed to prod along with no spits or sputters. Dust puffed in the windows, stirred from the ground by the tires of the lead truck. The truck ahead was carrying the horses, leaving a continuous, dusty cyclone behind it.

The desert of Nevada had hidden treasures in the folds of its canyons. One of those treasures was the wild horses that everyone called mustangs. Mustangs were the hardy descendents of those first horses that were brought to the Americas by Hernando Cortez, the Spanish explorer. This was the first time Theron had been considered old enough to go mustanging,

TS and The WOW

"You're too young," or "you will just be in the way," were the comments made every year until now. Always before, he had to settle for watching George come home with the new horses.

"Finally, I get to be a part of the roundup," Theron thought as he watched the sagebrush and juniper trees slide by in the truck's dirty window.

"Come on, pass them. This is a good spot!" said Uncle Joe.

"Yahoo!" Theron shouted, ready for the change. They passed the big truck, taking the lead to show the others where George had seen the animals last month. Suddenly, the window filled with the most wonderful sight. Wild horses ran across the hillside. The majestic stallion reared onto his back legs, then bounded down the hillside, leading his harem in escape from the threat of the invaders. George brought the truck to a stop, sliding in the dirt and tossing Theron into the stick shifter. Both of Theron's hands sprung up to halt his momentum. He caught a portion of the cold metal dashboard in one hand and the stick shift in the other. The men opened their doors and leaped out of the truck, as excited as young boys, to see the free-ranging horses. They had startled the herd that was now escaping into the red canyon, leaving only a dust-filled cloud and hoof prints on the ground. But it was those hoof prints that the men were counting on. The prints were fresh and couldn't be much fresher. The big truck rolled to a stop and Grandpa climbed down from the cab. The horses in the big truck snorted and danced. The mustang

TS and The WOW

stallion wearily turned atop the rise, snorted a puff, and walked a few steps, then broke into a trot.

"Magnificent, just magnificent," Theron thought as the animals disappeared, leaving nothing but the dust cloud. They passed out of sight over the hill. The men gathered near the trucks and began to unload the horses. There was an excitement that had been brought about by the sighting. Theron watched as George cinched the last strap on the saddle and swung his leg over his horse's back, sliding his dusty boot into the stirrup on the far side. The boot and the stirrup snapped together with a popping slap as the leathers made contact. The same boot seemed to wake the horse from her stillness and brought about an almost immediate gallop in the direction of the escaping horses.

"Stay here, son. We'll be back soon."

George had already formed a loop with his rope while racing in the direction of the herd. The rest of the men were shadows of that same motion, as if they were one in their purpose. It was only a second and they were all out of sight. Theron had nowhere to go, so he climbed up on the cab of the truck, metal clanking and popped under his weight as he sat down.

"This is a nice view. I can see a long way from here."

The morning sun felt warm and it was amazing how, at first, it seemed to be silent as the riders disappeared. But it was not silent at all, Theron thought. A bird chirped. It had come to rest on the limb of a nearby mesquite bush. The creek ran slowly by, making a sound as if water was being poured into a tin cup. Other small earth creatures moved on the dry mounds of earth, rushing down to get a sip of life from the stream.

"Hey little one," Theron said, referring to the chipmunk that stood near the stream and chirped as his tail spun around clockwise. Nothing had seemed this normal to Theron since the wolf had first appeared on his bedroom wall. With a look into the distance, Theron climbed down from the truck and off the embankment into the creek bottom. A green, spotted frog leaped from the bank into the water and hid itself under the bushes that were drooping into the water on the opposite side of the stream. Grasshoppers leaped ahead of Theron's steps, causing the tall grass to come alive. The day was drawing long. The sun had passed noon, and if it had not been for the cool water, Theron would have been past ready to go.

"It's not much fun being alone out here," he thought, wishing he were riding on the back of his father's horse. After eating a sandwich that Adeline had made for them, he remembered the double-faced coin in his pocket. It was from another world but was the coolest thing Theron had ever possessed.

"Now this will be fun." Some time had passed since he had had time for such things, but right now there was plenty of time to watch the faces on the coin and maybe they would know something about how to wrangle a pony.

TS and The WOW

"Not likely." Theron thought.

"Come out of there." Theron struggled to pull the coin from his pocket. "Let go in there."

The coin finally slipped free like a seed from its pod. First, he washed it in the water from the stream and then placed it in his open palm. One of the faces coughed and the second face on the other side of the coin laughed at him.

"I told you to hold your breath," it said. The coin rested in his palm, coming to life, as if it had been in hibernation in Theron's dark pocket.

"Are you awake?" Theron said, nudging it to roll on its edge.

"Nah, not quite yet."

Theron tried to look into the one exposed eye. He saw nothing but a milky haze. Theron set the coin on a rock in the morning sun, allowing it some time to awaken, and went to watch the minnows in the creek. They were fine, swimming in place until his shadow crossed them and then they would dart into the undergrowth or behind the biggest rock. Theron was on his hands and knees, leaning out over the water and trying to scoop up one of the minnows, when a noise, like a bugle being blown through a tight opening, startled him.

"Just the snort from the horses coming back," he thought. When the bush parted, the entire herd of horses burst into the stream. This time, there was no school coat rack in which to take refuge. The horses' entrance into the stream splashed

TS and The WOW

water, covering Theron. He scrambled into a crevice in the embankment, pressing himself in as tight as possible. Horse after horse passed by him until all that was left were the young colts that trailed them. Three young ones stood still ankle deep in the water, not noticing that Theron was even there. He watched them as they snorted into the water and drank their fill of the cool liquid.

"How could I catch one of them," he thought. "My belt!" He loosened the buckle and pulled the belt slowly free, trying not to alarm the colts. Theron moved out to the water's edge just a few feet from the ponies. When he was close enough, he leaped and put the belt around the tiny horse's neck. The horse bounced his springy legs up and down in the water and swung Theron around as he held the tether about his neck. Water splashed in all directions and the other two colts scattered up stream to their mothers. The captive horse struggled to free itself from the boy. "Ride-em cowboys!" Yelled one side of the coin who watched from the rock until he began to roll and splashed into the water. "Help," he screamed in the bubbles plopping into the water.

"Come on boy, I won't hurt you." The struggle ended with those words as if the colt understood his fate. The other horses were long gone when Theron led the white colt back to the truck. His belt had not been the best tool to capture a wild stallion, but was okay for this colt, just weaned from his mother. The size of fight in the tiny horse was great, but the boy had held his ground.

TS and The WOW

Dust rose in the canyon where the cowboys had chased the herd of horse's hours earlier. They were coming back.

"Maybe they have your daddy, Bright Eyes. They are going to be surprised when they see you," Theron said to the milky-white colt. The horsemen walked their mounts the last half mile back.

"An empty round up," Uncle Joe said. "Nearly had the stallion, but he grew wings and flew out of the canyon," George said. "That's my story and I'm sticking to it."

"Yeah, wings!" Uncle Joe repeated. They all laughed.

Theron walked with George as he led his mount to the truck, not saying a thing about his colt.

"What did you catch?"

"Just their dust, son."

"Dad, look what I got." The trailer door swung aside and there stood the pretty little pony. George smiled from ear to ear.

"Come and see this, boys. You aren't going to believe it."

"You skunked us, son!" George said as he patted Theron on the shoulders.

It had been about two weeks since Theron had brought home little Miracle. Everyone said it was a miracle that Theron could ever have caught him without getting his teeth kicked out. Twila wanted to call him Milky, but Miracle just seemed right. It was Theron's job to take care of his growing horse, but Twila had taken on the job of turning him into her pet. Every day she

TS and The WOW

would bring him a carrot or an apple. As she fed it to Miracle, she would pat him on the forehead.

"What's this?" Twila asked as she patted his forehead. Theron put his hand on the spot, pushing his fingers over it again and again. It was like an extra bone.

"How weird is this?" He exclaimed. With that, they watched him play, trotting inside the corral.

"Twila, is your room clean?" Adeline questioned,

Twila tucked the blankets under the bottom of the bed, and then moved the clothes from the floor as quickly as she could place them in the woven grass basket in the corner.

"It's clean!" she cried out while still in her room. The 1954 red and white Mercury Monterey was a lot of car for such a small woman as Adeline, but it was the only way for two girls to get out of town and do some shopping in the city. The mercantile was okay for some things, but when it came to things that girls really needed like new dresses or curtains with a feminine touch, you just had to drive the fifty miles to the south and visit JC Penney.

"It's girl's day out, "Adeline happily said while Twila turned on the radio. It took a few minutes to warm up before it began to play.

"And that was a little ditty by the Turtles," Adeline laughed. "Turtles, Beatles, and the Monkeys sound more like a zoo than three bands," Adeline laughed again. In ten minutes the car had risen into the Cottonwood Canyon with both Twila and

TS and The WOW

Adeline singing to the songs on the radio. The last turn had dissolved civilization away except for the occasional car coming the other way. The highway twisted back and forth on the hillside, climbing at a steep grade to the summit. The old car moved aggressively up the road, both occupants anticipating with the adventure that awaited them in the city. A short distance ahead, the clouds were dark. Soon the mother and daughter passed under the clouds and into the storm, leaving the sunshine and blue skies behind and passing through a windy door. The radio crackled. Then the voices died, replaced by a constant static.

"The top of the ridge is just ahead and then it will be downhill for awhile," Adeline thought, nervous at the weather change.

"So what color of dress do you want, Twi?"

"Maybe white cotton with flowers," she replied.

"Your daddy has always loved polka dots."

"So that's why," Twila said with an expression of discovery on her face.

"That's why what, honey?"

"Oh, when I was little, I asked Daddy what my Indian name was. He said, "You are Princess Polka Dot." She had loved that name ever since George had given it to her. At that time, Twila had been learning that Indians would get a new name when they came of age and had wondered what hers might

TS and The WOW

be. In a tender moment, she had become someone more. She was and would forever be Princess Polka Dot.

The car trudged through the rain that fell on the countryside. The sleek black road shined in the headlights and the wipers beat in time with the song that had come back on the radio. Rain fell now in a fury, the wipers unable to keep up. Something stood in the road on the big turn into Pine Mountain Canyon. Adeline crushed the brakes under her foot and cramped the wheel away from the person or animal or whatever stood in her path. The car first slid sideways, fishtailing, and then spinning around the body in the road. Suddenly, the road was gone, replaced by trees, bushes, rocks and streams of water careening down the canyon. Twila gripped the seat, bouncing up to the ceiling. Then her face smashed against the window. Adeline tried to steer and brake, with little response to either. At last a crashing, grinding groan came from under the car. It impacted rocks and, finally a tree, which stopped the car. Twila's face pressed against the front window, her body contorted with the curve of the dashboard. She could see directly into the bottom of the canyon a hundred feet below.

"Are you okay?" Adeline's motherly instincts inquired.

"I'm okay, I think. Mom, are you alright?" Adeline didn't want to alarm her baby, but Twila's red spot of hair had already told her.

"Mom, you're hurt?"

TS and The WOW

"A little, honey." The car groaned when Twila moved back to her seat, and then settled again. Lightning struck on the opposite side of the canyon and thunder rolled from it almost immediately, shaking the soil underneath them.

"Just sit back for a moment," Adeline said while holding her arm. Secretly, she was sure it was broken.

"Mom, what should we do?" Lightning flashed, a bolt striking the tree that was holding them. The thunder was instant and deafening. When it ended, the tree was in flames, the car lurching forward. Twila quickly sat back, preparing to crash in a fiery ball somewhere in the canyon's rocky muddy bottom. The tree roots released from the soil and rocks slid with the flaming remnants of the tree into the canyon. The rock held the old car for a moment and then it followed the tree.

"I love you!" Adeline screamed, the car tumbling down the cliff. Twila's mind focused on the elements.

"Open bubble, open," she thought again and again.

Somewhere, part way down the canyon, the air changed and a bubble opened. The car entered the water of the new world with a splash. The car started sinking only for a moment and then turned to the surface.

"Are you okay?"

"I'm still here, honey," Adeline replied.

The cut on Twila's forehead looked far worse than it really was. She put a piece of her shirt over it to stop the bleeding then looked out to assess their new predicament. The sky was

TS and The WOW

clear and the car floated like it was a boat, except for the water that was slowly seeping in through the space under the passenger back door that had not been properly shut.

"Looks like we are okay for now." The water splashed against the car, slowly turning it around in the water. It rotated a full turn in the space of three or four minutes while moving toward what looked like an island in the distance. Everywhere else was water as far as you could see. It was encouraging that the car was headed to the spot of land, Twila thought.

Adeline was resting in her seat, still holding onto her arm. Not wanting to alarm Twila, she hid her true pain. The car had revolved forty-three times at Twila's count. Adeline had counted thirty-four. She was aware of how special Twila was, so she tried not to be affected by her new strange surroundings.

"Twila, how did we get here?"

"It was a bubble, Mom. Kind of like the time on the front lawn when the yard changed and we were in the dinosaur world."

"But how do they appear when you want one?"

"I just think about one opening, because that is what Arlis taught me, and then one opens."

"Can you do it now?"

"I suppose I could." Twila had no idea what world it would open to, but being adrift in an endless ocean might not be the best place to be. She focused her thoughts and a bubble opened right in the path of the car. The Mercury Monterey

TS and The WOW

started to spin faster and faster until both Adeline and Twila were nauseous.

"Got to quit spinning!" Twila said, holding back the chunks she was about to blow.

At her request, the funnel in the water pulled the spinning car to its edge. Both Twila and Adeline knew that they would never reach the bubble. They were going to be sucked into the middle of the whirlpool. Through the bubble they could see a grassy field and stones the size of houses stacked atop one another in a teetering fashion.

"I wonder how they balance?" Twila questioned in her mind as the car spun backwards away from the opening. The stacked rocks looked like a giant snake, reaching miles into the air. The car tilted, sliding back-end first into the gaping hole in the water.

Twila kept thinking, "Bubble open! Bubble open, please open!" Car, purses, shoes, Adeline, and Twila tumbled into the abyss in the center of the whirlpool. The car bounced off the walls of water, tossing the occupants about in its interior. Adeline hung her good arm over the steering wheel, while Twila had braced both legs under the dash and was holding onto the door handle with a grip that would have crushed anything but steel. They bounced once more and then sank into the murky bottom. A flood of water tumbled in behind them. The fast moving current pushed the car along the bottom of the water, rolling it back onto its wheels. Water had started to come onto the backseat, and for a moment, things were still.

"Mom, are you okay?" There was no answer. Twila switched on the inside lights. Adeline, no longer conscious, laid half on the seat and half on the car floor. Suddenly, Twila felt alone and doomed. What could she do? She was just an 11-year-old girl. Terrified and in desperation she cried," Daddy!"

Above the water, bubbles filled in the hole where the whirlpool had been and left no trace that they had ever been on the surface. The gateway remained open into the world of the stacked rocks, but nowhere close to where the submerged car rested. Twila watched as the water began to fill the back floor, spilling in at her feet and starting to soak Adeline's clothes. It wasn't going to take long before the water would take over the air that remained and they would drown. Twila's red hair was weaving itself into intricate patterns, doing its business again.

"What are you trying to tell me?" Then she felt it. A large presence was outside the car, or at least something had just passed, bumping against the automobile.

"W...what now?" Twila asked herself out loud.

Adeline groaned. Then groggily she said, "What's going on?" She readjusted herself into a sitting position, pulling her feet from the water that had filled the floorboard.

"Mom, we've got to get out of here!" Twila was sure that if they didn't escape the car soon, it would become their final resting place. "Can you swim?"

TS and The WOW

"Sure," Adeline said, trying to convince her daughter as well as herself that she could. The creature outside brushed the car again, nearly tipping it on its side.

"What was that?" Adeline had been unaware of the lurking menace. The car rocked and then settled back into the murky bottom. Twila had climbed into the back. Pulling open the back seat, she punched out the cardboard that covered the trunk. Then it was easy for her to get the tire iron.

"Is it going to get us?" Twila asked, a quiver in her voice.

"Don't you worry. We are going to be just fine." Adeline's comforting words fell without touching Twila. She knew that they had to get out of the car and to the surface or die right there from drowning. She smashed the tool against the window several times before it fell away. Water rushed into the car and it was now or never. Twila helped Adeline to the window, and with three gulps of air, she was out and rising to the surface. Now it was Twila's turn. She gulped in air three times just like her mother had then out the window she went, leaving the family car behind in the depths of a foreign world. It was dark and murky. Twila was unable to see anything but a shadow of the car below her when she looked back, expecting to be swallowed by the sea monster. She was glad the thing that had bumped them was not behind her. Light from above coaxed her upward. Her lungs constricting, she released some of the air. Then she could see Adeline's feet kicking in the water. Something tentacle-like brushed against her legs. A large body glided under her like a

TS and The WOW

giant catfish, its body gliding through the water like a serpent. Twila cupped her hands and pulled herself through the water toward her mother. Somehow, she felt if she could get to the surface, everything would be okay. The cat-serpent circled quickly and thrust out a tongue four feet in front of itself, entangling both of Twila's gangly legs. She fought to reach the surface and get a breath. Panic filled her as she fought. She freed one of her legs, but drew no closer to the water's opening. For some reason, she thought, "I would taste bad, oh so bad." She hoped that it was true because she was about to be lunch for this cat-serpent thing. Then she thought it again with the same power as if she was opening a bubble.

"I taste so bad!" Her mind drew a picture of animals with sharp spikes and animals that were bigger and more terrifying than the thing that had her leg and was pulling her into its tentacle-covered mouth. The cat-serpent saw the images and knew that Twila was not an animal that he should eat. It released her leg and swam off, avoiding being eaten by the images that Twila had placed in its brain. Twila released her air and bobbed to the surface. Spent, she coughed out water and sucked in the wonderful air of this world.

"Twila, you're going to be okay," Adeline reassured her. "Keep breathing," she said, holding Twila with her injured arm and treading water with the other.

With her composure regained, Twila noticed the bubble was still open. It would be the best chance for them to get out of the water. They could use the backstroke for ten yards or could she just use the mind thing and lift them from the water?

Twila began to think, "Lift us out of the water." The water rippled and then…nothing. Adeline was struggling to stay on top of the water, obviously in pain. Twila knew that she would have to be clear of thought. This gift from God should work the same way it had on the cat-serpent. She had possessed it her whole life, but this was the first time she had tried to use the gift.

"I need to pray and ask God to help me," she thought. Immediately, she begun to pray, "Dear Father in Heaven, I am thankful for all my loving family and You preserving my life with the cat-serpent, but now we need Your help. Let me have the ability to lift Mom from the water to the land. Amen." Her thoughts became clear. She could see in her mind Adeline rising from the water, a vision so clear she could see the water dripping from her clothes. She, herself, was now above the water and floating toward the bubble and dry land.

Lifting things with her mind was a gift from God, but as she had learned, there was a need to do things in the bounds God set. Twila thought of this as they landed on the grassy plain where stacked rocks reached high into the air. Twila grabbed one just before the bubble closed behind them on the world that had swallowed the family car. Once again, they had made it home.

CHAPTER 14

The Stone and
The Never-Seen

The Winter Tree shivered, its leaves rustling as though it had felt moss growing on its backside. Theron sat down on the grass underneath the tree next to his sister who was playing with that strange stone she had found while they were on the world of Shopera. Stones there were not bound to the ground. In fact, they were a hazard to the flying creatures on Shopera. This stone seemed as though it were sick. It rolled gently over and over in Twila's hand, seemingly gaining comfort from her touches.

"I think that he's sick," Twila said while gesturing toward her stomach as if the stone might have a stomachache. The stone had no stomach or a head or any other part that might be described as a body part.

"Theron, how do you fix a sick stone?"

"Are you serious?"

"Look at it."

The stone was now hovering in the air, quivering.

TS and The WOW

"Maybe Arlis will know what to do." Twila cradled the stone in both hands as they walked through the sagebrush and then across the lava flow to the cave with a mouth. The water began to spin as if activated by the passing of Theron's hand and the orb key he had placed in its bottom. The orb was the key to transporting them to the Tween and Arlis. This had become like a game to the twins, a game sometimes and the very root to survival other times. Most kids had to imagine themselves in the situations that Twila and Theron found themselves in naturally. Today, they stood in the cradle of something much older, something that tied these two 11-year-old children to the very cosmos. They had not been allowed to be children in certain ways, but in other ways, they had the best of childhoods. The stone quaked in Twila's hand when the orb flowered into opening.

"Wow!" Theron loved the light show. To him it was like the fireworks on the Fourth of July every time this happened. Twila was better at this game. She took everything more seriously. The orb spun about the room, almost violently spraying shards of energy on the walls of rock. A rip appeared in the air, a bubble opening right in front of them.

"What's that?" Twila said, holding her nose.

"That stink's worse than anything I've ever smelled," Theron coughed.

TS and The WOW

Twila curled her nose and brow in an expression of displeasure. The smell dissipated and the violence of the orb's storm subsided, leaving only the bubble between worlds. For the first time, the twins seemed to be in control of the bridge to other worlds, not being drug into some chasm beneath the house or kidnapped by the growing green things on the bottom of Busher's Pond. This time, it was up to them to walk through the portal to this world.

"I think we're getting the hang of this. Come on, Twi!" Theron waved his hand, motioning her through the bubble.

The bubble in space snapped to its natural shape when Theron stepped through its rubbery boundary.

"That one was sticky." Theron wiped a hand across his face to remove the feeling. Twila was left standing in the cave watching her brother through this window to a different existence.

"Sometimes I wish he would just think before he leaped!" she thought, the stone still quivering in her hand. Twila hated the feel of the bubble on her face and she made a swimming motion with her arm as she followed her brother into the Tween. The world between this one and all the others, was by far the most unnatural. It was only in this spot that Arlis could be undetected. Only there, could Arlis rejuvinate. Twila was sure that, in some remote corner of the Tween, others like Arlis must exist. Yet she had only met Arlis and a few special creatures that had the key to these pathways. As far as she knew, it was his personal refuge.

Theron was already on the trail that led to Arlis' cottage in the glen, when Twila burst through the gooey bubble. The forest here was lush green and water showered all the plants with a generous caress of life. The trail to Arlis' cottage was groomed meticulously, cared for in a wild sort of way. A stone bridge crossed the small river, appearing to have stood there for centuries. Arlis was the same as always, stern yet pleased to see that they would find their way to him when in need. The thatched roof was damp and the sun was rising in the sky. Smoke poured from the cottage chimney.

"Come inside, you two!" Arlis stood in the doorway, inviting them into his cottage. Twila noticed that his blue eyes were a more intense blue here, if that was possible. She wondered if hers were that way, also. Theron's were, she could see that much. Theron's eyes were also intense, as though the energy here charged them both. Her face had tingled, her red hair relaxed, and she felt charged somehow inside herself.

"To what do I owe the honor?" asked Arlis. The cottage was strange. It felt as though it was bigger inside than outside.

"But that was not possible," Twila thought.

"It's Twila's rock. She thinks it's sick."

"Where is he?"

TS and The WOW

Twila unwrapped a cloth covering that she had put around the stone, hoping to stop its shivering.

"Let's put him here next to the fire for a bit."

Arlis put him on the hearth next to the fire. The fireplace was warming from the cool of the forest morning, yet even it was unusual, no log burned on its flame. There were only flames without any coal, wood, or even gas. Another of those differences from world to world. Twila wondered if she would ever get used to how weird things were beyond her side of the bubble.

Theron and Arlis were like peas in a pod, as Adeline would say. They rested in a large elaborately handcrafted pair of over-stuffed chairs. The material that covered the bottoms of the chairs was not recognizable, other than it must have been a hide of some kind of creature that had tiny white bumps all across its back.

"The rock is sick, so what can we do?" Twila heard Theron say, interrupting her examination of Arlis' home.

"Mom always said you can learn volumes about a person by where they live." Twila thought as she remembered hearing her mother's words as she noticed the furnishings of the cottage.

"Let's see how he's doing now." Arlis held out his index finger to touch the warming stone. He poked the rock. It had stopped shaking, and if it could have purred, it would have. Arlis caressed it with a finger.

"You're okay now, little one," he said. The rock seemed calmed by his voice, but still appeared just a little sick. Arlis' white hair glistened in the sunlight that emerged in the window. The same sunshine fell upon the stone and it begun to shiver more violently than before.

"It's sunstroke," Arlis said, pulling the stone away from the sunrays. Arlis took the stone to the basin on the countertop and gently bathed it. The stone became still again.

"How does a stone get sunstroke?" Twila asked Arlis.

"Each world operates in their own way. You see, in his world, the sun is filtered by a layer in the atmosphere that protects him."

"So is he going to be okay?" she asked.

"Now, you keep him wet and he'll be just fine, but he will have to go back to his world to survive," Arlis said, handing the little stone back to Twila. She cared for her rock all the day like it was one of her dolls or a baby kitten. The Tween was a safe place and as calm as a summer's morning where the water meandered its way across the countryside. The temperature was perfect with a gentle breeze, carrying smells that fit whatever moment you happened to be in.

Arlis took Theron for a walk into the woods near the meandering waters of River Tween. Twila stayed in the cottage, examining all the things on the walls, and of course, watching over her sick little rock. Nursing was in her nature and so what if it was a sick rock? It still needed attention.

"How are you feeling, Stony?" Twila had named her rock and Stony was his handle. Stony started to shake more violently than he had before. He was so very sick now. "I don't know what to do for you." Twila put her hand on the rock and rubbed it like her mother would her when she had a stomachache. It grumbled inside and shook more and more.

"This sunstroke must be the worst ever. Where are those guys?"

Stony rolled over and began to swell, just like an inflating balloon. As suddenly as Stony had swollen, he exploded, or

should I say she exploded, leaving seven little rocks the size and
shape of brown M&M's nestled at her side.

"You're not sick. You're a mama!"

"Where have you two been all day?"

"With Arlis. Look mom, Stony's a mom." Twila held out
her hand with the new little rocks exposed in her palm.

"You children need to be asking permission!" Adeline said. It was
as if she had not seen the new little ones at all.

It was soon agreed by all that life at the Salter house was
way too hectic and unpredictable for Theron and Twila to
wander to other worlds without their parents' knowledge. These
controls were long overdue. In 1969 it was still a time of
innocence when children could roam the hills, being children, but
Theron and Twila were a bit different, traveling from world to
world. There were dangers, unseen dangers.

The little rocks were now plump and round, healthy as
little rocks could be. Twila still watched after them like the little
mother hen she was. They were all tucked into their box. It was
small enough that Twila could carry it with her, or they could rest
in the yard under the Winter Tree in the bright summer sun.

"Rocks don't do much. They just lie there," Theron said
astutely, surveying his sister's obsession with the little black rocks.

TS and The WOW

"So what? I like them."

"Let's go do something," Theron pleaded, bored and also avoiding the weeding job Adeline wanted him to do in the garden. Twila placed her rocks into the box and the pair crossed the ditch into the field. The tree house was a great spot to sit in the summer breeze, during the morning hours.

"So what do you want to do, Theron?"

"I was thinking it would be fun to…" Smash, crack, kerplunk. Something fell from the tree across the wash. Theron stopped his words in mid sentence, his focus directed at the maker of the noise. Twila searched to see what had created such a ruckus.

"What was that?" She asked her brother, hoping he had seen what had fallen from high in the tree. The branches still vibrated from whatever it was that impacted them, but neither Theron nor Twila could see what had made all that noise. Theron's first impression was to scamper down from the tree house and search the ground for what had fallen. Twila grabbed hold of his arm and pulled him back.

"Just watch for a second, Jumping Jack Flash." Twila had seen too much to jump and run toward a noise just to see what made it. She was learning that being a balancer meant that, perhaps, whatever had fallen was not so friendly.

"I can't see anything, can you?" As far as Theron could see, the ground was clear beneath the tree. Twila had not taken her eyes from the tree since the noise had disrupted their conversation.

"There's nothing out there," she declared, noticing that even the branches had stopped moving. Both of them had begun wonder if they had really witnessed the sound or commotion.

"I'm going over there."

"Theron, be careful." Twila stood on the wooden planks of the tree house, one hand on a tree limb, ready to dash down to help her brother if help was needed. But for the moment, it seemed safer to stay right where she was. Theron straddled the fallen barbed wire fence, one hand pushing down on the wire to keep it from catching his Levis.

"I hate this stuff," he commented out loud, only to himself. The sand crunched under his feet as he crossed the wash, still remembering how unstable the sand in this wash could be. It was a hop, skip, and a jump, and he stood under the great Cottonwood tree from where the noise had first come.

"Nothing here!" he called out, while still looking around the foot of the tree. He disappeared around the back side of the tree. Suddenly, willows popped and a twig snapped. Something was running away from Theron.

TS and The WOW

"What's going on?" Twila yelled, climbing down from the tree. She was still unable to see where Theron had gone. The sound had taken him away.

"How will I explain this one to Mom and Daddy?" she thought. The pant leg of her shorts caught on the barbed wire as she passed over it. "Dang it!" She hurriedly loosened it. The sand of the wash slowed her steps as she ran toward the spot where she had last seen Theron. A noise came from behind the tree with more limbs popping and brush cracking. "It's coming for me," she thought, fear rising inside her heart. Twila stopped dead in her tracks, listening. She looked down, finding she was standing right in the middle of the wash, a spot in which she had declared she would never stop.

"Which way? Forward to the noise or back to the other side of the wash?" she wondered. No time to make the choice. She quickly ran to the wash bank opposite the side of the tree where the noises were coming from. Twila tucked herself into the underbrush like a rabbit hiding, watching. The noises stopped, then started again, coming ever closer to the tree front. Twila feared that Theron had been taken by one of the unseen and another had returned for her.

"Twila, where are you? There's nothing but footprints over here." Theron's head appeared from behind the tree.

"What are you doing down there? I know you're a scardy cat." He laughed at her. She stood up and stuck out her tongue at him, then giggled a little herself, feeling kind of stupid. Twila joined Theron at the base of the giant cottonwood tree.

"Where did it go?" she asked.

He pointed at a single track in the soft dirt. The track barely held its form in the sandy soil.

"Can you tell what kind of animal made it?" Theron was a Boy Scout, but that track was larger than any track he had ever seen an earth animal make.

"I think it's not from around here." Those were not the words that Twila wanted to hear.

"You mean they could be after you again, don't you?" Her question was rhetorical, but Theron answered anyway.

"Looks like something is watching us."

An uneasy feeling fell on the twins as they retreated to their side of the wash. Twila's red hair spun and Theron's red hair stood on end.

"Something's going on" Twila announced with a quick look over her shoulder. Something brushed up against her as it passed.

"What was that?" she squealed, her long legs dancing into the air. She shuddered. The unseen was now right in front of

TS and The WOW

them. Both now had a hair problem. Their hair was spastic. Both Theron and Twila froze in their tracks.

"This is just like a gunfight on the television show 'Gunsmoke'," Theron thought, not daring to speak the words. Twila's thoughts were wondering what the creature was that faced them down.

"I wish we could see this thing." At first it moved about, leaving tracks in the dirt.

"It must be heavy," said Theron, seeing the prints pressing themselves into the soil. It was the same creature that had left the prints under the tree. Twila took Theron by the arm, sliding slightly behind him.

"What is it?" she asked.

"It's the never seen.

"What's the never seen?"

"I don't know, I've never seen it," he laughed at her, trying to lighten her spirits. The never seen stopped dead in front of the twins. It intended to do something that involved the Salter twins, but neither Twila nor Theron felt they knew what it wanted. The never seen stood fast in his tracks, the only way that Theron could identify where it was that new tracks had not been laid down in the soil.

TS and The WOW

There was a shrill scream, the sound of a super vacuum sucking, and then a pop right in the spot where the never seen tracks were. Twila's red hair fell flat, just like her brother's, and the terror that had filled Twila's stomach gave way to peace.

"What just happened, Theron?" Twila still had a hold on Theron's arm.

"It's gone. You can let go now." She released her grip on his arm. They walked cautiously toward the footprints.

"You're sure that it's gone?" Twila glanced at Theron, wanting eye contact for assurance.

"It's gone, Scaredy Cat." Theron was frightened, himself, but he wasn't about to let it show. A measure of relief came across the duo as they crossed the ditch into the Salter yard. The Winter Tree leaned as far into the vacant yard as he could, wanting to protect the twins. He shivered his limbs as they crossed again into his domain. The tree sprang back, becoming once again the sentinel in the yard.

"Theron it's time to gather the eggs." Adeline's usual sweet voice seemed grating and gruff, incased in the early morning demand. Theron lay in his bed, not refusing to follow her order, but rather wanting to finish his dream. In his dream, he was a normal boy, nothing out of the ordinary. Just for a moment, he thought that he lived in dream during the day and his real life was when he was asleep.

"Come on, lazy bones. I need those eggs." George had rebuilt Theron's room and it was nearly the same as it had been before the earthquake. There were some differences, like the big window. The window he had put in place of the shattered one was twice the size of the old one. At first that seemed great, but in the night, when the moon was full, the room filled with light as if the paint in the room gave off light of its own. In the day, the sun illuminated every segment of the room. All this meant that Theron was unable to sleep in late and sometimes not sleep at all. Last night had not been one of those nights when it was hard to sleep. In fact, it was the best night's rest and sweetest dreams ever. Finally, he tossed aside the blankets that had comforted him to face this world, the real world.

"I want to go back!" he said in frustration with his life.

"What was that?" Adeline called in response to his words.

"Nothing, Mom," he called back as he pulled on his clothes.

The newly laid eggs were warm under the hens, only starting to cool when Theron placed them into his basket.

"Good job, girls." Soon the basket was heaped to the top with the white and brown ovals. Theron's thoughts were not on the chickens. He barely remembered to water and feed them

TS and The WOW

before he exited the pen. As he closed the door, the hens flapped and cackled up a ruckus.

"Now what?" He opened the door to discover all the hens and the cowardly rooster tucked tight into one corner. His red hair spun. "There's something strange going on here," he thought in a sing-song way. The hens seemed almost frozen, but nothing threatened them. There was nothing in the coop but the chickens. At least that was how it seemed as Theron stood in the doorway. Theron's red hair told a different story. There was something or someone there, and just for a second, an un-embodied, wide, toothy grin hung suspended in the air between Theron and the chickens.

"Oooo, my heck!" Theron shuddered and pushed the door closed until there was just enough opening to see inside. The grin turned toward the chickens, disappearing as it turned. Theron's red hair lay flat. The willies shivered up his spine, resting in the small hairs of his neck.

"I will never get use to this," he said, more worried about the wolf on the wall than the never-seen. The chickens resumed their activity as if the fox had never entered the hen house.

Theron slid the basket full of eggs onto the kitchen counter without a word. His face was long and his head was drooped as he passed Adeline. She let him go, not commenting, which was unusual for her. She was always the most attentive mother.

"Sometimes you just have to let them work it out on their own," she thought. It had been an hour since Adeline had seen Theron, so she wandered into his bedroom. He lay on his bed, looking at his coin collection and baseball cards, not really reading the information but just staring at them. He held up the Don Drysdale rookie card. It was his favorite because Don was a lefty and so was Theron. However, today it was not the fact that he was a lefty that attracted Theron to his card.

"What's going on, son?" The soft voice came from the doorway.

"Nothin'."

"It's somethin'. What's bothering you?" She didn't like her children to be in the place where Theron was headed. All the signs were there for a small bout of depression and Adeline wanted to remind him of one thing.

"Theron, tell me what's going on," she began to pry.

"Mom, I just wish I could be normal."

She sat on the corner of his bed, brushing her apron over her knees.

"What makes you think you're not normal?"

"I know I'm not the same as everyone else."

TS and The WOW

Adeline laughed. "Whatever made you think everyone else is normal? Why, you are the most normal person I know."

"But, I am a balancer and other people don't have to be a balancer."

"Theron, let me tell you, most folks think I'm pretty weird. They think because I do things my own way that I am from some other planet. For all I know, I probably am. It's not wrong to be true to who you are. In fact, I like being cut from a different cloth."

Theron knew that his mother often did things a different way than other older women, but he liked that about his mom.

"Yeah, that's you, but what about me?"

"You have to march to the beat of your own drum."

"What drum?" He was confused.

"Well, inside each of us there is a little voice that kind of guides us. You know, if you have a choice to make, like whether to help when someone needs help or to just sit on your rump and do nothing. What does the voice say inside you?"

"It says I should help."

"And how do you feel when you help?"

"I feel good."

"That's your drum. Learn to listen to your voice and you will always feel good."

Brightness came over his face as she hugged her son.

"One last thing dear boy, my daddy once told me something, that since then, I have learned to be a secret in the universe."

"What's that?"

"Happiness is a choice. I always thought it was the things others did that made me happy, but that is not true. You must choose to either be happy or to be unhappy. So what do you choose?"

Theron first thought about how the wolf wanted to take him into his world and destroy him, and now the Never-Seen was up to something. Life was not easy. But now he was in charge, in charge of himself.

"I choose happiness!" A smile grew on his face. "I think I understand now."

"You are special, Theron," she said, while running her fingers across his red spot of hair.

The Never-Seen lurked somewhere outside, perhaps watching the twins every time they went into the yard. They recognized something there had changed.

TS and The WOW

CHAPTER 15

To Ride Like The Cowboys and Water Dogs

Normally Martin slept in on Saturday; however, today was different. It was the start of his army leave and he was home and was not going to miss a second of time with his family. At 6:30 a.m. he dressed and then walked up the stairs into a morning filled with memories. The aroma of bacon greeted him, along with the sun's first appearance of the day.

"Good morning, honey. Would you get me some eggs?"

"I thought that was Theron's job," Martin said jokingly. "That's my mom, nothing has changed here," he thought. That made him feel good in a warm, welcome home sort of way. Martin reached for the basket, pulling it down from its hook on the wall and headed for the hen house.

The early cool of the morning felt great on his skin. Martin found it strange to have to duck to enter the chicken coop. It had been Theron's job for a long time. The hens were beginning to stir and the eggs were warm as he pushed the hens aside to take them. It was weird being in here, almost like he had returned to a life he had lived and thought was gone forever.

TS and The WOW

"I wonder if the tree still plays games with Theron?" he asked himself. Martin was ready for the Winter Tree. At least he thought he was. The door on the coop was jammed and wouldn't open when Martin pushed against it. The door was as solid as if the wood had turned to stone or had taken root, boring itself into the earth. Martin set the handle of the egg basket on a hook along with the feeding bucket that swung there, keeping it from the chicken poop. The basket swung back and forth as Martin put his shoulder to the door and pushed. It was solid.

"Theron, I'm going to get you!" he yelled. Martin backed up a few steps and then ran at the door. His shoulder impacted it with the same intensity as two mountain sheep butting heads. The door stood in place, not quivering at all. A second time he stepped back and then ran at the door, expecting the same action. This time the door opened and Martin flew out the door, first landing on his head, then his back. He rolled twice on the lawn, finally rolling to a stop at the foot of the Winter Tree.

"It was you!" he exclaimed. "Not funny!"

When Martin returned for the basket of eggs he kept one foot in the door and reached in to take possession of the egg basket. He snatched it from the hook and quickly turned to see where the tree stood. The tree hadn't moved. He stood solid, as if he had always been rooted right there.

"What took you so long?" Adeline questioned.

"Nothing here has changed, Mom." She knew by the tone in his voice that the Winter Tree was up to his old tricks. She

TS and The WOW

took the egg basket from Martin and washed the eggs in the flow of water from the kitchen faucet.

"What are you up to today?" Adeline asked as she broke a few eggs onto a hot griddle.

"Just going to the celebration in the city square."

Twila and Theron had gone early, helping the boy scouts put out the flags in front of homes in celebration of the Fourth of July. The country band had just passed the house, playing their instruments while riding on a hay wagon. Martin's 1965 Mustang Fastback was washed. The chrome rims shined and the eight-track played at a level to which George surely would have said, "You are going to break your eardrums, boy. Turn it down."

Martin pushed the gas just to hear the sound of the motor gurr, verlump, verlump and roar, then purr as he drove off to the town center. Several girls watched Martin as he arrived, closing the door on his sporty car. He was the coolest, as Twila would say.

"Martin, over here!" Twila's hand waved above the crowd. He turned, seeing his little sister, and started across the grass. Then Susan walked into view. Her long brown hair flowed in the air. As she turned, her hair whipped delicately against her face. She smiled at someone on the other side of the crowd. Martin gulped in a breath of air as he watched her. Everything else ceased to exist for that moment. Her sundress accented her alabaster skin and drew his attention until Twila yelled,

TS and The WOW

"Martin, you big dummy, over here!" Twila had been watching and went to where her brother seemed paralyzed. She grabbed hold of his hand, which brought him out of the "Susan world" and balanced him back into the real world.

"Not only do I have to balance the world, but I have to balance my big brother, too," she said and laughed at him. Theron ran past Martin and Twila. It was obvious that his clothes were soaked. They clung to his body and water marked his footprints as he crossed a sidewalk. Theron was chased by two bigger boys, each with balloons full of water. Danny slung one of his balloons at Theron, but instead of impacting on his back, the balloon bounced, smashing at Martin's feet. The boys turned and ran the opposite way, knowing that Martin was some kind of war hero and could mop the floor with them.

"My turn to balance things." Martin ran after the pair and Theron turned, delighted to see his brother chasing them. Mildred P. caught Martin's eye and tossed him a water balloon from the hoard she had stored in a number nine washtub. This was an annual event and the younger boys had failed to recognize that Martin was also a veteran of many, many years of water wars. The balloon left Martin's hand, targeted at the boy running slowest who was trying to get to the trees so he could hide behind them.

"Got ya!" The water balloon splattered on the back of the boy's white T-shirt.

TS and The WOW

"Oaf," the boy cried as he landed on the grass, sliding face first into the picnic blanket of the Moore family. Theron fed his big brother another water-filled balloon, tossing it right into his waiting hand. The balloon flew through the air at the second boy, impacting on the tree as he ducked behind it. Theron had found a position where he could sling his balloon at the boy. Splat! Water soaked the back of the boy's head and the collar of his shirt.

"Got ya!" Theron ran back to the protection of his big brother. The boys followed close behind him. As they came within throwing distance of Martin with their arms cocked and their balloons ready to throw, Martin stood tall and statuesque, waiting. The boys let their balloons fly. Both were airborne. The first hit Theron, just bouncing off and rolling in the grass. The second, an over-filled red one, went over Theron's shoulder and landed in the lap of Mrs. P. She laughed and then took arms herself, reaching into her stores in the washtub.

"The game is on boys!" She laughed a witchy kind of cackle. She winked at Martin and they separated, leaving Theron to guard the washtub. The balloon that didn't explode rested like a colored Easter egg on the grass. The boy who had thrown it raced to retrieve his unspent weapon. Mrs. P. went slyly around the back side of the tree and Martin swiftly made the frontal attack. His first balloon burst on the boy's back, startling him. He dropped the balloon a second time, dashing for cover from the other balloon in Martin's hand. He raced back to the tree where,

TS and The WOW

to his surprise, Mrs. P. met him with her second balloon, having already plastered his partner. He was now at the outside faucet refilling his water arsenal. The boy Martin was chasing, now thoroughly soaked, surrendered.

"I give!" he exclaimed, holding both hands up in the international sign of surrender. Martin rested back on the cement step of the old church, watching the gathering crowed. The water fight continued, but Martin was on the bench, out of the game, so to speak.

Martin watched the crowd, waiting for someone, but who? Most of the kids his age were either off to college or in the armed forces and in training in some fort like he had been. Martin leaned back with both elbows resting on the upper step. A balloon filled with water landed at his feet, splashing water onto is red stained, perfect cowboy boots. Water beaded on their polished surface, not penetrating the pervious leather skin.

"Hey, watch out!" Martin leaped to his feet, no longer looking into the crowd. He wiped the left boot on the back of his pant leg and then the other on the opposite pant leg. Then, as quickly as he had come out of the game, he was back in play. Mrs. P. watched the splashing from her lawn chair next to the washtub. She gently tossed him first a red water-filled balloon and then a yellow one.

"Go get'm, boy!" she cackled. The boy that had dropped his aqua sphere on Martin's shoes was running for cover. He hunkered underneath an evergreen bush that sat against a

TS and The WOW

building. The boy lay on the ground, sucking in a torrent of air, attempting to catch his breath. He was sure he had escaped Martin. He thought there was no way he was going to find him.

Music played on a loud speaker, a country hoedown with fiddlers and a cowboy singer, the kind that Adeline always played on her record player. Martin was being chased by the growing group of 11- to 12-year-old boys, some against him and others siding with him and Theron. The town folks were beginning to close in on them. Soon the grass seemed covered in blankets. Everywhere food and families encroached on the battlegrounds.

"Take the blanket sweetheart." George, Adeline and Twila were removing blankets and food from the 1956 station wagon where they had just parked on the street. Theron ran past and Adeline called after him to come join them. Theron just kept on running. Water balloons splattered on the car next to Twila who had just reached in for something. Water blotted the white flowered sundress.

"I'm gonna smack someone!" she yelled. Her red hair twitched, ringing a bit of water from its locks. Three boys had been chasing Theron and now they were on the run, laughing at Twila. Martin had seen the boys and took aim with the red balloon. It flew from his hand as if it were a fast ball he had pitched in the state baseball tournament. It impacted on target, the middle of his back like a perfect strike. He loaded the yellow balloon into his throwing hand as he ran, clanking down the street in his boots after the trio. Theron was now at his side with

TS and The WOW

a new supply of ammo. Martin took aim at the running boys, and without thought, he let the yellow one loose in the air. It was almost before it left his hand that he wanted it back. Two girls stepped in behind the running boys, directly in the path of the yellow sphere of water. It impacted the girl nearest, exploding water across her chest and all over the girl strolling stride to stride with her.

"Oh, Susan!" Martin yelled. The water covered the girls' once crisp sundresses. Both shuddered. Shocked, they tried not to cry. Susan had heard Martin's call.

"You monster!" she screamed.

Disbelief left Martin's bloodless face, replaced by horror at his scolding. Her shrill scream softened to a laugh as she saw how silly Martin looked. It was Susan Moore that he had secretly come to the gathering to see. Susan was a slender, brown haired girl with an olive complexion and amazing green eyes that, right at the moment, shot fire from them directly at a boy, or perhaps a man who was entangled in a bad moment.

"We got ya," four boys yelled as they unloaded a barrage of water balloons at the still stunned Martin. He took the drenching, still thinking all his chances with Susan were gone. She laughed at his predicament.

"I guess you deserved that!" Susan smarted at him, while bending at the waist and springing back in a playful way.

"Ladies and gentlemen, the races are about to begin!" the announcer interrupted the music. Soon the grassy area was lined by folks of all ages and the 5-year-olds were lined up for a foot race. It was obvious that none of them understood the concept of racing. The three little boys were being held on the shoulders by their dads and the two girls were having a dress-twirling contest of their own. The moms of all five were at the end of the racing path, coaxing their children to the finish line. It was a little red-haired girl that won, simply because she ran crying all the way to her mommy. The box of cracker jacks that she won didn't even bring a smile. Martin stood next to Susan who returned his flirty glances.

"Martin, there you are," Adeline called to him, waving for him to come and join the family. With his head ducked, he smiled at Susan.

"I'll be right back."

"Last call for 11-year-old boys and girls. Report to the starting line for your race!"

Theron already stood on the starting line, but Twila stood like a porcelain doll next to her mother. She wasn't about to mess up her new sundress in a sweaty foot race, although she was sure she could beat all the boys and probably all the girls. Theron stood ready for the whistle to start the race. Eight boys and four girls stood shoulder to shoulder in line for the 50-yard dash. It would go across the grass and past the

TS and The WOW

sidewalk to the other end of the town square. A twine rope was strung across the grass, each end being held by a large man, making the finish line.

"On your marks, ready..." Theron hated the wait for the whistle. It gave him the same sensation as when the doctor was about to give him a vaccination with a needle.

"Tweet, tweet!" The racers burst forward, each determined to be the victor. As quickly as their 11-year-old legs would propel them, they crossed the grass. Theron had never supposed that he would win the race, but he had taken a lead over Marlene, the fastest girl his age, other than Twila who stood in the crowd cheering him on to win.

"It's going to happen. I'm going to win," Theron thought. The twine rope was going to hang on his chest. He could see it all in slow motion. He had never been good at anything, but he ran all the time and, today, it was going to be his day.

"Faster, Theron!" called Martin, who was near the finish line with Susan. The finish was in reach and Theron was still in the lead.

"Aofa." Then a collective, "Oh, no," rose from the onlookers, each gasping for air. Theron slid on his chest through the grass. His tangled feet had taken him to the ground as though his shoelaces had been tied together. Marlene crossed the finish line, followed by everyone else, with only one exception. Theron lay on the grass, his chin bleeding from a grass burn. He rose to

TS and The WOW

his feet and then walked across the finish line dead last. Martin met his brother there.

"Are you okay?" Susan shared his concern and put her arm around Theron. "Come and sit over here," she said. Then she took a handkerchief out of her purse and blotted his chin.

"What a race! You had her beat." It felt good to have the praise of his big brother, and Susan could make any boy feel better. Marlene, the gangly red-haired girl, walked up to where Theron sat.

"Here's your crackerjacks. You would have won." Then she turned and was gone into the crowd. Theron blushed, almost connecting all the dots of freckles on his face.

The Fourth of July was a day of heroes, firecrackers, water fights, and girls in sundresses.

"Come on, Theron, you're my partner." Twila had entered Theron and herself in a contest of skill. "I'm sure we can win this."

"What is it?"

"It's called snap net." She handed Theron a pair of yellow sticks that were a half inch in diameter and 12 inches long. They were attached together with a spider-web like net that had a strange spring quality.

"You pop it like this." She pulled the sticks that she had in her hands apart and a bright red ball sprang from the net and shot ten feet into the air. Her dress flowed away from her body as she spun around to catch the ball back into her net. "It's easy, try

TS and The WOW

it." Twila tossed the ball into the air, aiming it at her brother. Theron snatched the ball from the air right on cue. That was unusual for him. Usually he was the clumsiest person alive. His red spot of hair twitched, laying itself flat to his head as if it were getting out of the way. Twila's red hair was minding its business, staying right where she had put it earlier. Each pair of contestants faced one another and snapped the ball to their partner.

"Each pair must step back one step!" called out the man on the loud speaker. Each contestant moved back one step, then snapped the ball at his or her partner. It was the fourth step back before anyone lost the ball, but after that, teams were falling like flies. Theron and Twila continued smoothly, using the twin-ness thing between them. The ball sprung from Theron's net on a perfect arch into Twila's net where she caught it again. Each partner stepped back another step. The process started again with fewer constants. Jack Sweeney with Marlene Jenkins and Jeff Hunt with Bonnie Darrington were all the contestants left other than the Salter team, each tossing the ball into the air as if it were synchronized swimming or team ice skating. Several more steps had been taken, leaving a good thirty yards between the partners. Bonnie seemed to be the only one having any trouble with the distance. She had stumbled backward on her last catch, nearly landing on her little sister who had come up next to her to watch. After a few more tosses, the distance had grown to forty yards. Twila popped the netting with the two sticks and the little red ball shot into the sky, much farther than it had been flying. It was far above the trees and far above the other balls that were in the air. Theron maneuvered his body under the place where it would fall.

"You'll never catch that!" Jeff yelled, just catching his descending ball. Theron watched the ball reach its apex and then drop toward the spot he had chosen. Judging it was hard. Just keeping his eyes on it seemed super-human. As the ball approached him, Theron could see he wasn't far enough back. He hurriedly stepped back and back again, stumbling and catching himself with one hand while holding the catching net in the other hand. All the others had passed their balls back and forth twice while the Salter ball was in the air. However, when Theron slipped, Jeff and Bonnie both stopped to watch like they were seeing a car wreck and their ball bounced on the ground in front of Jeff.

"Dang it!" Jeff exclaimed, slapping his hands to his side. Theron knew that he was about to lose again to Marlene, and now, to Jack Sweeny. He stumbled to his feet and leaned back, catching the ball over his shoulder. Twila cheered. Martin gasped with relief and sucked a new breath. Theron took his step back to match Twila's step. The ball popped out of Theron's net, gliding its way above the trees again. Marlene had just caught the ball. She smiled at Theron.

"Why had she done that?" he thought. He refocused on the ball that was spinning in a helix as it dropped to Twila's net. Twila seemed unaffected by the erratic movements of the ball. She just calmly waited for it to fall, then reached her net out, and

TS and The WOW

it was caught. Marlene had tossed her ball into flight. It traveled right to the arc, breaking a downward fall toward Jack. There was little time to watch the others. Twila, at nearly 40 some odd yards, had to snap the net with all her power to get it back to her brother. As she snapped the net, she was sure it would never travel high enough to fall close enough to Theron to stay in the game. However, the ball took flight, like a bird sprouting wings, and soared high into the sky. As it began to fall, it was on a perfect angle just within Theron's reach.

"Good job, Theron!" Martin called out. Sticks, nets and identical red balls lay in a pile where the disqualified constants had put them. Inside the pile, the balls shook, quivering like they were all one entity. Rolling like a rattlesnake in unison, they slithered from side to side, creeping up unnoticed.

"Come on, Marlene, you can do it," Sweeny called. Their ball hung in the air between them, their distance shorter than Twila's and Theron's. Catching it seemed easy. The ball train shot itself into the air and returned at the same rate as the one Jack had slung. Ball after ball bounced in front of Marlene and her ball hit her on top of her head and bounced lifeless with the others. Twila snatched the ball from the air and the game was over.

"You cheated!" Jack screamed and stumbled over three of the balls.

"We have a winner in the 11-year-old Zermetzel contest. Twila tossed the ball into the air, spun about twice and caught it, just how she had practiced it earlier. Marlene smiled at Theron.

TS and The WOW

"Congratulations. Now we are both winners." Theron kind of liked that.

"Yahoo!" Martin screamed, grabbing a stunned Susan by the waist and lifting her into the air. Some days are meant to be just about being happy and this was one of those days.

CHAPTER 16

Where The Wind Blows and Holes In Times

The morning fell into the calm before the storm. The sun drenched the mountains that had slumbered through the night with only the serenade of the coyote's song. From nowhere spilled the first wave of wind, down the canyon directly into town and the Salter's yard. Some folks called Enterprise "Windy Prize," because the wind would often find a home there.

The Winter Tree had moved to a spot where the garage took the brunt of the approaching storm. The tree's high branches groaned under the strain of the increasing winds. He pulled his limbs close to his trunk in order to stabilize himself. The chickens clucked anxiously, only stopping once in awhile as they paused to hear the change in the wind velocity. All the chickens huddled in one corner, sharing warmth as the wind battered the wood slats of the coop. Theron held onto the wooden door with both hands while entering the coop.

"Lousy wind!" he exclaimed. The chickens paused, their choirs of bock-bocking until the door was tightly closed. The eggs in the wall-mounted boxes were cool as if each hen had done her duty and then abandoned ship for the safety of the flock.

"Nine, ten, and eleven, only eleven today. Well girls, you're falling short." Theron spread the milo and grain on the floor. The chickens scrambled to peck at it. He filled the water pan and then held the door with the eggs tight against his body to protect them from the wind. The wind pushed him sideways in gusts. It took him by surprise when, for just a second, the wind stopped as he slammed the door to the coop behind him.

"Don't break them, son," George commented, holding the door to the house open for his son. Theron placed the egg basket on the counter and then unwrapped the scarf covering his face.

"It's dusty out there. I could hardly breathe. Only eleven eggs today, Mom."

"Did you water them?"

"I gave them water and grain."

The temperature had fallen. Even for a summer storm, it was cold outside, but the house was warm and a hearty breakfast was nearing completion. Twila was setting dishes on the table, obviously happy about something as she danced back to the utensil drawer for forks and spoons.

TS and The WOW

"So, why are you so happy?" Theron just had to know. The wind was blowing harder now and the screen door popped free from its latch, crashing and banging against the wall. George got up from the table, opened the door, and re-latched the screen door a little tighter. Then he locked the eyelet hook to keep it closed.

"Snow is what is going on. It's summer and we are getting snow!" George reported as he returned to his chair. Snow had begun to fall and the wind was building piles against the east side of the house and the garage. The Winter Tree wasn't living up to his name. Winter was not something he was happy about. He had bent over out of the wind, aligning himself with the west side of the garage.

Twila squealed when she discovered the snow. She loved the snow, but that was one of the differences between the twins. Theron loathed the snow and Twila loved it. In fact, Theron thought that, if he could, he would stop the snow and it would always be spring, with the temperature a comfy 78 degrees.

Twila jumped into her cloak, hat, and scarf with a feminine twist. Theron moped as he put on his things, not wanting to go back outside to face the storm.

"Its summer, not winter," he had begun to say to himself. "I want this storm to stop and it to be summer again instead of winter."

TS and The WOW

Twila opened the door, bracing for the wild blasts of wind and snow. Theron was right behind her, his shoulder lowered and hat brim tilted to take on the storm. But as they opened the door, something had changed. The wind had ceased and the snow was gone. Only a small pile rested against the east side of things. Theron had wished it were summer again and it was.

"That's weird," Theron said. "This was just what I was wishing for."

"Be careful what you wish for, it may come true." Twila repeated the old saying she had heard her dad say many times. Twila's mood was no longer jubilant, but still happy. She was now was cradling a spring-like snowball in her hand. Twila's eyes sparkled deviously as she threw the snow at Theron, hitting him in the side of the face. He scooped snow into his hand as Twila ran ahead of him.

"Now you're gonna get it." His throw was close, but narrowly missed hitting her shoe.

"Missed me, missed me. Now you gotta kiss me!" The thought of kissing his sister made him spit on the ground.

"Yuck, I ain't kissin' nobody, especially not you!" By the time they reached the school, the snow was gone and it was too hot for a coat. The coat hooks were filled in the hall and the kids were in the gym playing while waiting for the whistle to blow,

TS and The WOW

calling them to order. Stranger things had happened to Theron and Twila, so even though it was August and it was always warm in Enterprise this time of year, the unexplained was normal here. When the whistle blew, Mr. Park, the gym teacher, came out and put his hands on his hips, waiting for all the kids.

"Everyone ages 11 to 13 forms a line right here." He pointed in front of himself.

"Today is the perfect day for junior league tryouts," announced Mr. Park, walking back and forth in front of the line of children. That was no surprise to anyone. That was the reason they had faced the strange August snowstorm just to be here.

"Attention! You boys in the back, listen up!" Mr. Park was ready to start and was not going to take any messing about. "Boys, line up under the far basket, girls, over here." He pointed to the basket on the end of the court where he stood. "Mrs. Park will take you girls. As for you boys, you get me," he said with the grin of a drill sergeant.

This was the first year girls would have a team. Things were changing. Theron had coaxed Twila into trying out. She had thought she would never make the team. However, it was her uncanny shooting that put her on the first string.

"Salter, Theron Salter!" Coach Park called out. Why in the heck had he singled him out? Theron wondered. He hustled over to where the coach stood, tripping over his own toe.

TS and The WOW

"I'm a dork," he thought. Coach Park placed his heavy hand on Theron's shoulder. That was a sure sign that he was about to be cut from the basketball team, Theron thought.

"Son, you got more hustle than anyone on the team. Now, just learn to shoot and we can use you. For now, you are second string. Pick up your uniform over there." Twila had all the reason in the world to gloat. She was a starter and Theron was only a sub; however, she didn't gloat because she knew how much her brother had wanted to be on the team.

"We both made it!" Twila announced, as they passed through the door where Adeline was making lunch.

"Great job, you two."

Morning came and it was spring-like weather. Even the wet ground had now dried out. The Winter Tree had moved to his favorite summertime spot. His leaves shimmered in the morning sun, bright and green, but that was not unusual. He always had green leaves. In fact, he always had the same leaves. Theron gathered the eggs and this time there were twenty-two.

"Well girls, you doubled your efforts today!" Theron said to them.

A week passed and nothing had changed. Not even a breeze had managed to blow in town and the average temperature was 78 degrees. It was strange not to even have a little breeze in the morning in 'Windyprise'.

TS and The WOW

"Is this the calm before the storm?" Theron questioned his father.

"Just enjoy it while you can. After all, you are only 11 years old. You should just be a boy for awhile," was how George responded to his son's question.

As calm as the weather had been, so had been the events of the Salter's' lives. Theron was glad that, as of late, there had been no reason to repair any entry bubbles. It was just nice to be a kid and enjoy his summer. All around town there was talk of how the depths of winter had struck all over the state, just like it had in Enterprise. It was gone here, but this was the only place where the mountains that had been smothered in snow had suddenly returned to summer. The end of August was approaching and it had been weeks now with the most fabulous weather imaginable. Theron loved it. George, on the other hand, was a little worried.

"If we don't get the usual storms, things will dry up and wither away. Right now is the usual monsoon season and we haven't seen a drop of water," George declared. "Do you suppose that...?" George left his statement hanging, realizing his thought had to be exactly right before he disclosed what he was thinking.

Theron and Twila came home together from the school, each sporting the T-shirt that represented their respective basketball teams. The shirts fit them, unlike the rest of the clothes they were quickly outgrowing. That was a problem for both of them, perhaps a little bigger problem for Twila than for Theron, or should I say a smaller problem? Twila had grown an inch more than her brother had and that was the way all her clothes fit.

"Mom can we have a slice of your bread?" Theron asked. He waited there three seconds, not long, but he needed the edge to be taken from his hungry stomach. Theron buttered a slice of Adeline's homemade bread, and then looked for cinnamon and sugar, hoping to make cinnamon toast out of it. They had sugar but no cinnamon.

"I want some cinnamon," Theron thought.

A soft brown powder began to cover the counter top where his slice of bread was. Theron and Twila noticed the powder and stood back away from it.

"What's that?" Twila pointed her finger at the powder as she asked her question in shock. Theron sneezed, took a breath, and sneezed again as he blurted a single word.

"Cinnamon!"

Cinnamon continued to come from thin air, filling first the counter and then flowing over and covering the floor of the kitchen.

"Dad, Mom! Come quick! Theron just wanted it, and then there was cinnamon everywhere!" Twila explained excitedly. Theron hadn't realized it was him.

"Theron, you have to stop it," George said.

"How do I stop it, Dad?" The cinnamon continued to pour off the counter, covering the floor, and now was nearly level with the tops of the cabinet doors.

"Think, Theron. What were you thinking when this started?"

"I just wanted cinnamon and it started to come from nowhere."

Then just think, 'I want this to stop.' Theron thought, "I want the cinnamon to stop." The same weird way it started, it stopped.

It took a couple of hours to clean up the mess, but Adeline had never imagined so much cinnamon. She thought she could make Dutch apple pie and cinnamon egg custard and she would come up with some new ways to use cinnamon.

"Theron, did you think about anything else the way you did the cinnamon?" George asked.

"Like what? What do you mean?"

"Like the snow storm a couple of weeks ago."

TS and The WOW

"The snow storm," Theron repeated. "Dad, could I have stopped the snow like the cinnamon?"

"Theron, we have got to let the storms come again. We need the water it brings."

'Make it snow," Theron said, but thought a lot more of how it should be in August.

"No, do not think of snow just think of the kind of weather we usually have this time of year."

It was hard to tell if it was Theron that made the weather revert to monsoons or if they just happened. Anyway, muggy afternoon storms came once more. It rained so hard that it covered the ground in huge puddles Theron had to be careful not to think that he wanted it to be spring or it would be. He was careful not to think in the form of "I want it to be" of any kind.

Twila, on the other hand, loved to dream that it was winter and cold. Snow crunched under Twila's feet. A good "wintery sound," she thought. The summer weather was okay, but there was nothing like the winter world. She liked the cold on her face and watching the steam from her breath. Most of all, she liked watching the flakes fall in the light from the street lamp as she passed under it. Home was only another block away and the darkness made the falling snow seem so silent. Lights from a car came toward her as the car slid in the fresh snow. The lights cast shadows in the falling flakes like they were resting on a moving

TS and The WOW

wall. The sound of the engine whirred away the silence and the car came right at her like the driver didn't see her standing there. Whoever it was that was behind the wheel hadn't seen her. Twila leapt out of the way as the car slid into her, tossing her off the road and into the cold deep snow at the side of the road. Her eyes popped open.

"That was so real! But I was just thinking it, wasn't I?" She felt the bed under her and she was at home. In fact, she was in her room with its four secure walls.

"That was weird." She closed her eyes and lay back on her bed, running her fingertips over the white crocheted bedspread. The rows of bumps kept her right there in the room. Or did they? She felt her finger no longer touching the cloth. Was she floating in the air?

"Got to open my eyes," she thought. Twila forced her eyes open, straining and pushing her eyelids with the same muscles that usually brought vision with little trouble. She could feel a force tugging at her skin and the sensation of traveling through the wind. Her eyes were left free, and again, she could see her room and feel her bedspread beneath her.

"I'm in my room, but I am having a come apart. What is going on here?" She sat up on the bed and waited for the world to spin away out of control. It didn't. Theron walked into the doorway.

TS and The WOW

"Want to do something?" he asked, while leaning his head in through the open door.

"I'm kind of sick."

"Sick? You look fine to me."

"I guess I am only dreaming. When I close my eyes, its zam doodly do and I am off flying through a hole into some other place.

"That sounds cool."

"You would think it was cool."

"Show me what you're doing. I want to try this."

"Do you think it's one of our gifts? If it is, I could do without this one."

"Just show me what you're doing."

"Lie back on the bed and hold on to my hand. Be sure that you don't let go of me." Both of them lay back on the bed and closed their eyes as Twila instructed.

"Now what?" Theron wanted to get this started.

"I just started to think…"

Before she could answer his question, they were both swept into that wind tunnel and the sensation of falling through a hole.

TS and The WOW

"Stop this," she thought, but it was too late. They had passed the hole and were falling.

"Don't open your eyes. Don't open your eyes," Theron thought to himself. Yet, just for a moment, he opened his eyes to see both himself and Twila crashing near terminal velocity toward the lavender mountains below them.

"Fly like a bird!" Twila screamed to her brother.

"I can't fly!" He screamed in return.

"Like this!" She held out her arms and tucked her legs behind her. Almost immediately she slowed her fall. Theron shot like a rocket away from her until he could assume the same position. When he did, he slowed his fall, then flapped his arms a few times, gaining total control like Twila had done. She swooped in next to him and they both landed in the top of the tallest tree in the lavender mountains.

"This is awesome! We can fly!" Theron's excitement was only matched by Twila's gratefulness that she had landed safely. She clung with both arms to the branch where they had landed. Theron teetered, wanting to try the flying thing again and especially wanted to see if he could glide to the ground below.

"What's that?" He pointed to something moving on the forest floor. Then he swooped just like a bird to the ground. "Theron, come back here," Twila said. Then she let go of the branch, first falling then swooping to the ground next to her

TS and The WOW

brother. "You're crazy, you know," she said, still getting her feet on the ground.

"Wasn't that so cool? We were flying!" Twila's eyes told a different story. She was neither glad to be flying nor happy about trying to figure where or even when they were.

"In one of the worlds, I suppose," she thought.

"Look at that. What kind of animal has a nose like that?" Theron had to see closer. The creature's head bore its face into a log with its nose twisting like a drill. Soon it passed its whole body inside the cavity where it disappeared inside the tree trunk.

"Where did it go?" Twila had not seen the creature disappear into the tree trunk.

"There it is." Theron spotted it rising again to the surface, leaving its nose like a lump or a branch on the trunk. The lumps along the animal's back resembled the fingers of a hand, wiggling with intent as though they were about to snatch a strange bird-like creature that hovered above its head. Another face rested where its chin should have been. That face was watching Theron, as Theron watched it, waiting for a reaction to its presence. The animal appeared to have its eyes on Theron, yet was not threatened. The finger-back double facer watched something else with its dominant face. Theron noticed that something else behind the small stand of trees was a hole in a very large tree, a hole big enough for the finger-backed double facer to climb into.

TS and The WOW

The twist drill nose animal flopped as it raced toward the open hole. It scurried up the tree and disappeared into the hole.

"Hey, look at this," Theron said to Twila as he climbed the tree, swinging his right leg up into the hole.

"What do you think you are doing?" Twila reached to pull him back, but he disappeared into the hole. At the same time, someone tapped her on the shoulder. She jumped, turning in the kung-fu pose and hoping that whatever it was would run so she didn't have to. Her long gangly legs quivered as she landed from her leap. She was shocked by what faced her. Theron stood right in front of her.

"How did you do that?"

"What do you mean?"

"You climbed in and then there you were." She pointed to where he now stood as if it had been in an instant. To her it was in an instant; however, to Theron the time was much longer. He had climbed in and out and walked back to find the animal, the finger-backed double facer, and then returned to where she stood back by the tree.

"You're crazy. You just appeared there." She was sure that the finger-backed double facer had done something. She stuck her head inside the hole in the tree. There was nothing there. The finger-back was gone and the hole was just a cavity in the trunk.

TS and The WOW

"Where did he go?" she asked her brother.

"He just disappeared before I got into the hole." A noise rose from behind a group of lavender tree trunks that stood split away from the main body of their once majestic group. It was the spinning sound of a whirling drill nose. The nose burst through the trunk and then the full head of the finger-back double-facer came out, freeing it from the oddly-colored wood.

"There it is." Theron's finger pointed toward the animal. Quickly, Twila, followed by her brother, approached the odd forest. Not getting too close, warily they watched the animal weave in and out of the trees, chewing their trunks for food. The finger-back double facer was not bothered by the twins, meritoriously going about its business as though it knew something that they did not, something that kept it safe from intruders in his forest world.

"Theron, not so close," Twila whispered. Theron had crept ever closer to the animal. He wanted to touch the fingers that dressed the creature's back. He placed his own finger to his lips, shushing her while he waited on top of the stump next to where the weird animal would pass. Theron was sure that he would be undiscovered where he sat. The finger-back's nose preceded him like the white cane of a blind person crossing the street. Then the waddling body passed under Theron, its fingers undulating along its back. Theron thought it would be nothing to reach out and touch the fingers, kind of like catching a horned

TS and The WOW

toad in his own desert home. A big horned toad, it weighed more than the boy and seemed to have a quiet temperament until he reached out, touching the fingers.

Twila gulped in air, trying not to scream. She was repulsed by the thought of touching it. Theron had no time to scream. The sticky slime spewed from the fingers on the animals back and stung his hand, paralyzing it. The fingers were fingers in every sense as they snatched hold around Theron's hand and bounced, as a kangaroo would, toward the tree with the hole. Twila screamed, "Theron!"

Theron bounced across the forest floor, still tied to the fingers. Twila leaped from her hiding place to give chase, but by the time she reached the tree, both the finger-back double facer and Theron had passed through the hole and were gone. This time she was not going to wait for Theron's return. She climbed into the tree, where she found nothing but the same hole she had climbed into, just as Theron had told her. In the moment she sat, time stood still on the outside of the tree. A bird chasing a bug was about to fly past the hole at the very moment she climbed into the cavity. There it was, frozen in time or ever so slightly moving. The air did not move and the bug and sounds all froze.

"I could reach out and move that bug or the bird," she thought. She didn't want to watch nature feeding on live prey. She reached out and turned the bird so that it was flying off at a ninety-degree angle from the bug. It was stiff and frozen. She

TS and The WOW

watched for several seconds. Nothing moved until she climbed down from the tree. Even then, she walked away from the tree before the bug's wings made sounds and the forest was alive again. The bird swooped away, losing direction and smacking into a low tree branch.

"Oops, "Twila laughed, putting her hand to her mouth. Some of the bird's plastic-like feathers spun to the ground. Under the tree where the bird fell was something else.

"That looks funny," Twila said aloud. She stepped closer to the object under the tree and picked it up. "Theron, is that you?" His garbled voice came from the other side of the log beyond the tree and where the object lying in the undergrowth had been.

"Yeah, what happened?" Theron's head rose over the log.

"There you are! How did you get away from that thing?" He rubbed his head.

"I don't know. Where did he go?"

"I haven't seen him."

Theron's head stuck for a moment to the log as he got up. He wiped the rest of the goo on the log, climbed over it, and walked up to stand beside his sister.

"What the heck?" He said, taking notice of the object that his sister had found. It shined in the ray of sun that came through the treetops.

"Put it inside you sweater, Twi."

Together they tied it up inside her warm-up jacket.

"Can we get out of here?" Twila had had enough and just wanted to be home. Adventure was Theron's middle name, but hers was Marie. Twila raised her hands and a bubble sprang to life near the Black Ridge and they stepped through it.

CHAPTER 17

Valley Of The Mountains and Water Their Roots

The night had enveloped the valley of the mountains, and as usual, when the sun dropped behind their majestic shadows, the world became cold. The darkness was full and final, only being touched by the plethora of stars glittering in the sky. The Salter Twins lay in their beds for the first time since they had been swept away into the world of the finger-backed double facer. The sheets felt silky and cold on Twila's feet, so different than it had been for the past few weeks. Theron had already fallen asleep, that sound sleep that only comes upon the young when their youthful energy is expelled, leaving their flesh a sloppy bag of bones. The morning brought with it a storm. Grey clouds paused in the sky to gather in the soothing mellow valleys of rain. Theron again had collected the eggs. Breakfast was spitting and sputtering in Adeline's pans upon her stove as Twila wiped the sleep from her eyes.

"Good morning, sweetems," George said as Twila wandered into the kitchen. She was still clad in her ankle-length nightgown. She had a fondness for the cozy feel of the flannel.

"Morning, Daddy," she muttered.

TS and The WOW

"Twila, after breakfast, let's get you some new clothes."

"New clothes? For real, Mom?" Twila had noticed some changes happening to her body and so had Adeline.

"It's time for some new clothes and a 'you know what," Adeline said with a whisper and passing her hands across her chest.

"You mean a bra?" Twila whispered back. It was a mother-daughter time and George and Theron did their best to step aside of that conversation.

The wind blew as the rains began to fall, pelting Theron's face where he had stood on the pond bank, watching the droplets of water as they bounced on the pond's static surface.

"I can't tell if the droplets bounce or if water is leaping from the pond into the air to catch them." Such things were always perplexing to Theron. The occasional water droplet, joined with millions of its brothers, and Theron's clothes were becoming soaked. Lightning flashed across the sky and thunder rocked the air.

"That was close," he said aloud. Theron was too far from home to return without slipping and sliding in the mud while racing bolts of lightning. Without thought, he raced toward the cave, jumping sagebrush and leaping from lava rock to lava rock as he traversed the hillside. Another strike of lightning split a tree atop the lava bluff, accompanied by clamorous thunder, ringing loud and loll-bashing down the hillside as if it were in pursuit of Theron himself. He bounced, running like a rabbit being chased by a fox, right to the mouth of the cave.

"All roads lead back here," he thought. The water showered the rocks, creating a mini waterfall that spouted water out into tiny streams, washing off the rocks and on down the hillside. Theron ducked past a waterspout and on into the cave where it was dry to await the end of the downpour. After a few minutes, the rain ceased and Theron emerged from the cave into the fresh breeze and the damp earth.

"That's the weather in the desert. If you don't like it wait five minutes." There was only a brief stop to check the sky "Looks like I can make it home." Off he went.

Theron's Red Ball Jets left a defined shoe pattern in the soft wet soil right alongside a track that had not been there before the rain and went unnoticed by Theron. The tracks were deep and nearly three times the size of Theron's prints. The giant tracks were made with bare feet. Something extremely large was just moments ahead of Theron, or had it been chasing him? "What's this?" Theron wondered, discovering the track as his foot slid inside one of the giant footprints. Theron turned about and started to follow the monstrous prints. They led into the lava flow where they disappeared. "Too rocky here, wonder where they go?" Theron thought. Climbing the lava flow was always a

TS and The WOW

game to Theron. He had to wind around on the rocks, creating a pathway over the stones. The lava had been cast from the bowels of the earth thousands of years ago to form the Black Ridge Mountain. Atop the lava flow, stood three trees that seemed to Theron to have been in that spot forever. The tree that had been hit by lightning still smoldered from the strike. It had split it clean in two. A pungent smell of wet burning cedar emanated from the broken tree. The remaining trees stood like the masts on a ship. For a moment, Theron could see himself out on the ocean, sailing to the Panama Canal, when a fresh piece of bark that had been stripped from a tree caught his eye. One tree's red inner skin was exposed. It looked dry underneath where all else was soaked by the rain. "He'd been here!" Theron noticed a footprint under the tree. It was same as the others he had seen near the entrance to the cave.

"Better watch yourself," a voice inside his head called out warning him. He responded, feeling his spot of red hair weaving and unweaving itself. A bubble swept past, engulfing him inside it, as he looked for whatever it was that had made the footprints.

"I'm scared. Why am I not running away? This could be a trick." Thoughts ran rampant through his head. Theron now stood in a valley of a mountain range different from home. "Not again!" he declared.

The foliage dressed the valley in colors of the brightest reds and vibrant purples. The grass, if you could call it grass, was slick like a watermelon rind and carried the zigzag pattern throughout the lowlands. The grass covered the countryside, alternating with light oranges and soft blues.

Tracks and more tracks. Theron had discovered the trail of the big footprints. The grass was squashed, imprinted with those giant footprints, leaving an easy trail to follow into the purple woods. But was he following them or being led into a trap? That thought never crossed his mind.

"Should I follow the trail or should I turn and find the bubble to get home?" His question hung in the air for just a moment until his thoughts changed. "Curiosity killed the cat, at least according to Mom," Theron thought.

"Glad I'm not a cat so I should be fine." Adeline had also said that. Curiosity lived in Theron, it was true.

A flash of pinkish-purple light illuminated the forest, exposing several bazaar dwellings near where the trees met the watermelon grass. Theron just had to see who or what lived there.

"Mom would skin me if she knew what I was about to do." He heard his own words and was amazed how they seemed to hang in the thick air. His words didn't fade. They popped like soap bubbles in the air here.

"Hey, you're a monkey's uncle," he called out, just to watch the air bubbles form and then see them burst after hanging suspended in front of him for a moment. "That's enough of that," he said still aloud. Bubbles popped.

It was time to either head to the structures or head for home. When he walked in the watermelon grass, it sloshed under his weight. It didn't break through but left a perfect imprint of the bottom of his Red Ball Jets in the orange and blue zigzags. The air here was cool, almost to the point of bringing his breath to steam, but the air was too thick to create steam. Besides that, he didn't feel cold.

The forest had seemed so far away when he started his trek across the watermelon grass to the row of cottages. Again the pinkish-purple light showered the sky with brilliance, seemingly like the northern lights that Theron had heard of in school. Theron stood in front of the row of buildings. There was no street, no traveled roads, and nothing to suggest that life traveled in and out of them except the footprints that were smashed into the groundcover. The cottages were dull in appearance compared to the surroundings. Gray seemed to be their only color, lifeless, like an unvisited barn or a stand of dead trees in a growing forest.

"Why am I not nervous?" Theron wondered. His red hair had stayed in the same spot and not moved, stiff, as if it had been sprayed with Adeline's Aquanet hairspray. The trail on the melon grass ended in front of the second building.

TS and The WOW

"What now?" he questioned aloud then put his hand over his mouth hoping not to be discovered. But it was too late. His words were already hanging in the air. He tried to pop them and shut off their sound before someone or something discovered him there. The buildings seemed to be single residences, but were well over normal human size. Large double doors, woven from once purple forest trees, fit snuggly together, showing just a sliver of light from under the threshold. Good judgment told him that it was time for his retreat to his own world, but he had to see what was behind door number one. He knocked, first brushing his knuckles timidly on the tall doors and then tapping them with the zeal of a door-to-door salesman. His knock hung in the air, bursting from their bubbles the same as his words had done. There was a clamor inside with the sound of things sliding on the floor and the tramping of feet. Theron's red hair stood at attention, not moving and not warning him of danger. The door opened just enough for a single, enormous, hair-covered hand with four fingers and a thumb to emerge. It held the door's edge, pulling it aside. Theron's eyes bulged and his heart thumped fast. First, it was faster than a rabbit being chased by a coyote and then, not at all. Blood drained from his face, leaving him pale. There he stood. It was real. He was real, with a voice as deep and fitted to the immense body as was the doorway in which it stood.

"Salter, we're expecting you." The deep words grew much bigger bubbles than did Theron's, each one bursting near

TS and The WOW

Theron's face. Hearing his name brought even more shock, raising the short hairs on the back of his neck. How did this creature know his name? However, his red spot of hair was not brought to dance in the least. This was strange. Usually it was first to become activated as an early warning.

"Perhaps I shouldn't be frightened," Theron thought, careful not to utter words that might give him away. In the open doorway now stood an English-speaking giant, a big-foot, a Yeti or a thousand names that have come about from a legend.

"Enter, young one."

Theron had experienced a great deal in a short time as a balancer, but this was a live dream.

"What should I have expected?" He questioned in his own mind. "This will be okay," he thought, entering the house and patting down the red spot of hair. His heart still pounded with excitement, pumping blood back to his pale face.

"You're a Yeti."

"And you're a human."

"You can talk."

"Yes. We speak your language, and others, Theron."

"What do, I mean how do you know my name?"

"I led you here. We need your help."

TS and The WOW

"My help?" Theron questioned. What help could he give to someone as large as this Yeti?

"I am Samja," he said, closing the massive door behind them. "Theron, my people were not Yetis or Bigfoot as the people of earth world called them. We are the Jmanna. Translated, we're men of the forest." Samja stood nearly eight feet tall and was covered from head to foot with a glistening white fur. Theron thought that Samja must never need a coat in the winter. Yet he wondered how he stayed cool in the summer. His hands were just like Theron's but were covered on the back by the same white hair that covered the remainder of his body. When Theron had become comfortable, Samja told him about the control his people had gained. They could cause a bubble anywhere, anytime they wanted. That was how they could travel into Theron's world with such ease. All they had to do was envision the bubble and one would appear.

"That sounds just like what Twi and I do," Theron thought, recognizing the similarities. When Theron thought about the bubble, he saw the very molecules that made the bubble in his mind. He would change the number of electrons and neutrons to make the elements become something new, kind of like changing water into wine he supposed.

"But there is a problem. Something has changed and some of us can no longer open entrances to the forest."

TS and The WOW

The Jmanna are losing the ability to enter other worlds and balance their forests. Many Jmanna were trapped in other worlds with no way of getting home, no way but with the help of, Samja and Theron. Even Samja was losing his power to travel to other worlds and he was the most accomplished traveler among the Jmanna.

"So are there Jmanna in my world?" Theron inquired.

"Many care for the forests of your world. There are Jmanna in each world. You see, we are caretakers of every world's forest."

"So Jmanna are real Smokey the Bears."

"I have heard Jmanna called bears, perhaps you see us as smoking bears. All Jmanna will soon be caught in one world or another if you do not help."

Theron was a balancer and it was his calling to set things straight. The door was, heavy and hard for Theron to push open. It opened just enough for Theron to exit into the setting of the orange sun. The sun was passing into the distant lavender forest making the trees glow looking ready to burst and to change into something from a dream of heaven.

"Wait young one," Samja called after him as he pushed the door fully open. The enormous hairy figure lumbered his steps toward, Theron.

TS and The WOW

"The door opened further and a small group of Jmanna followed Samja. Most of them were the same stature as was Samja but one of the group was not. She was near the same height as Theron. Coja made no effort to avoid Theron. Walking right up to him, she put both arms around him and hugged until he grunted from the tightness. Her flowing white hair was curled into ringlets, showing a mother's loving care. So, which one of these creatures was her mom? Theron had no idea. They all looked so similar to him that it was impossible to tell them apart. Samja put his hands on Coja's shoulders to move her back from Theron. The Jmanna, had been watching Theron since he was born. They had known of the earth child that would be the balancer in his world and they knew that he would be the one to help them when the time came. It was prophesied that this day would come, and the Jmanna would be bound in their world. Even the youngest among them had feared this day. To them, Theron Salter was a name that would bring their families home to them. To the cheers of the crowd, Samja showed Theron how to return to the spot where he had traveled to reach the earth world.

"Here young one, go to your home here. But you must bring them home. Remember them."

Theron's red spot of hair twirled like the blades of a chopper in Vietnam, readying to carry the wounded home. When the bubble formed in front of him, his eyesight allowed him to see into his world, and the other five worlds. He had discovered

TS and The WOW

that bubbles were always there, but it took concentration to access them. It was just the changing of one element into another that brought a bubble into a visible existence. He remembered being in Sunday school and hearing of the story about the 'Good Samaritan.' That was what he had to be to help these beings, a 'Good Samaritan.'

"I kind of like that," he thought. Theron thought that any one of them could crush him with just one hand. He felt a good spirit, and a safe feeling from them.

Theron's red hair, seemed to bring the bubble into vision, or was it just his gift of being in the right place, at the wrong timethat did the job? Theron looked back at the Jmanna, then turned and stepped through the bubble onto the black lava ridge of his desert home.

He was home, no longer in the valleys of the lavender mountains or the watermelon grass, everything here was normal. The earth was now dried, only slightly damp from the rain that had fallen earlier.

"Theron, where are you?" Called Twila. She was searching for her brother.

"Here! I'm here!" he called, anxious to tell her about the Jmanna.

"Twila look at this."

"What is it?"

Theron pointed at the imprint of the Samja foot he had left behind.

"It's a Bigfoot."

"That's pretty obvious, it's a very big foot."

"No, blockhead, it's a Yeti."

"Aren't they from Nepal?"

"Not really. They are from the valley of the purple mountains, another world!"

"So how do you know that?"

"They need our help."

"And how do the two of us, help a bunch of giant Yeti?"

He explained the whole story to her as they walked home. They arrived just as the golden sun of their world closed its day resting behind the Blue Mountains in the distance.

It was morning, and in a hurry the ritual of breakfast passed.

"Come on Theron, we have to find some Bigfeet."

"I know," he said, while shoving a third biscuit into his pocket for later. This reminded Theron of the round-up, but this time it was Jmanna he was in search of and not horses. They had spent the day in the forests of three worlds, only delivering home

TS and The WOW

six Jmanna. Many more were lost. Without communication or a pathway home they were stranded, same as the, Swiss Family Robinson. Not lost on the islands of the seas, but in worlds where they were only visitors.

A week passed with Theron and Twila diligently carrying out their mission. One by one, the locations where the Jmanna were stranded were discovered, until there were only a handful of refugees left unrevealed. It would prove to be more than they had bargained for when Samja announced that his two brothers were lost in the world of the great desert, in the dying forest of Eltergo. A shiver ran up Theron's spine at the mere mention of Eltergo. "Did he have to go there to rescue the Jmanna?" he questioned himself with his head in his hands. The answer was obvious. He was bound to this man's job even though he was a mere boy. Reluctantly, the twins prepared for the last stage of operation, "Smokey goes home," as Twila had dubbed it.

What fears did Theron have? They were fears of being caught by a mad wolf man, his nemeses, the wolf on the wall. "Why had Arils left them to do everything all alone? After all we are just kids," Twila thought, not mentioning her frustration to her brother. In her sight, Theron was never afraid. He was the strong one.

With the sun's touch on the shoulders of the mountains the rooster crowed and a new day began. Theron was already finishing his chores, when the Winter Tree rustled his leaves in a

TS and The WOW

panic. Theron twisted his body in stride toward the noise. His egg basket swung in his hand, nearly pouring the eggs on the ground. There at the edge of the yard stood Samja. He was being greeted by the Winter Tree.

"He acts like he knows you," Theron said.

"Yes, he remembers."

Just "what" the Winter Tree remembered was unclear, and never told to Theron. He just had to continue to wonder. Samja explained that he had been in the Earth forest and he himself could not get home.

A rather strange sight crossed the vacant field neighboring the Salter property. A tall hairy humanoid and a pair of children one on either side of the bear-like figure disappeared over the wash bank into the wash bottom hidden from view. They stood in front of the cave with a face. Theron focused his thoughts, gathering the molecules into a bubble. As he did the air took on a smell of old dirt, a waterless dead smell.

"Is this how we will smell when the wolf kills us?" Theron thought. Twila's eyes flickered with concern of the same thing when Twila's eyes connected her thoughts through Theron's eyes. The dry desert air sucked the breath from their open mouths, as they entered the lonely, desolate, world, wilting their enthusiasm.

"Samja, which way do we go?"

TS and The WOW

"To the drying forest." He pointed to the hillside that was covered with the remains of a once glorious forest. This was the same forest where Mebo and Theron had escaped the green trolls. Every moment was filled with heads turning to discover the origin of the slightest sound. The dead limbs and trunks of the trees hid the twins, and Samja's tall frame became one with the forest blending nearly unseen. Deep in the forest, was a single spot where it seemed to flourish. Here things were green, and put off a scent of sweet floral. Water flowed here.

"Is this where they are?"

"Yes, this is their place, Miss."

Yet, where were the two Jmanna? Samja threw his head back listing to something.

"What was that?" Theron asked, watching his reaction.

"Was that them?" Twila's hopeful look told the story of her fear of being in this place. A long low howl rolled over the dead land and into the oasis. No one had to ask what that was.

"Let's get out of here." Twila tugged on Theron's arm. Tree limbs crashed, as they were broken, and the dead dirt spun into the air. The creature that ran through the forest was being pursued, pursued by Theron's nightmare. Samja blended into the forest. Twila and Theron attempted the same thing crouching in the green bushes. The fugitive broke into the oasis. It was a single

Jmanna. Samja appeared in front of him, releasing his hiding place.

"Now, Theron, we need a bubble to get out of here."

Theron crawled from under the bush ready to open a window. The two Jmanna stood shoulder-to-shoulder anticipating the bubble opening while watching the trail for the appearance of the wolf. Twila waited under the greenery, while Theron's mind pitched the molecules changing and the bubble opening. Then he heard the noise that haunted him. The wolf howled and growled commanding that the forest be set on fire. Theron lost his vision of the bubble when the trail filled with an enormous troll. He was sure the wolf would be next. The Jmanna blended into the foliage while Theron slid under the green bush where his sister had waited.

"Did he see me?" he whispered, fearing he was caught. The troll turned around on the trail, scratched his bottom and sucked the drool back into his mouth. The fire was burning the dry trees, belching, crackling, and spewing smoke into the already hot air. The troll walked on until he reached the green spot in the dead forest. Sitting down, he waited for something. His bulky body settled into the bushes just next to Twila. A hand and arm rested so close to her that she had to turn her head so as not to breathe on it.

TS and The WOW

The fire popped and crackled. Smoke filled the air. The smoke that smelled of dead carcasses was making both Twila and Theron gag. The red spot of hair on Twila's head wormed its way through the underbrush where she lay like it was a periscope. She tugged the worming hair back not wanting the troll to see it. Theron's hair spun but stayed close to his head. It was the warning of the red hair that brought his thoughts back to the opening of a bubble.

Theron slid himself back out from the undergrowth and when the troll looked the other direction he concealed his body behind a live tree that had smoke blowing around it. Trees exploded, bursting from the inside out where the remnants of life still existed in them. The bubble opened right smack in front of the giant troll. Surprised, he sprung to his feet watching through the bubble for whatever was about to enter into his waiting arms. Theron motioned to Twila to jump through the opening. She hesitated, afraid that the troll would capture her.

"Go now!" Theron yelled at her. As he did, the troll turned his attention toward Theron who was clouded in a shroud of smoke. It was just a voice that commanded him the troll thought. Fearing the wrath of his master whose voice he thought had spoken, he leaped into the bubble. Both Jmanna appeared from their covering and followed after him.

"Go, Twi, get out of here!" Theron struggled to keep his thoughts on the bubble and its creation. Twila scurried like a

TS and The WOW

rabbit from under the bushes where she had hidden and leaped through the bubble. Theron was next and last to retreat. He had watched for the third Jmanna to show himself, but that wasn't going to happen. He could hear the creatures coming toward the green spot where an open bubble could lead all of them into another world. The bubble was about to close, when he stepped one foot through. As he did, something hit him, spinning him about and tossing him through the opening. He tumbled into the watermelon grass, his bottom imprinting a smile in the foliage. Twila was safe standing beside Coja and several other Jmanna.

"Where is the troll?" Theron asked, wary of the monster. Just before the bubble closed his question was answered. He heard, "oof, oof," and saw the troll bouncing on his butt into the puddle of the oasis splashing water on to the flaming trees. Smoke mixed with steam belched through the bubble just as it closed.

The Winter Tree was up to something. He had been in the corner of the yard, not with all the other trees like usual. When the family talked about the Winter Tree they used the words strange, unusual and freaky. With regularity they used the word bizarre. For example, when cats flew from his branches without warning it was described as "a bizarre happening," and when he locked Theron in the chicken coop it was "freaky" and nearly always "strange." The Winter Tree was not predictable. He

TS and The WOW

had a mind of his own. Yes this tree had a mind, and a capable one at that. He was playful and fun loving, but always protective over his family, the Salter's.

"According to the astronauts what shape is the earth?" asked Mr. Prince.

"Round," called out Larry, a boy in their class.

"Not quite."

Twila raised her hand. Mr. Prince pointed his hand toward Twila indicating that she should answer.

"Egg shaped."

"That's right, but not exactly like an egg, just a little oblong."

They had started a new school year. Twila liked school. She was smart, and could memorize anything. She was master of a photographic memory. Theron however, was another story. School was hard for him. He had to struggle just to spell with the right letters. To him it made no sense having just one way to spell a word. After all, to was spelled three ways. There was to, too and two. Now that made no sense to him. Theron thought it was more fun to work in the shop with his dad, or to draw, or paint something. Art was his passion.

"You will be a starving artist." Those words rang in Theron's head every time he thought that he would become an artist.

Three ships on the bulletin board sailed for the new world. Of course, the Santa-Maria was Theron's work. The other two looked like they were sinking he thought. The yardstick smacked Theron's desk.

"I asked you a question young man!"

The sounds shook Theron from his daydream, without an answer to the question, a question he had not heard. Mr. Prince repeated the question.

"So what did the world believe about the earth when Columbus set sail?"

"That it was flat."

"That's correct. People thought that there were sea monsters, also that you would fall off the edge of the world, if you sailed too far."

Theron snickered at the comment. He felt a little like Columbus, plus he had seen those sea monsters first hand. Later in the day Mr. Prince had arranged an activity. Everyone would plant seeds and then watch to see the seeds germinate, sprout, and grow into plants. Theron kind of liked that idea. His mom grew a garden every spring and he liked watching the new plants grow. It would be interesting to watch the seeds grow. The class

TS and The WOW

had removed the tops from milk cartons, leaving a square wax-coated box. The box was filled with soil, where the seeds could germinate. Twila pushed a pencil into the soil, and then placed a few flower seeds into the cavity, brushed the dirt in to the hole and poured a sprinkle of water over the soil. Twila's red spot of hair had not made any movement in weeks, but today it tugged at her head. Something was not right. She sensed something unusual about the seeds that Theron was planting in his five grow boxes.

"Theron, what kinds of seeds did you plant?" Arthur asked. Theron smiled and didn't reply to Arthur's question.

"What did you plant?" Theron asked.

Arthur had planted beans, Danny squash, and Larry had planted watermelon in all of his five containers. School ended with a blaring ring of the final bell of the day.

"Put your things away and don't forget your homework," announced Mr. Prince as his parting blow for the day. At least that was what it felt like to Theron.

"Homework," Theron muttered under his breath. He felt that since school had started this year, that was all he did, more homework. Twila didn't mind homework. It was easy for her.

"Theron, is your homework done?"

"Almost, Mom." Theron sat next to his books, one closed and the other open to a group of fractions. Twila leaned over his shoulder.

"Just divide the bottom into the top."

"That's all you have to do? I'm done."

"Good, its bedtime you two."

School started with the ring of the bell. There they were again dragging off their coats, to hang them on the hooks in the hall. Each child filed into the classroom where Mr. Prince already stood. He was next to the spot where the cartons had all been placed. The window was covered with green plants. The plants had lifted all but four of the milk cartons into their limbs. The boxes were suspended in the growing branches, where they dangled like Christmas tree ornaments. The four cartons that were not lifted were right where Theron's cartons had been. Three trees had sprouted from the cartons and were taking over all the sunlight coming in the windows. The fourth carton held a single cactus, which squirted water onto the roots of the other three. The water seemed to be like miracle grow to the plants. As water doused the roots, the plants grew.

"Something in this window is not the way it was when we left last night!" Mr. Prince said, directing attention toward the row of cartons. The plants were now three feet tall, and the cactus was rocking from side to side trying to loosen the soil on its roots.

"Everyone out quickly now!" Mr. Prince said urgently. He called out, "Theron Salter!" as he was about to exit the door with the other children.

The red hair quivered and then dropped to a flattened mass on his head. Theron placed his homework on his desk and preceded his trek to the window where Mr. Prince stood with his hands on his hips, still watching the amazing growth rate of the new plants.

"Can you explain this mess, young man?"

Theron had little time to answer and even a shorter amount of time to see for himself what he was talking about. He quickly scanned the plants and knew he had to come up with something quick.

"It's a miracle!"

"Clean up your mess, young man!" He shrieked, waving a finger. "Detention after school, young man," He said, nodding his head and twisting his lips together in satisfaction, smacking like he had finished another sandwich or chunk of cake.

Mr. Prince was not certain how Theron had gotten into the school overnight, but he had somehow, he was sure of that. His plants had to be one of his jokes.

TS and The WOW

Twila watched her brother once more take the punishment for something he could not explain. She helped him stand up the plants and clean up the mess that was left.

"The Winter Tree will like the company," Twila said as they carried the plants home. But it was anything but joyous when Theron placed the plants in the backyard. Theron turned around for just a second leaving his back to the Winter Tree. When he turned back around the Winter Tree had planted his trunk and roots next to the holes Theron was digging.

"Now what do you want?" Theron dug the holes to plant the trees thinking that it was like family to the Winter Tree. Theron was sure that he must be lonely.

"Theron come in here for a minute," Adeline called from the back porch. Theron responded and poked the shovel in a standing position, in the pile of fresh soil. Theron finished his dinner and then returned with Twila to plant his new trees and cactus.

"Where did you put the trees?" Twila questioned, seeing only a cactus remaining. The holes that Theron had dug were filled in and the Winter Tree had retreated to the edge of the yard where the trees all stood in a row.

"What the heck are you doing?" Theron stared at the tree then scolded him knowing full well that he understood every word. No sign of the little trees were ever found, but the cactus

TS and The WOW

became popular with the other plants in the yard, as he expelled water on the dry ones whenever it was needed.

CHAPTER 18

The Traveling Coin and Whisked Away

The Boy scouts pitched their tents in the Little Pine Canyon next to the stream. Its trickling babble was barely heard above the sounds of clanking tent poles and the arguing about how the four tents were to be set up. Theron felt a little out of place being a first year scout, or a 'tenderfoot' as it is called.

"You get some wood for the campfire," one of the older scouts commanded Theron. The older boys seemed to be in charge and Theron was relegated to taking orders. This was okay because he had chosen to follow the order to gather the wood for the campfire, which left him on his own, while the others attempted to set up camp. The lifeless gray sagebrush stumps seemed to be the most ready supply of wood. Theron's woodpile was quickly growing, however, the more it grew the farther upstream he had to walk to fill his arms. He didn't mind this because the greater the distance from camp the sharper the pleasant sounds of the brook became. Small frogs croaked, birds whistled and even a chipmunk whirred with chatter.

TS and The WOW

"You're pretty cool," Theron said out loud, and the chipmunk stopped his chatter for a few seconds. The wood was stacked and the camp was set. When night came to the camp it was a Boy Scout custom to sit around the fire and tell stories. Stories that brought the fear, that made a chill go up your spine, and raise the little hairs on the back of your neck.

"No one really likes this feeling, do they?" Theron thought, knowing he could tell a story or two that would frighten everyone. Then from the darkness rose a laugh, deep and gravely and a cacophony of terror spread on the troop. The laugh was without form, without parts. Fear gripped the boys in sudden silence. Sticks stirring the coals in the fire were drawn back as a weak protection.

"Where is that coming from?" The Scout leader Mr. Hunt asked, breaking the silence that had followed the laugh. The boys huddled closer together by the two men that lead them.

"Danny, is that you?" Roger called out into the darkness.

Theron watched the trees from up the creek, where the light of a gas lantern faded. Danny burst from the darkness with another blood-curdling scream. All the boys cowered behind the leaders.

"Got ya!" Danny said, laughing at his friends cowering behind Mr. Hunt. Theron was relived. Nothing to worry about, he thought.

TS and The WOW

Then the coin in his pocket began to twist and then turn as if responding to a call from a force outside this world. Theron's pocket bounced as if it had a heartbeat, pulsing faster and faster while, Theron struggled to remove the coin from his pocket. When he plucked the coin from his pocket his hand danced in the air led by the rhythm already focused inside the coin.

"Man, what are you doing?" Danny was quick to ask.

"Looks like he is dancing," Jeff interjected.

Theron pressed his arm down to his side, still bouncing just a little against his body.

"That was real cool, you're such a bozo Salter," Danny said, thinking he was witty.

Theron had started collecting a coin from each place he had visited throughout his whole life and this one came from the time he visited the world of Arlo McFarland. He had found it hiding in a corner of the blockhouse where he and Mebo met. The coin twisted sharply, leaping from the boy's hand. It made a plink sound as it hit the rocky ground. Bouncing once, then twice more, it rolled to a stop standing on its edge. Each of the two faces swelled and protruded off the sides of the coin. Theron stepped back away from his prized coin, no longer wanting to pick it up until he knew for sure it would find its way back into his pocket. It had nearly ripped a hole in his pants. He looked about to see if anyone had seen what had just happened. Luckily no one had. He was glad to see that by some miracle no one had noticed the coin.

"You're such a weirdo Theron."

"Yeah, what is it with the hand thing?"

Three of the boys mocked the motion of Theron's hand. Theron was accustomed to being teased. He ignored his tormenters and tried to keep his eye on the troublemaking double-faced coin. Theron wondered how the coin could be standing on its edge right there on the rock where it had rolled.

"Theron, where did you go?" Arthur called. He was one of the boy scouts that didn't fit in either. No one except Theron treated him like he was important. Theron had crept into the shadows, away from the crowd and the light of the fire where the coin had landed. He stepped his Red Ball Jet on the coin, hoping it would not start spinning again. The coin was having none of that. It tossed him into the air. Theron landed on his back in the bushes.

All this had not gone unnoticed by the other scouts, who were snickering.

"Smooth move Exlax, see ya next fall."

"Danny, you think you're so funny," Theron thought.

TS and The WOW

"Lay off Danny. That's enough." Mr. Hunt's eyes pierced the boy. Danny's glowing delight disappeared. He ducked his head to hide from Mr. Hunt's glare. Theron felt stupid, but watched as the double-faced coin sprouted legs and ran to hide. Arthur had walked to Theron and never noticed the coin.

"You okay?" He asked, reaching a hand down to pull his friend from the ground. Theron tried to snatch the coin from its place behind the rock, but it ran to a crack and wedged itself in the crevice. Theron reached into to where it was wedged. He tugged at it, but the coin braced itself and held its place.

"It's stuck," Theron almost said out loud, but kept it in his thoughts. The coin had a mind of its own and was not coming out. "For now, you will have to stay right where you are!" This he did say out loud. Arthur had followed him and would never understand what was happening. This was an everyday event in Theron's life, however, the "ordinaries" as Twila called them would be freaked.

"Did you lose something?" asked Arthur. Theron smiled widely and said,

"Just lost a coin, but its okay. Let's go back to camp." And with that he left the coin in the dark crevice for the night.

Flashlights flickered in the hands of the other boys who were coming over to see what was going on. Not able to easily explain the coin or its ending up in the dirt, Theron directed

TS and The WOW

Arthur back toward the lights and began gathering a bundle of brush.

"Hey you guys, Mr. Hunt said that it's time to grub," announced a boy whose face hid behind one of the lights.

"I can get that stupid coin in the morning," Theron thought.

The sagebrush gave off a smell that wrapped itself around the potatoes and chicken being cooked in the deep black pots. Everyone's plates were filled with the western gourmet food. Theron ate his food like it was on fire, finishing ahead of everyone.

"Got to see a man about a horse," he said and slipped away to the rocky hiding place and the double-faced coin.

"Come out of there," he coaxed. The coin braced its swollen sides even tighter in the crack. Theron shoved a stout stick into the crack.

"Suck it in," he commanded the faces on the coin. The rock moved and the stick struck the coin. It popped free flying through the air and into the creek, just making a tiny splash. The coin swirled, twisting and turning, seemingly holding its breath. The coin landed on its tiny legs at the bottom and quickly turned sideways into the current so it wouldn't be swept away. Theron rushed to the water ready to scoop the coin out.

TS and The WOW

"Where did it land? I can't see it." The boy's arm thrust into the water about where he thought the coin had fallen. His fingers walked the bottom of the stream over the sandy granules on to the water-rounded rocks hoping to feel the coin. "I wonder if he can drown?" he thought and suddenly he touched the runaway.

"Come to papa." Theron clamped his thumb and forefinger over the coin. "Got ya." The coin gasped for air as it came from the water. Theron laughed as he looked at the coin that was hugging his finger, his legs dangling in the air. Theron knelt with his hand stretched out like the great King Kong. The coin grasped his giant fingers and slung itself into his palm. Theron brought his treasure closer to his face and looked into the eye on the right side of the double-faced coin.

"So Mr. Trouble, what are you?" With a voice as tiny as was the coin its self sounded the reply.

"I'm just a lost coin."

"You might be lost, but I'm not," cried a voice from the other side of the coin. An argument ensued, one side of the coin arguing with the other side about who was lost and who was not. Theron laughed again and the left side of the coin kicked his thumb, obviously annoyed by him.

"Ouch, now what am I going to do with you?"

TS and The WOW

"We're just a coin and coins are just traded. We don't decide what to do."

"So do I trade you or keep you?"

"Yes sir, that's right. Trade or keep."

"So why were you running away?" Theron was full of questions. He had never had a conversation with a coin, or for that matter seen one run away from him and hide. "Well I did lose one in the stream when they were on the round up. He remembered, wondering if that coin could still hold its breath under the water. "So why were you running from me."

"We just landed there."

"You mean you weren't running away?"

"No. That's what all loose coins do, right?"

Theron had lost coins before. They always seemed to get lodged in corners or cracks just like the double-faced coin had just done.

"Do all coins have legs and talk where you come from?"

"Just the most valuable ones!" the left side of the coin said with an uppity snap wanting his value to be appreciated.

"That's the other side of the coin," the right side said. "I'm sorry master, lefty can be a nose in the air grouch. I think something got caught in his face when he was engraved."

TS and The WOW

"I'm not the pain, he is!"

"Yes you are, misprint face!"

"Come on you guys, don't argue."

"You argue with the female you." He meant Twila.

"He's right. I listen to you the entire time master," the left side of the coin said.

Arthur appeared from behind a pine tree and headed right toward Theron.

"Clam up you guys. Here comes an earth boy and he won't understand."

They argued for a moment more. Theron wrapped the fingers of his hand over them and muffled the last grumble from the left side.

"What you doin'?"

"Just lookin' at stuff."

"It's dark. What you lookin' at?"

"I'm not really lookin', more listenin'."

The frogs croaked and Arthur simply said, "Oh, I see."

The coin squirmed under the pressure of Theron's fingers as he squeezed a little too much.

"The leaders want us all back at camp."

TS and The WOW

Theron was as gentle as possible with the captured coin while walking back to camp, but heard continued complaints from the left side. First it was too tight and then Theron's palm felt sweaty.

"All right boys, I've got a tale to tell." Mr. Hunt was a cougar hunter and had spent many nights in the forest. The sun had gone down long ago as the boys grouped about the fire watching the sparks roll off the sagebrush logs and into the night sky. Theron thought that his real life was a better tale than any tall tale that might be invoked across the flames tonight. All he had to do was tell about the coin that rested inside his palm and the boys would want to hide, and the leaders would run away. He was sure of it.

"Mr. Hunt, tell your story", the boys coaxed. They wanted him to tell the stories about his grandfather. What could he do, but tell the story?

"Well, my grandfather was a mountain man, the last of his kind. He was a real cowboy with boots and suspenders, all the things that make a mountain man ready to survive in the forest. He loved to take me fishing and one time we went fishing on the old lake, up in the mountains, where the dam was nearly broken. Old cars had been put in to help strengthen the dam. Granddad wanted to fish over by the old cars. He said that he had seen the monster of the lake near there, and wanted to catch that monster fish. We went near the dam and the whole day I caught fish. My

TS and The WOW

Granddaddy never caught a single one. I was near my limit and still he had not caught a single fish. Then it happened. He hooked the monster and his pole bent into the water and his line whirred as the fish ran. After quite a battle he brought the fish near the boat and it was the monster he had sought out to catch. He told me to get the net. I reached for the net and as I did it touched his line and the fish threw the hook from its mouth. Well boys, mountain men are a strange breed and my Granddaddy was not going to let that fish escape. He tossed his hat in the bottom of the boat and pulled off his boots and then dove into the water. I saw bubbles in a line all the way to the old cars and then for the longest time there was nothing. I pulled off my shoes and was ready to try to rescue my Granddaddy. As I was about to dive in he came out of the water next to the boat."

"Do you have your knife?"

"I pulled out my pocketknife, opened it and handed it to him."

"He's holed up inside one of those old cars and I'm going to get him."

Granddaddy put the knife in his teeth and then swam down toward the cars. It was the same as before. I saw the bubble trail to the old cars and then for the longest time nothing. I was sure Granddaddy had perished. All of the sudden he came out of the water and tossed the knife into the bottom of the boat.

TS and The WOW

"Where is the fish?" I asked.

He climbed into the boat and then said, "The darn thing outsmarted me. When I got back down there he had rolled up all the windows and locked the door."

All the boys that hadn't heard the story were trying to figure out how the fish could lock the doors and roll up the windows. It was the other leader that explained that it was a tall tale. The double-faced coin grunted in Theron's hand, "Smart fish." There were stories about bears eating birds and then learning to fly and stories about a monster that lived in Little Pine Park where they were camped. At the end someone wanted the story about Cougar Joe, King of the mountain. The coin rested in Theron's hand quietly listening until it fell asleep, snoring with tinny disintegrating puffs that were just loud enough for Theron to hear. The tent was filled with boys from one end to the other and as you might expect, the talk went on long after the torches were turned out. The last moment Theron could remember he was talking and then peacefully dosed off in the middle of a sentence.

Morning was cold, but the sleeping bag couldn't stop the need to address nature's call. The fire was warm when Theron sat down next to it.

"Have a good rest son?" Mr. Hunt asked. He already had hotcakes and bacon already on the griddle. Theron just nodded

TS and The WOW

yes. He was glad that his leader had gotten up early to start the fire. Bacon sizzling in a skillet alongside some fresh eggs smelled wonderful.

"How great is this?" Theron said, taking in the smells and being next in line for breakfast.

"Eat 'em up guys."

"Are we going hiking when we're done?" Theron could see the ridge of the canyon and figured the stream bed was just asking to be hiked. Besides, he had heard a story of a hidden Spanish treasure somewhere in these parts.

The troop started up the canyon exploring as they walked through the woods. Theron carried the coin knowing that if he left the coin in the tent it would be wedged in some small crack where he may never find it. At first he carried it in the palm of his hand, but it was just too awkward to hold it tight all the time. He reminded himself that he wasn't going to put the coin back into his pocket, however, the compass pouch that was on his belt would work nicely. He could remove the compass leaving the flap tucked behind the case so the coin could see out. That worked for awhile, but the left side kept arguing with the right side. He wanted to see the countryside.

"Just turn around once in a while," Theron said to the right side. That stopped the chatter for awhile. The limestone canyon was growing narrower as the eight Scouts and their leaders walked upstream.

"Let's rest here, boys," called out the Leader. About that time the boy's packs hit the ground and they began to explore in all directions.

"Beware of snakes!"

"We will," one boy replied for all the Scouts. Theron was sure he would find Spanish gold, or a sword, or just one of those funky helmets with the razor on top like those that he had seen in history book drawings. Arthur had been at Theron's side the entire hike. It was beginning to annoy him trying to appease the coin and not be heard talking to it. The canyon walls were growing steeper and higher, seemingly impossible to climb. The distance from one side of the canyon to the other was now only about fifty yards. In the distance off twenty yards or so, Arthur and Theron had lost sight of the rest of the troop.

"Hey, look at this." Theron looked at the weird rock. It looked like a giant mushroom, but it was the other side of the rock that caught Arthur's interest. In the shadow of the rock was a tranquil pool of water shielded from the heat of the day under an outcropping. The pool seemed guarded by the mushroom sentinel. It was only a few minutes and the pool was filled with dusty, dirty boys.

TS and The WOW

"Cannon ball!" Arthur screamed, and then leaped from the mushroom rock into the water. The water was deep and soothing to the boys. Theron lodged the coin in a crack on the side of the high rocks so the left side could see as much of the action as the right side did. Where the water came into the pool was a waterfall from the cliff and it splashed across rocks green with moss and ferns that were unusual to the desert.

The boys rested in the sand, eating some food they brought from their packs and just talking about who had jumped the farthest from the rocks. Suddenly from under the water rose a giant bubble. The water in the pool exploded when the bubble broke the surface. It was followed by a second and a third, each releasing gas that had been trapped in the depths of the water for how long no one knew.

"Now that was a bad case of gas!" declared Arthur. They laughed, but the stench from the gasses lingered in the air. The boys scrambled to get away from the pond, their food, shirts, trousers, and shoes all left on the bank. As they scattered, the waters parted and a fourth gaseous balloon displaced its putrid contents. When it burst, water was sent rolling over the banks, consuming all their possessions in the wave, and then sucking them into the pond's void. The spot where the pond had been now contained something as old as time, something that brought fear to both man and boys, even terrifying the little coin who was still wedged in the rocky crevice. The coin was now eye to eye

TS and The WOW

with a yellow-eyed beast and shaking with fear that Theron might trade him to this thing. The left side of the coin closed its eye, then pushed tighter into the crack trying to wedge itself even more.

"Theron, what is that thing?" Arthur's voice was at a whisper and quivered as he spoke. Both young scouts hid behind the mushroom rock looking out.

"Why me?" Theron said, finding himself trapped in nothing but his wet underwear. He wanted to retrieve his clothes that floated on the water of the pond next to the great yellow-eyed beast.

"I wish Mr. Hunt were here." Arthur nearly cried when he said that. The scrawny pale-skinned boys rounded the mushroom rock ever so quietly. The displaced water now flooded the base of the rock nearly to their knees. Something brushed his leg swimming past also wanting to escape the creature. Theron could see the beast and worse than that, he could smell him. The yellow-eyed beast had wedged itself in the pond, wearing the bank like a band around its middle. The monster's long neck was exposed along with a head that seemed to be composed of nothing but teeth and those huge yellow eyes. The giant neck swung the head at Theron trying to take a bite. Fear regained its hold on Theron's heart. Arthur reached out from where he had concealed himself, inside the mushroom rock. He was in a cavity where both could retreat into comfortably.

TS and The WOW

"Salter! MacKay!" The Scout leaders were calling after the boys. A reply was a little awkward. Surely it would give away their hiding place.

"Theron, Art!" They continued to yell. How could they reply without chance of the creature finding them? Theron motioned to Arthur to stay where he was. Theron had something in mind, but he didn't want Arthur to mess him up. His fingertips felt the rough texture of the mushroom rock as they glided over it. He moved along to the side of the great yellow-eyed beast. Almost with surprise he saw the coin in the rock.

"Come and get me!" The insolent left side of the coin demanded. Theron put his finger to his mouth, hoping that he understood the human sign for shush up.

"Well what are you waiting for?" the coin blurted out. The yellowed-eyed beast sniffed through a hole in the top of his head. He was sniffing for the scent of something to eat. "From the look of his inflated rubber-like neck he was capable of eating a refrigerator or even something as big as a '57 T-bird with ease," Theron thought. The long porcupine-like hairs stuck straight into the air from the top of its head down its neck, each hair spilled with colors of purple, green and all shades in between.

"Awesome," Theron said under his breath. "Come on then, let go."

TS and The WOW

The coin was holding its place. Then it let go. Theron's red clump of hair had been warning him for some time that he had no business standing knee deep in the water in front of this throw back to the dinosaurs, but he wanted his trousers back. The great yellow-eyed beast had not noticed him but still sniffed, trying to smell something tasty. Theron reached out for the clothing that floated near him. First he fished out a pair of pants. This pair belonged to Arthur. A second scoop brought two things from the water, first an armload of water-soaked clothing and then the attention of the yellow-eyed beast.

"What do I do now?" Theron found himself climbing the limestone as fast as he could. The rubberneck swung its head after him. One eye watched behind him. The other searched for an escape.

"Come on, come on, concentrate," Theron told himself rushing for cover. The head swung against him toppling him from the limestone into the water below the mushroom rock. The momentum of the head swung past like a ball on a tether. Theron rolled to his knees in the puddle and hurried for the cavity in the rock where his friend still hid. The head came back, mouth open and teeth snapping. Theron ducked nearly to the ground, narrowly avoiding the open mouth that now looked like a bucket on a steam shovel.

"Hurry, hurry, get in here!" Arthur said as he reached one hand out to pull Theron into the hollow spot in the rock. As

TS and The WOW

Theron tucked his last body part into the hollow spot as the hungry, yellow-eyed beast pressed his ugly face to the opening. It snarled a hideous belch at the boys.

"Woo, that's some bad breath." Theron waved his hand in front of his nose just out of the reach of the yellow-eyed beast. The coin rolled free from between Theron's fingers, bounced on the rock and rolled into a crack. The left side squealed, and then wedged itself tight in the crack. Suddenly awake, the creature's quills became erect. His massive mouth opened and jabbed toward the boys inside the rock. They remained just out of the predator's reach.

"At least we got our clothes." Theron handed Arthur his shirt and trousers. Back to back they dressed while the yellow-eyed beast watched trying to figure out how to get his meal. They waited knowing that the monster had to get bored sometime. The huge head of the yellow-eyed beast began to wobble, the long balloon neck growing tired.

"Let's climb out the top. Maybe it won't notice." The mushroom rock had a hole on top and they went right out of it.

"Give me a leg up." Theron locked his fingers together and Arthur stepped into his palms. It was only a short climb from there and he was on top of the rock. Silently a rope landed on the rock coming from the cliff above. Arthur looked up to see Mr. Hunt grasp the other end of the rope. The man motioned for him to put the lasso loop around his waist. When he did he got the thumbs up from Mr. Hunt who pulled the rope. Arthur looked like a fish being reeled in as he disappeared over the hanging ledge. The wild yellow-eyed beast swung his head toward the escapee, snapping at his feet.

"This is my chance," Theron thought, excitedly dashing from the hiding place. Then he remembered the coin. He darted back to where it had lodged itself in the crack. He fell to his knees and retrieved the coin.

"Glad you found us," expressed the left side of the coin. Theron tucked it into his pocket, something he thought he would never do again. The body of the yellow-eyed beast broke the band of dirt around its middle to free it from the pond and lunged toward Theron. The bulky body landed on the dry ground with its webbed feet flailing and it's snapping teeth right at Theron's heels.

"Up here!" Arthur called, now standing next to Mr. Hunt. Theron frantically climbed the limestone rock, gripping it with both his hands and bare toes. Mr. Hunt leaned down to reach Theron's hand and yanked him upward to the top of the rock just out of reach of the monster. Together they climbed to the top ridge of the cliff. The monster was infuriated by the escape and tossed its body high into the air above the pond, releasing the rest of his body that had been below the surface. Arthur watched, tucked behind a tree as the animal pushed free. Water rushed

TS and The WOW

back into the cavity where the pond had been only partially refilling. The creature's head sniffed and snorted while the tongue of the amphibian spread a putrid slime all about.

"Never seen anything like that before. How about you boys?"

"Nope. What do you think it is? Arthur asked the adult. Theron remained silent having seen things similar, but Arlis had warned him not to say anything, at a time like this.

"Well, he can be the last one we ever see if we can push that off the cliff." Mr. Hunt pointed to the ledge just above them, having noticed a rock the size of a '52 Buick teetering on its edge.

"If we can get him back to the pond it will line up perfectly," Mr. Hunt said, calculating the point the rock would leave the cliff to where it might land.

"Hey, you monster!" Theron screamed to change the creature's intention of moving downstream away from the little pond.

"Hey, you ugly bugger, I mean you stupid!"

The head of the giant yellow-eyed beast turned to focus on the voice on top of the hill. The quills had jutted forward and wings were unfolding as the creature moved around toward the pond.

"It's now or never!" Mr. Hunt exclaimed. Theron, Arthur and Mr. Hunt all sat on the hillside behind the teetering rock. They placed their feet on the backside and pushed until their faces were red.

"Push like you never have before!" They grunted, using all the power they had inside. The rock quivered and then it began to move away from their feet. Moving down the hillside crushing everything in its path, the rock began to tumble end over end, mashing six-foot trees, whatever was in its path was devastated, cutting a trench in the hillside. The crashing sound of the rock suddenly disappeared, leaving the top of the cliff and becoming airborne while at the same time becoming silent. Mr. Hunt and Theron hurried to the canyon edge.

"Wa hoo! Direct hit," The man called out in satisfaction. The great yellow-eyed beast was smashed back into the bottom of the pond from where it had come. Like David who fought Goliath they had smote the giant with a single stone. This stone could have taken out a tank but it was still just one stone. The force of the impact cast dust and particles of stone into the air. When the air cleared, the giant yellow-eyed beast was gone. Forced back into the pond, bottling it like a cork and driving it back to where it came from. Theron and Arthur whooped and hollered all the way back to the creek bottom.

TS and The WOW

Twila had experienced the twin thing with her hair twisting and untwisting.

"Sometimes it was a pain to have a brother, especially one that was always in trouble," she thought. Her hair had stopped dancing, so Theron must be okay she surmised. Yet, she thought she should ask her dad who was working in his shop.

"Hey, how's my favorite daughter?"

"I'm your only daughter Dad!" She always smiled when he played with her in that way. George leaned over the workbench reaching for a tool as though it should just come to his hand. His nimble fingers grasped the screwdriver. Then he turned to the Boltiere ball and began to work on the lower base. Twila spun around on one foot trying to remember why she was visiting her father's shop. His shop was filled with inventions constructed from spare parts. Some worked, while others were total disasters and waiting to be reused in the next attempt at something amazing. The device that was the most interesting resided in the corner of the shop, seldom worked on and still unfinished. George called it a de-fragmental Modulator. Today he was working on it. It was suppose to be a doorway into another world. It looked like a doorframe with coils of copper tubing twisted around the opening. It had a hand riveted copper tank and several vacuum picture tubes all in a line behind the doorway. The seat that looked like a horn was the highlight.

TS and The WOW

"Oh, yeah, that's it!" Twila had remembered what she was doing in the shop. "Daddy, do you think Theron is okay?"

"Sure, honey. He's with good men. He's okay." That was all it took for her to feel okay about the hair twisting warning. After all it had stopped, no longer tugging. Twila sat on the horn of the de-fragmental Modulator. She called it the DFM. That was just easier for her. She had seen the machine when George turned it on. It sparked lighting and she supposed that the magnets that were all over it had something to do with that. It was cool to see the doorway spin the same way a gyro did, disappearing as it spun. George worked beneath a single floodlight focused into the heart of the great ball that was attached to the base of the machine.

"Hey Twila, would you hold this?" George handed Twila a glass tube that was twisted in a spiral. "Plug it in there," he said while pointing to a slot in the opening at the top of the ball. George had parts in both hands and a tool tucked against his chin. As she plugged the part into the prepared slot of the machine, the machine sparked and puffed a column of smoke into the top of the ball. The DFM began to whir. George spun around, placing the other parts into their appointed places. Lights came on and the whir turned into a chugging sound.

"Get down from there, Twila." George was not sure what might happen with his creation, so no chances with his baby girl. The machine glowed with intensity, first flashing and then

TS and The WOW

bursting beams of light into all corners of the workspace. For a moment Twila was blinded by the first strike of lighting. George had protected his eyes with welding goggles, neglecting the potential for Twila's eyes to be stabbed by the light from the rotating ball.

"Here, honey, put these on." He shielded her face from the intense light with his body while she slipped the visor over her eyes. "Now that's better," he said as her eyes adjusted first from the balls of light that seemed to hang in front of her, then to the blazing light from the ball that was captured in the purple shield of her new eye wear.

"That's awesome Daddy. What does it do?"

"Are you okay, girly bob Jones?" That was a pet name he had given his daughter. Twila's vision had settled and she was beginning to be all right.

"Sure, I'm okay." She was more curious than worried about her eyes. "So what is it?"

"I call it a de-fragmental modulator."

"I know that. What does a de-fragmental modulator do?"

"Well, for one thing it will burn white spots in your eyes."

"I know that too."

to another place, kind of like the radio does with sound."

TS and The WOW

"And like the TV does with a picture, right?"

"That's the idea. So we just place something in the portal space and then crank this lever." As he spoke he put a screwdriver on the portal and then pushed the lever. The screwdriver disappeared. Twila clapped her hands together delighted it had worked.

"Where did it go?"

"That's my problem. I can't figure that out. See, when I turn it off this happens." The whir of the machine ceased and the light fizzled inside the ball. For a moment, all their senses adjusted.

"Clunk. Ping." The screwdriver reappeared in the air above the platform and then fell to the portal platform. It shattered like it was made of glass. George tugged at his hair, frustrated that he could not figure out what was happening. The door opened and Adeline walked in.

"Are you guys ready for some supper?"

"I am," Twila replied while George stared off into space thinking of where he was going wrong.

That night Twila wondered where the screwdriver had gone and why it came back as glass. The house was quiet, the sun drooping on the horizon. Soon coyotes howled in a distant canyon.

TS and The WOW

"It's nice to hear familiar sounds," Twila thought. One of those sounds was music coming from the Lawrence Welk band on television when she entered the living room. To Twila, familiar sounds meant everything was okay. Twila was calm and peaceful as she crawled into her bed. She dosed off to sleep and began to dream. Her eyes fluttered into a deep sleep, dreaming of wonderful things. At first she saw Theron along with two of the other Scouts throwing rocks and skipping them on a tiny pond. Then in her dream a door opened into another world, which allowed something to creep into her dream. She couldn't see what had come in, but it felt large and raised the hair on the back of her neck. It came into her room first and then quickly escaped the house, expanding the walls in the hall with its body as it pounded its way outside. The monster traveled to where Theron and his Boy Scout brothers rested inside their tents. In her dream it chased after the Boy Scouts, her brother and their leaders. She was positive of the intent of the unseen animal. He wanted dinner. She shook, but fear trapped and bound her to her mattress. Fitfully she awoke, tossing aside her cover that had her snared.

"What was that all about?" she said out loud. One foot on the floor with her nightgown pulling tight at her knees, she sat on the edge of the bed in the darkness of the late night. For a moment she paused to take it all in. "Just a dream," she told herself.

TS and The WOW

Twila's eyes adjusted to the darkness and everything looked normal. Flushed with relief for the nightmare to be gone and her eyes to be normal, she sighed.

It was the wee hours of the morning just before sunrise when the Scout master's truck tires crunched the cinders in the driveway. The door slammed and Theron said goodbye. The front door opened with a creek and Theron entered the house, worn to a frazzle and with dust caked on his face from the ride in the back of an open pickup. He curled up on the floor of the living room amidst his dirty clothes and his rolled sleeping bag to sleep. The coin rolled out of the compass pouch into a circle until it dropped to Theron's side, not looking for any crack to hide in, just was as glad to be here as was Theron.

Saturday morning cartoons were playing on the TV when Theron finally awoke. Twila was glad to see him safe at home. She had been watching the cartoons for a couple of hours hoping that they would rouse her brother.

"Twila, come and help me!" George called. Together they went to the workshop. "Put on your glasses." George handed Twila a pair with darkened lenses. "You look like a movie star with your shades on."

She did look a little like a very young Grace Kelly. George threw the switch and the bolalliter ball sparked a few times, lighting inside the glass. Light intensified as the machine began to

TS and The WOW

whir. Parts made noises that Twila couldn't identify. It was fun to watch something her dad made, work. George held a screwdriver in his hand, adjusting something. As he did so, first one of the noises dampened and then the others, one by one until they were all finally gone. Only a pulsing whir was left coming from the bolalliter ball.

"That's better."

"You're going to do it this time, Dad."

"Now hold this up while I attach it." George handed her a ball that contained a homemade gyro. Its stem had four holes in it that lined up with four holes on top of the bracket above the bolalliter ball. Without notice or being fully connected, the new ball lit.

"Looks like it's going to work."

"Should I turn it off, Dad?" Twila received a nod and turned off the switch. As she did, the machine's whir ceased and the light in the balls disappeared, sparking no more. The mounting screws were tightened to finalize the position of the gyro ball.

"Toss the switch, sweetems."

Twila threw the switch. A spark of light drove the gyro into a spin. It grew in speed, faster and faster. As it did, a gate opened on a box at the back side of the machine. Through the opening of the gate there was cast an intense light, which passed

TS and The WOW

a set of lenses and then cast a moving picture on the wall of the workshop. It was like looking in someone's window. Twila recognized the window. It was Mrs. Sweeny's. She was dancing with her son. She was teaching him how to dance. What a sight! The enormous lady moved with grace, but the boy looked uncomfortable at her feet and moved like a duck being chased across the yard by a dog. George was surprised that it had worked.

"It's doing it! It's workin'!" he said.

Twila giggled at her classmate's predicament. George turned a dial on the side of the machine and the Sweeny's were gone and a new picture appeared on the wall. For a moment it was Klin and Arlis Alger. His image only fluttered in and then went out. Image after image appeared on the wall, first the Hershey's and then the Tiltons. People from all over town were right there on the wall. The horses in the corral ran across the picture that was becoming more and more sharp. The image was tuned, appearing that it was not an image at all, but a window in which the father and daughter were watching life as it was going on through their town. One of the horses snorted, spraying snot all over Twila.

"Ew, that's real!"

"It can't be real. It's just an image." George reached toward the window, apprehensive but forcing his hand to search

TS and The WOW

around for the wall. His fingertips touched the snout of the horse that had snorted on Twila. George jumped back and started to shut off the machine. The image changed to Theron and Adeline in the house.

"Dad, how did you do that?" Theron called. Fearful, George still tried to shut of the machine when its focus drew in on George, Twila and the machine. Shockingly, they were face to face with themselves. George moved the controller as far the other direction as he could. A wind blew through the window drawing an unnatural gale of wind inside the workshop. It blew about the room and exited through the window image, causing a great suction and pulling George through the window. Twila had lowered herself to her knees, groping the floor for the machine plug.

"Dad, Dad!" She screamed.

Finding the cord with her hand she yanked on it until the connection was broken. The window stayed open for a moment while the machine slowed down and the wind stopped. The light returned to that of the simple shop.

"Theron! Mom! Mom!" Twila ran screaming from the workshop. Both Adeline and Theron stood at the screen door.

"It's Daddy, he's gone."

"Where has he gone too?" Adeline asked.

"The machine ate him."

TS and The WOW

Adeline wanted to laugh but then realized their family was different.

"Now let's see what happened."

"We were right here and we saw you and then us. We saw ourselves."

"You saw yourselves?"

"Yea, and then Daddy fell into the window. Now he's gone." They stood by the silent machine. "Turn it on." Adeline said. The machine came to life and Twila adjusted he control knob that George had been in charge of just a moment ago. The window showed the horses and the corals. She moved it a little more and the living room was in view. Just a bit more and they could see the inside of the workshop a few feet from where they stood. Twila picked up a ball that was on the floor and tossed it into the window. As soon as it went through the window it bounced out from nowhere on to the floor of the shop.

"That was strange." Theron Said.

"But that doesn't explain what happen to your Father." Twila moved the knob and for a second it was the three of them in the window and the suck of wind started. She quickly moved it on past and the wind ended. "Slowly now", Twila was instructed by her mother.

"There he is."

TS and The WOW

"He's ok."

George, was standing next to a telephone. It was ringing. "Hello Dad," Theron called out through the window. He placed the phone back on its hook.

"I'm ok just at my sister's house."

"Who are you talking to?" Lilly, George's sister asked. "No one. But come get me."

The window worked only in one direction but George would someday change the world with his DFM.

CHAPTER 19

Hidden and 1918 Red Rider

Fall turned the lilac bushes into something wonderful according to Theron. The blossoms were gone, along with Theron's allergies leaving only and abundance of leaves. Now that their pollen was gone he could walk into their covering and hide from his sister. Theron sat in the bushes concealed just like he imagined his brother Martin had been in Vietnam. He even wore the camo coat Martin had worn there.

"Twila, I think your brother is so cool."

"Sally, you've got to be kidding, Theron's a bug!"

The girls walked past the row of bushes, pausing right in front of the hidden boy.

"I'm not a bug!" Theron thought resting in his hiding place wanting to tell her so.

"You think Theron is cool? You mean you like him like a boyfriend?"

"Well, he is kind of weird some of the time, but his eyes. They are so beautiful." Her head tilted to the side as she made the statement.

"You are as weird as he is," Twila said. She would never have thought that Sally would be sweet on Theron. After all, she was her best friend not his. Being twins was hard sometimes. It was like always having a part of you that people thought was you, but had little to do with who you were. It probably made sense that Sally would like Theron. After all, he was Twila's twin and they were best friends. Theron sat in the bushes trying not to let on that he had heard their secret, yet he had. He blushed as he thought about how pretty Sally was. Sally was the girl he had like for weeks, but Twila had hurt his feelings telling Sally that he was a bug. It was not so much that bugs were bad because Theron liked most of them. Bugs were cool. He pressed his finger down on a pill bug that rolled itself into a ball. He wished they would move past the bush, or maybe he could roll into a ball also.

"Maybe I should just curl up into a ball since I'm a bug," he thought.

"I guess it's okay if you like Theron," Twila said hesitantly. Sally smiled at her, but Theron was the one that felt its warmth. The bush rattled and the girls heard the movement in the undergrowth.

TS and The WOW

"What's in there?" Sally asked. She supposed it was someone spying on them. Theron held his breath as the girls searched the bushes with their eyes. The girls were watching the lilac bushes and following the sound that rattled the leaves. Theron was sure he was about to be discovered. He was sure that Sally had seen him and was looking right into his eyes. He clasped both legs in his arms making himself as small as possible. Something in George's garage exploded with a noise kind of like the Fourth of July cannon firing. The noise was so loud and the percussion so intense that the pressure sucked away all three of the eleven-year-olds' breath. Twila screamed in terror.

"Daddy!" The girls ran just a step ahead of Theron, who had leaped unnoticed from the undergrowth. Theron stepped over the neighbor's cat that had been in the cool bush alongside him as they raced toward the garage. Theron ran faster than the girls, being the first to arrive at the pile of rubble. Sticks were still falling from the sky, with fire burning portions of the walls that still stood. It looked like a bomb had exploded on the left side of the garage. At first it seemed there was no way anyone could have escaped alive.

"Daddy was working on one of his machines in the there," Theron blurted out, with a need to inform his sister.

"Daddy! Daddy!" Twila cried. Theron had thrown himself into the rubble.

TS and The WOW

"Dad!" he called. The screen door to the house opened and Theron turned to see the look of total shock on his mother's face. She was frozen in her fear. In the back corner of the garage lay the machine that George had been working on. It laid bent, glass shattered, yet mostly intact. It moved. George groaned and then coughed.

"He's alive!" Theron's heart swelled choking his throat. Theron tossed rubble aside with strength he never knew he had. Twila joined him and even usually prissy Sally in her dress dug in the ruins. Theron's red spot of hair had formed a flower-like pattern, as did his sister's. Theron moved a large chunk of wallboard aside. The girls watched, still not believing what they were seeing. Both Sally and Twila were crying. Adeline had come to her husband and son's aid, capturing her emotions inside and choking back the thought of what they were about to see. George lay on the floor under the wallboard.

"That was exciting!" George exclaimed. Adeline could see blood on his face, but there it was, that sense of humor he always had.

"You all look like you saw a ghost" George said with a smile.

The Winter Tree had come to the edge of the building where he was shaking his leaves, building a wind strong enough to blow out the remaining flames.

TS and The WOW

"He's okay," Adeline choked out through her tears to the girls. George leaned on his wife and son to maintain his balance, moving to where the door had been. He looked back at his missing shop. "Guess we will have to do some redecorating." Doctoring was in the nature of the Salter women. They dotted and pampered George like a wounded bird. It was a week before George's hearing returned and the cuts on his face healed.

"Yes, Mrs. Sweeny, it is a miracle that he is alive," Adeline said on the telephone putting to rest the gossip that George had been blown to tiny pieces. He would always say he was spared because he had not fulfilled his purpose and the good Lord had one for all of us, something great to accomplish before we pass on. All the neighbors had gathered the rubble into a pile next to what was left of the building. The Winter Tree had been nervously keeping his distance at the other end of the yard, but he kept a watch on the strangers. Mr. Sweeney had climbed over the wall into the rubble and was snooping through the remains. The Winter Tree had been upset by the man when he had cut off a small limb from another tree in the yard, whittling it into a tooth pick. The Winter Tree twisted his limbs into his helicopter mode and then untwisted, making a noise that brought everyone to attention. When they looked his way, every leaf lay still. Not a breeze blew and all was calm. Mr. Sweeney stopped snooping intent on investigating the noise. He walked the yard for nearly thirty minutes without figuring it out. He lifted his hat and scratched his balding head. He put his hat back on and then went home without figuring it out.

"It's a miracle that George was not killed," Adeline repeated to everyone in the neighborhood. George agreed it was a miracle, but for a different reason. His survival was secondary to his Red Rider motorcycle that had survived without a scratch in the devastation. There was one other thing that had been tucked away for years that survived. The bike, along with the stone box, had been hidden from the world underneath a tarp in the corner of the shop. Adeline thought the box belonged to a woman named Pandora. But it had survived and maybe it was due to that, that George had lived through the explosion. He had removed it from the fireplace vault earlier that week just to examine it, placing it under the tarp so that Adeline wouldn't be frightened by it. Right next to the tarp the machine that had caused the explosion was twisted, the shattered glass walls gone. It was a total loss.

The Salter's were thrilled when the community wanted to help them restore the building. Folks were going to do an old fashioned barn raising. One thing about living in Enterprise, if you were a member of the town you were family. Saturday came and building materials arrived by the truckloads. Women came with biscuits in their tins, meat on platters, food enough for an army. The backyard had become picnic central.

TS and The WOW

"Theron, bring that wheelbarrow over here," George directed his son. Twila dashed past, her arms loaded with soda bottles.

"Over here young lady," a man on top of the new wall called out to her. Others reached for the cold drinks as she passed.

"More to the left with the truss, that's it. Nail her down boys," Mr. Busher said with authority. It was only hours until the last nail was driven. Where rubble had been yesterday, now there stood the shop, a shop that George thought was gone for good. It was easy to put in the contents. There were only a few things, one motorcycle, an ancient stone box and various remains of the old shop.

"Nothing explosive this time," Old Man Busher insisted. George looked at his remaining things.

"That's no problem," he agreed, knowing that it would be awhile before he could afford any materials to build projects.

The Winter Tree had stood silently, watching all the activity, uneasy for the invasion of his domain. The moment came he had waited for. The door to the house closed and the yard was silent again. He lifted his roots and spun about like a giant ballerina in the shadows of the evening. His roots narrowly touched the ground in his exercise of stealth. The roots were replanted as he towered over the bushes next to the new

TS and The WOW

structure. He rattled his leaves in approval and took his position of rest for the night.

The last light had been dimming in the evening skies for hours when it all began. The silence in the house was first broken by the clanking sound of stacked plates being slid away from one another. The airborne dishes flew from the cupboard. Forks, knifes, and spoons marched on the counter top. Lights flickered, dancing the same motion as the kitchenware. Finally the light switched on. It was not the light from the electrical bulbs that eliminated the goings on. The light came from the source that had brought these inanimate objects to life. George snored on as Adeline in her night curlers shook to awaken him.

"George, there's something in the kitchen." When his snoring paused he rose to a sitting position on the edge of the bed and slipped on his boots, figuring any good cowboy should die with his boots on. He wiped the sleep from his eyes.

"My rifle is in the closet in the living room, isn't it?" he whispered.

"A lot of good that is." Adeline said as she quickly stuffed hard objects into an old sock. She handed it to George. He took one look at it and put it back on the bed.

"I'm not David and I'm sure Goliath is not in the kitchen fixing something to eat." He picked up the stick that he had carved a design on during their last camping trip.

TS and The WOW

"This will have to do." He cracked open the door and peaked out, expecting another wolf on the wall or some other creature like that. The room was light and dishes, food, and even chairs were marching about the room. The only thing that did not belong was the stone box resting on the countertop.

"Not again," Adeline muttered, her hand resting on George's shoulder for comfort. She stood behind him wanting to be close but not wanting to face the terror of the box once more. The man in his pajamas and the wife in her gown and curlers inched toward the commotion. Light streamed from the stone box that seemed to play a silent musical tune that the entire group of objects danced to.

"Do something!' Adeline poked George in the ribs, prodding him to action.

"Hold on, I'll take care of this." He pushed her hand away. George slid his feet across the tile floor. He moved ever closer toward the box on the countertop. Adeline remained in the safety of the doorframe.

"What are you going to do?"

"I'm shutting the lid on this thing." With the stick held high above his head he approached the box dodging plates as they flew past. The stick crashed down as if Hank Aaron was swinging his bat to put the ball over the fence. The wood splintered as it struck the box. The lid bounced closed and then opened wider. George swung again. The stick splintered in half, a portion falling to the floor. The box lid closed as a clamshell to protect its soft inner body. As suddenly as it had started the utensils fell to the ground. The dishes hovered a moment longer and did the same, crashing in piles in the now dark room.

"Get the light!" George called to his partner. The room lights came on showing the mess. Adeline had been looking over George's shoulder.

"It was that box, wasn't it?" She vividly remembered her flying bread encounter with that thing eleven years ago. That memory shook her emotionally. This time the box had to go.

"What is going on, Dad?" the children queried.

"Nothing to worry about, go back to bed." George took the box, with Adeline's persisting nudges, outside to the storage vault where he would leave it for the night.

"How did you get in here?" George asked the box. He held open the door with one foot and switched on the flashlight while letting the door close on its new spring closer. He placed the box on the rock bench. When he did, his fingers slid across its side triggering something inside. A tray at the bottom of the box opened revealing a hidden occupant. The curled edge of an old ancient paper was exposed.

"What's this?" George pulled at the edge of the paper. It was wound on a spool and was fourteen inches long when stretched out. "This is curious. Were you trying to get me to find this?"

The other survivor in the rubble of the ruined garage was the1918 Red Rider. Where the red polished surface ended the chrome pipes finished the spectacular lines of George's vintage Red Rider motorcycle. Some might say he liked it, but they would be wrong. He loved it. Pride in his motorcycle brought a ray of happiness across his face as he spun the tire in the cinders of the driveway. The smile on his face looked out of place on a canvas that had been so solemn lately. It was ever since Theron and Twila had become balancers that he had become so worried. So many amazing things had happen to his family and especially Theron.

"Why the twins? Wasn't it enough that Adeline and he had waited so long just to have the twins? " He muttered with disgust. It may have been the twins' calling, but balancing had become the job of the whole family.

"For the moment we are free, just regular people," George thought. "Come on Theron," George said waving his hand for him to welcome Theron on board the bike. Theron swung onto the back of his dad's motorcycle and off they road toward Busher's Pond. Twila and Adeline stood in the black cinder driveway watching the father and son duo ride away, shifting gears as smoothly as the old bike would.

Sagebrush broke and dust sifted down to the ground in the trail created by the Red Rider. Neither father nor son looked back. They were just enjoying their moment and the ride.

"Nothing better than the outdoors, and the companionship of my son," George thought.

"Ride 'em cowboys!" screamed the boy on the back. George twisted the bike, sliding it sideways to a stop on the bank of Busher's Pond. If he had stopped any later, they would have been looking at the pond from the long green growing things that lined the bottom. Yes they were back. The muffler made a sound something like the repeat of a World War I rifle once or twice muffled and then the motorcycle stalled. Theron swung his leg from the bike into the water-filled side of the pond. He balanced on his tiptoes, spinning like a leaf caught in the center of a dust devil. George brought his leg blindly off the bike to hear the splash where he stepped. He turned his head just in time to see the water ripple and his boy covered in green, being drug away into the water from where the green things had risen. The chilly bottom of the pond gripped Theron, pulling him under the water. George reached a hand to aid his sinking son. Theron gulped for a breath of air as he was pulled under again. Theron struggled away from his entanglement, reaching his father's hand. He was about to reach the bank when the green things began the tug-of-

TS and The WOW

war, each pulling against the strength of George's hand. They tugged against him, rolling to tighten their grip first around his legs, then assisted by more of the green things tying themselves together until they formed a chain, linked to the bottom of the pond.

"Fight them son!" More green things shot from the pond bottom and strengthened their hold on him. Soon the boy was covered with their slimy green texture.

George yelled, "You can't have him!" He was not about to lose this struggle for the very life of his son.

Theron snorted for air trying to keep his presence of mind to fight. George dug both feet into the soft ground letting the Red Rider fall into the water. It sizzled for a moment, then sank into the green things, leaving a rainbow oil slick on the water. George's arms ached and Theron would take a breath each time his father pulled his head above water.

"You will never win," George groaned. The green things scrambled as though they had been commanded to release their grimy, slimy grip from the boy. Theron was pulled into his father's arms, spitting and then panting for air that he had lost. The green things looped around the tires of the Red Rider, weaving their way around each spoke and then dragging it into the depths of the pond, fading away into a bubble as Theron had when he was taken from the raft. Steam rose from the hot

TS and The WOW

engine of the bike as it sank. Air formed a giant bubble that burst in the pond's center, appearing for a time to be the mouth of a slimy creature lying just under the pond's mud-covered bottom. The bubble erupted, swallowing the bike, subsiding, then totally disappearing, Red Rider, green thing, and all.

George and Theron rested on the pond bank knee deep in the mud stirred from the once placid pond, now filthy from the struggle.

"I thought I lost you boy," the father said, holding his son to his chest while pulling drying, dieng green things from his leg. The ones with life retreated back into the water as fast as they could and settled into the soil to root again on the floor of the pond. Breath after breath pumped first in and then out of Theron's lungs until he once again breathed without struggle. "I hate this pond! That scarred me, Dad. I thought they had me again." He was wet, muddy, and exhausted, yet his father's strong arms had saved him, winning the battle as he had declared he would.

"You're my son and I would never let them take you. You will always be safe with me."

It would be a long time before any Salter's would swim or play in Busher's Pond. Not because of the pond or the water, but because a father and son had come to know each other's love. And it was their way to respect life itself.

TS and The WOW

The Red Rider, caked in pond mud and wrapped in green things, tumbled through the bubble and into a foreign world. Water pushed the bike to the edge of a different pond and the rocky beach of a dark foreboding cavern. Hands plucked the motor bike from the water. Their job completed, the green things retreated into the depths of the pool where they seemed more natural. The two pairs of hands that brought the bike to its normal riding position were dead looking and the two humanoids that possessed them were a lifeless fading green color. Water dripped from the frame of the bike, trickling back into the pool. The darkness of the cavern hid the features of those who had stolen George's treasure. It was now in their control and one of the green-handed creatures climbed aboard the bike. The phantom kicked the start pedal like he had done this a thousand times before. The alien world roared with the new life of the strange machine. The pasty green rider balanced the machine in the dim earthen chamber where the cavern walls glowed with the eyes of all the creatures hidden in the darkness. Their eyes showed, resembling sparks in the darkness, curious of the rider and machine. The rider twisted the throttle handle, lurching the bike forward and unleashing a deafening echo that bounced from wall to wall. The bike rider shot through the cavern toward the opening as fast as he could, the tires slipping and sliding on the damp and loose rocks. The opening to the outside world was at first a sliver of light. That sliver expanded beyond the shoulder width of the rider. The bike and rider burst from the darkness

TS and The WOW

into the light of the world. From the outside it looked like the planet spat the rider and machine into the air. This foreign warm world's landscape was dry. There were endless dry dunes of sand and the earthly engine was worked as it had never been worked before. The thief's hooded cloak had concealed the face in the darkness of the cavern. But here in the wind generated from the motion of the motorbike the hood was pulled free to his shoulders. A hideous face sat upon the shoulders of the rider. Arlo McFarland rode George's Red Rider. He cackled a wicked laugh that rolled into a wolf's howl at the ridge crest. It was evil that coursed through his veins. He was only partly satisfied for now with his prize. Only he knew why he had taken the motorcycle and let George win the battle for Theron.

What was next? Twila and Adeline piled the groceries all across the yellow and white speckled counter top. The smell of the paper bags mixed with the ripening cantaloupes gave a sweet musty smell to the room. Twila thought she should either really like the smell or be disgusted by it. She simply ignored it.

"Twila, put away the milk please." The glass bottles hung on plastic straps and as Twila removed them from the counter they clanked together. She brought them to the floor and set them in front of the avocado-colored refrigerator door. The door popped when it released the magnetic seal.

"Where should I put the spuds?"

TS and The WOW

"The cold bin next to the sugar."

"I thought that was where the flour went."

"Well put them downstairs in the fruit room."

"I like doing this, its fun to be..." She struggled for the right way to say what she was feeling. "...to be normal."

In that moment Twila was the most normal person she had been in a long time. This was as it used to be before the calling, and becoming a balancer.

Theron pulled off his boots before going into the house. He had been warned by his father that Adeline would find a willow and tan his hide if he went into the house wearing his muddy boots and clothes.

"That's a no brainier," Theron thought, although he had done that very thing time after time. George told their story to Adeline, nearly sobbing at the loss of his prized motorcycle. Then adding if he had to choose he would rather have his son.

If they had known what sequence of events had been set in motion because of that machine, George would have buried his motorcycle encased in six feet of cement to keep it away from Arlo McFarland. For all they knew it was now in the murky mire of Busher's Pond, guarded by the weeds and green things.

A moss-like fungi clung to the castle walls. The guard, a Troll, sat his lumpy green body above the gate. His drool fell over the edge and into the trench that had once been a mote. His gaze was locked on something just beyond the long grasses skifmuss in the distance. Four other trolls walked the grounds, each with a specific area to guard. The bigger they were the uglier they seemed to be. The castle shifted its shape as the doids let go of their hand holds and reshaped it. A troll on the ledge rode the change like riding a wave. When the change was over he rested higher in the castle, in a window opening.

A clamor came from inside the structure ringing through the valley all the way to the skrnifins. The project was secret and was held in the utmost of confidence. McFarland directed the construction of the machine that would soon take the thread that tied all worlds together and place it in his hands, to do as he would with them.

"That's it! He declared, to his aids of mayhem and conquest. The one-eyed wongle, picked up the Red Rider with his massive hairy arms. His telescopic eye located the spot and placed the cycle in the slot that seemed predestined for this driving mechanism.

"Make it run!" screamed Arlo. The Red Rider sputtered, only a machine but seemingly aware it was about to become a part of something terrible, something unspeakable. It sputtered once more, coughed, spit, sputtered again and began to run

TS and The WOW

with its usual powerful roar. The machine groaned, its gears tugging and clanking to come into motion. Sparks orbited the ball in the machine's center and gradually a glow came from within the globe. Soon the machine caught up with the rolling speed of the Red Rider. The machine produced a pulsing, purring sound, a sound unnatural to machines. Cogs spun and a weather-vein-like propeller whirred into action. A cylinder chamber resembling a circular phone booth began to rise from within the platform where a door was cranking aside. Arlo gave a wolf howl that penetrated the stale air. The booth was solid glass or something near glass. Nothing gave notion that it had seams of any kind except the open door. The wahnagel pressed a bar that had a handprint that fit his three-fingered palm in the control panel. This raised a seat from the bottom of the booth. Smoke, steam, or fog poured into the room from the cylinder's opening and in its midst was that single chair, ornate from top to bottom and laden with crop circle hieroglyphs, carvings of an ancient origin. Knobs, switches, and dials covered its arms obviously once a king's throne.

Arlo McFarland moved to the stairs and climbed to seat himself in the ancestor's throne. His face was withered drawn and gray. No part of his countenance shined. He was dead on the inside. Long locks of his gray hair hung on his shoulders his age apparent. The only color more than gray on his body was a patch of fading red hair in his goat whiskers.

TS and The WOW

The chamber started to spin. Fog rose and the sides of the chamber closed over him. As it spun, he was human, then wolf, then human and somewhere in between. The fog in the chamber was gone, along with the occupant who had disappeared. With the howl of a wolf, everything ceased and was still, except for the sound of the Red Rider motor put puttering to a stop.

CHAPTER 20

Return To The Canyon and Photo In The Falls

"Could the answers be found in the canyon? Would the answers be found in the canyon?" George wondered. After twelve years this was their first return to the river. George was determined to find out why his family was thrust into the balance, it was long overdue. He had many unanswered questions. Adeline was ready just to get away from the house. Besides, she wanted to see what hid in the droplets of the falls.

"Twelve years...I wonder if?" she thought holding her question inside, not wanting to think what was in her heart. Adeline recalled the last time she had seen the falls, and was sure that a man had been trapped in its waters. "How could someone be part of the water?" She was left to wonder as she prepared for their trip.

From Enterprise it was only a three hour drive to the north rim of the Grand Canyon, but from there to where the boats put in the river was another hour or so.

"Everyone ready?" called George. "Where's Theron?"

TS and The WOW

"He's feeding the chickens, here's his bag." Adeline set a gym bag on the floor next to all the others.

"Load up, let's be on our way." George was ready to be on the road and out of town.

Theron walked across the yard. As he did he realized the Winter Tree was bending nearly in half. He had twisted, with his branches touching the ground.

"You're looking a little sick, old boy." The tree rustled his leaves and untwisted his trunk, bringing his branches off the ground.

"What's wrong?" Of course, the tree was not going to tell him, but it was Theron's habit to talk to everything as though it would respond somehow. The Winter Tree had sensed that the family was about to leave. The tree rose to his full stature, dropping a cluster of leaves on top of Theron's head.

"Cut that out!" Theron brushed the leaves from his hair. The back door opened.

"Come on Theron, Dad's ready to go!" Twila said while waving her hand motioning him to follow her. Theron turned away from the Winter Tree to follow his sister to the car, never noticing the leaves on the ground. They imitated a petroglyphic crop circle pattern forming a single word, "Peril."

Relief poured over the family as they closed the doors on the old car.

TS and The WOW

"Did we forget anything?' George wanted to know. "Bathroom!" He ordered.

"Check," Theron said.

"Roger dodger commander!" Twila teased.

"Let go already," Adeline said, anxious to get away. This time it was going to be a family trip for everyone except Martin.

"Too bad Martin's not here," George commented as they pulled onto the street that passed their home.

"That would make things complete," said Adeline. Her heart was a little heavy to have her eldest son was so far away. He still had six months left before he would be coming home permanently from the Army.

"Slide over girly." Uncle Herbert said when they stopped to pick him up. He was going to bring the car back and then pick them up on the bottom of the river. He squeezed Twila to the center of the back seat. She liked him, he was always telling strange jokes about pickles that danced or something strange that made her laugh.

When they stopped for gas, the breeze blew a gentle whisper. Similar to Grandpa Salter's whistles when he whittled and rocked on his porch in the evenings. It was a good feeling, calm, and peaceful. The next stop was high atop the rim of the canyon to view the great wonder of the world. There were ooohhs and aahhhs .

TS and The WOW

"What's the big deal?" Theron moaned, unaware of the secret held by his parents. "If you like this, you will love the land above the water in the world of Shopera. Now that's a wonder!" he said.

This was a pretty big hole, impressive, but Theron was concerned about the Winter Tree.

"Do you think the Winter Tree is okay back at home?"

"Aw, he's just lonely. Spoiled brat, that's what he is," Adeline said.

"Do you think the Winter Tree is okay?" Theron asked his father.

"I'm sure he can take care of himself," was the reply George offered.

"I think you will love the river trip son." Adeline was working her motherly instinct. She herself was apprehensive as she thought of the screamer they had heard in the canyon so many years ago, but she and George felt that there were answers to those long lingering questions hidden behind the falls. What untold story would they learn in the bottom of that canyon? After all, that was where all this weirdness began.

Amazingly the water appeared calm, deep, but calm. The rafts rested on its surface, glazing past the dock hardly showing motion. Their boats were being held nose upstream by ropes tied off to the dock. Three men were loading the boats with food and

TS and The WOW

sleeping bags and strapping everything down, securing it all with sailor knots.

"Close the car door behind you son." George sometimes felt the boy was mindless when it came to closing doors and cleaning up after himself. Theron felt oddly peaceful, just as Adeline had predicted he would when they reached the river. Banging the door closed, Theron wandered back to the river to watch it flowing into the canyon. He wasn't sure if it was the walls of the cliffs that closed in on him that brought back the memory of being captive in the castle, or had it just been a long time since he had felt this still or peace inside? 'Goodbye' was said to Uncle Herbert then he and the car disappeared around the bend.

"Now there are a few things you folks need to know about this here river. First, never trust the water. Secondly, always wear this here May West," the boatman said holding up a life jacket. Twila put the full face of her jacket over her head locating the straps and tying them off in big bows across her chest.

"Is this right?" she asked the handsome boatman.

"Well, little missy, that's bass ackwards." He tried not to laugh, but just had to snicker once. Twila undid the strap and the boatman removed the jacked and turned it about. Her eyes watched his handsome face as he did his job.

"Now tie those strings missy."

TS and The WOW

Twila kind of liked being his little missy.

After putting on their life jackets the family boarded the boat. The boatman quickly moved to the back. Theron and Twila took their turn and slid over the squashy rubber pontoon. George and Adeline sat upon the storage box in the middle of the raft. The boatman's long dark hair slightly covered his face.

"He could be one of the Beatles," Twila thought. Twila tried not to be obvious, but had a hard time looking away.

"I guess you folks should know my handle. I'm Delbert, your boatman and your request is my command." One hand swooped in front of him and the other to his back in a bow. Delbert the boatman had noticed her glances and smiled at Twila as he bowed. "Cast off that line," he called to the other crewmember unlashing the other rope himself. Delbert was too involved with getting the raft underway to be bothered with a skinny kid half his age, but she watched the boy-man intently. He tugged on the rope that tied them to the dock front and tossed it on board. The raft moved away from the dock, became part of the current and pulled off into the river. Delbert leaped on board, stumbling, bouncing and then falling right into Twila's lap. He quickly regained his poise and stood up. His face blistered with shades of red, the same color as Twila's.

"I'm sorry missy," he said, "Darn wet shoes, got to watch that," he muttered loud enough for everyone to hear. He moved to the rear of the boat and grasped the motor. Starting it, the raft rolled about and he moved it in to the deeper calm water. He was pleased, recovering well he thought from his stumbling start. Twila was recovering from her own little embarrassment. She found herself exposed to the crowd. It was like all the awkward young girl in her had come to the surface and rested on her face for the entire world to examine.

"Go away!" she commanded in her mind, wanting the red color to fade from her face. In a moment she recovered her natural color and acted as if nothing had happened, but she was totally afraid to look anywhere in his direction. Delbert had wanted to forget the moment, but he had to sneak a look at the little beauty. When he thought the passengers on his boat were admiring the upcoming rapids he noted her once more. In Twila he noted her gangly yet so very regal presence. The red spot of hair was strange. "Weird, but it fits her," he thought. That would be the last of it. After all, he was eighteen and she was just a kid yet to understand how beautiful she was.

"Looks like you've got a boyfriend sis," Theron teased.

"Shut up." She whacked his arm. Theron had not let the encounter pass without notice. After all, he was connected to her and when she felt strong emotions the red hair on the side of her head curled into to a sleek ringlet. His red hair twisted uncomfortably whenever such events occurred making him a part of her love life. Theron patted his head where the red hair squirmed about.

"Okay, okay I'll stop this time."

"Look at this." George had wanted to show the kids the wonders of the river ever since they were born. He missed Martin and wished he had been there. At least for him that nightmare of Vietnam was over and he was safe.

The river tossed the raft into the air as it went into the first rapid.

"Wa hoo!" George screamed his best cowboy call, thrilled to watch his young ones experience the ride. Theron grasped the rope that tied down his gear in the middle of the raft. Twila hung onto her brother hoping he would hang on for the both of them. The entire time George was thinking that this was a small rapid and they had a surprise yet to come. He smiled. Theron had forgotten the feeling of watching his uncle drive away and stranding them. He was pleased to be on the move down the waterway, nervous, but nervous in a good way. Apprehensive about the rapids, but he was game for the experience.

The canyon at first had been wide and lined with a plethora of forest growth. Now it changed. The trees where more sparse and the walls of the canyon grew ever higher above them. The red sandstone riddled with cracks, long deep fissures and overhanging stones as big as a house brought thoughts of all

TS and The WOW

kinds of disaster or mayhem. The first day on the river they had only experienced three rapids of any consequence.

"This is great fun," Theron spouted out to his father having had a change of attitude. George, Theron and Twila all sat on the front of the raft with their legs over the pontoon and hanging on to the ropes, facing the force of the watery waves head on. The soaking was the best part. The water was cold, but the air temperature was in the eighties or nineties. Theron's thoughts of falling off the boat into the water were long gone,

"This trip is all Dad said it would be," Theron thought.

"We'll be a pullin' in here folks. This is tonight's camp," Delbert announced, moving the raft to the shore. The beach was just a small sandy bit of land with a few odd-smelling clumps of bush. The sun was setting when all the bedrolls were laid out. Dinner was cooking and a wash of good food, wild plants, and muddy water smells caressed the camp.

"Some fine memories were made today darlin'." George sat next to Adeline on a driftwood log to eat the fabulous meal, or grub as the boatman had called it. Twila and Theron were sitting cross-legged in the dirt with their plates in their laps.

"What is this?" Twila inquired of the meat, holding her piece in the air on her fork.

"Just something we picked up off the side of the road."

"You're kidding, aren't you?"
TS and The WOW

"Yeah, it's squirrel."

Twila contorted her face not knowing what to believe.

"You can eat it, Honey, its good." Adeline bit into her portion and seemed to enjoy it. Privately the Salter's had thanked God for the meal and their safety on the river, knowing they would need His watching eye while down here in this hidden place.

Night finished its fall and it was one of those miraculous nights when the stars took the sky into overdrive, touching every part of the canyon with heavenly light.

"Come sit with us, Theron," Adeline said, wanting Theron to come near the fire where everyone had congregated to tell stories and sing some camping songs.

"Sit tight, Mom, I'll be right there."

The younger boatman put a few more logs on the popping fire. Twila and Theron sat to one side and George and Adeline on the other side of the log. The other folks that had accompanied them on the river assembled in around the blaze. Randy and Candy Sweet from Hershey, Pennsylvania and Todd, Jane, and Anna Oliver of Prescott, Arizona filled the rest of the raft. Anna was the only other young person on the trip.

Anna was a pretty twelve year old, having long black hair and being just barely taller than Theron.

TS and The WOW

"Are you going to play us something on that thing?"
Randy Sweet wanted to know. Delbert was strumming the strings
of an old box guitar that looked like it had been down the river
for more years than Delbert had lived. The tune was luscious, a
complement to the water rushing past in the river. Adeline
snuggled close to George partly because she was cold and partly
because she was sitting in the same spot where a memory had
haunted her for nearly twelve years. It was right here where they
had faced the moment when that terrifying scream had attacked
their dreams, turning them to nightmares.

"We're all going to be okay here aren't we?" Adeline
whispered into George's ear.

"We will be just fine honey," he assured her.

Sparks like fireflies floated in the air over the water's edge
and died as Delbert strummed strings of a calming melody.

"Mom, you were right. This is a great place," said
Theron, who stood behind his mother and father looking on.
They were not the only ones he was watching. He had noticed
Anna. She was sitting with Twila and they had become fast
friends, ever once in awhile including Theron in their talk. It was
okay with him. He kind of liked being able to do his own thing
and then be a part of the real important things. So far, there was
nothing very important happening, he thought. Besides, he had
folded Mebo into a small enough package that he was in the

TS and The WOW

corner of his bag waiting to be watered and awakened from his flattened slumber. It was still warm here. In fact, it was much too warm to sleep under all the weight of the sleeping bag. Theron had chosen to sleep on top of his bag. He would wish he had been deep inside the protective cover later that night.

"May Anna sleep over here by Theron and me?"

"If her mother doesn't mind," Adeline told the girls.

Theron's bag had its place and he wasn't going to move it, not for some girl. The girls brought their bags to the sandy spot near the edge of the orange cliffs where Theron had his bag.

"There's not enough room here," Anna said.

"Yes, there is. Theron move your bag that way a little."

He looked as his bag, looked at the girls and looked at the bag again.

"Can't you..." He stopped his words before they came out and just moved his bag. It was weeds in his face if he looked one way and girls if rolled to look the other way.

"What if she snores, what do I do then?" he thought. The sound of a lone coyote on a distant peak was the only sound Theron heard before he was deep asleep. The river flowed on through the night as it had throughout time, a never-ending parade of water passing the spot of a sand bar where they lay sleeping.

TS and The WOW

"Snore sputter, snore sputter, sputter," came from all around, no worse than the frogs that were croaking or the crickets chirping. Everything was at peace, calm within nature, until the first drops of rain began to fall. Droplets fell high on the towering red pinnacle, gathered into puddles, and then formed a stream to tumble down the rocks watering everything in its path.

"Oh, what the heck is that?" Theron woke from deep sleep with water splashing on his face, falling from the rocks and the sky in unison. The rain began to cover the entire camp.

"I'm all wet!" Twila muttered.

"It's raining!" Anna exclaimed.

"Get under here kids," George called.

Anna, Twila, and Theron scampered under the tarp that was covering George and Adeline. They were already soaked to the bone, so the tarp covering did little to dry their already water-basted bones.

"It was warm before this dang rain! Now I'm cold!" Theron said in disgust.

Twila and Anna tucked under the tarp. There they sat watching the rain pour off its corners to the ground where it blended seamlessly with the water of the river. Huddled like chickens in the corner of the coop Anna tucked her arm and shoulder tight against Theron.

TS and The WOW

"She's warm and drier than I. This is kind of nice," he secretly thought.

The storm ended like turning off the garden faucet and it was over. All the water soaked into every part of the parched earth and in twenty minutes the ground was dry and appeared to be thirsty once more. Only the sleeping bags were still wet dripping dry on the rocks.

"Well that was a rude awaking," George said a little louder than if he had used his normal voice. Morning had come like Grandma's slobber kiss, making everyone take notice.

"It will be all dry soon and you will want to get wet," Adeline said drawing a picture in their minds of the sun taking charge of the skies and every one of them sweltering in its packs of heated light. But right now the fire the boatman had made felt good.

Theron sat on the only real dry spot. It was where his sleeping bag had covered the ground. He had his back to a large rock and held both of his knees to his chin. Then he heard a noise. The noise was coming from his gym bag that had filled with water from the cliffs

"Let this Mebo free."

It was Mebo. The water had awakened him. The bag's zipper opened and Mebo poked his face out.

TS and The WOW

"Mebo, you okay?" Theron was glad to see his friend, but explaining him to the other passengers was another story. "You have to be quiet."

"Mebo want more liquid." Theron gave his pal the water he wanted. Mebo swelled to a larger size, ending his growth with an elastic pop. The sun had been up for awhile but had not found its way into the canyon bottom. There was still the shadow world of the early morning.

"What have you got there, Theron?" Anna asked?

"Just my basketball."

"I love basketball. Show me your best move."

Theron balanced Mebo to his back, turning his face away from the girl's view. Mebo did look like a basketball at least that was what Theron had always said. Theron spun the ball on his finger. Mebo closed his eyes through the spin. Mebo found it hard to stop spinning in his head even after Theron had stopped spinning him.

"That's about all I can do without a ball court."

"That was cool," she said, satisfied.

"Come on you guys, bring me your stuff." Delbert was packing the boat for the next leg of the river trip.

Mountain goats standing atop the highest ledge in the morning sun watched the boat move away from the sandy beach

TS and The WOW

to depart. The animals had patiently awaited the humans leaving so they might regain their watering spot once more.

"Did you see that?" George's finger pointed to where the animals were standing on the cliff, but the boat rounded a turn on the river at the same time and no one else saw them.

"I don't see anything," Adeline said.

"Aunt Louise's toe, I called it," Twila adamantly said. This was a game the Salter family played. You see when someone says they see something but no one else can verify the seeing, it's just like Aunt Louise's toe, not there. Aunt Louise had an accident, cutting off her toe with an ax. The famous wood chopping accident, a story repeated nearly every Thanksgiving since it happened five years previous. She buried that toe in the yard beneath the wild elm tree where she visited occasionally. So Aunt Louise sported an empty space between her big and her third toe of her right foot. The game was called finding Aunt Louis's toe. It was big family points to recognize that absence of Aunt Louise's toe, which to any Salter that meant the other person who saw something where nothing existed was as crazy as Aunt Louise.

The water splashed against the boat in a soothing, lulling movement. Adeline rested in the morning sun enjoying her return to the canyon.

TS and The WOW

"No screams in the night, that's a good sign," she thought to herself. She had always loved the sound of the flowing water and the moment couldn't have been better as she dragged her hand on the water, leaving a trail only for an instant behind her fingers. George sat much higher on the front of the boat looking like his namesake George Washington crossing the Delaware. Theron and Twila were on the storage box with their new best friend Anna.

"My dog is a Saint Bernard and last week he was licking the neighbor's Chihuahua. In two licks he had swallowed the poor thing. My daddy jumped on him and just like that, the tiny dog shot out. He ran away shivering," Anna said.

"I guess he saw something that made him sick to his stomach," Twila said.

"Yeah, a Saint Bernard's stomach," Theron commented.

All three laughed. The sun had crept into the canyon and suddenly, it was hot.

"I would like a little of that rain from last night right now," thought Theron.

"George where is it?" Adeline asked in anticipation.

"A few more rapids, a few more turns," he replied.

Adeline was looking for the reason she had come to the canyon. It was farther than it seemed on the previous trip. The

TS and The WOW

rapids came up against the boat to change her focus to the rafting adventure.

"This is so cool," said Theron.

"Awesome," Anna chimed in.

Not to be out done, Twila used one of her words in a way only she could, "Insmackulatious," she said with a smile as they rolled over the rapid while seated on the front of the pontoon, one hand swinging loosely something like that of a cowboy on his bronk. They laughed at the water splashing full force into them, nearly dislodging them from the boat. Mebo peeked out from the bag to see what was going on. He ducked back into the bag, after seeing the rapids and swells of water that they were riding upon. He was growing greener and greener as they went over the swells in the river. Delbert guided the boat out of the rapid and into the smooth waters.

"Were going to camp here," he said. George thought they would have reached the falls today.

"Isn't there a falls just ahead of us?" He asked the boatman.

"Yes, there is a falls, a small one. You could hike there on that trail." He pointed to the trail that lead out of the camp up the hillside and onto the cliff.

"Looks a little dangerous," Adeline said.

TS and The WOW

"Not as long as you're back by nightfall, you'd be okay," Delbert politely said.

"Let's go Addie, this is our chance."

She hesitated and then realized that if they were going to search the cave, it was now or never.

"Come kids, we're going for a walk in the falls."

Theron tucked his bag containing Mebo behind a bush, telling Mebo in a whisper, "You stay there until we get back." Mebo wasn't happy with being left behind. After all, he had just woken up in this great place. He had never seen so much water and he wanted to explore.

"Can I go to the falls?" pleaded Anna, to her mother.

"If it's okay with the Salter's," looking at Adeline in a way of getting her approval for her baby to go with them. She wanted to say no, but how uncomfortable would that be for the only other child not to be allowed to discover the falls? In the way only mothers know, she agreed to add Anna to her brood.

Mebo had wiggled his way out of the bag, rolling himself through the weeds and hiding from the other travelers. Only the weeds gradually bending and rising would have given any evidence that he was on the trail behind them.

"Theron, you be last. It's your job to help the girls."

George knew Adeline would need him. Theron climbed like a mountain goat and was well practiced. He climbed the Black Ridge nearly every night. The girls didn't need much help. They were just fine on the climb.

The Trail started off meandering through the weeds, but quickly climbed into the rocky edge of the canyon wall, twisting back and forth on itself until it turned into a path of stone. It was like walking a corridor in a fancy building with a floor of polished stone. It was a rocky ledge on the riverside and an impenetrable wall on the mountainside. Large birds flew in above them circling and waiting. Mebo had rolled his way up the trail, enjoying his freedom from the bag.

"Mebo like this place," he said to himself while pausing to look out over the canyon and the river below. The sight of the canyon made him shake, being afraid of high places. The red rock and water were all new to him, very different from his home. It was also a desert, but not quite so colorful, nor did his home have a river like this one.

George pushed aside a tree limb that had grown over the trail that had become jungle like. Water seeped out of the rock walls and moss, bushes and loose rocks had overtaken this part of the trail. The trail began its descent into the canyon.

"George, can you hear the water falling?" Adeline asked, touching him on the shoulder. The water poured off the rocks to

TS and The WOW

the pool below. It was different to see the falls from this height. Before they had only seen it from the river and as they stood at the foot of its majestic flow.

"George, is this it?"

"Yes, it has to be the falls."

"This is cool!" Theron said. Both girls just smiled enjoying the falls.

"This is so beautiful!" Twila said as she exclaimed her astonishment. When the group stood at the bottom of the falls, each had their own expression of wonder. George, with his cowboy hat tilted back, watched one drop of water fall from the ledge all the way to its ripple in the pool. He and Adeline gazed into the sheet of falling water looking for something.

"Was he here?" Adeline wondered.

The cool water was inviting to everyone, but there was something more hidden in the water and the memories of George and Adeline were about to come full circle. The girls waded into the water. It was cool on their warm skin. George pulled off his boots and socks, but the cowboy hat stayed in place. Adeline followed George into the water.

"It was right here wasn't it?" The water poured into the pool just beyond the spot where they stood. Theron wasn't so ready to get into the water. There was something about this spot that just didn't seem right. His feelings were on edge and his red

TS and The WOW

spot of hair was fidgeting. Theron was sure that his sister was having the same hair raising experience. She looked at him in a way of confirming his thoughts.

"This is it." After wading a few more steps into the water George reached in and pulled up on the handle that had been in the water undisturbed these twelve years. Everything was real. It was the way they had remembered it, not just a fantasy or a dream as it had seemed. The stone behind the falls rolled aside only part way.

"Dang it, it's stuck!" The handle was wedged by a large rock that had fallen in the passing of years.

"That's all I got," George said, while pulling on the lever, grimacing and clenching his teeth. The lever stood part way out of the water exposed to view.

"What do we do with Anna?" Adeline asked George. It was hard enough to keep the secrets of the Salter household in their town. How were they going to get Anna to keep them? Both girls swam across the pool to where Twila's parents stood gazing at the falls and hiding the lever behind them.

Twila and Theron were not the only ones who noticed something change in the air. When the door had opened Anna squirmed a little, "Twila, let's go back to the boat," Anna pleaded, feeling nervous. Twila looked at both of her parents and then said, "Come, on let's go."

TS and The WOW

"You be careful girls." Mothers were mothers all the time and this was no exception. In a moment the girls had climbed to the point where the trail was lost to sight. But they were being watched by Mebo, who had seen them coming just in time to hide in the rocks above the trail. He rolled slightly as they passed. Sure that they had heard him, he held his breath.

"What was that?" Anna said. They had heard a noise, so the girls put an extra bounce into their step, their nervousness exposed. The girls had scarcely passed when Mebo felt something wet behind him. Its touch made him swell to his next size trapping him between the rock where he had hidden and the one just behind him. The animal's nose was wet and poked at Mebo once more. His skin made a popping sound with the elastic bounce as he grew again to the next size. Now he was trapped for sure, stretching tight to against the rocks. The animal was startled by the popping sound scurried away without Mebo ever seeing his curious visitor.

At the waterfall, Adeline opened a pack that contained the reason they had returned to the falls.

"Here it is," she exclaimed, after searching the bag. In the pack was a photo, a photo of the falls taken the last time they were here. For twelve years it had left an uneasy feeling both in her and George. She had taken several rolls of film of the canyon, but the photo she held in her hand had caused wonders, dreams and visions of what or who the image in the fall might be.

TS and The WOW

Perhaps now it would be revealed to her just who he was. Three Salter's stood in the spot where the photo had been taken and looked over the image on the paper. It was a photo of the falls with little change except for the face that had been imbedded in the water droplets as they fell. Adeline wanted to twist her face in a way that might bring back the image so she might see it again in the droplets of water. How had the water configured to show a face in the falling droplets?

The face seemed familiar. Was it because she had seen it for twelve years or was it because she knew the face from some other place, some other time. Adeline pondered this thought.

"All those years and now I don't feel any closer to knowing what this means," Adeline said

"We are closer than you might think, Honey."

"Dad's right." Theron pointed to his red hair spot. It was twisting like a clock and bouncing like a sprung spring.

"Well it's now or never," George said with just a slight hesitation in his voice. He pulled on his pack, and then waded through the water to the cave. Adeline and Theron followed him. Each of them passed under the falls and then climbed to the opening of the cave. It was a tight squeeze getting past the partially open door and the fallen rocks.

"Smells weird in here," Theron said.

TS and The WOW

Moss grew from the ceiling to the age-worn steps that spiraled upward carved on the wall. Water trickled down the steps from the room above. It was all just the way George had remembered it, down to the moss-covered, hand-carved steps. The moss on the steps had grown thicker in some spots and withered dead in others. The years had changed it little since they had walk there last. It was dark in the staircase. Adeline held on to George's hand and Theron held on to hers. Flicker, then with a flash came on a beam of light from George's flashlight that poked its way up the stairs.

"I am glad I brought a light," George commented.

"You're just the perfect Boy Scout, always prepared, honey."

The stairs led them to the room where their mysteries had started. Just possibly they would find answers. At least, that was what they hoped. George scraped the light on the side of the wall, which echoed in the staircase tube. The light broke loose cobwebs and George did his best to avoid anything that slithered into his path.

"What was that?" Adeline screamed, as something scurried over the hand she held on the cave wall.

"We're really here," George said, knowing this was the birthplace of many Salter legends. All the years of tales of the stone box, and the cave in the canyon were word pictures of a

TS and The WOW

distant past. But today, right now, this was suddenly all real. It was a coming out of imagination, the face of reality Theron thought.

"Come on in, son." George stood inside the room where the water basin still ran with its aqua blue water that poured over the edges of the bowl and ran into the ring at the bottom of the basin carved in the floor. The water then flowed into the floor to hide somewhere inside the earth. Theron trotted over the last riser and entered the room. George was tapping a rod on the ceiling. He tapped a few more times and dirt slid away from the outside of the isinglass ceiling, letting in light. It was a natural window.

"How cool is that," Theron said.

"Neat, huh?" George replied.

Dusk had come outside, so the flashlight was still the main source of illumination inside. There was just a faint glow of the prism colors from the isinglass.

"Look, Dad." Theron pointed to carvings on the walls. They were in rows, lines of circles. It was the text of worlds, the common language of the seven.

"Theron, what do they say?" asked George.

"Let me see." He ran his fingers over them as if he was getting a better look at them.

TS and The WOW

"It's talking about an ancient treasure and of seven cities. It says each city is made of gold. They each are from a different world, and they have been hidden."

There was a broken spot in the carvings that had fallen away to rubble on the floor. The wall was cracked, leaking water and growing lime in that spot on the wall where the etchings continued. Theron did his best to read on.

"The Protectorate, that's like a balancer I think."

"What about the Protectorate?" George was impatient, but continued shining the light on the wall to aid the fading light coming in through the isinglass.

"The rest is something about a map protected by a stone guardian."

"Is that all?"

"Yes, Dad, that's it. What do you think it means?"

"You have heard about Cortez and the seven cities of gold haven't you?" inquired George.

"George, do you think this is the seven cities of gold that the Indians knew about?" Adeline asked.

George removed the stone box from his pack and placed it back on the floor approximately where he had taken it from years ago. He paused for a moment, removed the lightening rod and placed it in a leather pouch in his shirt pocket. He patted the stone box on the lid, as if he were saying goodbye to an old friend.

"Your home, this is where you belong."

"What's this?" Theron had his hand in one of two carved holes in the wall. George and Adeline removed their attention from the box, both relieved it was no longer in their possession. Especially Adeline felt peaceful thinking of her home and her new freedom from the box.

"Mom, Dad, look at this!" Each of them ran their hands over the holes, becoming reassured that man made them. The flashlight flickered, and then went out, making it dark and moist. This was one of those times when everything seemed to come in so tight, closing in around a person.

"Dang thing!" George said, shaking the light to make it work.

At that moment a pleading scream came from the other side of the wall. It was ripe and strange, oozing its way out of the holes carved in the wall. George, Adeline, and Theron all recoiled back away from the wall and the scream from on the other side. Adeline stumbled. Theron stumbled over her and fell to the floor as they tried to escape from the room.

"Oops, what the heck?" Theron said when he hit the floor.

TS and The WOW

"George that's it, the scream!" Adeline saw a vision of the night on the river when she had first heard the scream. The scream had become etched in her soul. It was so terrifying to her that she began to cry.

"Its okay honey."

The screamer cried again bringing the hair on Theron's neck to attention. His heart pounded with the ferocity of a thousand wild beasts trying to become free from their metal cage. George shook the flashlight once more. It flickered and a beam of light poured from it.

"Let's get out of here while we can!" George led them to the staircase. Theron's courage mounted. He tapped George on the shoulder, looking at him and then at Adeline.

"Mom, let me look through the holes. I have a feeling." Theron trembled as his red hair jittered, twitching into overdrive. Could he look through the holes and see what made such a painful noise? He was driven inside himself to make right whatever was unbalanced. He took the light and shined it into the dark cavity beyond what now seemed to be eye ports. He placed his face against the wall allowing one eye to see through the hole.

"Move the light down just a little," he thought catching something at the lights edge. As the light moved, Theron came eye to eye with the screamer, who also wanted to know who was on the other side of the wall. Startled, he yanked his head back

TS and The WOW

away from the wall. His heart nearly leaped from his chest. Slivers of rock dislodged from the roof of the cave, bouncing to the cave floor. The room quaked and the walls shuddered, it seemed to be preparing to release the prisoner on the other side of the wall.

"Have I touched some key or am I the key that has caused this?" Theron wondered as he dodged the falling stone.

"There's another room in there and someone is in there," he said.

"Could this be the pathway to one of the seven lost cities?" George asks aloud.

The eye Theron had seen was yellow, not blue or brown or even green. Theron sat on the floor of the cave away from the holes, quivering and fearful.

"I think it's the wolf!" he cried out as the shower of stones ended.

"Is everyone okay?" Adeline called out through the dust.

"I am okay," George said as he moved to her side.

"Me too," Theron said as a single stone the size of a peanut fell conking him on the head. It stunned him for a second. His eyes blurred and his vision changed, first totally out of focus and then something weird happened. He no longer saw too dimensionally. The blood pumping to his head had opened a hidden door in his brain exposing an additional cone of sight.

TS and The WOW

Suddenly he could see the rocks melting away and the DNA of the creature on the other side of the wall.

"Something's happening!" he said in an alarmed voice. He could see blood pumping through a human-like body, but there was something wrong with that body. The creature on the other side of the cave wall was not just a human, but also some kind of dog-like creature. This new vision panicked Theron.

"Come on you two, we're getting out of here." George was taking no chance with his family. If the wolf from the wall was on the other side, he was staying there. They were going back to the boat. "Theron, come on right now," he demanded.

Theron should have recognized the sign. His red hair had warned him, but he had not been listening. He was glad his sister wasn't there.

"At least Twila is safe," he thought.

The water fell like a curtain over the opening of the cave. The first breath of air was the sweetest breath that Adeline had ever taken into her lungs. She stood on the rocky bank of the pond near where the waterslide cut into the sandstone cliff. She watched as both her husband and her son struggled with the lever to close the door to the cave, hoping to keep the creature imprisoned behind his wall. The door made a grinding sound as it thudded into its closed position.

"That should hold it," George said.

TS and The WOW

The sun had gone down but the moonlight had not yet entered the canyon, resting only on the rim and giving off just enough light to see. The water curtain infused with light like the flashlight had done in the cave bursting to life with the image of a man. It was the photo she had taken years ago. When the door was closed Theron and George joined Adeline in her spot out of the water on the bank to watch what had mesmerized her. Adeline stared at the image in the water droplets.

"Daddy. It's my daddy," Adeline said with tears in the eyes of a daughter seeing a father that had disappeared when she was young.

"How could it be her father?" Theron wondered.

"What is this, some kind of trick?" George said.

"How could he be the figure in the falls?" Theron thought. He had not aged since she was a young girl and had last seen him.

"Dad! Daddy!" she screamed, tears flowing down her cheeks. The fall luminance dimmed when the figure trying to become more than an image, struggled to reach out of the falls. Light faded danced on and off, going blank and disappearing with the image locked in another world. All that was left was the sound of the water splashing on the rocks and into the pool of water. George held Adeline in his arms as she sobbed.

TS and The WOW

"It was my daddy!" She felt his loss a second time in her young life.

The moon finally rose over the canyon walls, creating a vision that the canyon that was now a fairyland. The scream from the prisoner in the cave shattered the moment, bring action to the trio. They stayed close to one another as they traveled on the trail back to the raft. Theron walked behind his parents on the trail, his red hair spot still twitching its warning. He checked over his shoulder after every few steps.

"Nothing back there," he kept telling himself.

"What's that?" he said in his own head, hearing the rock tumbling just above him on the trail. His heart suddenly pumped with the fury of a fire engine, but the red hair had ceased its twisting. Mebo bounced to the trail behind the boy, startling him.

"How did you get here?"

"Too much water," was all he said. Then he rolled into line behind the Salter's. Theron was a little more at ease now that he was no longer the last one in the darkness of the trail. The fire was strong, a beacon in the night. Soon they were back at the raft and the camp where dinner was ready for them.

The morning came without disaster befalling anyone in the night. The creature in the room must have been truly trapped in the stone prison. They passed the waterfall, just a picturesque jewel of the Grand Canyon. The raft rolled into the next rapids

TS and The WOW

down the waters of the Colorado, leaving the wolf and the connection to Adeline's daddy behind.

CHAPTER 21

Home Again and Loose Among Us

"What a mess," declared Adeline.

The countertop was covered from one end to the other with debris from their trip down the river. "At least we are rid of the crazy stone box," she said aloud just thankful it was gone.

That box had been her nemesis and finally it was back in the cave where it belonged, and she was in her kitchen where she belonged. "Trash, Trash, Theron and Twila's trash, everywhere I look more trash." She sorted at the mess in disgust until she came across the photo of the man in the falls.

"Daddy, could it be you?" she questioned her memory. Was he really the man that she had seen in the curtain of water? Well it wouldn't matter now that they were long way from the falls and even if they could get to the falls, what could they do to help him?

"Could the falls be a gateway to one of Twila's and Theron's worlds?" she wondered. The photo was real and the man in the picture surely resembled her father.

TS and The WOW

"Honey, where do you want this?" George carried in a couple of sleeping bags that still had sand clinging to them.

"The washroom please."

"Twila, come here!" Twila went to her mother. "Would you put this stuff in the workshop?"

Twila scooped the pile from the counter into her arms and then went out to the workshop. Theron was watering the chickens and gathering the eggs. The neighbors had taken care of the chickens, but it had been a couple of days since they were tended to. The egg basket was so full that Theron was afraid to let it swing at all. He balanced it like he was walking a tight rope high between two skyscrapers. The Winter Tree sat in the middle of the yard enjoying the water from the hose that Theron had turned on him.

"Bet that feels good," he addressed the tree with some satisfaction for watering him. Theron walked underneath the tree. At the same time Twila walked out of the workshop looking toward her brother. The tree was glad to have the family home, but he was always the Winter Tree, full of the unexpected. He waited until Twila was watching. As Theron walked under his limbs, he reached down and snatched the basket of eggs from him. He nimbly tossed an egg to a fork in his branches. Theron could see what was about to happen and he ran toward his sister for cover. The tree began to toss eggs in volleys at Theron as he

TS and The WOW

ran away. A rain storm of white and brown eggs tracked him with radar precision. The eggs looked like hail stones in the air. Twila saw the eggs coming. Expecting to be showered with her brother, she focused in on the eggs.

"Stop right there," she thought. It was as if she had the right to command the eggs anyway she wanted to. The fleet of flying ovals hung in the air weightless. Theron turned to see the eggs come to a sudden stop in the air. At first he couldn't believe what he saw, and then he plucked each one from the air as you would pick plums from the limbs of a tree. He folded the bottom of his T-shirt upward to cradle his fragile pickings.

"Got you this time!" Theron said teasing back at the tree the same way it teased him. With his shirt filled and all the eggs gleaned from the air, Theron stuck out his tongue at the tree. "I win," he said, then turned to walk into the house. Splat! The Winter Tree had concealed one egg that now ran down the back of Theron's head, neck, and shirt.

"He wins," Twila laughed.

Theron couldn't help himself. He laughed also. The Winter Tree had recovered from whatever it was that had bothered him when the family had gone on their trip. He seemed glad to have them home, moving all about the yard and playing jokes on Theron, his favorite target. But fall was on its way and school was about to start and for Theron, that meant he should try to get in as much outdoor time as possible. His favorite thing was to get out into the hills to look for the arrowheads that the Indians had shot at animals hundreds of years earlier. It wasn't an easy hobby, yet to him it was cool to find something that had been untouched for a couple of hundred years. It was a strange connection that he felt whenever he would happen to find one. Theron finished his chores quickly.

"Mom, is it okay if I go hunting arrowheads?"

"Fine honey, just be back before lunch."

Theron skipped off the back porch letting the screen door slam behind him. With his Red Ball Jets on he felt that he was just like Morph Man, able to change into any animal and run and jump faster than lightning could strike. The comic book "The Adventures of Morph Man," hung half out of his back pocket as he climbed over the fence and scurried into the wash. The tattered copy had been with him through the summer, his example of a super hero. He imaged being just like Morph Man able to change into anything he wanted.

"If I changed into a rock, what would pass me by?" he wondered. Then he saw himself as a rock and the neighbor's dog taking a leak on him. "That wouldn't be so cool," he said out loud.

Theron meandered along the edge of the wash, passing Busher's pond, it was out here in the sandy wash banks where he

TS and The WOW

found the unbroken Indian stone tool. What was that? Theron bent down to one knee next to a piece of brush and picked up a sleek black arrow point. "It's perfect." It never ceased to amaze him that something so delicate could be lying on the ground for so many years without being busted into a thousand pieces, like the plates and bottles left by the pioneers had been. Most of the morning had passed. The sun now was high in the sky. Theron was feeling parched without having water to drink.

"Time to get home for lunch," he thought, tucking the arrowhead into his pocket for safekeeping. He had kept it in his hand while hunting for more, kind of superstitious that if he put it into his pocket it would signal the end of finding any more. "Not bad work for a Saturday." Theron stood on the top of the wash bank surveying the land below him. He leaped off, plunging his Red Ball Jets deep into the soft sand. Quickly he pulled his shoes free and darted down the wash until he had reached the trees that lined the edge of Busher's Pond.

Someone was coming toward Theron. He walked with purpose, not glancing to either side but intent on his target. The old man walked toward him, not broken and bent but with an impressive stride and bounce in his step. Excitement was in his voice, unlike his natural demeanor.

"Come, son, we must hurry. You're family has been taken by the wolf from the wall!"

TS and The WOW

way back to the Salter home with the same power in their steps as those that brought Arlis to Theron. The Winter Tree greeted them with a frantic display of limbs twisting and leaves flying all about the yard until he was nearly bare to the trunk. The yard was covered in a foot of leaves and for the first time the tree was bald.

Inside the house evidence of a crime was everywhere, chairs were turned over and mother's favorite glass statuette of a deer and her fawn lay broken on the floor. Mebo was flattened, with all his water in a puddle next to him.

"Can't they leave us alone? What did I ever do to deserve this?"

For the first time Theron had reached the limit of an eleven-year-old. His body felt shock and tears rolled over his cheeks. The old man took him in his arms and comforted him like a surrogate grandfather.

"Calm now, we have work to do." His words brought composure and a purpose as Theron choked back his emotions and wiped the tears from his eyes. Arlis poured water over Mebo. Rapidly the flattened Mebo swelled to the size of a basketball, ending his expansion with the now accustomed pop.

"Mebo awake now!"

"Do you remember what was going on here?" Arlis asked him.

TS and The WOW

Mebo looked around at the tattered room awakening his memory.

"The man wolf. This be a man wolf take them." It was just as Arlis had suspected. This was the work of Arlo McFarland.

"How was he able to come to the earth world?" wondered Arlis. Until now he had been bound in his own world.

The front door opened and in walked Twila. Theron, puzzled, ran to her and grasped her shoulders.

"You're okay!" he shook her.

"Sure, but the question is, are you?" She was surprised by his behavior, thinking he had lost his mind. Neither of the twins' red hair spot had alerted them. This danger had come as a total surprise.

"Twila, mom and dad have been taken." She wearily looked about the room.

"Where's mom and daddy?"

"He's got them."

"Wait a minute, who's got them?"

"I've been trying to tell you. It's the wolf from the wall. He's got them."

"Mebo, tell us what happened here." Arlis prodded.

"The man-wolf wanted Theron. He says the map of seven or the mom and daddy be done. He say Theron bring map to room of seven worlds."

"What map, I don't have a map!"

Arlis stroked his whiskers and looked at the children knowing that Arlo McFarland was up to no good. Maybe he would try to seal their abilities in the one spot in creation where their powers are bound and the worlds would lose all balance. That would mean chaos for all of them.

"How do we get to the falls?" Twila asked her mentor. Knowing that was where the room of the seven worlds was.

"I can't take you there."

"You have to take us there!" Theron demanded in a way he had never done before. His parents needed him and being a balancer was not as important as they were.

"Let's go, sis, we can get there on our own." For the first time Theron looked at Arlis with contempt in his eyes.

"How can we get to the labyrinth in the canyon, behind the waterfall?" She said.

"How are we going to get back into the canyon?" asked Theron.

TS and The WOW

"I will go, better together than alone," said Arlis knowing they needed him and just possibly the three of them could face the wolf.

"But you don't have a map and neither do we," Twila said.

"What is this map he wants?" Theron inquired of Arlis.

"Two thousand years ago each of the seven worlds took their most precious treasure to a city in their most protected spot in creation. These treasures where formed in the foundation of each of the worlds at their very beginning. Each treasure is a link to the beginning and also the end of creation," he explained. "If any one person were to control all the treasures, he would be the most powerful being ever in any of the worlds. Many have pursued the map, trying to posses the treasure," he added.

"Only balancers were trusted to know where the cities were a long time ago. One balancer was made guardian over all seven cities. A group of men and creatures banded together to take the treasure for their own. The council of tribes hid the cities and the balancer who is named Quetzelquatl hid the location for all time. The cities are somewhere in the earth world."

"I know this story. Cortez wanted the seven cities of gold," Twila said.

"Was he a balancer?"

"A very wicked one."

TS and The WOW

"We can't let the wolf get them!" Theron exclaimed thinking he must protect his family and the hidden cities.

"But what about mom and dad?"

Theron was just as concerned as Twila and he did not intend to let either of his parents become lost to that monster. It was Twila that noticed a strange smell in the house as she cleaned things from the floor. A smell of wet dog permeated the air.

"So what do we do?" Theron asked the man who had feared taking the twins to the labyrinth behind the falls.

"There might be a way. Come with me," he said.

They both followed immediately, Twila dropped the couch pillow back on the floor. He led them into the yard where they passed the Winter Tree. The tree had grown a new crop of leaves to cover his limbs. He stood in the spot of the yard where he had first taken root, his spot. In front of him, instead of a pile of leaves, they were one stacked on the other like bricks in a house, forming a hollow cylinder. Arlis led the twins. They were followed by Mebo who rolled up to the stack of leaves.

"Now what, are we going to be like a tree and leaf?" Theron's witty comment was not far from the truth. Arlis stood in front of the leaves and with a wave of his hand the leaves re-stacked themselves in the brick pattern, leaving an opening for the group to enter its center. A stiff breeze rolled in the leaves from all corners of the yard.

TS and The WOW

The wind thrust its vigorous breath against the outside of the leaf pile, closing the door and then twisting the leaves into a tornado of fallen glory. The leaves swept high into the sky taking with them the four creatures, two human, one Eltergoen and one from the world of the Tween, leaving only the tree in the yard with his leaves shuddering in the last bit of the wind.

The group became particles passing through a tunnel or a pathway of travel to the waterfall in the bottom of the canyon. The column of leaves twisted across the river, silent, and unseen. They touched ground and fell away from the passengers. The particles of the travelers formed leaving the four bodies standing on the sandy banks of the river. Leaves blanketed the water for a moment, and then passed on down the river into the beginning of darkness. Arlis stood on the shore at the head of the group with his chest thrust forward. Each one gasped for a breath of air as their particles grouped them into the personages they were.

"That was weird," Theron said.

Twila clutched Theron's arm with both of her hands, wanting to hold on to something that she felt was secure. Theron was neither secure nor brave. He shivered with fear. Darkness cloaked their arrival, yet that feeling of being watched drenched over them. Theron waited for that impression to change, but the weight of eyes on them remained. His red hair spot had woven into a distinct W.

TS and The WOW

"How do you make this work, you know the vision thing?" questioned Theron. Arlis looked at the boy, motioning to him to be quiet. He had other things on his mind. With a look of stupidity Theron ducked his head so that Arlis knew he would be silent from that point on. The sound of the falls pouring onto the rocks and into the pond was all that made a sound. The moon had passed its fulfillment last week when they had been in the canyon, leaving only the stars to shine down on them this night.

"What's that in the falls?" Twila pointed to the water twisting and flickering with light like a million tiny fireflies as it fell from the ledge to the pool. In the aurora of light a man's image appeared. It was the same man that Theron had seen with his parents.

"It's Grandpa." Theron said in a whisper.

"He was trying to say something, can you hear him?" Twila asked.

He looked right at her as though he recognized her. The light in which he basked was a magnetic rainbow of colors, flushing through his figure in the curtain of water. He was obviously distressed, trying to present his message and not being heard. Theron tried to see into the fourth dimension as he called it. Finally his eyes focused on the man in the falls. Suddenly, a pathway of sight cut like a tunnel into the fourth dimension esposing the man's molecules. Every part of his molecular

TS and The WOW

structure was tied to the water and it held him like a prisoner in its shackles. He was human, not an illusion Theron could see the life stream DNA that defined him as human. Theron's fourth dimensional sight passed deeper to the cliff wall and on into the labyrinth of chambers hidden there.

"I've got x-ray vision just like Morph Man," he thought. The tunnels where Theron could see were strange rooms, some filled with water and others empty except for the carvings in the crop circle language on their walls.

"The rooms must have contained something once but, they are empty now, maybe they contained the treasure of the seven cities." Theron said. "There are a bunch of rooms back there," he added. Theron wanted to see what was beyond the stone wall like he had done inside the cave. But it looked more like the television had gone off the air than seeing into the next room

Twila kept her eyes glued on the man in the water curtain. Her ears waited for the words to come. His lips moved, but no sound came from them.

"What is he saying?" she asked, hoping that Arlis could tell her.

"They look like they might have stored something," Theron blurted out interrupting. "They're empty now, but this had to be where the seven cities were hidden, at least for a while."

TS and The WOW

His eyes caught hold of the stream of water that flowed through the caves the common thread binding them all together

"This water is weird!" Theron said as he watched it pass bubbling by. "Look at that," he said with surprise.

"Look at what?" questioned his sister Twila.

"It's made of tiny crop circles the same as the carvings on the cave walls."

"You mean its DNA is a crop circle?"

"Where is it going?" Arlis wanted to know, keeping his eyes wide open for Arlo McFarland not knowing how he had escaped the world of Eltergo.

"You should see where it goes. Maybe it will lead to your mother and father. I must release the man from the falls," Arlis said.

Yet something more was going on inside their mentor. He watched as the youngsters entered the water and then found the lever that opened the stone door.

"What are we doing?" Twila asked as they entered the staircase fearful of what lurked in its corners.

"We are doing the only thing we can, we're saving our family," Theron said, adding, "We will be okay," in an attempt to reassure his sister.

"Right, and don't forget the wolf is in there, too." Twila said mockingly. Twila had not forgotten why they stood in the bottom of the canyon or why Theron and she had to follow the path of the water through the labyrinth. She was terrified at what might be lurking in that dreary hole, but she knew they had to enter the murky grip of darkness. Theron was the only one who could see the water in the darkness, so the brother and sister entered bound by blood and calling. Theron feared the room where he had seen the wolf, how could he possibly have been freed from his stone prison. It was true that the water poured into other rooms, both Theron and Twila could hear it splashing. The water splashed into a pool somewhere in the darkness.

The fourth cone of sight had given Theron cat-like vision. With his new sight he could not only see through walls of stone but also, like a nocturnal animal, he could see in the darkness. The whole room with its isinglass ceiling and the ball that begat the water in the pedestal bowel was clear to him. Twila trusted him, holding his hand to lead her and comfort her at the same time. "Hey little brother, I'm glad you're with me."

"We have got to climb down there." Theron pointed downward, hoping to show his sister the hole in the floor where the water tumbled into the pool below. His efforts were wasted on the girl that felt as though she was blind. The water tumbled down deeper into the cavity of the earth. Cautiously they searched each room for George and Adeline. Then to his

TS and The WOW

amazement Theron saw something moving in the next room. Was it his father? He hoped so.

"I see someone, there's something in there." Theron said. Twila gripped his arm afraid it was the wolf.

"Quiet!" she shushed, reminding her brother who might be there. When they climbed into the pool room Theron could see someone was submerged to his shoulders in the pooled water.

"He's drowning!" Twila exclaimed, breaking the silence and seeing through the darkness more clearly than she had. In the same moment Theron saw his father.

"It's Dad!" he called out, making George aware for the first time they were there. The words of the man in the falls shot free from the other world, echoing in the cavities of the mountain and striking Twila in the ears with surprise. The shocking reality of his words penetrated her, causing her to stand fast in her tracks.

"The wolf!" he warned, and then garbled words followed by a clear simple statement.

"Save my little Adeline!"

"Theron! I can hear the man in the falls, He said to beware of the wolf and to save mom."

"That is just what we intend to do," Theron replied as though their friend in the falls could hear his words.

TS and The WOW

"How does that strange man in the falls know mom?" Twila said.

Theron's eyes had returned to normal, leaving him stranded in the darkness of this place. His energy draining, he sat on the cave floor.

"Come on, Theron, you can't stop now. Dad needs us." Twila had watched the man in the water. The figure was her father and he was drowning. Tables had turned. She now was the one who had to take the lead. She tugged at Theron's hand until he struggled to his feet. She now was energized, wanting to rescue him. They struggled, wading into the water and coming ever closer.

"Dad, are you okay?" Twila asked the man in the water.

Outside where Arlis and Mebo had remained, Arlis had recognized the figure of the man trapped in the droplets of water in the falls. Letting down his defense Arlis began to work on helping the man escape his prison. Thinking he would be the help they needed to save George and Adeline. In the shadows of the canyon where animal's eyes flickered in watchful interest, there rose something so ancient and so dormant that when it first loosed its bounds the stink of age spewed from it. It caused critters of all kinds to scurry away escaping the electric smell. It poured out over the water of the falls as a green mist. The mist of power sealed at the beginning of time inside the mountain now loose over the falls.

"For what purpose might this power have come forth?" wondered Arils. He had known of the power of the canyon, but had supposed it was myth. Lightning shot from the falls to the sandy embankment where Arlis and Mebo stood. Again and again it shot like rockets at them exploding with fury. The crashing sound around them drowned the words of the man in the falls who beckoned, pleading to help him.

"Behind the rocks!" commanded Arlis. In that very moment a lightning bolt slammed into the back of the man in his white linen suit. Arlis stood silent, disbelief glazing his eyes, when he tumbled face first into the river. Mebo, watched from the rocks as his friend Arlis fell into the water and floated down the river into the darkness. The lightning ended and the green mist was sucked back into the rocks by some hidden vacuum. The man in the falls had watched on, wilting at Arlis's demise. Mebo rolled into the water pursuing Arlis. The scream of the wolf haunted the night as the lightning struck one more solemn time in the water of the falls twisting and turning the water in a vortex and tossing water into the cliff and the trees. Nature fell silent, including the man in the falls.

TS and The WOW

Inside the cave small stones fell from the rocky ceiling into the pool, narrowly missing Twila.

"Don't cry, I need your help. It will be okay, sis."

"But our family is going to die."

"No we're not, we are going to help Mom and Dad."

There in the depths of the earth were two eleven-year-old children. Yes, they had experienced many terrifying things during the year, but always with the thought that they would overcome anything. The connection with Arlis was close, helping them and guiding them through every experience. Now that connection was abruptly severed and both of them felt it. It was gone and they were all alone. They feared Arlis was forever gone.

"Twin power," Theron said putting out his pinky finger to his sister. Shaking and reluctant she locked her pinky with his while remembering how they felt about being twins. Together they could do anything. With her tears wiped away only sniffles remained. They had to focus on saving their parents.

"What do we do?"

He took his sister's hand and together they waded to their father.

"Over here kids." It was a voice in the darkness, but it was one they both recognized. They rushed to his side. Theron knelt in the water and put his arms under his father's back and

TS and The WOW

head. He grunted and pulled up on him, bringing his head out of the water. Twila cried a tear of joy.

"Daddy." She kissed him on the cheek.

There was little question that the wolf from the wall was waiting for them somewhere inside this labyrinth. It would have been a good idea to have a plan, but all their plans had gone with Arlis.

"Where are we?" Twila whispered. Her words echoed in the cave.

"The writing on the wall in the first room called this the water room." Theron whispered back.

"We have to get dad out of the water." Twila said.

Theron struggled, forcing one hand into his wet pocket, withdrawing his pocketknife.

"This will do it!" He jammed the knife into the lock that secured the chains, but it did nothing to unlock it.

"That didn't work." Theron said recognizing that the lock was a type he had seen on pirate's chest in movies. He searched through the stuff he carried in his pocket. There was his flint stick, a couple of coins one of those being the two faced coin. "What about these." Said the left face of the coin, nudging his hand. "Right the skeleton keys." He had thought the keys he found in the box at the mercantile were cool and had carried

TS and The WOW

them with him, just in case he found a treasure. The lock was opened by the third of five keys. "Thought I was a goner." George said standing on his wobbly legs for the first time in many hours. He hugged his twins. "How in the heck did you find me?"

"Arlis brought us." Twila said.

"Where is he? We are going to need his help to get Addie from that creature."

"We think he's…" She didn't want to face the fact that he was gone and not saying it left possibilities she thought.

"Oh, I understand." The dry bank felt good where they sat, but the gloom of the darkness was close about them and they feared every noise as if the wolf was returning.

"My flint and steel," Theron thought, reaching into his pocket and pulling out his striker flint. He struck it with his knife and sparks flew.

"What can I burn?" Theron said, as his hand ran across the comic book in his back pocket. It had gotten wet, but with some coaxing it might burn. His favorite issue of Morph Man given to him by Martin was his treasure.

"Not Issue 6, the introduction of Megawatt from the planet Daptrea." Theron struggled only for a moment. Then it was strike, strike. The flint against the knife sprayed sparks in the darkness. For a few seconds Twila could see the faces of both her

TS and The WOW

brother and her father then darkness again. Theron pushed the blade across the flint, throwing sparks onto the comic book. At first it would not light. Theron crumpled the edge in his hand and then tried again.

"You're still my hero Morph Man," Theron said when the book started to burn, lighting the room. No longer was the room as dark as the inside of a cow's stomach, something Theron had heard George say many times to describe incredible darkness.

"Ditto, you're my hero too," Twila said.

"You kids look for something to burn before this goes out. Hurry now!" Twila found a pot near the hole where they came into the poolroom. It contained a tar-like substance.

"This will burn." Theron lit the pot contents and the room filled with light. Suddenly things seemed hopeful, something that had been hard to reach a short time earlier. Chips and chunks of fresh stone that had fallen shined in the new light.

"The stones look like stars in the night sky," Twila said noticing their glimmer.

"We have got to find Addie," George announced.

"How do we find her Dad?" Theron was weary of the task of exploring this underworld.

"We must go deeper into the cave," George replied. That was not what Theron wanted to hear, yet he had known that

TS and The WOW

would be the answer. Without hesitation Theron crawled to his feet, then into the hole, dangling his bottom into the darkness of the new room and wondering what might bite it off. Twila held his arms, lowering her brother into the unknown, but they had to go in there. His feet slipped several times on the side of the wall of the cave before he reached the bottom. "I'm down."

"Hand me the light." Twila took the pot into her hands and leaned into the opening headfirst. The light exposed the nature of the new room. It was similar to the upper chamber, but the walls were cut to hold the mud and rock dwellings of some long-gone civilization. Crystal water from the upper room ran out from a slot in the wall into a hollowed-bowl in the floor, where it swirled around a crystal whirlpool funneling still deeper into the earth. Twila made an oofing sound when she lowered herself into the new room, followed by George, the last to come from the darkness of the upper room.

"Can you see mom anywhere?" Twila trusted the new gifts that each of them was learning to use and Theron had seen things through walls. Theron strained to see through the walls as he had before, first squinting and then throwing his eyes as wide open as he could. Nothing happened. He tried the same exercise again and again until he was sure that it just was not working inside the cave.

"What was that?" a clanking sound like a hammer pounding on pipes brought everyone to attention. George already

TS and The WOW

stood erect scanning the room. Anguish rose inside their stomachs and a sweaty fear ran inside their veins, but this was not enough to dissuade them from their rescue. Terrified, each envisioning his or her own demise at the hands of the Wolf from the wall, they stepped forward. The wall bent and narrowed into a tunnel.

"What now?" Twila wanted to know.

"Follow the tunnel, that's where the clanging came from," George said, leading his children into the hollow tube. It bent and twisted. Within seconds the sound of running water disappeared, but the clanking became more clear, each strike against the pipe resounding in the echo from the stone walls.

"That hurt!" Twila said loudly enough to be heard over the clanking sound. She placed both hands over her ears and began to think of a bubble opening. As she concentrated intently the wall blended seamlessly with the world of the Yeti. A bubble had opened right there inside the tunnel.

It was easy to see that this was the world of the Yeti. The purple forest of the Yeti world where the watermelon grass was in the fall of the season was turning a yellow and muddy brown instead of the bright oranges and purples it had been. Theron could see Samja's cottage in the tree line and his first impression was to get help.

"We have to follow the tunnel," George said, pulling at Twila's arm and directing her away from the bubble opening.

The labyrinth wound through the sandstone. The only constant had been the trail of crystal water that was now gone. Passing through each room, Theron wondered what they were used for. Each of the rooms was carved from stone and each room bore a message in the crop circle language, but there had been no time to stop and read them. Perhaps they should have, thought Theron. They approached every corner with the caution of scared rabbits, wide eyes and rapidly-beating hearts, ready to find the rhythm of running away.

"He's got your mother, let's hurry." George was not concerned about himself. He had expected to die right there in the darkness, with the water of the room of the seven worlds, but his children had saved him and now he had but one thought, to save his Adeline.

The second Mebo had rolled into the water he began to swell, popping and crackling as he grew. Quickly he reached the size of a rubber raft. He moved over the water being pulled by the current wherever it went. Each time he would pound against a rock, water would squirt from his body reducing his size, then the water would soak back into his skin and he would make the squeaking sound popping at the end of the cycle and becoming a new more impressive size.

TS and The WOW

"If I be help for the Arlis, must be now," he thought, realizing he had little control over his growing frame. Arlis floated face down on the water just ahead of Mebo, caught where the water swirled into an eddy. Mebo forced his ball-like body against a rock that jutted out of the water. A fountain of water shot from him. He shrunk to half the size he had grown to, then drifted into the eddy and spun just behind the lifeless figure of Arlis Alger.

They all rested in the flicker of flame that came from the pot. The pounding on the pipes had increased in volume and then had suddenly stopped. It was silent, except for the breathing of the trio and the new sound of water trickling down a stream.

"Theron, come over here," George said still using his whisper voice.

"He's gone, daddy." Twila's red spot of hair had stopped doing anything. It lay limp, covering one eye before she wiped it back away from her face.

"Where did Arlis go?"

"I don't know. One minute he was here and the next he's gone, we both felt it." Theron started out ahead of the group using only the edges of the light to navigate by.

"That boy is going to be the death of me!"

"He is going to rescue mom," said Twila. George stood, ducking even though the ceiling was still a foot or two above his

TS and The WOW

head. He wanted to catch up with Theron. Carrying the pot light he led the way pursuing his son with the hope only a father possess to intervene before something happened to his family.

With his second sight returning Theron had found another tunnel into the cavity of the earth where the water pooled again.

"I guess it's in the water again," he thought as he splashed into the pool from a ledge, struggling not to make noise. Once settled into the water he scoped the layout of the chamber still ahead of his father and sister.

"First things first. Where is mom? I'm sure I saw her in there," he thought, swimming to a spot where he could stand in the water. The water had only gently rippled as he moved. "There she is!" he said surprised by the light in the cave and how easy it had been to find her. He saw his mother seated in a glass-enclosed chamber. Adeline seemed to be yelling at Theron. "Had she seen him?" Theron questioned. What she spoke did not pass through the walls of her glass prison. She waved both hands to warn him away. Theron walked toward her, ignoring the warning. She waved her hands frantically and screaming to be heard.

"I'm coming mom, hang on!" His red hair spot twisted, ringing the water from itself and then tying into a knot so tight that it hurt.

TS and The WOW

"Stop that, not right now!" He slapped at his wild hair, not heeding the warning. Water drained from his clothes to the sandstone floor making it a deeper rusty red nearly the color of blood. He had no more stepped from the water into the light and onto the sandstone shelf when he felt a presence he had felt before. His bones shuttered knowing he was in trouble. This time the wolf was not on the wall.

"You're mine this time little one." The words set the red hair spot to ringing the rest of the water from its strands. Theron turned to his left, dripping the blue water from his clothing. He shivered again, partly because of the cold and partly because of the clarity of his fear. Frantically he looked for the embodiment of the voice. In a rocky cavity near where the light emanated stood a figure in its shadow.

"What, what do you want me for?" He stuttered as he spoke.

"I don't want you, I want what you have boy!" The gruff growling voice rolled off of the walls like the background tune in a horror movie. The beast leaped from his advantage point on the high rock in the shadows. He landed next to Theron teeth exposed, growling low and guttural, eyeing him with his deep yellow eyes.

"I want the map to the seven." He was speaking as if any balancer would understand his slang.

TS and The WOW

"I don't have a map," Theron said trying not to cower from the monster that paced around him.

"Are you the earth balancer..?" The Wolf said, dragging the last word out until it sounded alien.

"I guess I am." Theron shrugged his shoulders as he replied.

"Give me the map and you can have..." The creature paused and stroked his chin with a long bony clawed finger. "...your mama. Now you would like that wouldn't you?"

Theron wanted to be as far away from the half-man, half-wolf as he could, but his mother was trapped like a dessert under glass. Adeline tried to smile at her son, wanting to help him but having no way. All she had was her smile. The wolf glared at her.

"Or, would you rather she be mine?" The awful thought of his mother forever trapped with the wolf in his sandcastle burned an image of horror on his brain.

"No, no I will give you whatever you want." Theron knew that lying was wrong, but surely God would forgive him this time.

"That's better boy, give me my map."

Strangely, Theron's thoughts became clear and vivid. He began telling a visual story of the seven cities. Where had his vision come from he wondered?

TS and The WOW

"The wolf-man wrenched Theron's arm to his back. The brute bellowed his breath over Theron's neck while pushing his face against the glass booth where his mother was incarcerated. The booth door made a clanking noise accompanied by a sound of a high-pressured suction release when the wolf opened it.

"In there, boy…." Again he dragged out the last word to its alien sound. While pushing the boy the wolf-man was forced to see his reflection in the glass. The face of a man not the face of the wolf creature peered back at him. The walls of the glass chamber opened like a banana peeling away its outer layer and leaving Adeline in its middle. Theron was thrust in by the side of his mother.

"Be with your mama, cub boy." Adeline hugged Theron, finally having comfort from her son, although she wished he had never come to her. Another glance into the reflection in the glass showed a man's image and for a second, someone else. The machine's banana-peel sides closed again, trapping both Theron and Adeline inside. The wolf danced gaily around the cavern almost tasting his certain triumph.

"Should I starve them or drown them?" thought the wolf as he plotted his next move to get the map from his prisoner. Theron and Adeline sat on the floor with their backs against the glass hiding their faces from the wolf. They didn't want him to see the despair on their faces and their worry for George and Twila who would soon fall into this same trap.

TS and The WOW

The fire-pot flame flickered, coming close to the end of its fuel and struggling to give light in the labyrinth where Twila and George had left it in the tunnel.

"Come on, daddy, I see them, they're down there inside that glass case." Twila pointed to the prison in the low end of the room.

"Down!" George said putting his hand on Twila's head and pushing her behind the rock just as the wolf looked their direction. Her red spot of hair wove around his arm, locking her in George's control. When she was safely under the rocks the hair unwound freeing her. Twila was frustrated that her own hair would do that. George had always protected his little girl. She wished she was home safe. However, that was not the way it was. She was here and more a part of what was occurring than ever.

Theron and Adeline watched as the water began to cover the floor where a short time before it had been dry. Water would soon be inside the glass booth and shortly after that they would have to stand just to stay above the water.

"Are you ready to give up the map?" growled the wolf from where he preached on a ledge, his head hanging low, teeth bared in his most threatening way. "Give it to me!" he demanded.

"I don't know what it is you want," Theron replied in frustration. The wolf leaped into the shallow water and put his hands on the glass booth. His hideous face pressed to the glass and his yellow eyes penetrated deep into Theron's heart.

"I don't have a map and I can't give you what I don't have."

"You have it balancer, I know you do," demanded the wolf. "You escaped me in my world. You won't be so lucky here boy."

Theron tried to see through the wall, but it just wasn't working. He was unable to see with the second sight. His thoughts were different, too. This booth left his red hair spot lifeless and nothing worked the way he had become accustomed to things working. He was out of balance.

"It's this glass tube," he said pounding on the wall with his fist. "It's blocking my gifts." The wolf was growing impatient, frustrated with the new balancer's denials.

As he paced he chanted saying over and over, "The map to the seven must be mine." He would stand on his back legs and lean on the glass until the water reached where his paws were on the glass. "The rising water would soon be as high as their heads," thought the wolf. "Then the boy will give in and the map will be mine at last. Then I will no longer be a wolf on the wall, in these worlds. I will be king of them all!" he thought. His greed and lust for power showed upon his ferrous face.

TS and The WOW

It must have been his obsession with Theron and the map that kept him from seeing two figures lowering themselves into the pool from the tunnel of the upper chamber. George told Twila that it would be of most importance that they do this thing as quietly as possible. Twila lowered herself into the water first. She was as near silent as a water snake entering the current of a stream. George took his turn clinging to the handholds that were carved into the wall of the cave. His large body was clumsier, and he splashed, causing a ripple on the pool. The ripple went unnoticed as it reached the opposite shore.

The wolf continued yelling at Theron to give him the map. The water, chest deep to Twila, made her cling to the pool edge to balance. She felt as if she were swimming in the cement pool at Veyo, o how she wished that were so. Swimming there in the resort fed by volcanic hot spring, was a soft memory.

"I hope there is nothing strange in the water," she thought. She could see the wolf taunting her mother and brother like fish being teased by a cat in a glass bowl. Fear had no part in her thoughts right now. Whether it was in the water or that thing taunting her family, she had to help them without fear. Theron and Adeline were balancing each other standing knee deep in the flood that was filling the fishbowl in which they were sealed. Adeline hugged her son holding him close.

"Mom, we will be alright," Theron said, knowing he could do nothing to help. Adeline choked back her tears, not sad for herself but terrified for her child.

"Surrender my map and you can go free? I don't know anything about your map!" screamed Theron for the tenth or eleventh time.

"Then you and your mommy, little balancer will die!" Theron felt a tug from the red hair spot that had been lifeless awakening him.

"It's about time!" he thought. He tried to see past the walls with his second sight, but nothing happened. His hair spun and twisted like it never had before.

"What's going on?" Adeline said, noticing Theron's hair problem.

"Mom they're coming, Twi is here," Theron said, calmly seeing them in the pool but trying not to let the wolf take notice of his interest in the water. The wolf stood on his safe shelf and looked Theron in the eye.

"For the last time boy, where is my map? Don't deny it. You are an earth balancer and you know what I mean!"

They were just shadows in the water as they glided through the pool to where they could stand. George motioned to Twila to wait where she was still deep in the water.

TS and The WOW

George leaped to attack. He ran from the water splashing and screaming, reaching the wolf with surprise. George gripped both arms around the monster's neck. The wolf tossed violently all about the room, carrying the man with him. Twila swam to the booth and tried to release the water that was approaching the top of the tank. If the water was not released soon it would swallow them. The wolf smashed against the booth like a battering ram with George's body between him and the glass, shaking the man loose. The blows against the glass stunned George for a moment. The booth was rocked by the impact, pulling Adeline and Theron underwater. Then it settled upright, Theron and Adeline returned to the air pocket rising to the top and each gasped for air. Twila had been unable to release the water that was about to fill the tank. The wolf leaped on top of George again knocking him back away from the glass booth. He struggled to swim, just reaching Twila.

"They're going to drown!" Twila said. Treading, the wolf-man shook the water from his body and stood on his ledge watching and waiting for the water to close over the family and devour them all.

"What's this, another little one?" the wolf-man said seeing Twila for the first time. "How sweet, you brought me a little girl one," he said in his threatening growling voice.

"Twila, get out of here!" George commanded his daughter. The booth was filled and Adeline and Theron were

TS and The WOW

drowning. It was act now or never. Twila's face grimaced as her body floated on the water. She concentrated on one thing and one thing only. As she struggled inside her thoughts the wolf – man plotted. "With one swift blow he could kill the girl right now and the family would watch her die." He thought, sneering with his yellow eyes pulsing and his breath rolling from his flared nostrils. He leaped high into the air, his teeth bared and his claws reaching, all for the destruction of one little girl.

"Open bubble, open bubble, Twila chanted into the water. A bubble opened. The wasteland of a dry parched ground appeared on the other side of the opening. Water poured out into the desert through the bubble.

The wolf-man already airborne in his attack could not change direction. The water sucked Twila with it rushing through the bubble. Lightning rocketed its way from several crevasses smashing against the floor and walls and striking the glass cylinder that contained Theron and Adeline. The lightning bolts were followed by the deafening sound of thunder. Its sounds rolled through the bubble and into the desert land. The wolf smashed headlong into the waterless bottom of the cave and began to change. The change crumpled his body from wolf-man to wolf, being drawn by an unseen force into the bubble.

George lay next to the wolf resting from the strain of treading water. Looking up he saw that the glass bottle-like prison draining. Theron and Adeline lay lifeless at the bottom of the

TS and The WOW

tank. Twila, covered in sand particles, raced back through the bubble opening to help them.

"Mom, Theron!" she screamed. They were gone, "dead," she thought. With a leap the wolf landed on top of Twila knocking her to the rocky floor. His yellow eyes focused on her crystal blue ones.

"You are nothing, not a balancer like your brother. You are nothing!" He growled, his paws holding her shoulders pinned to the ground. The force from the bubble tugged at him, his grip no longer sure.

George rushed to Twila's aid. Her arms pinned under the weight of the wolf from the wall. The wolf saw the man coming. Turning his head, he said in anger, "Come one step closer and she is dead."

George paused in checkmate with the villain. The red hair twisted to a long strand and like a hand wiped the rest of her hair away from her eyes. The room became light with the power of a hundred thousand candles. Creatures that were lurking in the dark were caught by surprise and scurried off into the darkness to hide, the brilliance too great.

"Off me you beast!" Twila thought, the weight of the wolf lifted from her and there he hung in the air. The wolf's body contorted being pulled into the open bubble. First a wolf, then half a wolf and then just a scribble like a crayon drawing in the air.

"You can't be a balancer, you're a girl!" He screamed, as his remnants were sucked into the dry sands of the desert world.

No female had ever been a possessor of the gifts of a balancer. Twila was the first. The little eleven-year-old girl had faced the yellow-eyed monster and won. She turned, stood tall to face the open bubble and said calmly, "Away." The desert world was lost behind the stone smashing all around as the bubble closed.

"Are they going to be okay?" Twila asked George who had retrieved their loved ones from the glass chamber to hold the lifeless bodies of his wife and son. He touched Adeline's limp arm to find a pulse. Theron had coughed up water as George lowered his head.

"She's gone," he said, pulling her to his chest. He hugged his sweetheart tightly and felt a shock of lighting at his chest. He let her go for a moment and then hugged her tightly a second time. Adeline coughed up water and came to consciousness. George hugged her again with tears of joy.

"Insmackulatious!" Twila said jubilantly screaming, "Mom, Theron! You're both okay!"

After tending to his loved ones, George smashed the glass of the booth to small bits. Its shards rolled to the sandstone

TS and The WOW

melting like icicles into a puddle being absorbed into the spongy rock. He pulled the spent lightening bolt from its pouch in his pocket.

Hopefully Arlo McFarland, the wolf from the wall, was trapped in his own desert world. The remains of the booth withered dying then smoldering in ash sinking towards death as a phoenix at its end. The cave was large and finding the way out was difficult.

"Our family is the best," George said holding on to his sweet Adeline and looking with pride at his twins.

"So, what was the map he wanted?" asked Twila.

"I don't know. Could it be this arrowhead from the stone box?" Theron replied as he pulled it from the corner of his pocket where it had carried it for months. The stone shined in his hand. It did look like a key not a map. More perhaps like a bolt of lightning than a key. Theron eyed it and as he did he noticed a light from inside it glowing. He held it in his hand as he climbed from the lower rooms back into the basin room under the falls knowing that it was good luck as long as it was in his hand. Retracing their steps they returned to the cave behind the falls. Theron wanted to see the ball in the basin, now that the threat of the wolf from the wall was gone.

"What is this?" Was it something new or just something he had not seen? There was a slot on the side of the water basin the same shape as the stone he had in his hand.

"I bet it will fit," he said mostly to himself. He set the jagged rock profile into the empty shape. The ball in the basin opened peeling like an onion and exploding into the room. Water flowed freely, showering the room and the people with sparklets of azure blue water. It washed the isinglass and the stone walls until they shined with a golden glow. The basin moved aside leaving a hole in the floor. The floor spread at the hole and the wall covered with the writings in crop circle separated exposing a gateway.

"What is that?" Twila said, gasping. George and Adeline still held on to each other watching as the room had rearranged itself. Theron walked slowly to the gateway watching the water flow away into the missing floor. In the room behind the gate a figure stood.

"Hello, hello!" Theron called out. His insides twisted fearing it was McFarland returning for revenge. The man stepped forward from the shadow into view. It was the man in the falls. He was free and in the earth world if he passed through the gate.

"Daddy, oh daddy," Adeline said, her eyes welling with tears. He was her daddy, her long-lost daddy. George watched his wife fill with joy.

TS and The WOW

"What's that dad," inquired Theron. George unrolled the scroll from the stone box.

"It's a map I found. Look it has seven circles with that crop language scribbled on it."

"That's what the wolf wanted from me." Theron realized. "And you had it the whole time."

.

.